THE SHERIFF'S AMNESIAC BRIDE

From Mills & Boon® Intrigue

His hands burned as he touched her everywhere. His lips were set afire by her kisses.

"I want you, Jericho," she whispered against his mouth. "I feel alive with you. What's between us is right. I know you feel it, too. Show me. Please."

The sound of her urgent plea knocked the sense back into his muddled brain.

He gently took her by the shoulders and set her back from him. "This isn't right." He eased her up into his arms and slid her into the pickup's front seat.

Striding around the cab, he slipped behind the wheel and started it up. "You must belong to someone – somewhere. If we give in tonight and tomorrow your memory comes back, you'll never forgive yourself – or me. I won't take that chance."

SOLDIER'S SECRET CHILD

He whispered, "You wanted me then and you want me now."

Then he kissed her like there was no tomorrow, because he knew there might not be. As honour-bound as he felt to help Macy now that he knew TJ was his son, he was also sure that he was not cut out for family or civilian life.

She responded to him willingly, going up on tiptoe to continue the kiss. He slipped his hands beneath her buttocks and lifted her until her backside was on the edge of the counter and her legs were straddling his.

Macy shivered as the hard jut of his erection brushed the centre of her, awakening a rush of desire that dragged a moan from her.

The sound penetrated the fog of want that had wrapped itself around them, tempering their kisses, and creating a short lull during which she managed to murmur softly, "I'm sorry. I should have told you about TJ."

First published in Great Britain 2009
Harlequin Mills & Boon Limited,
Eton House, 18-24 Paradise Road, Richmond, Surrey TW9 1SR

The Sheriff's Amnesiac Bride © Harlequin Books S.A. 2008
Soldier's Secret Child © Harlequin Books S.A. 2008

Special thanks and acknowledgement are given to Linda Conrad and Caridad Piñeiro for their contributions to THE COLTONS: FAMILY FIRST mini-series.

ISBN: 978 0 263 87320 7

46-0909

Harlequin Mills & Boon policy is to use papers that are natural, renewable and recyclable products and made from wood grown in sustainable forests. The logging and manufacturing processes conform to the legal environmental regulations of the country of origin.

Printed and bound in Spain
by Litografia Rosés S.A., Barcelona

THE SHERIFF'S AMNESIAC BRIDE

BY
LINDA CONRAD

Linda Conrad was inspired by her mother, who gave her a deep love of storytelling. "Mum told me I was the best liar she ever knew. That's saying something for a woman with an Irish storyteller's background," Linda says. Winner of many awards, including the *Romantic Times BOOKreviews* Reviewers' Choice and a Maggie, Linda has often appeared on the Waldenbooks and BookScan bestseller lists. Her favourite pastime is finding true passion in life. Linda, her husband and KiKi, the dog, work, play, live and love in the sunshine of the Florida Keys. Visit Linda's website at www.LindaConrad.com.

Chapter 1

Uh-oh. Big trouble.

"Shut up, lady." One of the two men in the front seat swung his arm over the seat back and smacked her across the cheek. "You're in no spot to argue. You say you can't remember? Well, that ain't my problem."

The driver didn't turn around, but muttered, "When we get back, the boss'll make you talk. And he won't be as nice as we are. You took something that didn't belong to you, and that's a no-no."

"But...but I really can't remember." She rubbed at her stinging cheek. "I don't even know who I am." Tears welled up and she fought the panic that was quickly crawling up her spine. She didn't dare cry. Hardly dared to breathe.

Caught in an internal struggle for clarity, she'd been trying to bring up memories from her past. She was desperate to remember anything at all. Even her own name escaped her, and it had been this way for what seemed like hours.

Where there should've been something, there was a huge void. Darkness. A little pain. But nothing even vaguely familiar.

She didn't have a clue as to why these men had forced her into the backseat of this speeding car. Or where on earth they were heading. Everything out the window seemed as alien as everything in her mind. She didn't know what she was doing here. Or who these horrible men were who kept insisting she tell them where "it" was.

The only thing she did know was that these two goons were carrying guns. Big ones. They'd waved them at her when she tried to tell them she couldn't remember.

Oh, God, help her. She was going to die if something didn't give soon.

Putting her hands together, she silently prayed for a break. Some way of escaping this car and these two men.

As if God had answered her prayer directly, a church spire appeared out the front windshield. The car slowed.

"What the hell is all this traffic about?" The driver sounded irritated as he slammed his foot on the brake. "It ain't Sunday, damn it. Get out of our way, you idiots!"

Oh please, let me find a way out, she silently begged. Let this be the time. Let this be a place where I can find sanctuary and someone who will save a desperate woman with no memory.

Then, quietly, an answer came to her from out of the emptiness in her mind. *The Lord helps those who help themselves.*

Sheriff Jericho Yates glanced up toward the Esperanza Community Church steps looming directly ahead and slowed his pace. He wasn't chickening out of his own wedding, but there was truly no sense in getting there before the bride-to-be would be ready to start.

"You're sure you want to go through with this, bro?" Fisher, his older brother and the best man, slowed his steps too.

With a serious face but eyes that always seemed to be laughing behind his sunglasses, Fisher Yates, U.S. Army captain home on leave, rarely showed any emotion. But at the moment, it was Fisher who looked panic-stricken by the thought of this wedding.

"Hell, yes, I'm going through with it," Jericho muttered as an answer. "I gave Macy my word. But I don't want to piss her off by showing up too soon. We've been best friends ever since I can remember, and I couldn't hurt her feelings by embarrassing her like that."

"Well, I remember when there were three of you best friends—back in the day. You and Macy and Tim Ward. I thought the whole idea of two guys and a gal hanging out and being so close was a little weird at the time. And sure enough, it was Macy and Tim that eventually got hitched. So what were *you* all those years? The dorky third wheel?"

Jericho straightened his shoulders under the weight of his rented tux and rammed his hands into his pockets. He would not let Fisher get to him today. His slightly shorter big brother, who was only just now back from his third tour of duty in the Middle East, could be a pain in the ass. But Jericho felt he needed to make allowances for Fisher—for possible psychological problems. Or whatever.

He opened his mouth to remind Fisher that the three of them, he and Tim and Fisher, too, had all been half in love with Macy in high school. But then, Jericho thought better of jamming the truth in his brother's face right now. Tim had been the one to win the prize. Jericho also remembered that Fisher had taken off in a hurry to join the army after Macy picked Tim to marry—and his brother had never looked back once.

"No," Jericho finally answered, forcing a grin. "I was the best friend and glad about my buddies hooking up and being happy together. I was also the friend who stood by Macy when Tim got sick and died six years ago. And today, I'm the friend who's going to marry her and give Tim's teenage son a new father."

"Yeah, you are. And right friendly of you, too, bro. But as you said earlier, you and Macy aren't in love. What's the real deal? I'm not buying this friendly daddy-stand-in story."

Jericho wasn't sure he could explain it to someone like Fisher, a guy who'd never had anybody depending on him—except, of course, for the men in his squad. Well, okay, his brother probably would understand loyalty and honor, but not when it came to women or kids or best friends. Fisher had never let any of those things into his life.

"The real story is that I'm not *in* love with Macy…."

"You said that already."

"But…I do love her and want the best for her. And that kid of hers and Tim's already seems like family to me. I'm his godfather, and I think I can make a bigger difference to his life as his stepfather. I mean to try."

T.J. was the foremost reason Jericho had been so determined to go through with this wedding when Macy had brought up the subject. As kids, Fisher and he had done without a mother after theirs had abandoned them. But they'd had the firm hand of a father to raise them right. As a tribute to his dad, Buck Yates, still by far the best father in the world, Jericho would bring T.J. into the family and do for him what Buck had done for his two sons. Give T.J. the greatest start possible.

"Act like a best man, why don't you, and just shut up about love and real stories." He poked Fisher lightly on his dress-uniformed arm. "We need to waste a few more minutes out here, bro. If you've gotta keep yakking at me, tell me what your plans are for after your leave is over."

Just inside the Community Church, waiting behind closed doors in the vestibule with her maid of honor, Macy Ward fidgeted with her dress. "What do you think everyone in town will have to say about me wearing off-white? Maybe I should've worn a light blue dress instead."

The dress was of no consequence, but Macy didn't want to say what she really had on her mind. Her maid of honor, Jewel Mayfair, was also her boss. And although she really liked Jewel, being too honest in a case like this might not be the best idea. Even though Macy was about to be married, she still needed the job.

So as devastated as she felt by the nasty looks she'd received from Jericho's brother at the rehearsal last night, and as much as she would love to pour her heart out to another woman as kind as Jewel, she would instead keep her mouth firmly shut on the subject of Fisher Yates. Anyway, he was about to become her brother-in-law. So the two of them would just have to find a way of getting along.

But Macy felt nervous and jittery about more than just an irritating old boyfriend in uniform. She was dwelling on something much more important. Her son T.J. had been giving her fits over this upcoming marriage. He'd said he didn't want anyone to take his father's place. Though her boy liked Jericho well enough, and eventually Macy felt sure he would come to love and respect the man as much as the rest of the town.

What was not to love? Jericho Yates was the best man she knew. He was kind, loyal and so honest it almost hurt her heart. His honesty had recently made her feel guilty because she had not been absolutely honest with him or anyone else in such a long time.

"What's wrong, Macy? You don't look happy. You should be ecstatic. Today's your wedding day."

"I'm okay, Jewel. Honest. It's just…" She decided to confide in her boss, at least a little. "Jericho and I aren't in love. Not like a man and woman who are about to be married are supposed to be."

"No? But then why get married?"

"My son." Macy plopped down in the nearest chair, disregarding the possible wrinkles to her dress. "T.J. needs a father badly. And Jericho will make such a great dad. I'm the one who convinced our poor county sheriff to take pity on an old friend and do me the honor. I knew he would never tell me no."

"But now you're having second thoughts?"

"Second, third and fourth thoughts actually. I'm about to ruin a good man's life and saddle him with a wife he doesn't love and a kid who's a handful.

"I like Jericho," she added hastily. "A lot. I don't know if I can do this to him."

Jewel knelt on the carpet beside Macy's chair and spoke quietly. "If you ask me, he'll be getting the best part of the deal. You don't seem to understand how really beautiful and special you are, and I'm not sure why you don't get it. You're a terrific mother and a fine employee. I'm both your boss and your maid of honor, a double threat at the moment. So I'm the one who's here to remind you of what everyone else already knows. If you decide not to go through with this wedding, it'll be Jericho's loss, not yours."

Macy's eyes clouded over with unshed tears, but she bit them back. Jewel had become the dearest friend. But when everything was said and over, Macy just could not go through with this sham wedding. At least not today.

"Jewel, will you back me up if I postpone the wedding?"

Jewel put an arm around her shoulders. "Sure, honey. But why don't you go out and talk to Jericho about it first? Maybe you can catch him on his way in."

"Come with me?"

"All right. But we'd better hurry. The guests are already arriving. There's a major traffic jam outside."

* * *

Outside under the cottonwoods and next to the church, standing with his brother Fisher beside him, Jericho had been biding his time. He turned when he heard someone calling his name.

"Sheriff Yates!" The voice was coming from his deputy Adam Rawlins.

Jericho watched as the man he'd hired not long ago hurried toward him. Adam was dressed in his full deputy's uniform because he'd been on duty today and hadn't planned on attending the wedding. Rawlins was a good man who had come to them with terrific references from a deputy job in Wyoming. And Jericho was mighty glad to have found him.

"Sheriff, we've got ourselves a traffic tie-up out here on the highway. Someone called it in and I thought I'd better come over and direct traffic."

Geez. The entire county must be planning on attending his wedding. Who all had Macy invited? He'd left the plans up to her because he'd been so busy for the last few weeks. What with that case of identity theft a while back and then an actual dead body and a murder investigation out on Clay Colton's ranch that had just been put to bed, the sheriff's business was booming lately.

"All right, deputy," he told Rawlins. "Thanks for the quick thinking. I'll be out of pocket here for a few more hours and then I can help you out."

The deputy nodded and raced back toward the highway, apparently all ready to set out traffic cones and organize traffic lanes.

"Aren't you and Macy going on a honeymoon, bro?"

Fisher laid a hand on Jericho's arm, reminding him of his presence and of the upcoming nuptials.

Jericho winced and shook his head. "Not funny, bubba. You already know the answer to that. Besides, Macy and I are planning on spending some quality time with T.J. over the next few days. I thought I might take him hunting like Dad used to do for us. I hear the wild boar hunting has been good up on the north Gage pasture."

"Yeah, wild boar hunting the day after your wedding does sound romantic." Fisher scowled and rolled his eyes.

Jericho shook off his brother's sarcastic comments. He didn't care what Fisher or anybody thought of this marriage to his best friend. Macy was a great lady and a great friend, and Jericho vowed to do right by her and her son—regardless of anyone else's opinion.

Still twisting her hands in the backseat and waiting for a good opportunity, the woman with no past and a questionable future bit her lip and stared out the car's window. There was so much traffic here. Surely one of the people in these other cars would see her predicament and come to her aid.

"Son of a bitch, the traffic's even worse now." The car wound down to a crawl as the driver turned around again to speak to her. "Don't get smart, lady. You call out or make any noises like you need help and we'll shoot you. I don't give a rat's damn if that special item the boss wants is ever found or not. The choice between you giving us the answer and you never being able to answer again ain't nothing to me.

"You got that?"

She nodded, but the movement seared a line of fiery pain down her temple. Another couple of pains like that and she might rather be dead anyway.

"Terrific," the goon sitting shotgun said. "Just look at that, will ya? A local smoky. Out in the middle of the highway, directing traffic. Crap.

"What's going to happen, Arnie?" The man in the passenger seat was beginning to sweat.

"We're not doing anything wrong," Arnie answered with a growl. "We're regular citizens just driving down the road. Nothing to worry about. Stash your gun under the seat until we pass him by."

The driver bent and buried his own gun, then twisted back to her. "Remember, sis. No funny stuff. I swear, if you call out, you're dead."

Shaking badly, she wondered if her voice would work anyway. But right then, the miracle she'd prayed for happened. Their car came to a complete stop, almost directly in front of the church.

She bit her lip and tried to guess whether it would be closer for her to head for the sanctuary of the church or to run for the policeman in the street ten car-lengths away. The truck in front of them inched ahead and she decided to break for the church—it was her only real choice.

For a split second she stopped to wonder if she might be the kind of person who made rash decisions and who would rather fight back than die with a whimper. But then, whether out of fear or out of instinct, she knew it didn't matter.

If she were ever going to find out what had happened to her in the first place, she would have to go. Now.

* * *

Jericho heard a popping sound behind his back. Spinning around, he scanned the area trying to make out where the noise had originated.

"Was that a gunshot?" Fisher asked, as he too checked out the scene in front of the church.

In his peripheral vision, Jericho spotted a woman he'd never seen before. A woman seemingly out of place for a wedding, dressed in fancy jeans and red halter top. And she was racing at top speed across the grass straight in his direction. What the hell?

Another pop and the woman fell on the concrete walkway. From off to his left, someone screamed. Then tires squealed from somwhere down the long line of cars. When he glanced toward the sound, he saw a sedan with two men sitting in front as they roared out of the line and headed down the narrow shoulder of the highway.

Chaos reigned. Car horns honked. People shouted. And the sedan spewed out a huge dust plume as it bumped down the embankment.

Jericho took off at a run. He dropped to one knee beside the woman, checked her pulse and discovered she was breathing but unconscious and bleeding.

"Is she alive?" Deputy Rawlins asked, almost out of breath as he came running up. "I got their plates, Sheriff. But I didn't dare get off a shot with all the civilians in the way. You want me to pursue?"

Son of a gun. It would figure that he didn't have his weapon just when an emergency arose.

"Stay with the woman," Jericho ordered. "You and

Fisher get her to Doc O'Neal's as fast as you can. My rifle's in the truck, and…" He looked over his shoulder toward the church door. "Tell Macy…"

Right then Macy appeared at the top of the church steps and peered down at him. He was about to yell for her to get back out of the line of fire. But within a second, he could see her quickly taking in the whole situation.

"You go do what you need to, Jericho," she called out to him. "Don't worry about us. Just take care of yourself. The wedding's off for today."

Chapter 2

It was one of those spectacular Texas sunsets, but Jericho had been too preoccupied to enjoy it. Now that the sun had completely dropped below the horizon, he retraced his steps to the Community Church and the pre-arranged meeting with his deputy.

"Sorry you didn't catch them, Sheriff. I searched the grounds like you told me when you called in, and I came up with just this one bullet casing. From a 9mm. Pretty common, I'm afraid."

Jericho felt all of his thirty-five years weighing heavily on his shoulders tonight. "Yeah, but just in case there might be anything special, send it off to the lab in San Antonio. Okay?" It wasn't often that a trained lawman witnessed an attempted murder and couldn't either catch—or identify—the perpetrators. So why him? And why on his wedding day?

The deputy nodded and put the plastic evidence bag back into his jacket pocket.

"What happened with the victim?" Jericho asked wearily. "Is she still alive?"

"Last time I checked she was sitting up and able to talk, still over at Doc O'Neal's clinic. But she wasn't giving many answers."

That figured. Why make his job any easier?

"Did you run the plates?"

Deputy Rawlins frowned. "Stolen. Not the car. The plates were stolen in San Marcos day before yesterday."

Jericho's frustration grew but he kept it hidden as he rolled up the sleeves of his starched, white dress shirt. "When I checked in the last time, everyone else was okay. That still true?" He was concerned about Macy. How had she handled postponing the wedding?

"I never saw an assemblage of people disband so quickly or so quietly." The deputy removed his hat and fiddled with the brim. "Mrs. Ward was amazing. Once we were sure the immediate danger was over, she told everyone to go home and that she'd notify them when there would be another try at the wedding. Had everybody chuckling pretty good...but they went."

"I'd better call her."

"Yes, sir." With a tired sigh, Deputy Rawlins flipped his hat back onto his head. "Doc O'Neal needs someone to take charge of the woman victim. Says her condition is not serious enough to send her over to the Uvalde hospital, but she isn't capable of being on her own, either. You want me to handle it, Sheriff?"

"No, Adam. You've had a long day and you've done a fine job. You go on home. I'll clean up the odds and ends."

The deputy nodded and turned, but then hesitated and turned back. "Sorry about the wedding, boss. Don't you think that whole shooting scene was really odd for broad daylight? What do you suppose it was all about?"

When Jericho just raised his eyebrows and didn't answer, Adam continued, "Wait 'til you try to question that woman victim. She's a little odd, too. Wouldn't say much to me. But she's sure something terrific to look at."

"Thanks. Good-night now." Jericho would talk to the victim, and he would take charge of her and this case. But he had a mighty tough phone call to Macy to make first.

As Jericho stepped into Dr. O'Neal's clinic, his shoulders felt a thousand times lighter. Macy had been wonderful on the phone—as usual. She'd tried hard to make him feel better about ruining the wedding. She had even told him that she'd been considering postponing anyway. When he asked her why such a thing would occur to her, she said they would talk tomorrow.

In a way, he was curious and wondered if he'd done something inadvertent, other than being the sheriff, to make her mad. But in another way, his whole body felt weightless. He had meant to marry Macy today. Still did, in fact. He'd given his word. Besides that, recently he'd come to the conclusion that it was important for him to become a family man in order to honor his father.

But before Macy had suggested it a couple of weeks

ago, he had never planned on marrying anyone. He'd begun thinking of himself as a lone wolf. The idea of turning into the old bachelor sheriff had somehow taken root. He'd had visions of ending up like his father and having a girlfriend or two stashed away—ladies he could visit on Saturday nights. But in general the single life suited him just fine.

Now that Macy was hedging, Jericho felt ashamed to admit that her change of heart would seem like a reprieve. His only sorrow if they didn't marry would be T.J. But maybe things around the county would settle down enough now for him to spend more time with the boy despite not being his stepfather.

"Sheriff Yates." Dr. O'Neal met him just inside the front door. "I'd like to speak to you in private before you see the patient. Let's sit out here in the empty waiting room."

Jericho followed the doc. "What's wrong? Did the bullet do serious internal damage?"

Dr. O'Neal sat down on the flimsy, fake leather couch and removed his glasses. "No. Her gunshot wound is superficial. The bullet went right through the flesh on her left side and completely missed her ribcage. She twisted her ankle when she fell, but it's not broken or sprained. She also has some old bruising and a few nontreated cuts that appear to be at least twenty-four hours old. All things considered, her physical condition is unofficially 'beat-up' but not serious.

"That's not the worst of it, though," Doc added thoughtfully.

Jericho leaned against the edge of Doc's desk. "What are you trying to say?"

"She can't tell me how she got the bruises or the cuts. In fact, she doesn't remember a thing before this morning. I'm no expert in head trauma, mind you. But even with the small bump on her head, I don't believe she's suffered any major jarring of the brain. Certainly there's not enough outward damage to suspect a physical blow caused her amnesia.

"There *is* a condition known as a *fugue* state or psychogenic amnesia," he continued. "It's caused by a traumatic event so frightening to the patient that they flee from reality and hide themselves in another, safer life—one with no memories. I don't have a lot of training in psychology, but I do remember learning that this kind of state may last for months or years."

"Amnesia? But it's just temporary. The memories will eventually come back, right?"

"Hard to say," Doc hedged as he blew dust from his glasses. "I understand that in some cases snippets of memories will flash through the mind and memories may fade in and out until the full picture emerges. Sometimes…nothing comes back at all."

Jericho took a breath. He couldn't imagine how hard that would be. To never be able to bring back the memory of growing up or the memory of his mother's face. What would that do to…?

He jerked and straightened his shoulders. Whatever would possess him to think such a thing? His mother had been a drunk and had left the family when he was only a kid. Truth be told, he hated her. Why would he care to remember what her face looked like? That was one memory he wouldn't mind losing for good.

"Let's go talk to the patient, Doc. What's her name?"

Dr. O'Neal shrugged. "No clue. She doesn't remember and your deputy said he couldn't find any ID in her clothes or at the church scene."

Now, that was *one* thing Jericho would hate to forget. The Yates name meant something. There were generations of Yates men who had been lawmen, sportsmen and landowners. It was a name to be proud of and to do right by.

Sheriff Yates. He'd worked hard to get that title. He'd paid his dues as deputy, been appointed when the old sheriff retired, and finally had been elected on his own merit. He anticipated continuing to be a man worthy of everyone's respect. And it was high time to do his job.

As Jericho walked through Dr. O'Neal's office door to meet the mystery woman, he didn't know what he expected to find. But it was definitely not the most gorgeous woman he had ever beheld.

Yet there she sat on one of Doc's plastic chairs. Miss America, Miss Universe and Venus de Milo all wrapped into one—with a bad haircut and wild, sky-blue eyes. Jericho had to swallow hard in order to find his voice.

"Good evening, ma'am. I'm Sheriff Jericho Yates. How're you feeling?"

She lightly touched her temple, but continued to stare up at him, those strange electric eyes boring holes straight into his. "The headache and the four stitches in my side are the worst of it. No, I take that back. Not knowing my own name is the worst of it. Did Dr. O'Ne 1 tell you that I can't remember anything? He says I ha ￼ 2 amnesia."

"Yes, ma'am. I understand. But we need to talk about what you *do* remember. Can you start with your first clear memory and tell me everything that happened up until the time when you were shot?"

"Um…I guess I could do that." She reached up and rubbed the back of her neck. "But can you sit down first? I'm getting stiff just looking up at you. How tall are you anyway?"

Jericho found a chair and dragged it over while Doc moved to sit behind his desk. "Six-three." They both sat. "There you go, Red. Is that better?"

"Yes, thanks." Lost and feeling vulnerable, even in the presence of someone as safe as the sheriff, the woman had to take deep breaths in order to calm herself down.

"Did you just call her 'Red,' Sheriff?" The doctor was scowling over his desk pad.

The sheriff looked perplexed. "Well, I suppose. We've got to call her something. 'Hey you' just won't do and she has all that bright red hair. Seemed to work."

"Bright red hair? Do I?" She put her hands in her hair. "But that doesn't feel right."

"Don't upset yourself by trying to force the memories of your lost past," the doctor said soothingly. "Not yet. Give it some time." He turned back to address the sheriff. "Jericho, I want you to take things slow. Pushing her to remember will only make it worse.

"Oh, and I don't believe 'Red' is the least bit feminine," the doctor continued. "It doesn't fit this beautiful young woman and it doesn't sound respectful to me. Can't we come up with something else?"

Still with her hands in her hair, she worried that more

seemed wrong with it than just the wrong hair color. Though God only knew what she meant by that.

"Okay, Doc," the sheriff conceded. "How about 'Rosie?' That's in the same color type."

"Rosie's okay with me," she agreed quickly. The name didn't nauseate her nearly as much as the wrong feeling about her hair.

"Okay, Rosie," the sheriff said with a deliberate drawl and a tight smile. "You can call me Jericho. Now tell me what you do remember."

She wasn't sure she could do this. Every time she thought of how terrifying those men had been, her whole body started trembling. Looking up at Sheriff Jericho for support, she was surprised to find an odd softness in his eyes as he waited for her to speak.

She'd thought he had looked so tough. Scary-tough, with all his hard angles and rough edges, when he'd first walked into Dr. O'Neal's office. Now, it seemed that at least his eyes held some empathy toward her, and the idea made her relax a little.

"The…um…first thing I remember clearly is two men pushing me around. One was pointing a gun at me while the other kept shaking me by the shoulders, hard. I felt as though I'd just woken up from a deep sleep. But now I'm not sure that was the case."

"And these two men didn't look familiar?"

"Not at all."

"Where was this? What do you remember of your surroundings?"

"After a few minutes, I decided it had to be a cheap motel room. But I…never found out whose."

"Okay," the sheriff said as he rubbed a thumb across his neat mustache. "Don't strain for answers. Let's just take this nice and easy."

She must've been wearing a frown as she'd tried to bring the images to the front of her mind because that tender look had returned to Jericho's eyes. "Can you tell me what the men said to you?" he asked gently.

"Oh, yeah. They wanted to know where some special thing was." At his curious expression, she shrugged her shoulders. "I never found out what the 'thing' was they were looking for. But they said I had stolen it and their boss wanted it back."

"You believe what they were saying was the truth? Like perhaps you had stolen something?"

Yeah, God help her, it kinda did. But with that strange thought, she began shuddering again. A lone tear leaked from the corner of her eye. "I don't know."

"Sheriff…" The doctor cautioned him with his tone.

Jericho scowled briefly then nodded. "Sorry, Doc. I won't push.

"Okay, Rosie, what did the men say or do after you couldn't give them what they wanted?"

She sniffed once and wiped her hand across her face. "They beat me up a little. You know, like slapping me and punching me in the arms and shoulders. And the whole time they kept demanding that I talk. I was so scared they were going to kill me that what they were doing hardly even hurt."

The doctor cleared his throat. The sheriff fisted his hands on his knees.

"What did they say then?" Jericho asked in a rough voice.

"Finally, they looked at their watches and said I was going to go with them to see the boss. That he would make me tell where it was. Then they pushed me outside and into the backseat of their car."

"Did anything outside look familiar?"

Dr. O'Neal huffed and opened his mouth to chastise the sheriff's choice of words.

"Oh, yeah. Sorry again," Jericho put in quickly. "What I meant was, what did it look like outside the motel room?"

"I couldn't see much. But what I did see wasn't anything special. Like the poor side of lots of small towns, I guess." Now how would she know that? She couldn't even come up with her own name and yet she knew what the poor side of town would look like?

The sheriff gave her an odd look. "Do you know where you are now?"

"Your deputy told me. Esperanza, Texas."

"Does that hold any meaning for you?" Jericho glanced over at the doctor and then held up his hand in self-defense. "Don't answer that, Rosie, not unless something comes to you. I shouldn't have asked."

Jericho was more than a little frustrated. He didn't want to hurt her by asking the wrong questions. But the only way he could help her was by getting answers. He promised to think longer before he opened his mouth.

"Okay. Let's get back to the men. Can you describe them?"

"I guess so."

But while Jericho watched her open her mouth to try, he noted her wincing as another one of those slashing pains must've struck her in the head. "Never mind. Give it a rest for tonight. We'll try it in the morning. In fact, if you're feeling well enough by then, you can go through mug shots."

Rosie sighed and her shoulders slumped. She glanced up at him from under long, thick lashes with a look so needful, so vulnerable, that it was all he could do not to sweep her up in his arms and keep her bogeymen at bay. He'd never before acted as some female's sole link to the world and to safety. He was just a county sheriff. But whatever had frightened her badly enough to erase her memories needed to be dealt with soon. He vowed to be the one to take care of it.

"Jericho," Doc interrupted his thoughts. "Rosie needs a good night's sleep. We've determined that she doesn't have a concussion, but we haven't got any place to make her comfortable here. What can you do for her?"

"Leave this place?" Rosie folded her arms over her very generous chest in a self-protective move that stirred his own protective instincts even further.

There were no motels in Esperanza. The nearest one was a half hour away. It was too late to call anyone in town to find her a place for the night.

"But what if those goons come looking for me again?" Rosie's voice was shaky and her eyes wild and frightened again. "Will they? Do you think it's possible?"

Hell. It actually was a possibility that those men might double back and finish what they'd started. Rosie needed to be in protective custody. But where could he be sure she would be safe and comfortable? The deputy's substation in town had only a small holding cell. That would never do.

"Don't you worry, ma'am. You're coming home with me. You'll be perfectly safe and comfortable there. I've got a spare bedroom and it's all made up." Had he really just said that? He stood up and stretched his legs.

"Your spare room should be okay, Jericho," Doc said. "But there's something I must tell you both first.

"I haven't said anything to Rosie about this yet," the doctor continued. "Because I don't know if it might spark a memory and cause her some pain. But both of you need to know that there should be *someone* who cares about her and should've missed her by now."

Rosie sat forward in her chair. "What do you mean?"

"While I was examining you, I discovered you're around two months' pregnant." The doc said it carefully, gently, but there was no way to make that news go down easy.

"No." She put a hand to her belly. "Can't be. How could I forget something like that?"

The doc went over to put his arm around her shoulders. "It's possible that you didn't realize you were pregnant before you lost your memory. Two months isn't very far along. If you don't start getting your memories or haven't found a family by the time you're feeling a little stronger, come on in and see me for prenatal instructions.

"And in the meantime, watch your diet. No caffeine. No alcohol, and definitely no smoking. My examination tells me you've never carried a baby to full term before, but I'm sure you won't have any trouble. There are just some things you'll need to know."

"Yeah," Rosie said. "Like who I am and who the baby's father is." She shot Jericho a rolled-eye smile.

It was such an intimate gesture. As though the two of them already shared some gigantic secret from the rest of the world. In that split second, her smile miraculously swept away one of the invisible shackles to his normal restraint.

He could almost hear the snap of an old, half-forgotten anguish relinquishing its hold on him.

With a competent smile, he offered her a helping hand at the elbow. "Let's go. All of this will look better in the morning."

She stood and he did something he hadn't done in so long he could barely remember the last time. As they walked out of the doctor's office, he pulled her closer and they walked arm in arm together toward the truck.

Chapter 3

The moment Rosie stepped into Jericho's huge log-cabin home it seemed clear she'd made a mistake. Oh, the place was beautiful, with its handcrafted furnishings, sleek open spaces and heavy-beamed ceilings.

After taking a few steps past the wide front door, she spied a state-of-the-art kitchen, including dark granite countertops and stainless-steel appliances, that appeared prominently just beyond the stone fireplace.

Decorated in tans, browns and natural woods, the place certainly looked comfortable. And since Jericho was sheriff, it should be safe.

But where were the feminine touches? The walls held few decorations, save for a large fish mounted on a brass plaque and a couple of birds, or maybe they were ducks, stuffed and stuck on wooden planks. A bronze statue standing on a hand-hewed coffee table was the only other decoration she saw. Even the kitchen seemed stark and empty. This was definitely a man's home. A single man.

"Uh," she began. "Aren't you married? Where's your wife?" Why hadn't she thought to ask that before she agreed to stay here?

"I'm not married." He walked to the grand, airy kitchen and opened the refrigerator. "You want something to eat or drink? There isn't much. I was, ah, supposed to be on my honeymoon tonight."

She relaxed a bit. At least he had a girlfriend. "What happened? What stopped the honeymoon?"

He turned from the open fridge. "There was a shooting right outside the church. The wedding was called off."

"Ouch." She winced and slid onto one of the barstools at the counter. "I screwed it up, didn't I? I'm so sorry."

Leaving the refrigerator door standing open, Jericho crossed the kitchen and leaned over the counter in her direction. He laid a hand on her shoulder and the electric jolt his warmth caused against her skin both shocked and surprised her.

"Don't be too hard on yourself," he said. "Seems the bride-to-be was about to call the whole thing off. Temporarily, anyway. I'd bet she might even be grateful that you gave her the perfect excuse." He took his hand away and stared at it, as if he too had felt the sizzle.

With his hand gone from her shoulder, Rosie decided she could almost breathe again. "You don't sound very upset. Are you heartbroken?"

Turning his back, Jericho cleared his throat and went to the open fridge. "Naw. It was going to be one of those whata-you-call-'ems? Marriages of convenience. Macy Ward has been my best friend since we were kids. I volunteered to marry her and take over being the father to her out-of-control teenage son."

He glanced around the kitchen and then back into the nearly empty refrigerator as though he had never seen them before. "But I'm not sure where I figured we would make a home together. This place isn't set up for a wife and kid. I built it with my own hands, me and my dad, and I certainly don't want to move out of it and go to town.

"I guess I hadn't really thought the whole thing through well enough."

Maybe it was because of her jumbled state of mind, but she was having trouble processing everything he'd said. "You mean you two don't love each other but you were going to get married anyway? I didn't know things like that really happened." She shook her head. "Just so you could be a father to her son? Wow."

What was that she'd been spouting? How would she know anything at all, let alone about marriage? Was she married? She didn't feel like she was. Damn. The harder she thought, the hazier everything became. She must be more disoriented than she'd thought.

"Yeah, I guess that's about right." Jericho shrugged a shoulder. "You want tomato soup? I've got a can or two I can heat up and soda crackers to go with it."

Was this guy for real? "Sure. Soup will be fine." Maybe the whole thing was some terrible dream she'd been having. Any moment now she would wake up and find herself back to being…

Nope. The best she could do was to remember she'd been running for her life and had fallen at the feet of one deadly gorgeous, *single* Texas sheriff.

And tonight she would have to adjust herself to a whole new persona. Mother-to-be. Without so much as a smattering of memory of her own mother.

Not to mention, without having the first clue as to who the baby's father might be.

Hmm. All that might be more than she could handle for one night. Maybe she'd be better off doing what the doctor said and just go with the flow. At least for tonight.

So far she'd learned this Sheriff Jericho guy might be too good to be true. Marrying the best friend he didn't love in order to give her son a father? Good for him. And by the same token, that ought to mean she wouldn't have to worry about him forcing her to do anything against her will. Mister Knight in Shining Armor must be the ultimate good guy. Who woulda thunk a man like that really existed?

Rosie tried to let her mind go blank as she watched Jericho fumble around in the kitchen. But she couldn't get the idea of him being unattached out of her head.

As she looked down at her left hand, it made her chuckle to think that she would know about married women wearing wedding rings on the third finger of their left hands but she didn't know whether or not she was married herself. Her fingers bore no rings at all. But that didn't tell the whole story. What if she'd taken off her rings? What if they'd been stolen?

Sighing in frustration, she went back to studying the man.

Then wished she hadn't.

Wide, muscular shoulders flexed as he reached for dishes in the cabinets. His dark blond hair and sexy hazel eyes made him as handsome as any movie star. Her glance moved down along his torso as it narrowed to lean hips. She forced herself to turn away from the sight of his fantastically tight butt. But she didn't completely lose sight of his long arms and even longer legs. The whole picture was developing into a hero, all lean and formidable. Like the sheriff in a white hat from an old-time movie.

The good guy. The *sexy* good guy.

He set a bowl of steaming soup in front of her and sat across the counter with his own. "This must be tough on you."

Heartfelt concern shone from those deep hazel eyes as he gazed intently in her direction. The more she watched them, the darker the irises became. Soon they were steel gray, and suddenly sensual. Hot.

She quickly took a sip of the soup and nearly burned her tongue. "Uh, yeah. It's hard not knowing where I came from or who I am. I wish I knew what those men were after."

Jericho lifted the spoon to his mouth and blew as he studied the beautiful woman across the counter. He was having trouble keeping his mind from wandering. Wandering off to things he would love to do to her, for her, with her.

Her stunning eyes had lost that wild, crazed look, so

he'd been studying the rest. The body seemed made for sex. At five-foot-ten or so, she wasn't quite his height. But she also wasn't a dainty little thing, one who might break if he didn't watch his step. Somewhat on the thin side, she looked like a model. But unlike the models he'd seen on magazines, her lean body just made those fantastic breasts seem all the more voluptuous. And those legs. Don't get him started on those long, shapely legs. Even encased in designer jeans, he could tell how they would look naked—wrapped around his waist and in the heat of passion.

The mere sight of a good-looking woman had never done things like this to his libido in the past. He couldn't imagine why she was so different. But the why didn't seem to matter all that much. She just was, and he had to find a way to stop thinking about her like that.

She was pregnant. No doubt she belonged to someone—somewhere.

"Is the soup okay?" he asked, trying to push aside the unwanted thoughts. "Is there anything else I can do for you before I settle you down for the night?"

Ah hell. Just the word *night* made him long for things he had no business even considering.

"Soup's fine." She took another sip and a bite of the crackers. "But I feel so…I don't know. Like I'm not grounded. Like I'm flying around in midair. It's probably because I can't recall my past and my family. And this baby thing… That really threw me.

"Maybe it would help if you told me something about your family," she went on to suggest. "Would you mind? I think just hearing that someone else can remember and knows who they are will give me hope that someday I'll get my memories back. Does that seem too nosy?"

He was good at questioning victims and criminals. And he'd forced himself to become a decent politician in order to get elected. But talking about his life to a complete stranger was totally out of his realm. He had a strong instinct to keep his mouth shut, but she looked so vulnerable, so needy.

"There's not much to tell." But he guessed he *could* give her a few basic facts. "I was born and raised right here in Esperanza. My dad is Buck Yates, and he was born right here in town, too. Dad spent years in the service and now he owns the farm-supply store in town. Of course around here, that means he sells mostly guns and tack, some deer blinds and a lot of game feeders."

Jericho let himself give her one of his polite, running-for-office smiles as he continued. "My older brother, Fisher, is a captain in the U.S. Army, just home on leave from his third tour of duty in the Middle East." He shrugged and ducked his head, not knowing where to go from here. "That's about it for the family. Want to hear about my friends?"

"You didn't mention your mother. Has she passed away?"

If only she had simply died. "Our mother took off when Fisher and I were kids."

"Took off?"

"Disappeared. Haven't heard a word from her in nearly thirty years. She might be dead by now for all I know." Good riddance if she was.

He stood, picked up his empty soup bowl and eyed

Rosie's almost empty one. "You want another bowl of soup? Or anything else?"

Without answering, Rosie glanced up at him and he spotted dark, purplish circles under her eyes. The lady was whooped. His protective instincts kicked right back in again.

"Let's get you into bed for now. We'll have a fresh start in the morning. Okay with you?"

"I am tired. Thanks." She slid off the barstool and he watched her hanging tightly on to the counter as if her legs were about to give out on her.

He dumped the dishes into the sink and went to her side. "Here, take my arm. I won't let you fall."

For a moment, it seemed that she would refuse. Jericho saw her try to straighten up and steady herself. But within a split second, she started to slide.

There was no choice. He bent to pick her up in his arms. A lot lighter than he'd imagined, her body hugged his chest as she threw her arms around his neck and hung on.

"I feel ridiculous. I can't even remember my own name and now I can't walk under my own steam. It's a good thing you're here, Sheriff."

Yeah, maybe. Or maybe this was going to turn into his worst nightmare.

Jericho carried her down the hall and into the spare room. Setting her down in the corner chair, he pulled back the covers from the double bed.

"This should be comfortable enough." He had to turn away from the sight of clean, fresh sheets just waiting for bodies to mess them up.

"It looks great," she told him. "But I wish I had a pair of clean pajamas. These clothes are getting gamy."

He stood there for a second, picturing her naked again. Finally, making a tremendous effort, he started thinking with his head instead of another part of his anatomy.

"How about I lend you one of my T-shirts? I've got one or two older ones that've turned soft from washing and I don't wear them anymore. Would that do?"

She nodded and gave him a weak smile.

When he brought a shirt back into the room and handed it to her, his sex-obsessed brain produced another thought. This one worried him.

"Are you going to need help getting undressed?"

"No, I'm feeling stronger, thanks. I think the food helped."

"Great. The bathroom is right across the hall. There are towels in the closet and an extra new toothbrush. Use whatever you need."

"Thanks again, Jericho. I'll be fine. See you in the morning."

Glad to know she would be okay for the night, Jericho eased out of her room and headed for his own. He probably wouldn't fare as well with his own night. The thought of Rosie lying in bed in the room right next to his would keep him tossing and turning.

Sighing, he shrugged off his by-now-filthy dress shirt and tried telling himself it would all be okay. He had a plan. He would just start thinking of her like he would a roommate.

Well, that plan didn't work out so well. Jericho dragged himself into the shower the next morning and turned the faucets on full cold. *Roommate, my foot.* When had a roommate ever kept him lying awake for half the night with daydreams of long, silky legs and ripe, sensitive breasts?

Irritated at himself, he swore to do better today. And it would serve him right if he was too tired and miserable all day long to concentrate.

After his shower, he stood before the mirror, preparing to shave. A couple of things were going to have to change today, he silently demanded of his image. He needed to get a line on Rosie's relatives. Somewhere people must be missing her. The sooner he found them and returned her to her previous life, the better off he would be. Let someone else protect her.

The second thing that needed to change was the way she dressed. She didn't have a change of clothes, and she needed to cover herself up real soon.

But the thought of how she dressed reminded him of something else. Another chore he must do, first thing. Maybe he could combine the two. Yeah, that should work.

Rosie opened her eyes when a dash of sunlight hit her eyelids and irritated her enough to wake up. She glanced over at the bright sunshine peeping through the wood-slatted miniblinds and wondered what time it was.

Rolling over, it hit her. A gigantic black void. The gaping abyss in her brain suddenly threatened to swallow her whole.

Gasping for air, as though someone had been choking her, and flailing her arms against a sea of nothingness and nausea, Rosie let her mind grab hold of the only thing it could. The one thing she saw clearly. The memory of Jericho Yates.

Immediately her heart rate slowed and warmth replaced the stone-cold numbness she'd felt when she awoke to find nothing familiar. Jericho had made one hell of an anchor last night. He'd tethered her to the earth with quiet concern and a sensual smile.

Fighting to remain in the moment and trying not to think either backward or forward, she sat at the edge of the bed and took stock. First was the physical. Her head wasn't pounding as it had been last night. The stitches in her side were barely noticeable. She rotated her ankle and found only an echo of the pain she'd experienced.

Okay, so she felt a little achy and sore, but she would live. Well, unless the bad guys came back.

Her second concern—and the real question—remained the same as before: How was she going to get her memories back? The doctor said not to push it. The moment she'd tried to find some thread of memory, panic had set in.

Taking another deep breath, she came to the conclusion that she had no choice. To keep from going stark raving mad, she had better just go along minute by minute. Living hour by hour and feeling her way.

Standing in the kitchen drinking coffee, Jericho heard Rosie opening the spare room door and going into the bathroom. The sudden jolt of anticipation at seeing her again competed with the practiced calm he had almost perfected during the hours since his shower.

But just then someone knocked on the front door.

Jericho figured Rosie's goons wouldn't have the guts to confront him in broad daylight, and they definitely wouldn't be knocking when they came to call. So this must be the person he was expecting.

He checked out the window and saw her car. Yes, it was his best friend. He wiped the smile off his face and went to let her in.

"Morning, Macy. Thanks for coming." He stood aside and allowed her to come in.

When she entered the room, everything felt easy, even somehow more homey. "Good morning, Jericho. I had every intention of talking to you this morning anyway. It's my pleasure if I can be of some help at the same time."

As a best friend, Macy Ward couldn't be beat. As a potential spouse…he would just as soon skip it.

"I wanted to say how sorry I am about the ceremony, Mace. You know I wouldn't have ducked out on it if I'd had any choice."

Macy went straight into the great room and dumped her armload of folded clothes on the nearest chair. "I know. You're a good man, Jericho Yates. That's one of the reasons I twisted your arm into agreeing to marry me."

"Now, Mace. You aren't holding a gun to my head. I volunteered to help you out with T.J."

"Yes, you did. And I love you for it." She turned and touched his arm. "You are really a good guy, my friend. Too good to get saddled with a wife who won't ever love you the way she should. I can't do it to you.

"I'm calling the wedding off permanently," she blurted. "You're off the hook for good."

Relief mixed with sadness and kicked him in the gut.

He didn't want to get married, but he would do anything to help Macy out in her time of need.

"What about T.J.? How are you going to take control of him now?" When she didn't answer, Jericho stepped up again. "Look, I can make some extra time for him this summer. Just as soon as I find a link to our mystery woman, my schedule should lighten up."

Macy smiled softly. "T.J. is a big part of the reason I'm canceling our wedding. You know he's in the middle of doing that community service project you arranged for him over at the state park this week. He's not pleased about having to make up for the toilet-paper and mailbox mangling incidents, but I hope he's learning his lesson and is staying out of trouble.

"And then earlier this week Jewel agreed to let T.J. work at the Hopechest Ranch for the rest of the summer." Macy's smile brightened. "The hard work should be good for him. But that means you don't have to worry about making time for him. He'll be plenty busy."

Several emotions flitted through Jericho at break-neck speed. Disappointment came first. Then another level of relief. Finally, a streak of annoyance came and went. Now he would have no excuse for not spending all his time with Rosie and working on her case.

"Do you think T.J. is going to be broken up about the change in marriage plans?" He hoped not. Deep down the kid was really good and Jericho hated to see him hurt.

Macy shook her head. "Don't worry about it. Actually, he's been pretty antsy over us getting married.

I imagine he'll be happy to hear his mother will continue being single."

Jericho didn't like the sound of that. "Is he still upset over my giving him community service? I only did it to keep him out of the juvenile system. I…"

"No, Jericho," she interrupted. "You did the best thing for him. You're not trying to be his friend. Me neither. It's our job as adults to do the right thing. I really believe T.J.'s biggest trouble with the wedding is Tim's memory. He saw you as Tim's friend for so long that he couldn't quite get past the changeover to having you take Tim's place."

"But I wasn't…I wouldn't."

Macy chuckled at his mumbling protests. "I know. And T.J. would've found that out if he'd had the chance.

"But calling it off is for the best," she continued. "For all of us. This way, you'll have the opportunity to find someone who you can…"

At that moment, Rosie cleared her throat to announce that she was interrupting. She still had on his old T-shirt but she'd slipped on her jeans underneath it and her hair was wet from the shower. The sight of her in the hallway simply set his veins on fire.

The difference between how he'd felt seeing Macy and how he felt right now seeing Rosie seemed extreme. And he didn't care for it one bit.

Chapter 4

"You must be the one Jericho's calling Rosie. I'm Macy Ward." The woman rushed over and reached out to capture her hands. "Jericho's old friend. It's gotta be terrible for you, not having any memories. I was so shocked when I heard. You poor thing."

Taken aback by such an effusive greeting, Rosie felt torn between laughing and running for her life. But there was just something about Macy Ward that made her want to smile.

Slinging her arm around Rosie's shoulder, Macy hugged her close. "I brought you some decaffeinated teas and a few things to wear, honey. Just to get you by for a day or two. I can't imagine not having a closet or even a purse to call your own.

"Oh, makeup," Macy added with a start. "Darn. I should've thought of that, too."

"Um. That's okay. I don't know if I wear any." With that thought, Rosie lifted the back of her hand to her mouth in an effort to hold off what might turn into a sob.

But she stopped in midair, struck by the wayward idea that she might be a nail biter. Checking, Rosie was relieved to find her nails seemed intact. And manicured and polished at that.

So she was a woman who took care of her appearance. Spent money and time on it. Not that anyone could judge by the way she looked this morning. One glance in the bathroom mirror after her shower, and Rosie had nearly fled screaming. In addition to the bruises and cuts, her disaster of a hairdo could not possibly be normal. Not only didn't it look like she'd spent any money or time on it, but it just didn't *feel* right.

Rosie nearly broke down again as she wondered how long it might take her to get a clear idea of what her hair was really supposed to look like. Would that ever happen? It was possible, she supposed, that the memory would never return. But thinking that way made her knees weak.

Macy turned back to Jericho, who had been standing there with his mouth gaping open. "Jericho, fix Rosie this tea and us some coffee, will you? Maybe you could even scramble Rosie a couple of eggs. You *do* have fresh eggs?"

Being called down by Macy seemed to shake Jericho out of his reverie. "I've got a few eggs, and the coffee's already made. What are you going to do?"

"I'm going to help Rosie change. The things I brought should be a close fit to her size. She's a little taller and thinner than I am, though. So we'll have to see." With that, Macy spun them both around and headed down the hall.

Rosie heard Jericho mumbling from over her shoulder. "Well, sure. Y'all help just yourselves. I'll cook."

Fifteen minutes later and she was still feeling a bit weepy. Macy had been trying to brush her awful hair into some semblance of a style. Of course, without much luck.

Rosie thought things in general seemed a lot better. Macy bringing clean underwear had been a real blessing. Putting clean clothes on made Rosie feel almost human again. They'd discovered Macy's slacks were about an inch too short and the shoulders of her blouse were big enough for a Rosie and a half—yet the buttons in front barely closed. Still, clean clothes had made a world of difference in how Rosie saw her situation.

"I'm sorry I messed up your wedding yesterday, Macy. Are you upset? Can you reschedule?"

The other woman turned and captured her in a big bear hug. "You're a sweetheart for thinking of me when you have so much trouble of your own. But not to worry. The wedding is off for good. You didn't mess up a thing."

Rosie's curiosity was piqued and she decided she didn't care about sounding too nosy around this sweet woman with the blazing white smile and two tiny dimples. "Why did you call it off? Did something happen between you and Jericho?"

"Come sit down with me for a moment," Macy said as she led her back into the spare bedroom and plopped on the bed. "Let me tell you something about the man who's taken you in."

Curious, Rosie eased down beside her. She didn't remember a thing about her past, but maybe it would be smart to know a whole lot more about her present.

"When I was born in this small town," Macy began, "there were several boys who lived on my block. I guess I was kind of a tomboy as a kid because two of those boys who were my age became my best friends. I never had much to do with the other little girls in town."

It was nice hearing Macy talk about her past. Somehow her story seemed to be grounding Rosie.

"One of those two best guy friends was always acting as my protector and big brother. Countless times he saved me from bullies and rescued me from runaway horses and from out of trees." Macy's dimples showed at the memories. "By the time I was twelve, though, it was the other one who'd captured my heart. I developed a huge crush on that one and it quickly turned to love. We married the minute we were old enough."

"Jericho was the big brother of the two." Rosie was sure Jericho hadn't been the lover.

"Of course. He's still doing it, too. My husband, Tim, died about six years ago and Jericho stepped in to make sure my son T.J. and I were okay. I'm not sure what we would've done without him."

"But Jericho's never been married?"

Macy's smile dimmed slightly. "No. But in my opinion, it's just that he's never found the right woman. Everyone who knows him loves and respects him. He could've had his pick of any woman in the county."

"But not you? You're sure?"

It was a sad smile that Macy wore by the time she answered. "I wish I felt differently. But no. I'm sure. Jericho and I are like brother and sister. We'll never get past that. I know he's relieved to be getting out of our marriage agreement. But he's still the best man in the entire county.

"Who else would've agreed to marry his best friend just so her son would have a father?" Macy shook her head sadly and patted Rosie's hand. "Enough about me. How are you feeling? You look a bit pale. Are you queasy? Let's go get you something to eat."

For a split second when Rosie appeared out of the bedroom wearing Macy's clothes, Jericho had been absolutely positive the image he saw was all wrong. This mystery woman did not belong in cotton slacks and long-sleeved, button-down shirts, of that he was sure. He envisioned her as being more into silks and fancy designer duds. But then when he blinked once, the lost woman with no past was back and it didn't matter what she wore, his heart went out to her.

As the three of them sat around his kitchen table and Rosie ate breakfast, Macy babbled on about the current happenings in her life. Jericho suspected she was doing it to make Rosie forget her predicament.

"My boss, Jewel Mayfair—you'll love her when you meet her, Rosie. Well, anyway, she's had a kind of rough life. But her uncle is Joe Colton. He's that senator in California who's running for president, you know?"

Jericho cut in, "Macy, Doc O'Neal said we shouldn't

expect Rosie to bring back memories just yet. She's supposed to relax and just let things come to her on their own."

"Oh, but…" Rosie interrupted. "The name Joe Colton does ring a bell. He must be really famous."

"Or maybe you were just interested in politics." Macy added her own conjecture. "I know that the presidential campaign has been really heating up on TV. Jewel says her uncle has lots of influential backers. But since our Texas governor entered the race against Senator Colton, Jewel says things haven't been going so well. And I can imagine that's right. Governor Daniels is really hot. I voted for him for governor, and he can probably count on my vote for president, too. But don't tell Jewel."

Rosie chuckled, but then put her head in her hands. "I don't know. Everything sounds familiar but nothing is. The harder I try…"

Jericho would've liked nothing better than to take Rosie in his arms to comfort her just then. But Macy leaned over and lifted a gentle hand to Rosie's shoulder.

"Then don't try, sweetie." She turned to Jericho. "Maybe you could help Rosie by finding out the kinds of things she likes to do when she's relaxing. For instance, you know I love to read romance novels. I'm positive that wouldn't change about me even if I couldn't remember anything else."

Okay, Jericho had always figured he made a pretty good detective when it came to catching criminals. But this kind of detective work seemed a little over his head.

"Uh, what kinds of things would you suggest she try?" he asked Macy.

Macy raised her eyebrows and then tilted her head to study Rosie. "Most women would love a good relaxing day at a spa—along with some chocolate. But there aren't any spas around here. And I always love a good relaxing day of shopping, which is also in limited supply in Esperanza, Texas, I'm afraid.

"Um…" Macy looked around the great room as though something might come to her. "Maybe she has a hobby. Like sewing or knitting. Or…" She swung her arm around to indicate Rosie should look at the room. "Decorating. Does anything about this room speak to you?"

Rosie blinked a couple of times and then glanced over Jericho's furnishings. "It just says *man's man* to me," she said with a shrug. "Except I guess for the Frederic Remington bronze on the table over there, and that antique Navajo rug on the wall behind the leather couch that I suspect is worth several thousands. Those aren't museum-quality pieces, by any means, but they're nice examples of the style."

Jericho knew his mouth was hanging open. And judging by Macy's silence, she too had been surprised by Rosie's sudden show of knowledge. He'd almost forgotten he'd even bought the Remington at a charity auction. And the Navajo blanket had been a housewarming present from his father that he barely noticed anymore. Those were the only two things in the whole house except for his rifles that were worth much. Rosie had spotted them right away.

He finally got his voice back when Rosie turned to him. "Hmm," he said for lack of anything more definitive. "I suspect you've been either an art collector or a museum volunteer at some point in your life, ma'am. What do you think?"

"I don't know," she said with a heavy sigh. "I don't seem to know anything. I can't explain why those things just popped out of my mouth."

Macy stood and bent over Rosie to cuddle her around the shoulders. "Jericho, this poor girl needs to relax and not think too hard so her past can ease back to her. You've got to find something to help her."

He stood, too. "My job is to keep her safe and alive first, Mace. I'm worried that whoever tried to kill her will come back around for another try. We're just going to have to let the memories come as they will and see how she does."

An hour after Macy left, Rosie's head was still buzzing with Jericho's words. *Those men might come back for another try? Oh, God.*

"You awake?" Jericho poked his head inside the spare room where she'd been trying to take a nap.

Just the sight of him made her stomach muscles flutter.

"Yes," she said as she sat up at the edge of the bed.

"I've been on the phone with my deputy. And he's gathering some mug shots off the Internet for you to look at later today. You willing to give it a try?"

"Of course I am. I want those men caught." Thinking of those awful goons made her body shiver in dread.

"Easy there." Jericho took her hand and helped her stand. "I've also been giving some thought to hobbies that might make you relax. You still don't have a clue as to what you like, do you?"

"No." But having said that, Rosie's mind tricked her into thinking about one way to relax she wouldn't mind trying at all. Sharing a relaxing kiss—with the man whose soft hazel eyes were gazing into hers right now.

On second thought, Rosie admitted that kissing Jericho might not be as relaxing as all that. Just standing next to him now was shooting jazzy little sparks of lust right down her spine. Kissing him was bound to become more intense than relaxing.

How could Macy have turned him away? He was so hot.

"When I want to relax," Jericho began in his fantastic Texas drawl, "I always find being outside with nature is a great way to shuck your stress. Does that sound like something you might want to try?"

She shrugged, not able to concentrate on anything much more than a pair of to-die-for hazel eyes that were turning a gorgeous shade of sea-mist green that matched his shirt.

"What did you have in mind to do outside?" she asked. But in the next moment she wished she'd kept her mouth shut. She sure knew what she'd like to be doing—either outside or in.

"Well, usually I fish or hunt," he answered as though he had no clue what was on her mind. "Both real relaxing. But I suspect those might be too tricky for someone without memories. And it would take us too long to get out to the right spots for them, too.

"I was thinking, though," he added. "That you might be willing to take in some fresh air at the same time as I gave you a small lesson in self-defense. I have a target set up behind the house in the woods so I can practice with my service weapons when I need to. Think I can talk you into trying a little target practice? Maybe you'll find that relaxing."

"Self-defense?" Oh, Lordy. Just the idea made her anything but relaxed. "Do you really imagine that I might need to know how to shoot a gun?" Her stress quotient jumped at least a hundred percent.

Jericho grinned at her. "What makes you think you don't already know how?"

"I...don't... Maybe you're right. I should try lots of things before I just say no automatically.

"But do you truly think shooting somebody might be necessary?" she added warily.

"Slow down." He took her hand and slid his arm around her waist. "We'll go nice and easy. Just give target practice a try. Probably never going to need a weapon for any reason, but I'd just as soon you were comfortable around them all the same.

"Besides," he added with another grin. "I want you to meet my two hounds. I've been keeping them outside in their dog run for your benefit. But I know they'd like meeting you. Maybe you're a dog lover. You might even find out you've always liked target practice. Some people find it totally relaxing."

"Damn it all to hell, Arn." The hired goon called Petey swore again and spit out the window of their idling car, almost hitting a willow tree. "Unless she's dead, we can't go back without the chick. We'll be the ones in dead trouble. So what're we going to do?"

"The boss just now told me on the cell that he's sure she ain't dead, stupid." Arnie pocketed his cell phone and ran a sweaty hand through his hair. "No body looking like hers has showed up in no morgues. She's not even been booked into any hospitals round here. The boss can find out that kind of stuff."

"Crap! Can we skip then? Maybe get lost in Mexico?"

"Listen, you idiot, don't you know the boss has contacts in Mexico? He has contacts where you wouldn't even believe. There's no place you can hide from him. Just calm down and let me think."

"So where could she go?" Petey wasn't calm and he couldn't seem to keep quiet. "I know I plugged her at least once. I'm not that bad a shot, and I swear to God I saw her go down. There was a bunch of people around the church. Too many for her to crawl off into some hole to die."

"Shut up a second." Arnie rubbed a hand across his face and tried to think.

In a few seconds, Arnie was trying out his thoughts aloud. "Okay, so we know there was some kind of smoky at the traffic jam. He maybe made the tags. But we dumped them right away, so no sweat there. No chance in hell he got a decent look at our faces, either. I figure we're golden on that score, too. We're still just a couple regular dudes with nothing to hide.

"But the chick…" Arnie screwed up his mouth to think harder. "Somebody helped her. Took her in. Probably the smoky, or maybe some kind of doctor do-gooder in that crowd."

Petey started to whine, "But if somebody's helping her, she'll turn us in. Turn in the boss, too."

Arnie nearly cracked his imbecile of a partner across the mouth. "Weren't you paying attention, idiot? She said she couldn't remember nothing."

Petey shrugged. "I figured she was lying. Trying to save her skin."

"Yeah? Well, what if she wasn't? What if some sucker is helping her and she can't tell them nothing?"

"Then we're in the clear. Let's get out of here."

Huffing in frustration, Arnie rolled his eyes. "We've gotta find her. The boss ain't gonna give up just 'cause she's lost her mind. I'm guaranteeing you, we don't bring her back, and we're dead meat. Finished. You understand?"

Petey nodded his head but couldn't get a word out of his trembling lips.

"Fine," Arnie said almost absently. "So we're gonna go see what we can find out about her. Somebody will know something in a town as small as Esperanza, Texas."

"How? Who's gonna tell a couple of strangers anything?"

"Shut up, Petey. I'm doing the thinking. In every small town there's a couple of places where people know stuff and don't mind spreading it around. If you was a woman, we could go to the beauty parlor. You find out all the gossip in them places."

Petey opened his mouth as if to complain, but Arnie threw him a sharp look.

"I saw just the right place for us back down the road a ways," Arnie said. "You know, I think you and me are in need of new hats. I've been meaning to get me one of those cowboy hats, anyway. Pulling the brim down over my eyes will make a perfect disguise. And I'm thinking you'd look pretty decent in a John Deere cap."

"Aw, crap, Arn. I don't like caps. Can't I get the cowboy hat? Where are we going get this stuff anyway?"

Arnie put the sedan in gear and pulled out of the roadside park. "Do me a favor, idiot. Do not say one frigging word while we're in the store. Not one, you hear?"

"Yeah. Yeah. But where?"

"Where every old codger in town usually shows up every day," Arnie told him with no small pride in his voice. "And all of them cowpokes can't wait to spill their guts around so they don't have to go back to work too fast."

At Petey's frustrated look, he gave it up. "At the farm-supply store, of course."

Chapter 5

"Is this the correct way to hold it?" Rosie asked as she grasped the weapon with both hands and pointed it at the target. "It doesn't feel right."

Jericho scraped both his sweaty palms down his pants legs and tried to figure out how he'd managed to get himself into this fix. It was one thing wanting the woman to be able to defend herself and quite another completing the mechanics of the thing without touching her.

He'd been standing a minimum of six feet behind her, spouting instructions at the back of her head. Now he lowered his eyes to take in her slender back, narrowing to the tiny waist. A little lower and his gaze stuttered across her small but firm butt encased in Macy's old jeans. Then his wayward eyes strayed further to look their foolish fill as his stare wavered on down those long, sexy legs. Holy mercy, but those long legs could sure give a man dreams he ought not have.

His attraction to her could not be tolerated or indulged. Too close, and he was bound to give in. She was too tempting, with her sexy body and her vulnerable but bright eyes. He knew with his whole being that if they ever made love, he might find he wanted to keep her forever. Or some other such nonsense in the same vein.

Jericho had a good life here. His father lived and worked nearby and they talked nearly every day as family should. He'd grown up with all the people of this town. People like Macy and Tim, Clay and Tamara Brown and Clay's brother, Ryder, and his sister, Mercy. Some of them were gone now, either dead or moved away. But still Jericho's roots here were strong. He didn't need anything else in his life.

The people of this town and county knew and respected him. Depended on him. That was where his energies should be focused. Not on a pair of lost, sky-blue eyes.

Okay, so maybe on some particularly lonely nights, being single in a small town wasn't all he'd ever wished for. It could be stark and depressing. That was a fact.

"Jericho?" Rosie turned to see why he hadn't answered. "Is this right?"

Tamping down his hormones, Jericho stepped up to the task. He slid in close to the warmth of her back and wrapped his arms around her in order to show her the correct stance by example.

The zing of electricity between their bodies almost knocked him back again. But the sheriff of Campo County had to be stronger than all that.

"Not exactly," he murmured into her ear. "Here, I'll put my hands on top of yours to show you the right way. Just relax."

The minute the words were out of his mouth, he knew they were both in trouble. Each of them took a deep breath, straightened up and cleared their throats.

Rosie's body trembled against his chest, but he felt he had to finish what they'd started. After a few more minutes, he couldn't have said how he'd ever managed to stand his ground and show her the correct way of pulling the trigger while keeping her eyes open and aiming at the same time. But, he had, and she'd hit the target—twice. So he backed off and took back his weapon.

"You seem to be a natural at shooting," he told her as he clicked on the safety. "But to tell the truth, you don't seem very familiar with guns. How does it feel being outside?"

"Weird. Like maybe I don't get out in the sunshine too often. But I kind of enjoy it." She stared into the woods behind the tree where he'd set up the target. "I'm not crazy about the wild though. Isn't it kind of scary in the woods? I don't think I'd care to go in there."

Jericho chuckled and took her elbow. "Okay, then. We'll cross hunting and fishing off our list of possible ways to relax." He headed them back toward the house. "Let's go to town and see if Deputy Rawlins has some photos for you to look at."

Rosie smiled at Jericho's deputy as he shook her hand. At just about six feet tall, Adam Rawlins seemed to be in great physical shape. But even with all his muscles, the deputy still didn't appear as formidable as the sheriff.

"We'll catch those bastards," Adam told her with a polite smile. "Don't you worry, miss."

She walked with Adam toward a computer that was stored in an alcove at back of the sheriff's office. Meanwhile, Jericho went to one of the two large desks in a different section of the large room. Even just a few yards away, Rosie felt bereft without him by her side.

Adam pulled two folding chairs up in front of the computer and motioned for her to have a seat in one of them while he sat down beside her. "Let me show you how to work this. It's pretty easy."

The deputy smiled over at her and she knew he'd intended to put her at ease. But his perfect brown hair with every strand in place and his sympathetic brown eyes that were studying her carefully didn't come close at all to settling her nerves. His hair wasn't the same dark blond color as Jericho's and didn't occasionally go astray due to having strong hands stab through it with frustration. Not like Jericho's. And the plain brown eyes of Deputy Adam weren't at all the same as Jericho's hazel eyes that could change from gray to green—all depending on the weather and what the man was wearing that day. Nothing about the deputy sitting next to her did a thing for her nerves.

Trying to hide a secret sigh, Rosie returned her attention to the computer. "Yes, I think I've got it," she told Adam. "The program doesn't look all that complicated. You don't have to sit with me. I'll call you if I run into trouble or if I spot anyone who looks familiar."

"Yes, ma'am." The deputy gave her a half smile as he stood and walked toward his own desk.

Rosie shot a quiet glance in the direction of the tall man wearing a long-sleeved white shirt and uniform tie standing across the room and bending over a desk loaded with paperwork. In contrast to sitting beside the deputy, just the sight of Jericho sent her pulse racing and her stomach bouncing. Whenever Jericho touched her, little firecrackers exploded inside her chest. Her palms grew damp, and her thighs trembled. Learning to fire a gun at the target this morning beside him had been a trial of fighting lustful thoughts and urges.

Things were so unsettled in her mind. But one thing stood out clearly. She wanted that man to want her. Badly.

"Is she all right over there by herself?" Jericho asked his deputy.

Taking a quick look in the direction of his boss's gaze, Adam nodded his head. "Yep. Frankly, I think the lady's better at using that computer than I am. Seemed to pick up on it right away."

"Yeah? Well, that should tell us something about her. I just wish I knew what it was besides the fact she knows computers."

Adam threw his boss a hesitant smile. "Yes, sir. Do you have any ideas regarding how we should go about starting our investigation? Where we should begin if she doesn't spot anybody from those mug shots?"

Jericho released a breath and turned away from the sight of Rosie's long legs bunched up under her as she sat at the desk. He rubbed absently at the back of his neck.

"Start with missing persons. Check all the wires to see if someone of her description is listed.

"She's a real looker, don't you think, Adam?"

The deputy nodded. "Except for the hair, I do."

Jericho frowned at Adam's truthfulness, but then shrugged it off, believing the choppy cut and unnatural color only added to her appeal. "So someone in this county or nearby must've seen her at least once before she ended up shot at the church's doorstep. She didn't just appear in the back of a car in Esperanza out of thin air.

"Why don't you start asking around?" he suggested. "Check the gas stations and the truck stops. And go on over to my dad's feed and supply store. Everybody in the county shows up there sometime or other during the day. Find out if any of the ranchers spotted her or one of those goons driving through or stopping to ask directions."

"You bet, boss. I'll go right now. You can help the woman with the computer if she finds anyone familiar, can't you?"

Yeah, Jericho thought. He could help her. And he would, damn it. Nothing else mattered quite as much to him at the moment.

Frustrated and tired, Rosie clung to Jericho's arm as they strolled down Main Street and prepared to cross at the corner, heading toward Miss Sue's town café. It seemed as if over the last couple of hours she'd stared into the faces of hundreds of men, all terrifying and snarling at her from the computer monitor. But none of them had been the ones who'd hurt and kidnapped her.

Worse, being outside in the fresh air now after

studying all those criminal faces was giving her the creeps. Every man who either drove by or walked in her general direction made the hairs on her arms stand straight up. Some kind of internal instinct must be calling out, demanding that she run and hide. Stay out of sight.

Definitely someone somewhere wanted an unknown thing from her badly enough to send goons after her. She was positive they wouldn't give up so easily.

"You okay?" Jericho asked as she took a couple of deep breaths. "Still want to grab a bite at Miss Sue's? You wouldn't want to miss her pecan pie."

"Um…yes. I guess so." Rosie looked up into Jericho's face and found a concerned expression, half hidden by the brim of his uniform's cowboy hat. "It's just that I can almost feel someone watching me. Waiting for me."

Jericho stopped directly in front of the café's door. "I take gut feelings seriously, ma'am. So I can't say for sure it's not possible that those guys are in town and waiting. But I guarantee you they won't be inside the café. And I promise I'll be guarding your back when we leave.

"All right with you?" he asked. "We have to eat sometime, and while we're here I can check with some of the folks about your case. What do you say?"

She threw a quick glance over her shoulder and saw nothing but an ordinary small-town street and loads of bright sunshine. "I say, I'm with you, Sheriff. Lead on."

Jericho did just that. He walked them inside, and hesitated long enough to flip his hat on a peg next to the door. He then found an empty table in the center of the room, away from the huge curtained windows that looked out on Main Street. Rosie could've kissed him for being so thoughtful. In fact, she could've kissed him just for being so broad-shouldered and steely-eyed. And, actually, she intended to find a time to test his kisses as soon as she could get him alone.

The tough but friendly sheriff greeted every person in the café with a smile and a personal word. Rosie guessed he must know them well since he'd lived here all his life. But no one looked the least familiar to her.

The café itself seemed old but spotless and well cared for. Homey. The mismatched wooden tables and chairs were all full of smiling, happy people who seemed to be enjoying their food. Shouldn't a place as comfortable as this feel as though she'd been here before? She'd wanted it to be familiar. But it wasn't.

Jericho ordered for them, since she hadn't a clue what she might like to eat. Within minutes their lunches were delivered.

"Why do I have a salad?"

"Well now, that's easy. I've found that pretty, thin ladies like you seem to go for salads at lunchtime. Does something else sound more appealing? If so, Becky will be happy to fix you anything you want."

Without warning, her eyes filled with tears.

Swiping at them, she tried to explain. "I hate this. I hate not even being aware of what I like to eat. I hate looking into people's eyes and not knowing if I've ever met them before." She gritted her teeth and fought back the sob threatening in her throat.

He put his hand over hers on the table and squeezed. "It's hard, I know. But the doc said for you to take it slow. Pushing could make things worse."

"Forgive me, but the doctor doesn't have goons hiding nearby in the shadows who want to kill him," she said with a whine in her voice she didn't care to hear but couldn't seem to help. "None of you can know how hard this is."

"True," Jericho said with another light squeeze of her hand. "But most of the people in town will be happy to watch out for you once they learn about your problem. Give them a chance."

Somehow certain she had never been able to depend on anyone the way Jericho was saying she should depend on the whole town, Rosie heaved a heavy sigh. "I'll try."

"Good. And in the meantime, why don't you give the taco salad a chance, too. You might be surprised."

That made her smile. And relax a little. At least, she relaxed enough to discover that the taco salad tasted pretty good. And that she'd been really hungry.

Just as they were contemplating ordering the pecan pie, a nicely dressed woman with short golden-brown hair stepped into the café and looked around. Her warm eyes skipped over every table as though she were searching for someplace to sit. The sight of someone like that who looked a little lost, got to Rosie. She immediately thought of this woman as a kindred spirit.

When Jericho spotted her, he stood and issued an invitation for the woman to join them at their table. Instead of being frightened, Rosie warmed to the thought of getting to know the lady with kind eyes and a friendly smile.

"Rosie," Jericho began after the woman had been seated with them and they'd all ordered pie, coffee and a glass of milk for Rosie. "This is Jewel Mayfair. She's Macy's friend and her boss at the Hopechest Ranch."

He tilted his head toward the woman he'd introduced as Jewel. "This here's our mystery lady, Jewel. I've been calling her Rosie because we don't know her real name."

Jewel extended her hand across the table. "Hi, Rosie. I've heard about you and what happened yesterday from Macy. I was certainly sorry to hear about your troubles. Are you feeling okay now?"

"I'm okay. It's just…frustrating…not knowing anything."

"I'll bet. But I'm sure it will all come back."

As she'd said those words, Jewel's expression had turned melancholy. She looked so depressed and forlorn suddenly that Rosie couldn't help but reach out.

"Are you all right?" Rosie stared into the other woman's face for a moment and discovered deep circles under her eyes. "Aren't you feeling okay?"

"Oh, yes," Jewel told her quietly. "I just haven't been sleeping well lately. That's all."

"Is there something wrong out at the ranch?" Jericho asked. He turned to Rosie. "Jewel runs a new state-of-the-art facility designed specifically to help troubled teens. She tries to give them a stable home base and good hard outdoor work while they're in treatment. I think it's a great idea. Been needed in these parts for a long time."

Returning his attention to Jewel, he said, "There's nothing wrong with any of the kids, is there? Or anything I can do to help?"

Just then the waitress brought out their plates of pie and drinks.

Jewel emptied a sweetener packet into her coffee mug and took a breath before she answered. "It's nothing, Jericho. Just my same old nightmares finally getting the better of me, I guess."

"Nightmares?" Rosie hadn't thought about dreams. Would she have any? Would they be scary or about the good times from her past that she couldn't remember in the bright light of day? "Are they horrible? What do you dream about?"

Jewel looked startled by the question. Rosie could scarcely believe she'd asked such a nosy, none-of-her-business type of thing.

"Sorry. I shouldn't have asked."

Turning to Jewel, Jericho gently put a hand on her shoulder. A dart of jealousy flew into Rosie's chest before she could block it. Such silliness. What was wrong with her? She'd only known Jericho for about twenty-four hours. She simply could not have any feelings for him this fast. And besides, she'd been wanting to take Jewel's hand for support herself.

"You don't have to talk about this, Jewel," Jericho told her. "It's too personal."

So Jericho knew about Jewel's past. Maybe that was just normal for a small-town sheriff. Or maybe they shared something special between them.

"No, it's okay." Jewel tilted her head back to Rosie. "I'm a psychologist. We believe that the more you talk out your demons, the less hold they'll have over you. So I don't mind you asking.

"It's all ancient history, anyway," Jewel continued. "Not something I should be afraid about now. But I still have these nightmares that I…"

"I think I'd rather not remember the bad stuff," Rosie blurted.

Jewel actually lifted the edges of her lips in a half smile. "Sometimes I wish I could have a little amnesia—just about this one thing from my past. But unfortunately, it was a too-real car accident. When I close my eyes, it still seems as clear to me today as it did when it happened a couple of years ago."

"I'm so sorry," Rosie wished she could drop into a hole and cover her head. She didn't want to hear the details. "Were you injured?" she asked anyway.

The other woman sighed. "Yes. And hospitalized for a long time. But that wasn't the worst of it. My fiancé had been driving us out on a date in my car that night. He was killed instantly—along with our unborn child. I…"

Rosie couldn't stand to hear any more. She leaned forward in her seat and whispered, "But you're a psychologist. Isn't there something you can take to make you sleep without the nightmares?"

"No, there's nothing you can take for nightmares," Jewel told her with a note of familiarity that indicated she felt a bond to Rosie. "I've gotten in the habit of taking strolls around the ranch when I can't sleep. It's nice out—usually. The stillness of the night. The vastness of the stars in the heavens. The stock softly baying in their pens. Something about it soothes me. If you have bad dreams, you might try walking."

"Absolutely not." Jericho had been quietly listening

to their conversation, but now he broke in. "And you need to stop going out alone after dark, too, Jewel."

"Oh, Jericho…" Jewel began, skepticism showing in her voice.

"Listen to me," he interrupted. "Remember, it wasn't that long ago a body was found on Clay Colton's ranch land—in a spot right adjacent to the Hopechest. And you—"

He turned to Rosie. "Just yesterday someone shot at you in front of a ton of people at the church. I'd rather you didn't walk anywhere alone. If you need to walk, then let me know. I'll be there to watch your back."

Chapter 6

Rosie's eyes went wide, but then she ducked her head and quietly sipped her milk.

Okay, so maybe he'd come on a little strong. But the idea of anything else happening to Rosie had gotten him all riled up.

Jewel sat, looking down and ringing the edge of her cup with a finger. "I've invited my teenage half brother, Joe Colton, Jr., to come visit for a couple of weeks. I'm hoping the company will help, if that makes you feel any better, Jericho."

An awkward silence spread over the table and Jericho decided he'd be better off to step away from it. He looked around the room and spotted a co ple of county road workers that he might be able to qu stion.

"You two be okay here?" he asked, but without expecting an answer. "I'll take care of the bill. Y'all sit as long as you like. I'll just be right over there."

As he strode across the room, Jericho thought he heard the two women whispering behind his back. But he was glad Jewel had befriended Rosie. Jewel's California sophistication seemed a better match to whatever Rosie had been in her past than his rural upbringing would ever be.

He was still trying to puzzle the mystery woman out. She wasn't an outdoors girl, that's for sure. Though, she had definitely taken to the dogs. Both old Shep and the collie puppy Chet nearly loved her to death when she'd stopped to pet them on the way to target practice this morning. He'd been left standing to the side, wishing he could've joined in the fun.

Whatever relationship was developing between him and Rosie had become a primal pull that he was having difficulty ignoring. But giving in to it just wasn't like him. He'd always been a right-is-right kind of man.

After a few minutes of questioning the two county road workers as they ate their lunches and finding himself getting nowhere, Jericho was relieved to hear his name being called out. He turned to find the deputy coming his way.

"Glad I caught up to you, Sheriff." Adam looked calm and cool, even though he'd just come in from the heat of the day. "I wanted to give you an update."

Jericho thanked the road crew and found an empty table so he and the deputy could talk more privately. "Any of the missing persons reports seem promising?" he asked.

The deputy shook his head. "Sorry, boss. I went back through the files for the last six months but didn't come up with anyone who even looked close to our mystery woman's description."

The waitress brought them glasses of water, but they declined anything else. "All right. That's fine, Adam. We'll keep checking around. When you get back to the office, why don't you put out a bulletin to the neighboring counties concerning Rosie and her situation. Something should turn up shortly.

"What else did you get done on Rosie's case today?" Jericho asked.

"I went on over to the feed-and-supply store like you said," the deputy answered as he picked up his water glass. "By the way, your dad says to say 'hey.'"

Jericho nodded, imagining his father's Texas drawl and the casual way he always held his body to make sure everyone felt at home.

"And your brother Fisher asked about the wedding," the deputy added. "I guess he's staying with your father while he's in town, right? Anyway, he wanted to know if the ceremony has been rescheduled. Told him it wasn't any of my business."

Chuckling to himself, Jericho could just imagine Fisher's attitude with the deputy. "If anyone asks you again, Adam, you can say the bride has called the wedding off."

"Yes, sir." The deputy sipped his water. "I left word with your father to check with everyone who comes in the store to see if they can remember anything about the woman or that car.

"But I'm thinking now I'd better get back to the office," Adam added. "On my way home later I'll swing by the truck stop and check with a few of the drivers. See if anyone remembers seeing a woman with crazy red hair."

"Fine. Good work. Something is bound to turn up eventually. Maybe by tomorrow."

Jericho wasn't exactly thrilled about having Rosie stay at his house for another night. Either Jewel or Macy probably would've taken her into their homes for a few days—and maybe he should've asked them for the help. But he'd rather not take the chance of putting anyone else in jeopardy. Someone was still after Rosie. He could feel it in his gut.

Having the mystery woman stay with the sheriff ought to keep her safe. No one would be crazy enough to attack her while she was with him.

Rosie sat back in her chair at the table as she listened to Jewel and Becky French, the café's owner, discussing the first stages of a pregnancy. Maybe she ought to be more attentive to their discussion since she'd been the one to start the conversation by asking questions. But she couldn't muster a whiff of interest in the subject.

In her mid-sixties, Becky was short and plump and seemed like the perfect embodiment of a grandmother. In fact, the first thing the woman had done when she sat down in Jericho's place was to drag out pictures of her own grandchildren in order to show them off.

Something felt familiar about Becky. Rosie stared at her over the rim of her milk glass, willing herself to remember. But whatever had caused that spark of recognition in the first place blew away like a smoke trail in a strong wind.

Did she have her own grandmother somewhere who looked like this one?

Whenever a wisp of a half-remembered memory strayed just out of her reach, she immediately thought about not having anyone. The feeling of being all alone in the world overwhelmed her again and again with paralyzing fear.

What kind of person had she been? Did she have a big family? Lots of brothers and sisters, friends and neighbors? She could only hope that she'd at least been a good person. All that talk from those goons about her having stolen something was worrisome. Was she a thief?

She supposed that if she'd been dishonest the police would have some record on her. Perhaps the deputy had come up with something already. It was a scary idea, but at least then she would know who and what she was.

Looking toward the table where Jericho and his deputy were temporarily seated, Rosie wondered what they'd found out so far. If she was some kind of criminal, she wanted to know for sure. Even if that meant having to face justice somewhere.

She watched Jericho closely. Every single person she'd seen interacting with him so far seemed to have the ultimate regard for the man.

What she wouldn't give to have people think of her in that same way. Was it possible she'd been like that in her previous life?

Maybe she would never remember who she had been

before. Maybe they would never be able to put a name to her face. Then she could build an entirely new life. Starting from today.

If things went that way, Rosie wanted her new life to be like Jericho's. She vowed to make every moment count from now on.

Jericho and Adam rose from their places and walked toward her table. As he came closer, Jericho looked so strong and dependable. It made her want to curl up in his lap and let him protect her from everything. From everybody.

She wanted him. Wanted him to be her sheriff and protector. Wanted him to help her build a new life and become her family. She just plain wanted him.

"Everything good over here, ladies?" Jericho grinned and straddled an empty chair to sit down. "Maybe we should be on our way if you're done."

"Y'all stay as long as you want," Becky told him with a friendly smile.

"Well, that's very nice of you," Jewel said. "But I have to get back to work."

Jericho turned to speak with Becky while Adam took Jewel's elbow and walked with her toward the restaurant's front door. Rosie was left sitting there. She got up and eased toward the door herself so she could bid Jewel goodbye, too.

"I was wondering if you might be willing to join me for supper this Friday night?" Rosie could hear Adam talking quietly to her new friend and she slowed her steps to give them a little privacy.

She couldn't hear Jewel's response, but the other

woman was smiling sadly and shaking her head. Looked like Jewel must be turning the deputy down.

In the next second, Jewel turned and glanced longingly back at Rosie. She seemed to be asking for help.

Rosie walked over beside the other two. "I didn't get a chance to say goodbye, Jewel. Wait up."

Adam nodded his head at the interruption, excused himself and turned away to join the sheriff. Jewel hustled Rosie out the front door of the café so they could say goodbye and not be heard.

"Are you going out with him?" Rosie whispered.

"I can't. I know it's been almost two years since my fiancé died, and Adam seems like a nice enough guy. But I'm just not ready."

Rosie felt terrible for her new friend. "You need to start living again, Jewel. Look at my circumstances. If I don't find out who I am, I'm going to have to build an entire new life. And I won't be able to do it by hiding my head—even if that's what I'd rather do.

"If I can do it, so can you." Suddenly, Rosie's eyes welled with tears and she was forced to flick them away with the back of her hand.

Jewel took her other hand and squeezed. "You're such a dear person. But I suspect you're a lot stronger inside than I am. For me, it's just too soon."

Rosie felt ridiculous being so weepy all the time. Had she always been like that? She straightened up.

"I don't know why I'm so emotional," she told her new friend. "It doesn't seem like I was that kind of person before. But how can I know for sure?"

Jewel patted her shoulder. "Maybe it's because

you're pregnant. Anyway, that's how I felt during my first few months, too. I cried at every little thing. Then after the accident…. Well, I can't possibly have any tears left at this point. I must've cried an entire ocean."

Rosie wanted to hug her friend, but her instinct told her to back off for now. "Maybe you're right to be cautious about dating," she hedged.

She should give herself the same advice. But with Jericho… Well, it was just different with him somehow. She felt like they'd known each other forever. And when it came down to reality, perhaps it would eventually turn out that her *forever* had started yesterday.

"I'd better go check and find out if Jericho wants to go," she said quickly to change the subject. "Will I see you later?"

"I'm really busy at the ranch right now. But maybe Jericho can bring you out to see our operation and meet the kids sometime."

Rosie hoped so. This life might not be her real life, but she was feeling more and more comfortable here and in her new skin.

She said goodbye to Jewel and then returned to the café—only to find Jericho and Adam donning their hats and getting ready to leave themselves. Jericho was still busy saying goodbye to Becky.

But the deputy turned to her and then slid a glance over her shoulder. "Did Jewel go already?"

The tint of a blush rode up Adam's neck. Rosie thought the idea of the tough deputy having a crush on Jewel was sweet.

"Jewel said she had to go back to work, Adam." The

man's crushed expression made her feel bad and urged her
to keep on talking, hoping to take the sting out of his re-
jection. "Did you find out anything about my past so far?"

The deputy shook his head sadly and took her by the
hand. "Sorry, ma'am. Nothing yet."

Not as much a surprise as a wake-up call, she found
that Adam's hand in hers lacked the same energy as
Jericho's. There was no zing with the deputy. No sizzle.

"I wish there was something I could do to help," she
said. Then she thought of those goons' scary words
about stealing and quickly decided it was time for her
to push the issue, even if it meant learning an unfortu-
nate truth. "Have you checked to see if I'm wanted by
the police somewhere?"

The deputy reared his head back slightly, narrowed his
eyes and dropped her hand. "No, ma'am. Should we?"

She opened her mouth to say yes when suddenly
Jericho stepped in close and answered for her. "We've
been operating under the assumption that she's the victim,
deputy. And I still believe that'll turn out to be the case.
But maybe we should cover all the bases. Rosie and I will
come back to the office on our way out to my cabin and
let you take her prints and a mug shot. Then run them
through the Texas system and also through AFIS."

Jericho's eyes were dark and bright as he watched her
closely. He looked dangerous as hell. Rosie really hoped
she wasn't on the other side of the law from this man.
He was probably deadly against his enemies. And she
would much rather remain his friend.

The deputy nodded curtly and went on his way.

Jericho took a deep, cleansing breath. He was trying

his best to get his inappropriate jealousy under control. When he'd turned and found Adam's hand on Rosie, his temperature had flared. But feeling this possessive of a mystery woman was just insane. What if she turned out to be a criminal and was faking the amnesia?

No, his gut told him that wasn't right. She couldn't possibly be anything but a victim. Her eyes said that much.

"Come on," he told her.

As he took her elbow, electricity ripped through his hand. His fingertips burned with the mere touch of her skin. He felt more alive and dynamic standing next to this woman than he had in longer than he could ever remember.

"Let's go back to the station and get this over with," he said gruffly. "Then I think we'll stop out by my dad's store on the way back to the cabin. Okay by you?"

She nodded and slipped a hand into his. The sparks exploded between them again. Every time he touched her, no matter how casually, he felt as though he had been branded. He wanted desperately to make her his own. To brand her in return so that everyone would know to keep their hands off.

Unfortunately, the ideas of what he *should* do and what he *must* do were beginning to merge in his mind. Right and wrong had always been clear before. Now all he could visualize was the gray lying in between the black and white. Lust was making him think in ways he'd never done before.

Stupid. Stupid. Stupid.

The handsome and powerful man excused himself from the lavish party and slipped outside to the terrace.

As he went, a dozen beautiful women watched him walk by with lust plainly apparent in their eyes. Too bad he couldn't take them up on their unspoken offers. He had too much to lose right now to give it all up just because he couldn't keep his fly zipped. No matter how tempting.

Checking his cell messages, he found the one from his hired man, Arnie, he'd been expecting. It was about time. After listening for a few moments, he lit an after-dinner cigar and returned the call.

"But, boss." Arnie was hedging with a whine clear in his voice after being chastised for not completing his mission. "She's staying with the sheriff himself. We don't dare try to take her as long as she's with him."

"I said to make your move *now*. Before things get any further out of control. And I expect you follow orders. I want that woman here within a few hours."

"But boss…he's the sheriff."

"How many men does he have guarding her?"

"Just the sheriff."

The boss *tsked* aloud and chewed on his cigar. He never had trouble controlling his irritation. That's how he had gotten this far. But now he felt a pang of pure anger beginning to crawl up his spine. It made him weak. Unacceptable.

He blew out a breath and vowed to keep his cool this time, too. "Then do as I say. A small county sheriff in Texas is nothing to me. He won't cause you any trouble. Do whatever you need to with him. I can fix it later.

"But I want her back here by tomorrow," he added. "Or else. And no excuses this time. Do you understand me?"

Chapter 7

Rosie waited in the back of the farm-supply store with Jericho's father, while Jericho joked around and told stories with his brother. The two over-six-footers were standing in an aisle near the front windows. Afternoon sun hung low in an orange sky and flowed through the windows, bathing both men in a warm glow as they spoke quietly together.

No customers were in the store at this hour. Just the three Yates men—and her.

Jericho's father made her feel comfortable. Like she almost belonged here. She didn't mind waiting for Jericho and getting to know his father at all. At six feet tall himself, Mr. Yates was still in great physical shape. He wore his gray-streaked hair cut close to his head, and his tanned, leathered skin spoke of a lifetime of outdoor living.

"You sure have two fine-looking sons, Mr. Yates."

"Call me Buck, please. Everyone does." The older man shot a quick glance at his two boys and then turned to study her. "I always tried to raise them with strong values of patriotism and service, and that much seems to have taken hold. But raising good-looking, community-minded men hasn't helped me a bit in getting grand-children. I had hopes that Jericho might be on the right track with Macy, but…"

"Oh." Did Jericho's father blame her for getting in the way of their wedding? "Maybe it was all my fault that the wedding didn't happen. But Macy said…"

"Hold on there." Buck interrupted her with a grin. "I know those two weren't really meant for each other. Not over the long haul. As a matter of fact, my son never once in his life looked at Macy the way he looks at you. It's a good thing he didn't ruin two lives by marrying the wrong person before the right one came along. I did that myself and have regretted it ever since."

"The way he looks at me? He doesn't even know who I am for sure. What do you mean?" She pulled herself up a little straighter and held her breath. It had always seemed to her that Jericho's eyes were questioning her, so Buck's answer seemed all-important. But she wasn't entirely positive why.

Buck patted her shoulder. "He looks at you as if he could eat you in one gulp. As if the sun had never shone on the world until you showed up. It don't matter how long two people know each other. That kind of feeling only comes along once in a lifetime. And my son's got it for you."

Did Jericho feel the same things for her that she'd been feeling for him? How could something like that happen so soon? And in the middle of such terrible confusion and terror.

"I…uh…" Buck started to speak, but his expression had changed from pleasant and hopeful to wary and sad. "That is…I didn't do my sons any favors by not remarrying after their mother left us. I was so sure I could be both mother and father to them that I didn't believe we needed anyone else.

"Trouble with thinking that way, though, is that Jericho was too young at the time to do without a mother." Buck shook his head and frowned. "He never understood why she'd left and never quite forgave his mother for not coming back. I'm sure he blamed himself, but that couldn't be further from the truth. I think he must still have a lot of anger inside him that needs to come out before he can ever be really happy. That's why he's never found anyone before now."

Anger? But that certainly didn't sound like the Jericho Rosie was beginning to know. All right, so maybe he thought of himself as a dedicated bachelor. But was he single because he wanted to be or single because he didn't trust a woman not to hurt him?

Geez. Rosie suddenly decided she was thinking too much. Where had all these crazy amateur psychology ideas come from anyway? Was that what she had been in her real life? A psychologist?

No, that didn't sound right at all. But on the other hand, how could she know anything anymore? Her whole life before Esperanza, Texas was a big fat blank.

Just then, Jericho and Fisher came up the aisle toward them. "You ready to go back to my place?" Jericho asked her.

The warmth Jericho caused by standing so close flamed across her skin and made her wonder if going back to his house was such a good idea.

Yes, she suddenly decided, it was. Getting closer to him was all she wanted. There was nothing she needed more than to plaster herself as close to him as possible. Had Buck been right about Jericho's desire?

There were so many things Rosie couldn't know because her mind had blocked them. But Jericho's desire for her was one thing she had the power to discover in the here and now. And she vowed to force the issue if she had to.

Twilight had arrived. In the parking lot behind his father's store, Jericho unlocked his pickup and turned to help Rosie climb into the passenger seat. But when she stepped closer, he was hit by a blast of yearning so forceful it nearly knocked him to his knees. He wanted her. Badly. Yet he'd known that before. This time, though, it seemed like something more than lust.

As he took her arm, he tried to come up with why this need felt different. *Safe.* That was the only word he could think of to define what he was feeling. He'd been trying so hard to keep her safe that it never occurred to him she might be the one to make him long for security. But as he looked into her eyes, it was like nothing he'd ever experienced before.

Family. For the first time in his life, someone besides

his father and brother made him yearn to be part of a family. This lost woman and her unborn child needed him in a way no one else had—including Macy and T.J. On more of a primitive, survival level.

"Jericho?" Her eyes searched his.

He'd been standing here staring for too long. Abruptly, he threw his arm around her waist to help her into the truck's cab. But he stumbled in his haste, and she reached for his shoulders to steady them both.

Inside, he was anything but steady.

Too close, their gazes locked as a sudden change came into her eyes. She fisted a hand in his shirt and dragged him even closer, though the whole time her eyes stayed intent upon his. Automatically, one of his hands went to her hair, stroking, soothing, until it finally eased its way down to cup the base of her neck.

Time hung between them, like the magic first star in the night sky that hovered just above the horizon. Then came another change. She murmured something low, clamped her hands on both sides of his head and dragged him down for a kiss. Many kisses.

She nibbled and nipped. Licked and sucked with such desperation that Jericho could barely keep up.

His mind went blank. Nothing was making any sense. Nothing but the surety that if he didn't return her kiss right now, this minute, he was going to die.

Giving in to his own desperation, he slanted his mouth over hers and kissed her as if it were the last thing he would ever do. But instead of the end of something, he wanted this kiss to be the first kiss she remembered. His kiss—not some dude's from the depths of her murky past.

As he returned Rosie's wild lust, he put his whole being into it. He ran his hands along her body, drinking in every curve. Soft. Yielding. Sensuous. Jericho absorbed the details, wanting to experience them all.

His hands burned as he touched her everywhere. His lips were set afire by her kisses.

"I want you, Jericho," she whispered against his mouth. "I feel alive with you. What's between us is right. I know you feel it too. Show me. Please."

The sounds of her urgent pleas knocked the sense back into his muddled brain. Thankfully, just in time. Another minute and they would've been sprawled together across the front seat of his pickup. And though it was getting darker by the minute, they were still in the brightly lit parking lot of his father's empty store.

Jericho gently took her by the shoulders and set her back from him. "This isn't right." He eased her up into his arms and slid her into the pickup's front seat.

Striding around the cab, he slipped behind the wheel and started it up. "You must belong to someone—somewhere. If we give in to our hormones tonight and tomorrow your memory comes back, along with a husband, you would never forgive yourself—or me. I won't take that chance."

"What? But…" Her voice trailed off as he put the truck in gear and pulled out of the lot. She folded her arms over her chest and stared out into the night.

Gritting his teeth, Jericho silently fought an internal struggle with fluctuating ideas of right and wrong. And he also battled to bring his overheated body back into line.

Frustrated as hell. He couldn't wait to get home and into a shower. A cold one.

The ride back to Jericho's cabin through the dark countryside was long and silent. Rosie stared out into the night, wishing Jericho would say something. Every now and then, the lights from someone's house shone in the distance. She took those opportunities to sneak a glance over at the man doing the driving.

He gripped the wheel with both hands, so tightly that even in the darkness she could see his knuckles turning white. He had wanted her. She didn't know very much of anything right now, but that had been clear when he kissed her.

Perhaps his father was right and Jericho did want her in a way he'd never wanted anyone before. That knowledge would help her because she couldn't even say the same for herself. She wanted him, all right—but had she wanted someone else the same way once before?

Damn, this was so frustrating. She began wringing her hands in her lap. Needing to think this romance thing through better, Rosie ticked off the few points in her favor as the black night flew by outside her window.

The two of them were attracted to each other. That was good. They seemed to have a definite chemistry. That was also very good. So what was stopping them?

Jericho had been about to be married when she'd fallen into his life. That could be bad. But then Macy and Jericho had both made it clear they didn't love each other and the wedding was off. Good for her again.

So now how about her own past? She was pregnant

with someone's child. And of course, that had put a serious damper on Jericho's desire a few minutes ago. But deep down Rosie didn't feel that there was anyone else, even though someone had obviously been with her—at least once. She'd thought and thought, scoured her feelings, but the only emotions she felt from the fog of her past were scary. Fear. Not love.

And if there had been someone, why hadn't he reported her missing? That was the number one unanswered question making her feel positive she was alone.

"Hell." Jericho took his foot off the accelerator and peered through the windshield down his own long asphalt driveway as the outside lights from his cabin burned through the darkness before them.

Rosie looked up, too. "What's the matter? Is something wrong?"

Jericho left the truck idling for a moment. "Everything looks fine. But…" He rolled down his window. "The dogs aren't barking. And there's just something—not right."

He put the pickup into neutral, flipped off the headlights, and reached around to eye his rifle, which was hanging in a rack in the back window. "I'm going to turn the pickup around, drive to the main highway and leave you there parked and locked in the truck. Meanwhile I'll call the deputy to come meet you while I hike back here to check things out."

He turned forward without unracking the rifle. Instead, he pulled his cell phone out of his pocket—just as a loud ping sound hit the truck's front bumper. Dropping the phone, Jericho rammed the truck into gear, hit the gas and spun in a one-eighty.

"Someone is shooting at us!" Rosie shouted above the noise of the engine revving.

"Right. Get down!" He flipped open her seat belt and shoved at her back.

She slid all the way to the floor and covered her head with her arms. Rolling into a tight ball, she squeezed her eyes shut and prayed.

Jericho cursed under his breath as he straightened the wheel and stomped on the accelerator again. He wished for the cell phone that was now out of reach on the floor somewhere. They needed help.

Hoping he could escape, he raced wildly down his own driveway. Good thing he knew every inch of this asphalt drive. He'd built it with his own hands.

But just when his pickup was within a hundred feet of the highway, moonlight picked up the shadow of a massive SUV pulling into the driveway from the road and blocking their exit.

Slamming on the brakes, Jericho came to a stop. Sweet mercy. They were surrounded.

Another series of blasts, sounding like they must be coming from an assault weapon of some sort, exploded through the air. The shots completely missed them, but Jericho didn't figure they'd be so lucky a third time.

"Yipes!" Rosie screeched from the safety of the floor.

How many were there? At least two. One in the SUV and one nearer to the house. Jericho was fairly sure they hadn't managed to break through his carefully constructed security and gotten into his home. But he needed to get inside there himself. Inside was a way to call for help and plenty of firepower to hold them off until help arrived.

Reaching over, he grabbed a handful of Rosie's shirt by the back of her collar. "Take your seat again and buckle up tight," he ordered.

"What are you planning?" she asked shakily as she rose to her knees.

Even though he didn't answer, when he jerked upward, she pushed herself back into a seated position. Then he waited one more second to make sure she had the safety belt tight enough.

"Hang on and stay low." Without considering other consequences, he swung the wheel to the right and pointed his truck off the driveway toward the empty fields. Then he hit the gas. The pickup jerked and roared ahead, breaking through a wooden fence he'd only just finished building last month.

Jericho plowed his truck through the rangy field. With the headlights still off, he prayed silently that none of the pickup's tires would hit a recently dug prairie-dog hole. Damned varmints never stopped digging, no matter how he had tried to stop them.

He and Rosie were lucky on this night. He heard the pickup's four-wheel drive cutting in as needed, and on a few occasions, the tires spun in the dirt before he slowed and allowed them to catch again. It didn't matter that they were bashing through prickly pear cactus and past tall, spindly wildflowers. His good ole truck made short work of it. He refused to think about what this wild ride might be doing to the paint on the sides and fenders. What was a new paint job when it came to saving Rosie's life?

At last they'd almost crossed the open field and reached the tree line beyond. There was only a half-moon tonight, but he wasn't having any trouble seeing where he was going. He knew it all by heart.

"Stop! Watch out for the woods," Rosie shouted from her seat next to him.

Apparently she wasn't having much trouble seeing in the moonlight, either. Jericho hoped to hell the bad guys' positions had been far enough away that they weren't seeing their escape route quite as well. And God help them if these goons had night-vision goggles.

He slowed the truck just a little at the tree line and drove right between two tall ebony trees. Hearing Rosie gasp, Jericho wished he had time enough to explain. But for his plan to work, he had to keep concentrating on his driving.

If the bad guys were smart enough to listen, they would certainly be able to hear the pickup's engine, even though the truck would be hidden by the woods. Because of that, he should turn the pickup off as soon as possible. But fortunately, he knew that people unfamiliar with rural areas would not think to step outside their vehicles and pay attention to the noise. He had to hope these perps were city boys.

Dodging through the sparse trees, Jericho judged their position and decided it must already be close to his destination. Sure enough, another few feet and he felt the front tires making contact with caliche. The ancient road through the woods that ran from an abandoned homesite—situated maybe a few hundred yards behind his cabin—to the main highway might be overrun with weeds and pockmarked by the weather. But it would take him where he wanted to go.

And where he wanted to go was not back to the highway. He was counting on that being what the bad guys would figure. That he would make a beeline for the highway, trying to escape. But Jericho knew the stretch of highway running in front of his acreage was always pretty deserted at this time of night. So he turned his truck in the other direction and headed toward the old homesite.

He spared a swift glance toward Rosie and saw her hanging on to the door with all her might. She was badly shaken by this bumpy ride. But at least she was alive.

As the pickup neared the relic of the ancient cabin, Jericho cut the engine and let it glide up to the clearing. When he thought they were in the best spot not to be seen through the woods, he parked and took the first breath he'd had since the original rifle shot had hit the truck.

"We're right behind my cabin—out a few yards behind those targets I set up." He shifted and drew his service weapon. "Here. This is similar to the gun you were using to practice this morning. I want you to keep it and stay with the truck." He handed the Glock over and then turned to bring down his rifle.

"You're not leaving me here." Even in the darkness he could see her trembling.

"You'll be safer here. I'm going to sneak up to the house and get in through a hidden basement door. I won't be able to move as fast or as quietly with you in tow. Stay here where I know you'll be safe."

"Why are you going to the cabin? Why aren't we running for our lives in the other direction?"

"Trust me," he said. "They won't be expecting me

to head right for them. This'll be the best way—a real surprise."

Hefting the rifle with one hand, he quietly eased open the door but flipped off the overhead light. Then he reached around under his seat with his free hand.

When he straightened, he held up something small. "Here's my cell phone." He shoved it at her. "Call 911 the minute I'm out of sight. Tell them Sheriff Yates needs help at his cabin. And also tell them you're waiting in my pickup by the old Gaston place. They'll come, but it may take twenty minutes."

Before he stepped out, Jericho shifted close and seared a quick kiss across her lips. "Please stay put. No matter what you hear. I'll come back for you as soon as I can."

She blinked a couple of times and then stared down at the weapon still fisted in her hand. "Okay," she answered in a shaky voice.

Rosie watched Jericho slide noiselessly out of the truck and shut the door behind him. Within seconds he disappeared into the darkness.

She called 911 and the operator also told her to stay where she was. After hanging up, she was all alone again.

Her heart thudded so loudly in her chest that she was afraid it would give her away. Her eyes had adjusted to the darkness, but every shadow seemed to move. The black night began closing in on her.

She couldn't just sit here. If one of those men happened to spot the truck, they'd have her captured in an instant. Not sure she could use the gun and sorry she had promised to stay put, Rosie made the decision to move. To hide in the trees, away from the pickup.

Easing out her door, she carefully shut it again. Then, putting the phone in her pocket and holding the gun with both hands, she tiptoed across the caliche and into the forest in the same direction as she'd last seen Jericho.

Shaking badly and with her back against the rough surface of a tree, she stopped to catch her breath and listened for any sounds. Nothing. No night noises of any kind. No car engines. No whispers or footsteps close enough that she could hear.

She closed her eyes and tried to calm down. But then it happened. A loud click sounded through the night. Close by. Had it come from over by the truck? Was it the sound of a weapon being prepared to fire? Or was it someone's footsteps breaking a twig beneath their shoes?

It didn't matter which one. She had to get away. Adrenaline shot through her veins, giving her false courage and agility as she stepped out and made her move.

Chapter 8

Rosie had been holding her breath for the last fifteen minutes. Hadn't she? Hiding behind the largest target Jericho had set up in his backyard, she exhaled and peered toward the back of his cabin through the spotty moonlight.

Suddenly staccato bursts, which she thought must be guns firing, echoed through the night. But they seemed a long way away. Were sounds deceiving out here? And who had been doing the shooting—and who may have been shot? The next moment brought total silence again.

Weren't there outside lights in the back as well as the front of the cabin? It seemed as though this morning she'd noticed a few tall posts at the edges of Jericho's backyard that she'd assumed were lights or electricity. Now there was nothing but darkness.

Curiosity got the better of her. She had to find out what was going on.

Creeping out from her hiding place, Rosie wondered if she would be too exposed even in the dark by cutting across Jericho's yard. She slipped the gun into her waistband and dropped to all fours. Crawling might cause her hands and knees some damage, but maybe she would live longer by keeping a lower profile.

After slithering a few feet, her hands were covered in nasty burrs from the sticker bushes. Another yard and her skin began to sting. Ants! Cripes.

Was it worth it to stay low? Someone from above must've been watching out for her, because right then she felt the raindrops start against her back and neck.

Rain would be a good cover, she thought. So she stood, dusted off the ants and stickers as best she could and moved on through the windy mists, hopefully still in the direction of the cabin.

Did she know how to pray? Had she been a churchgoer in her previous life? Rosie couldn't say, but still, she tried begging for mercy in the only way she could imagine.

Please, God. If I was a bad person, then don't help me now for myself. But keep me safe for Jericho's sake. She knew the sheriff well enough by now to know if he lost her, it would devastate him.

The rain began coming down in sheets then, and she gave thanks for the shield it provided. But in the next moment she found herself totally turned around. What direction was the cabin? Rosie could barely tell up from down.

Frozen in panic, she swiped the water out of her eyes

and tried to reason. Should she keep on going straight ahead? Had she turned her body at all after she'd stood up and the rain started?

A disturbing noise reached her ears through the sounds of rain splashing against the dirt. It sounded for all the world like someone moaning. Jericho?

Had he been injured? If so, he would need her help.

Sucking up all her courage, Rosie put her hands straight out in front of her body to run interference in case she smashed into any trees or walls. And then she took her first tentative steps, going in what seemed to be the same direction as the moaning sounds.

Shuffling along, she went quite a few yards, totally blinded by the rain. Then the weather eased up a bit, allowing her to see the dark shape of the cabin straight ahead. She stopped to listen.

There. The same unsettling moans. Closer to the cabin's back wall. She inched ahead again.

Nearby. She felt she was almost on top of the sounds now. Did she dare call out?

Dear Lord, what shall I do?

Out of nowhere a siren's scream pealed through the night. Help was coming! Thank heaven. They were saved.

"Jericho," she rasped in as loud a whisper as she dared. "Where are you?"

Another blind step and Rosie tripped over something large and inert, lying on the ground. She put her hands out in front of her body to take the brunt of her fall. But it wasn't any use.

Down she went. In the next instant, her nose buried itself in mud and muck. Ugh. As fast as possible, she pushed herself up and tried to roll over to catch her breath. The mud clung to her, sucked her back down.

Damn it. All she could think was had that inert object been Jericho's body? Rosie forced herself up to crawl backward. She had to find out.

Quickly losing his grip on self-control, Jericho slammed the door to his empty pickup, still sitting exactly where he'd left it, and cussed under his breath. Where the hell was she? She'd promised to stay here.

He knew the bad guys hadn't had a chance to kidnap her. He'd been keeping them plenty busy over the last half hour. First with the surprise of having to fight off his firepower. And then with trying to get away after they'd heard the sirens heading their way.

At least they hadn't gotten away totally clean. He'd winged one of them as the guy had been making a dash toward his buddy in the SUV. Jericho was sure of it. He was also positive their SUV had taken several hits as he'd fired at their retreating backside.

Both Deputy Rawlins and a deputy from another part of the county had arrived at the scene at the same time. The other deputy had taken off in pursuit, but Jericho didn't figure he would have much of a chance of catching the SUV that'd had a few minutes head start.

Now where the hell was Rosie?

"Lend me your cell, Adam," he said to his deputy.

"Sure thing, boss." Adam threw him a phone and then began edging around the clearing with his flashlight studying the ground.

"There won't be any decent prints left after that rainstorm," Jericho told him. "I'm going through the woods toward the rear of my cabin. You go on back to the house by way of the highway and see if you can spot Rosie anywhere along the road."

They split up and Adam retreated carefully down the ancient caliche road in the direction of the highway. Jericho flicked on his own flashlight and headed into the woods at approximately the same spot where he'd gone in an hour ago.

In a few minutes, he came out at the edge of his property line. Going left, he found the emergency shutoff for the outside lights and turned them back on. Earlier darkness had saved his ass. Now it was keeping him from finding Rosie. She had to be somewhere close.

He stood for a second, letting his eyes become accustomed to the floodlight. Then, thinking he heard a snuffling noise, Jericho moved closer to his cabin. In the direction of that noise. Pulling out his deputy's phone, he put it to his ear and punched in his own cell number.

It began to ring, but the ringing was much clearer in his free ear than in the ear next to the phone. His own phone had to be somewhere nearby.

"Hello?" He heard Rosie whispering into the phone.

"Where are you?" he demanded. "You were supposed to stay put."

"Jericho? I need you. I'm out behind…."

Her sentence was interrupted when Jericho's flashlight beam roamed across her face. "Here I am. Help me, please."

Through the beam of light, Jericho saw her sitting on the ground in half shadow just a few feet behind his cabin. She looked like someone had covered her in mud and weeds. Her tear-streaked face was caked and intense. If he wasn't mistaken, she also seemed to be holding his old shepherd's head in her lap.

"What the hell?" He bent on one knee. Sure enough, Shep's body lay perfectly still and Rosie was murmuring something quietly in the old dog's ear.

"I think he's still alive," she said. "But…but…"

"They poisoned him." Jericho's blood raged. He had to grit his teeth against the idea of anyone hurting his animals.

Thrusting the flashlight into Rosie's hand, he carefully scooped up the dog. "Lead the way toward the kitchen door. As soon as we get him inside, I'll call for help. Then I'll need to come back out and look for Chet."

At the mention of his name, the collie appeared out of the shadows. With his tail between his legs and shaking his head as though to clear it, the collie didn't look all that strong, either.

"Good boy, Chet. We've got your buddy now. Don't worry. Come inside."

Rosie opened the door, flipped on the kitchen overhead light and stood aside so he could bring both dogs across the threshold. Jericho took one look at her in the bright light, and his heart sank.

Not only hadn't he managed to keep his dogs safe, but the one person he'd been determined to save tonight looked like she'd been dragged through hell.

Nice night's work, Sheriff.

"Thanks, Quinn. I appreciate it." In the early hours of the morning, Jericho stood at his front door, saying goodbye to his neighbor, Quinn Logan, a large animal vet. "I know dogs aren't really your business, but I'm not sure mine would've made it without your help."

Rosie stood back a few feet and listened as Quinn prepared to leave. She ached all over. And even though she'd washed her face and hands, her body was still covered in mud. However, she was much more concerned for her host than for herself. He'd been so pale and quiet as they'd tried to make the dogs comfortable and waited for the vet.

At first, after they'd come into the dry, safe house, he'd been all business and strong as he'd dealt with the deputies and made phone calls about their attackers. Then a little later, when they were sitting on the floor with the dogs in the kitchen, she'd caught Jericho trembling while he stroked the coat of his old shepherd. She almost knew how he felt. If Shep died because someone was after her, she would never be able to live with herself.

"Well, I didn't do much," Quinn told Jericho. "I wish I could've done more for the shepherd. Your collie should be fine by tomorrow. But it may be touch and go with the older dog for a few days."

"What kind of poison do you think they used?"

Quinn, a man about Jericho's height but with an easy-going manner and sensitive eyes, shook his head and took a breath. "Not sure. But if I had to guess, I'd say it was probably an illegal human drug. Maybe something like PCP, which is easy to get on the street, and acts like an anesthetic in animals. As a powder, it would've been simple to add it to hamburger and feed it to the dogs.

"If it'd been anything like a real poison, the dogs wouldn't have lived for this long."

Jericho cleared his throat and looked down at his boots. "Yeah, well…"

Quinn clapped him on the shoulder with a gentle hand. "There's nothing else you can do but wait. Get some rest yourself."

The vet tilted his head in Rosie's direction. "I'm thinking the humans in this house need as much attention as the animals. Both of you look like a strong wind might blow you over."

Jericho shot her a quick glance. His eyes softened as they took in her messy appearance. Then he turned to finish telling the vet good-night.

After he locked the door and set the security alarms, Jericho took a few steps in her direction. He held his hands out, and Rosie thought he might take her into his arms. But something stopped him and he dropped his hands limply to his sides, shaking his head with hesitation.

"Why don't you take a shower and hit the sack?" he said as he brushed past her, heading for the kitchen. "You heard Quinn. I'm just going to check on the dogs once more then collapse myself."

"Aren't you worried about those men coming back?"

"Not tonight." Jericho's lips actually quirked up into the semblance of a smile as he stopped and turned. "I'd bet those goons are going to be busy finding a way of tending their wounds without going to a legit doctor who would be bound to turn them in. They won't even think of us again tonight. Then, for tomorrow night and every night until we come up with answers, I've already lined up a watch system. My brother, Fisher, and a couple of deputies from other parts of the county have already volunteered to stand guard in shifts. I'm sure a couple of our neighbors wouldn't mind helping out, either."

"Oh, no. That's too much trouble because of me. Maybe I should leave. Go…" *Where?* Where could she go?

Jericho's expression tensed as he shook his head. "You're safer here than anywhere else. Let us watch out for you while we figure out where you came from. None of the people around here mind taking up the cause of your safety. It's what we do in these parts. We watch out for each other."

Rosie brushed her fingers over her burning eyes. "Thank you, Sheriff. I suspect your friends and neighbors will help because of you, not me.

"But I don't seem to have a lot of choices, do I?"

He stood watching her intently for several moments without answering. "Go on to bed. We'll figure out something eventually. And in the meantime, just remember you're safe."

Turning his back then, Jericho headed into the kitchen to look after his animals. Miserable, but out of both choices and energy, Rosie forced one foot in front of the other and made her way toward the shower.

At the very least she could clean up. It was one of the only things she could do to help herself.

A half hour later, Jericho stood barefoot in front of his bedroom mirror, staring at his own image. Naked to the waist, he bent over the dresser and beat his fisted hands against the top. What a jerk he was.

Damn it! He'd been so scared when he'd thought he might've lost Rosie. It made him sick to his stomach to think of it.

Gulping in air, he wondered what the hell was the matter with him. She wasn't his to lose. She didn't belong to him. In fact, she clearly belonged to someone else.

His dogs were resting easy now. He couldn't worry too much about them for what was left of the night. But he had a feeling he wasn't going to be faring as well as they did, what with Rosie right next to him in the other bedroom.

After he took a couple more deep, calming breaths, an odd noise reached his ears. Someone seemed to be in trouble nearby.

He stepped out into the darkened hallway and stood still to listen. The noise was much clearer from this spot. What he'd been hearing with the door closed was definitely the sound of a woman's sobs. Coming from his bathroom.

He'd thought Rosie was already asleep in her room. Something must be wrong with her. But what should he do about it?

It sounded for all the world as if her heart were broken. But maybe she'd been hurt. What if she'd cut herself and really needed his help?

Hell.

In three big strides, he was at the bathroom door. He tried the knob, hoping to peek in and check on her without her noticing him. The door was unlocked, so he held his breath and opened it.

When he could see inside, he found the bathroom

awash in limited, flickering light. Just the two night-lights were burning, but the overheads had been left off.

Rosie stood in front of the bathroom mirror, looking at herself through the dim light in the mirror. And sobbing uncontrollably.

"You okay?" he whispered. "Do you need help?"

She gasped, and it was only then he noticed she didn't have on any clothes. She didn't turn around but grabbed a towel and held it to her body, trying to cover the intimate parts.

But she couldn't cover her long, lovely backside. And he let himself take it all in. From the crown of her strange red-colored head, down her slender neck and past the slim torso all the way to her perfectly rounded buttocks and those mile-long legs. My God. She was perfect. He'd known she would be. But this was better than all his idle dreams.

"Go away. I'm…okay," she began with a stutter. "No, that's not true, Jericho. I do need help. I need…"

She started to turn, but then their eyes met in the glass and she halted. She blinked and licked her upper lip. "The doctor said it was all right to shower, but not to get the bandage too wet. It seems I got the dressing all muddy earlier. So then I tried to change it myself, but I…can't reach."

Jericho watched as the tears began again. They glistened against her cheeks in the low light and swamped her beautiful blue eyes.

"Let me," he said and took a step closer.

Rosie tried to stem the flow of her tears. What an idiot she must be. It was a simple thing. Just changing her bandage after a shower. But when she couldn't seem to help herself, she'd remembered how all alone she was and the tears poured in earnest.

Jericho was being so nice. But nice wasn't really what she wanted from him. She wanted—well, she wasn't sure.

Glancing up into the mirror over the sink, their gazes met—and locked. Oh, yes. That's what she wanted from him. Whatever that was, there in his eyes. Was it a hunger? A wanting so desperate he looked ready to pounce.

"Give me the bandage and show me where," he demanded roughly.

Her heart pounded wildly as his gaze lowered to the edge of her towel in the mirror. She could feel her nipples tighten painfully in response to that look. She wanted him to touch her there, relieve her aching.

"The bandage is on the counter," she said, but was surprised at how deep her voice sounded. "And the wound is on my side, under my left arm."

"Show me," he repeated slowly, and put his hand on her shoulder.

Her skin sizzled at his touch. It was too much temptation. She nodded and dropped the towel.

Rosie didn't know what to expect. Would he turn away? Every moment the unspoken question hung in the air her passion spun higher. Yet, so help her, she could not have blinked as much as an eyelid if her life had depended on it.

He didn't turn. He didn't budge. He didn't seem to be breathing.

Part of her wanted him to whisk her up and carry her to bed. But the part of her that could've moved stood transfixed as his hand finally…finally…flexed and began caressing her shoulder as he bent to place kisses against her neck.

Even in the shadowed lighting, the sight of his darkly suntanned hand, contrasting against her pale body, was exciting. The skin lying under his fingers grew heated and began to tingle.

He stepped in closer and she could feel his warmth against her back. Her sensitive skin flamed and flushed, igniting at every point they came together. She could also feel the hard ridge under the placket of his jeans zipper poking into the small of her back. The juncture of her thighs flooded with moisture and she watched her own eyes going wide in the mirror.

She opened her mouth to beg, but no sound came out. Wanting to face him, to touch him, she started to turn. But his right hand came up under her arm to her ribcage and pulled her back into his chest.

"Stay," he growled.

He rubbed his palm upward so that his fingers were in position to trace her taut peaks. She moaned. Wanted to squirm. Instead her head fell back against his shoulder as he pulled and lightly pinched her sensitive nipples.

Every movement felt so wonderful. So perfect. Had sex ever been good before? Not like this, she was sure.

Jericho's other hand slid around her hips, flattening against her belly. A downpour of sensation raced straight to the spot between her legs that ached for him, as his hand slowly inched lower through the curly hair under her belly button.

Her eyelids drooped and her knees trembled.

"Watch," he gasped.

Her lids popped open and she stared straight ahead at the sight of the two of them in the mirror. While with one hand he rubbed and provoked the tips of her breasts, his other thumb flicked over her feminine nub—stroking, tempting, tormenting.

The woman in the mirror looked so wanton. She was sensual, heavy-lidded, breathing through an open mouth and with startling rosy nipples that grew higher at every caress.

But as Jericho continued to tighten the string on her reserves, Rosie decided she didn't care how it all looked. She only wanted to experience an end to this growing pull inside her.

"Jericho, please." How sexy she sounded to her own ears. Every movement of Jericho's and every sound she made only served to build the tension higher and higher inside her.

He began murmuring soft words of lust into her ear in that lazy, erotic Texas drawl of his. Stroking and caressing, his fingers worked faster, harder, until she thought her whole body would burst into flame.

At last the tight rubber band inside her snapped in a flood of sensation as the orgasm washed over her. In the mirror, her eyes widened impossibly and her mouth dropped open in a very unfeminine scream.

Pulsating aftershocks hit her in waves of pure pleasure. Her knees buckled and Jericho lifted her into his arms.

He turned to carry her into the bedroom as she whimpered against his chest. This was going to be a long but fantastic night. She couldn't wait.

Chapter 9

"Hang on." Jericho carefully laid her down on the guest bed, flipped on the bedside lamp then turned and strode back out the door.

Hang on? What could he mean, and where was he going?

Rosie's senses still reeled. But she suddenly felt cold without him. He should be here beside her. She needed to touch him and make him feel every bit as good as he'd done for her. Together they were going to be spectacular. So why wasn't he here?

Minutes dragged by before he reappeared in the doorway, carrying something in his hand.

"If you're worried about protection," she began, "I can understand your concern. But the doctor's tests would probably have caught anything I might've had. And if it's for the other reason, wouldn't that be like locking the prison door after the criminals already escaped?"

"Turn on your side." Ignoring her comments, he slid a hand beneath her and urged her to turn on her right side, facing away from him.

Hmm. Was this usual? she wondered. Why couldn't she remember having sex? This was like being a virgin—at least in her mind.

Instead of sliding his body into the bed behind her, he raised her arm above her head and began rebandaging her wound. "This won't take but a minute. Then you can get some sleep."

"What? Aren't you coming to bed with me?" She couldn't see his expression as he worked on her side, but his tight silence told her everything.

"Jericho, I don't want to go to bed alone." She heard the tones of exasperation mingling with her near desperation and tried to calm down. "I want you to come to bed with me so we can finish what we started. You didn't…I mean, you didn't have your…um…turn. Let me touch you. Let me feel you inside me."

Instead of answering, she felt him patting down the edges of the tape around the bandage. Then he gently placed her arm down at her side and turned her over on her back. Staring up at him, Rosie became so frustrated she wanted to scream.

Jericho's eyes gleamed bright with what she would swear must be desire as he gazed down on her naked body. He reached over and placed his palm flat against her belly. The fire his hand caused seared her there and set her aflame once more.

She groaned and reached her arms out to him.

"No." He grimaced but left his wide hand gently but firmly against her flushed skin. "Tucked safely under my hand is someone else we have to consider. We can't just act without thinking through the consequences for everyone. Your child has a father—somewhere.

"I shouldn't have taken advantage of you like that," he went on. "The two of you need to know where you belong—*before* making any decisions you might come to regret. Tonight was all my fault. I've promised to protect you, and I mean to, even if it has to be protection from me."

He took a deep breath. "You've had a bad night. Mostly due to my mistakes. I'd appreciate it if you would sleep now."

Too stunned at his little speech to speak, Rosie blinked up at him as he lifted the covers and tucked her in. This guy was definitely too good. Or was that more like so good it could be bad?

As he turned off the light and backed out the door, she worked to bite back her neediness, closing her eyes and wishing a dream to come for what she really wanted.

But when the images came into her mind, she couldn't tell if they were dreams or not. Everything seemed so familiar. But then again…it might not be her own reality.

The soft evening air, tenderly perfumed with the scent

of flowers, ruffled her hair. The sounds of an orchestra played in the background. Gentle laughter and conversation floated lightly on a sweet breeze.

How strange.

She was floating, too. In a long blue gown. Shimmering up a staircase that appeared out of nowhere. A staircase that looked as though it must belong in a castle.

How amusing. And how thrilling.

Before her appeared a prince. Wearing a tux, his royal bearing quickly became a powerful aphrodisiac. Tall and lean, with dark brown hair combed in an impeccable style, he stood out above all the rest. She felt a tiny pang of regret, somehow missing dark blond hair that grew over the collar and always appeared messy.

But then the prince gave her a generous smile that eased into a deep dimple on his left cheek, and her heart fluttered. Thoughts of any other smiles flittered away as his eyes filled with romance, passion and sex.

The prince held out his hand to her, and she stepped into his arms. Music filled her head with sparkling, erotic diamonds of pure passion as they danced across a ballroom floor like a royal couple.

Was she a princess? Looking down at herself, she saw glass slippers on her feet. So...not a princess. She must be only pretending.

But she quickly decided she didn't care. Twirling around the dance floor, she felt beautiful—and powerful. Like nothing could ever hurt her, and like everyone in the room would want to be her.

A bolt of lightning suddenly shot golden flashes through the ballroom. With the boom of thunder that followed, spears of panic darted straight into her heart. She gasped, stepping back and holding a hand to her breast to still the fear.

Glancing at the prince for reassurance, what she saw instead sent chills up her spine. Dark, demon eyes glared at her with fury and hunger.

Sinister.

Evil.

My God. She stumbled back, turned and fled.

The music disappeared and she was barefoot, running through a field of blood. It was after her. The monster was hot on her heels.

Closing in faster and faster.

She had to hide. Ripping at her clothes, she stripped off the gown and streaked through the foggy night. Shivering now, and mewling like a wounded animal, she fell to her knees. But all around her was blood. A sea of it.

The contents of her stomach curdled with nausea as she tried to crawl away. But the simmering scarlet ocean clung to her, dragging her down. Tentacles reached around her body, tugging at her ferociously.

Dragging at her body.

Pulling her further and further down.

Clawing her way up, Rosie forced her eyes to open. Sunshine glittered into the room, nearly blinding her with its welcoming reality. She was safe. Safe in Jericho's guest bedroom.

Thank heaven. The sheets were twisted around her body, a reminder of her nightmare. They clung to her, tying her to the bed.

She fought them off and swung her legs over the side. Trying to clear the last bit of fog from her brain, Rosie stood up, took a deep breath—and nearly doubled over from the nausea.

That must be still part of the dream, right?

In the next moment, she found out that being sick to her stomach was unfortunately very real. She made a mad dash for the bathroom across the hall, praying she would make it in time.

At nearly midday, Jericho hurried his way through morning bathroom chores. He wasn't too sure he would ever again be able to spend much time in his bathroom. Images of what he and Rosie had done together last night surrounded him and punched him in the gut. Trying to shave, he'd felt himself suffocating on the visions he remembered in the mirror.

Dumb. Taking advantage of the situation last night had been a purely dumb-ass move. He'd always imagined himself to have more self-control. Guess not. At least not when it came to Rosie.

In only two days, the woman had gotten under his skin. Having her stay here in his home wasn't smart. Obviously he couldn't be trusted to keep his hands to himself. Maybe this afternoon he would be better off sneaking her over to one of the neighbor's houses to stay the night. If handled properly, the move could easily remain a secret and she should be safe.

Rubbing at a sudden ache in his chest, Jericho braced himself for seeing her again. Was she still asleep? They'd had a late night, which he hadn't done a blessed thing to help. He hoped to hell she'd been getting the rest she needed since then.

Jericho headed for the kitchen and the coffeepot. But before he could even leave the shelter of the hallway, Rosie's voice wafted through the air and met his ears. Coming to a halt, he stood and listened to her speaking softly to the dogs. In another second she began humming, sweet and low in her throat.

A disturbing memory ambushed him. He hadn't awoken to a woman humming in the kitchen since he'd been seven years old. Sharp, edgy memories of growing up and hoping against hope to hear those feminine sounds once more came darting through his conscious mind.

Waking up in his room upstairs at home, sneaking down to peek into his dad's kitchen and praying that Momma would've finally come home. He'd been so sure that any day now she would be back and tell him she'd made a big mistake in leaving him. Despite Daddy forever saying it would never happen.

Dumb again, Jericho told himself while he exhaled heavily and cleared his head. As an adult, he realized that the family had been much better off without his alcoholic mother. *He'd* been better off, too.

Still, what a surprise to suddenly find that aching need had never completely gone away. That it had just been lurking there in his subconscious. Irritated with himself for being so vulnerable, he stuffed the old feelings back into the dark corner of his mind and went into the kitchen to confront all his demons.

"Good morning," Rosie said and looked up at him as

he entered the room. She was sitting on the kitchen floor, trying to coax Shep into drinking water.

God, she was even more beautiful in the light of day than she'd been last night. If that was even possible.

Refusing to just stand and stare at her, he bent on one knee and checked Shep's eyes. They were much clearer and the old dog seemed to recognize his master.

Jericho cleared his throat. "It's nearly noon, but it looks like the day will be good one. The dogs are better."

"Yes." She gently placed Shep's head back down on his dog bed and stood. "I hope that means they're going to make it."

"I think it must. Though Quinn said it would take a couple of days to be sure." He stood too and turned to the coffeepot. "Have you had anything to eat?"

"Uh, no. I fixed myself some tea and made you some coffee. But I'm not really very hungry."

He glanced over his shoulder, really looking at her, and saw that her face was pale, her hair standing up on end as though she'd run her hands through it. "You okay?"

"I had a nightmare. But I think it might mean something. Maybe my memories will be coming back through my dreams. What do you think?"

His first thought, that her returning memory was the last thing he wanted, sideswiped him with unusual force. When she remembered, she would leave him and go back to her life. *Breathe.* After another moment, he got his bearings and mentally kicked himself for being such a fool. Of course she needed to remember. It was her life.

"It's possible," he said. "Doc O'Neal said the memories might come back in bits and pieces." Jericho tried to smile at her, to reassure her, but he didn't feel much like smiling. "What did you dream?"

"Most of it was silly—or scary. But I clearly remember looking down at myself and thinking I looked like a fairy princess. With long, beautiful and shiny hair." She reached up and tugged at her own short locks. "Not the horrible-looking mess that's there now."

He blinked a couple of times and all of sudden the image of her naked in the mirror last night sprang into his head. "You know, I believe you probably are a natural blonde. If that makes you feel any better."

She frowned. "No. That just makes things worse. I want to know for sure. I wish I had a picture. Being sure about my looks might make it easier for the rest of it to come back."

"Well, now," he said as the idea gelled in his mind. "I think we need an expert opinion. And maybe you might discover something you enjoy doing at the same time.

"Get your shoes on. I'll call one of the neighbors to come over and stay with the dogs for the afternoon. I know where we'll find just the person we need to figure it out."

Rosie once again stared intently at herself in a mirror. Only this time the mirror was at Sallie Jo's Cut N Curl, a few doors down from the sheriff's office. The person standing directly behind Rosie with her fingers sliding through Rosie's hair was the owner, Sallie Jo Stanton.

"What do you think, Sal?" Jericho asked from his spot, off to the side. "That red can't be for real. Can you tell anything about the natural color?"

"Hmm." Sallie was a woman in her early forties. Maybe a little heavyset for her bones, but her hair and makeup seemed impeccable and her clothes fit perfectly.

She combed Rosie's hair into sections. "Yeah, looky there. The blond roots are already growing out.

"Now why would you want to cover up your gorgeous ash-blond with that nasty red dye, sugar?"

Rosie lifted her eyebrows. "I don't know—for sure. But can you put it back to natural?"

Sallie shook her head and studied the hair a little closer. "The only way to totally get rid of the dark red color would be too harsh. I could strip it out, but that would ruin your hair and it still wouldn't be natural."

She lifted a section so Rosie could see it clearly in the mirror. "We can lighten it up some. Maybe end up as a strawberry blonde for a while. But the best thing will be to let me cut it shorter so it can grow out quicker."

"Shorter?" Rosie felt positive she should have long hair. All down her back, if she believed in dreams.

"This…I hesitate to call it a cut…isn't doing you any favors, hon." Sallie picked up her shears. "All these split ends and funny angles just call attention to the drastic dye job. Let me style it short for you.

"Think of it this way," Sallie continued as she combed through the hair once again. "Cutting is one way to get rid of that awful coloring job a lot faster. Then we'll lighten the rest and before you know it, you'll be blond again. What do you say?"

"Okay, I guess so."

Jericho stepped into her view in the mirror. "That's fine. You'll be good here for a while, right? I'm going over to speak to the deputy. He needs to revise his bulletin and recheck with the people around the county.

"We've been asking about a redhead when we should've been checking for any word on a blonde." With that, he tipped his hat at Sallie. "I'll be back in a couple of hours. That do?"

"Sure, Sheriff." Sallie watched Jericho leave with an admiring gleam in her eyes. "That there is sure one fine-looking man. If I wasn't already married…" Her voice trailed off, leaving no question what she'd do.

Yes, Jericho surely was fine-looking. And a fine-quality man, too.

Rosie suspected that Jericho would turn out to be the best man she had ever known. Over the last two days, between hiding for her life and almost having sex, she had fallen in love with him. And she had a strong sense that he felt the same way about her. Now all she had to do was prove it to him. There had to be some way to make him see that the two of them belonged together.

Rosie was determined to find it.

Deputy Rawlins checked his watch and discovered it was past five o'clock. It'd been a long, discouraging night last night and he should've been off the clock long ago. But he wanted to make just one more stop before he headed home this afternoon.

He'd already checked with some of the truckers at the truck stop yesterday. But today he had new information.

For fifteen minutes Adam spoke to as many of the drivers as he could find. Finally, he'd found one who claimed to know something.

"Yeah, I gave a ride to a drop-dead gorgeous blonde," the long-haul trucker said. "Five days ago. I have it in my log. A real looker, that one. She'd be hard to forget."

Adam asked for a better description.

"Oh man, hair and legs down to there," the driver said with a grin. "And a shape worth losing your job over— if you know what I mean."

Though not a perfect description, Adam figured it was close enough. "Can you tell me where you picked her up and dropped her off?"

"Sure. I picked her up sixty miles or so north on the interstate. Between Austin and San Antonio. At a joint called Stubbins Barbeque. You ever heard of the place?"

"Yeah," Adam said. He'd eaten there, the place was famous. "The food's good, even if the patrons are on the rowdy side."

The driver nodded. "Don't know that the lady ate anything. I'd eaten earlier, but old Charlie Stubbins lets drivers catch a few hours sleep in the back of his lot. So I was just about to get underway again when I spotted this babe running down the side of the highway. She looked like she'd seen a ghost. I figured a couple hours in the cab with a broad who looked like that wouldn't be such a bad thing. You know?"

Adam nodded, then continued, "Where'd you drop her?"

"I was heading across the border. Let her out just this side of the river, in the town of Rio View."

Adam got the driver's name, address and number, then sent him on his way. Jericho should be pleased with this new info.

At least now they had a handle on where to start looking. All they had left to do was ask a million questions at both ends until something popped.

And at the same time, they'd better keep watch on their backsides for an ambush. Adam didn't like it, but he guessed that this kind of thing was all part of the job.

Chapter 10

The hired gunman called Arnie eased his stolen pickup into the dark lot of a roadside bar near the Mexican border. He found a spot to park on the caliche and got out. At long past the midnight hour, and considering it was during the middle of the week, the place seemed usually packed. Dirty trucks and well-used four-wheel-drive SUVs squeezed into every inch.

Grateful to have already made it over the border and back, Arnie gave a moment's thought to his previous partner. He'd left Petey in that medical clinic in Ciudad Acuna. No one there spoke much English, but the medicos managed to treat Petey's wound and more or less agreed to keep him in the clinic until his arm healed. Arnie had just been glad it was cheap.

Also thankful that their employer had given him another chance, Arnie figured otherwise he would probably be dead right now. But this time around, the boss wanted things to go differently. And whatever the boss wanted, Arnie was willing to do. It would keep him alive a few days longer.

That's why Arnie was about to walk into this rough, sleazy out-of-the-way nightspot. The meeting had been set up for 1:00 a.m., and Arnie hoped to hell he managed to leave by 2:00 a.m. with both a new partner and a new plan. Most of all, he hoped to get out of the place alive and in one piece. If this turned out to be a setup, he would never know what hit him.

Inside, after his eyes got used to the low lighting, Arnie spotted the man he was supposed to meet. Located at a table in a dimly lit corner, the guy was sitting with his back to the wall. A group of dangerous-looking hangers-on surrounded him, leaning their elbows on his table. A chill ran up Arnie's spine as the man in the middle of things tilted his head and shot him a narrowed-eyed stare across the smoky room.

He'd seen this man before, of course. In a much different context. But even tonight in this backwater bar, the guy carried an air of respect. His dark brown hair had not a strand out of place. His lips turned up in a kind of sneer as his eyes followed Arnie's movements. But when Arnie got closer he saw that a dimple marred the strength in the man's craggy cheek. A shift in the guy's position at the table as he raised his bottle of beer caused a small beam of light to glint against the metal badge affixed to his breast pocket.

Swallowing his fear, Arnie gathered his courage as he strode through the crowds. It was too late to ask how he'd gotten himself into this.

Too late to do anything differently either. Arnie braced himself for the worst—and hoped to hell it would end with the best.

Rosie awoke sick to her stomach again the next morning. But she was no longer in Jericho's guest bedroom. Despite her protests, last night he had delivered her to his best friend's Bar None ranch for the night. Clay Colton and Tamara Brown were lovely hosts, but they simply could never replace the man she loved.

Rolling out of bed, she tiptoed into the guest bath and lost whatever was left of the contents of her stomach. Today's morning sickness was a big fat reminder of yesterday. But similar as it was, last night there had been no dreams. Not even one fuzzy glimpse of her past. She wondered if that was because she was no longer in close proximity to Jericho. Perhaps he was the catalyst for her returning memories. If so, that might be a good excuse to stay near him.

Washing her face and brushing her teeth, Rosie couldn't help feeling somewhat lost without the security of Jericho nearby. This morning Tamara had promised to take her shopping for clothes at a mall she frequented just this side of San Antonio. But afterward Rosie was scheduled to spend the rest of the day with Jericho, trying to trace her movements on the days before she lost her memory.

Checking out her new hairdo in the bathroom mirror,

Rosie was pleased with what she saw. The stylish cut and lighter color made her look almost sophisticated. Sallie had given her a little makeup, too, and as she applied a touch of lip gloss a picture began to form in her mind.

A picture of herself, in a dark gray business suit and crisp white blouse, getting ready for work. So…she must have a job. But if she did, why hadn't her boss reported her missing?

Why hadn't *anyone* reported her missing? Didn't she even have any friends that missed her?

Becoming frustrated once again, Rosie put away all her unanswerable questions and finished getting dressed. If that's the way her old life had been—no friends, a boss who didn't care if she showed up, and a husband or boyfriend who couldn't be bothered to report her missing—then she didn't want to remember.

She decided not to buy anything that looked like a business suit today when they went shopping. Getting something that was right for Esperanza, Texas—and its sheriff—would be a much better way to go.

Jericho helped Rosie up into the passenger seat of his pickup. Since he'd showed up here at Clay's ranch to pick her up a few minutes ago, he couldn't seem to take his eyes off her. She looked so different with the new haircut and new clothes that really fit.

Not bad, mind you. But different. Spectacular.

The bruises around her face had nearly disappeared, and it looked as though the long, lean woman had evolved into a real Texas stunner in her narrow dark jeans and a tight-fitting denim jacket. She seemed to belong at one of those big outdoor Texas-style charity events, held in Dallas or Houston, rather than in small-town Esperanza, Texas. She wasn't the Rosie he had been getting to know over the last few days.

But then, who was she?

"Where are we going first, Jericho?"

To find out who you really are so I can know who I'm falling in love with. "To Stubbins Barbeque. It's about sixty miles up the road. Ever heard of it?"

She put her thumbnail to her lips, lost in thought.

"For a moment...I thought..." She shook her head. "No, it doesn't sound familiar. But then nothing does. Why are we going there?"

"Someone said they thought they saw you at the place almost a week ago. I want to ask around now that your hair is lighter and see if anyone recognizes you. Okay?"

She squirmed a little in her seat. But when she turned to answer, her eyes were bright and she had a big, warm smile on her lips. "Great. Wouldn't it be terrific if we find someone who knows me?"

Past the words— Past the smile—

There was a sense of misery about her. When he looked deeper, he noticed a tiny lick of fear hiding in those brilliant blue eyes. If she was miserable because their time together might be drawing to an end, that was okay. He felt much the same way.

But the fear—now, that bothered him. He intended to protect her from those goons or any others sent in their place. Didn't she know that? What else was there for her to be afraid about?

Confused, but determined to stand beside her despite

whatever they might uncover, Jericho headed his truck up the ramp to the interstate and drove on toward the answers.

As they turned off I-35 at the exit for Stubbins restaurant, Rosie's nerves tensed and strained. Nothing looked even vaguely familiar. Still, the closer they drove down the frontage road, the more jittery she became.

"Any sparks of recall?" Jericho asked as he turned onto the gigantic blacktop parking lot.

The smells of mesquite smoke mixed with her panic and filled the air with doubts.

Yes. "No. Maybe." She rubbed at the hairs standing up on her arms. "Nothing specific. Just a bad feeling."

"I'm right here. But don't do anything that makes you too uncomfortable. Just let me know and we'll leave."

Jericho parked behind the big red barn of a building, turned off the pickup and rounded the truck to help her down. "Ready?"

Rosie felt as if she were being marched to the guillotine. "I guess so. What are we going to do?"

"We're going to find out if anyone remembers seeing you on the first of the month. That's when the driver claims he picked up a blonde."

"But…" The sign beside the entryway said the hours were noon to midnight. All the deputy had managed to get was a date. How many people had come and gone on that day?

Jericho took her hand and strode up to the cashier's booth. The woman behind the counter was bleached blond, skinny as a rail and watched them with sharp, hawklike eyes.

She coughed and cleared her throat before picking up a couple of paper placemats and raising her painted-on eyebrows. "Just the two of you?" she asked with what sounded like a smoker's rasp.

Jericho shook his head. "I'm Sheriff Yates from Campo County. We're investigating a shooting, and I'd like to speak to anyone who was working here on the first of this month."

The cashier looked a little taken aback, but she glared at his badge and the gun strapped in its holster at his side before she said, "A shooting *here,* Sheriff?"

"*Was* there a shooting here on that date?"

"We've had our share of knife fights and an occasional gunshot," she said by way of an answer. "But not last week. I worked that day—the lunch shift."

"I would imagine I need to talk to someone working later in the day. Could you tell us who worked the dinner shift?"

Rosie quietly tried to stem her unease. She shifted from one foot to the other and folded her arms under her breasts.

"Let me check." The cashier pulled a plastic-covered chart out from under the counter and studied it for a moment. "There's two waiters and a busboy who were here that night and who'll also be on tonight. Actually, they might be already in back getting set to start their shift. If they're here, I'll send them on out.

"Besides them," she added. "I'll have to check with the manager to see if I can give you a list of the others who worked that night."

The cashier asked them to wait and they stood in the small lobby, idly staring at framed pictures of prize bulls that sported blue ribbons and snorted at the camera. Rosie found it hard to think. She couldn't even manage to get a word to form.

A young man with dark hair and a big apron came out of the open half of the kitchen and walked up to them. The kid looked scared to death of Jericho, but he stood his ground and answered questions.

After one look at Rosie, though, he shook his head. "So sorry," the kid mumbled with a heavy Spanish accent before he went back to work.

Another young man, this one with his light brown hair tied back in a thong at the nape of his neck and wearing jeans, a checked shirt and a red vest that obviously was part of his uniform, stepped out of another back room. He immediately seemed to recognize her.

"Hey," he said. "You cut your hair. Shame. It was cool all the way down your back like that."

"You've seen me before?"

"Sure. You were in the other night with another woman. Older broad. Maybe your grandma? Don't you remember me?" He went on as if he didn't expect an answer. "I remember the two of you paid in cash. Not something we see a lot around here what with truck drivers and business people using credit cards and all. You two weren't bad tippers, either…for two single women."

A picture of an older woman who looked something like Becky French, only she was wearing a business suit, glasses and a worried expression, flashed in and out of Rosie's mind. She started to sweat. Trying hard, she couldn't bring back anything more.

Jericho asked the young man another question or

two but suddenly Rosie's ears were ringing. Her legs became spongy and she found herself leaning on the sheriff for support.

He slung his arm around her waist, thanked the waiter and pulled her outside into the sunshine. "What's wrong with you? Aren't you feeling well?"

"Something…" One look around the parking lot and a flood of images flashed in her brain like a movie on fast-forward.

Darkness and fear. Someone chasing her across the blacktop. A gunshot. A thud from behind her.

Blinded by fear, she couldn't breathe. "Ahhh." The muffled scream came unbidden from Rosie's mouth but it originated somewhere deep, primal. "Is she hurt? I have to run. Hide."

Suddenly Jericho had her in his arms, rocking her gently. "You're okay. What do you remember? Who was hurt?"

She couldn't stop trembling and found herself shaking her head as though that might clear up the images. "I…I can't make it come back." The tears started to flow. "For a second back there, I saw another woman sitting across the table. A friend, I think. But now I can't…the pictures in my mind won't come back."

"What about out here in the parking lot?"

Swiping furiously at her cheeks in frustration, Rosie glanced around the lot. "It's just bits and pieces. Some-thing that sounded like a gunshot—or maybe a car back-firing. Dark shapes moving through the shadows. Damn. Why can't I remember?"

Jericho half dragged her over to his truck, opened the

door and helped her in. "Stay here. Lock the doors and stay put. I'm going back for a couple more questions then we'll head out. You'll be okay?"

She nodded her head. But without her memories, she wasn't sure she would ever really be okay again.

Jericho spent the next half hour talking to the manager of the restaurant and then driving himself and Rosie over to the local county sheriff's office. He'd only met the newly elected sheriff of this county, Richard Benway, once. But had heard Benway was a good man.

Rosie's color had come back by the time they finished at the sheriff's office. It had been decided that Benway would open a full investigation as to what exactly had taken place in the restaurant's parking lot on the night of July first.

Jericho had loads of unanswered questions. The truck driver who picked up Rosie hadn't seen another woman, so what happened to her? Had she been hurt? Had anyone witnessed what took place? And how exactly had Rosie arrived at the restaurant in the first place? Driven? If so, what happened to her car?

Luckily, Sheriff Benway was willing to do the legwork. He had the authority and the extra manpower. But there were no guarantees the investigation would be successful.

Back in the truck, Rosie turned to him and asked, "What's next? Are we going home?"

It was a shock to his system to hear her calling Esperanza home. But he found he sort of liked it.

"This time of year," he began easily. "The sun doesn't

set until nearly 9:00 p.m. I thought we could drive on
to the border. Check out the town where the truck driver
says he let you out.

"You willing to give it a try?" he added thoughtfully.
"Are you too tired?"

"I'm okay. If there's any chance of finding out who
I am by going, then I'm there."

Jericho nodded and pushed down on the accelerator.
This time they would play it smarter and start at the
county sheriff's office.

But, unfortunately, he knew this county's sheriff.
Knew him only too well.

There'd been rumors for years about how Sheriff
Jesus Montalvo had gotten rich by turning his back
to the forty-mile stretch of border that his county
shared with Mexico. Like Jericho, Montalvo's county
had no big cities and a small tax base. But unlike
Jericho, Sheriff Montalvo of San Javier County had
managed to accumulate an enormous amount of land
and a few heavy bank accounts. The only difference
between counties was a wild forty miles of Rio
Grande riverfront.

Still, Montalvo *would* help. He had a large staff of
deputies and knew where all the bodies and secrets were
buried in his territory.

By the time they arrived in Rio View it was supper-
time. Rosie didn't think she was hungry until her
stomach started rumbling and she remembered that she
hadn't eaten anything today. Jericho called ahead and
Sheriff Montalvo agreed to meet them at a truck-stop

restaurant near where the truck driver had claimed he'd let Rosie off late on the night of the first.

As they entered the crowded diner, that same uneasy feeling from before began to niggle around the edges of Rosie's mind. She forced it aside, determined this time to either ignore the images and feelings or capture them whole and place them properly in her memory.

A waitress pointed out the booth where Sheriff Montalvo was waiting. They worked their way through the loaded tables and past row upon row of full booths made with brown plastic seats and linoleum-covered tables. Everywhere Rosie looked were men. Long-haul truck drivers. Cowboys and ranchers. Rugged-looking men who seemed too busy eating to pay much attention.

Until…she walked by. Then every set of eyes studied her carefully. It gave her the creeps.

She'd thought she would be glad to slip into the booth across from Sheriff Montalvo and get away from the stares. But when she came near enough to the table to get a good look, there was something about him that seemed darkly familiar.

Not knock-you-down familiar. But close.

The man sat slouched in the far corner of the booth, but the power of his position glowed around him. He wasn't wearing a hat and his brown hair was combed in a perfect style. His white shirt looked starched and crisp under his badge.

A couple of waitresses stood beside the booth, like two virginal handmaidens. Rosie could just tell that everyone in the place, probably everyone in the county, would treat this sheriff with deference.

She grew uneasy again. Did she know this man? And if so, would he be able to tell her who she was?

Easing her way into the booth in front of Jericho, Rosie suddenly surprised herself by wishing that Sheriff Montalvo would not be able to tell her a blessed thing.

Chapter 11

"Is it very far from here?" Rosie stared out the windshield into the growing silver-gray dusk.

Jericho watched her body tensing with every mile they drove and his gut twisted from wanting to do something for her. Montalvo hadn't turned out to be of much help. The San Javier County sheriff told them he hadn't gotten any reports of trouble or missing women. But something about Montalvo's body language had been saying that he at least knew of Rosie, though he swore he'd never laid eyes on her before.

As they'd waited for their supper, Montalvo prompted Jericho and Rosie to ask around the restaurant to see if anyone recognized her. No one did. But Jericho's instincts had screamed at him through the whole search. The diner crowd had looked at her with hints of recognition in their eyes, yet not one would even meet his gaze with their own as he'd been asking questions. Liars.

After supper, Montalvo had also encouraged him to check with a motel on the outskirts of town that might match Rosie's description of the one she'd seen on the day she had lost her memory. Montalvo even called ahead to get them an appointment with the manager/owner.

As they pulled up in front, Jericho decided Rosie's original description fit the place perfectly. A cheap motel on the poorer side of a small border town. Just as she'd described it.

The deepening purple shadows of nightfall obscured his view of Rosie's face as they walked to the motel office. But he could feel the nervous energy radiating from her.

At the office door, he stood still for a moment, holding on to the handle as the fluorescent light from inside shone out through the glass. "Something's coming back to you, isn't it?"

Her eyes were wide and bright and her face flushed. "This is the place," she whispered. "From that morning when those two goons grabbed me. I remember the neighborhood."

"Yeah. I figured it was. Anything else coming back?"

She shook her head and bit her lip.

"Okay, let's see what we can find out from the owner." He let her go in ahead of him so he could watch the reaction of the man behind the desk.

The owner turned out to be a portly guy in his fifties, dressed in shorts and a T-shirt turned gray from washing. The bald spot on the man's head was almost covered over by several thin ash-brown strands of hair. But not quite. From Jericho's viewpoint, towering over the man's five-foot-eight frame, the guy would've been a lot better off leaving the bare patch alone.

As they stepped into the room, the owner never blinked an eyelash or showed any recognition of Rosie. But then once they came closer, Jericho caught a glimpse of the man's pupils widening involuntarily at the sight of her—right before he quickly glanced away. The man knew her all right. Even if he wasn't going to admit it.

They introduced themselves. The motel owner seemed put out at having to answer questions. Too bad.

"So, you're sure you don't recognize this woman?" Jericho asked after the man had just said he didn't. "Take another look."

"Once is plenty, bud. The answer is no. Back off."

Jericho lost it in that instant. He grabbed the owner by the front of his shirt and lifted him off his feet and halfway over the counter.

"It's Sheriff Yates to you, *bud*. And Sheriff Montalvo said you would cooperate. Let's have some of that cooperation right now.

"This woman was here in your motel no more than four days ago. Take a better look."

"Jericho…" Rosie put her hand on his shirtsleeve and her expression said she didn't want this much trouble.

Jericho lowered the owner back to his feet but refused

to open his fist. In fact, he still held the man's shirtfront in a death grip.

"Oh…oh, yeah," the owner stuttered as he took another look at Rosie. "Ya see, I didn't recognize you. You've changed. You're the broad that had the long, blond hair.

"You left one hell of a mess in the bathroom of one of the units when you dashed outta here, you know? There was hair and blackish-red dye everywhere. Ruined a couple of our good towels, I can tell you that."

Jericho let him go and then threw a couple of bucks from his pocket onto the counter. "That should take care of any damages.

"Was she registered here?" he added, putting a demanding tone in his words. "Under what name?"

The guy shrugged. "I don't remember. Or, maybe I just wasn't on duty when she came in."

"You want to take a look at the register anyway?" Jericho's patience with this character was running thin.

After another ten minutes of avoiding giving any actual answers, the owner shrugged again and said, "Look, we're not in the business of asking questions about our guests. This place isn't located on any main highway. The people that come here do it for their privacy."

"And I suppose your guests all pay in cash?" Jericho was ready to pound this sucker into the ground if he hedged one more time.

"Sure. In advance. We don't take credit cards and only take checks from the people that live around here."

"Well…" Frustration was making Jericho steamy. "How did she arrive then? Not on foot, surely."

The manager narrowed his eyes at Jericho. "None of my business. There's a bus stop about a block down. Maybe that way. How should I know? Ask her."

Jericho's hands fisted once again, but just then Rosie touched his shoulder. "This isn't doing any good," she told him. "I'm not getting any flashes of my past here. Let's just go."

"Hey," the manager said as he tilted his head to give her another look. "What're all the questions for? Don't you remember?"

The way he had said it told Jericho the man already knew very well that Rosie couldn't remember her past. And probably knew why not. Someone had already told him. Or warned him. Sheriff Montalvo? The sheriff was the only one who could've let the owner know what was going on.

If that was the case, then Rosie was right. They weren't going to get anything else out of this guy. In fact, all of a sudden it seemed like he'd had been deliberately hedging his answers in order to keep them here longer. If the sheriff were somehow involved, then whatever was going on in Rio View and with Rosie went far beyond dangerous. It would have to involve something bigger and more secretive than just a woman who'd been kidnapped.

Jericho's gut was telling him he needed to get Rosie out of San Javier County. Fast.

"Let's go." He took her by the arm and rushed them both outside and into his truck.

Buckling up, Jericho mentally ticked off the various routes he could take that would get them back to Esperanza the quickest. Menacing darkness began closing in around the pickup as he pulled out of the motel parking lot and kept an eye on what was going on in the rearview mirror.

Rosie cast a sideways glance at Jericho's profile in the glow of the dashboard lights. His jaw was set and a slight tick pulsed under his right eye. The man must still be furious.

She had never seen him as mad as he'd been while he questioned the motel owner. He'd controlled it in the office as long as she stood by his side, but the whole time she'd been afraid that the thin string binding up his anger would snap at any moment.

But why should he still be mad? He had no reason to be mad at her. She couldn't help it if her memories were lost. Yet he seemed furious.

With no clue as to what he was thinking, she looked out the pickup's window as the few remaining buildings on the outskirts of Rio View flew past. Rosie noted that they'd begun picking up speed. When the city-limits sign sped by and nothing but black, moonless night took the place of outdoor floodlights and lighted billboard signs, she all of a sudden realized they were zipping down the highway way too fast. Good thing the roads seemed deserted at this hour.

She cast a quick look over to the speedometer and was stunned to see the gage touching the ninety mark. Asphalt rushed under the truck as she tightened her seat belt. She was not ready to die tonight just because Jericho was a little miffed.

"What's wrong?" she asked him, and was embarrassed by the squeak in her voice. "Are you mad at me?"

"No."

Well, at least he'd answered. But that wasn't enough of an explanation for her. "Then what's up with you?"

It was then that she finally noticed him checking the rearview mirror every few seconds. "Someone is following us." She'd answered her own question.

He shot her a sideways glance then went back to concentrating on the road ahead. "Not yet."

"Yet? How do you know for sure that…"

"Crap." Jericho must've stepped down harder on the gas pedal just then because the truck gave a roar, bucked and unbelievably the speedometer needle eased up past one hundred. "There they are."

Rosie twisted her neck so she could look out the rear window. About a half a mile back a set of headlights could be seen in the distance heading in their same direction.

"What makes you think that car is following us?"

"Gut feeling. That guy in the motel kept us there for far too long. He set us up."

"Well, what do they want?"

Jericho spared her one, quick glare. "Guess."

"Me? Oh, God." Her voice almost left her in the dust as the truck flew down the highway into the dark. "What are we going to do?" she rasped out.

"We're going to lose them."

But even through those determined words, Rosie could hear the other vehicle's engine roaring up right behind them. She turned again and saw a huge set of headlights bearing down on them. They were close. Too close. How had they caught up so fast?

"All we need is another mile…" Jericho's words were interrupted by a loud thump and a terrific jerk.

"They're ramming us," Rosie screamed.

Were they crazy? Ramming people while doing a hundred miles an hour could get them all killed.

While Jericho struggled with the wheel, downshifted then hit the gas again, Rosie turned back to see the other vehicle losing ground. Apparently they'd had to fight the effects of the bump themselves.

"There it is." Jericho tapped the brake, cranked the wheel in a ninety-degree angle and downshifted into second. The engine whined and the tires squealed, but the truck responded in a perfectly executed wheelie, hitting the hidden side road back on all fours.

Rosie thought her lungs would explode. The truck barreled down a narrow paved road with barbed-wire fence whizzing by on both sides. She gasped for breath, closed her eyes and hung on.

"Do you know where you're going?" Blinking open her eyes, she screeched past the engine's whine. This might turn out to be a dead end. Then what would they do?

Jericho was keeping one eye on the rearview mirror as he answered, "My dad and I used to hunt the leases in this section. If nothing's changed since then, I know every inch. There's a couple of places to lose them up ahead."

If nothing's changed? That might be a big if when their lives depended on it. Rosie shivered and prayed for all she was worth.

Jericho drove on through the darkened fields, forced to continue using his headlights and pushing his truck as much as he dared. But they hadn't gone far enough to be safe when he picked up the other guy's headlights once again in his rearview mirror.

Finally spotting what he'd been waiting for, he slowed just enough to make the turn onto a caliche farm-to-market road. The tires clanged over a cattle guard and spun briefly before they caught again. Stepping down on the gas after the truck righted, he noted that the fencing was gone from the left side of the roadway. *Open range.* Dangerous driving in the dark.

Figuring they had about five miles to go before they made cover in the woods just past Gage's Arroyo crossing, he hoped to hell they made it that far.

Jericho threw a fast glance toward Rosie and vowed they would make it, at least that far—and beyond. The other choice was unthinkable. Once they hit the woods he would find some place to hide the truck, for long enough to call for help. But that was presuming his cell would work out here. He counted on those woods being located in the next county over. A county with a sheriff he could depend on to come to their aide.

Taking his eyes off the road for a millisecond, he checked on the woman sitting next to him. Her body was stiff. Her breath coming in short staccato bursts, and her fists bunched and ready to strike. He approved. She was scared but ready to fight.

That was his girl. Beautiful as always, but tough when she needed to be. Good for her.

The road got rougher, and he peered out as far as his headlight beams would reach. Pockmarks, potholes and deep ruts kept his speed down to a roar as the truck behind them began gaining ground.

Holding his breath and gritting his teeth against the violent shaking from his truck, Jericho hit the gas again. The next time he looked into the rearview mirror, he'd gained a little ground.

Son of a gun, that was one gigantic mother of a truck. Taller, wider and faster than Jericho's, the thing loomed out of the darkness like a huge beast with blazing eyes. Resembling a fantasy dragon in this darkness, from a distance it even appeared to be snorting smoke out its sides as dust and caliche spewed from under the tires.

He wasn't sure if that description was bad news or good. Bad news because he couldn't outrun them. Good news because he should be able to outmaneuver them on the narrow, slippery back roads.

Wondering if the driver was more, or less, familiar with this range road than he was, Jericho fought the wheel as he tried to bring their surroundings into better focus. Where were they now? How far from the bridge?

There should be a couple of bends in the road up ahead where the packed caliche wound around the edge of a deep arroyo off to his left. He blinked and stared into the star-filled night, trying to judge how far.

At the distant edge of his headlight beams and seemingly right in the middle of the road, he caught the shadow of a mesquite tree. That told him the first bend in the road was coming up. Downshifting enough to take the curve on four wheels, Jericho held his breath waiting for the second curve.

"Jericho, watch out!"

Rosie must've seen the hulking outlines in the road a second before he did. A half dozen cattle had wandered out onto the caliche and were lying around soaking up the day's lingering warmth. Son of a bitch!

Jericho jerked on the wheel and went right, knowing the arroyo was to the left. And hoping against hope to miss any more of the cattle that might be off to that side.

The minute the pickup was off-road, it skidded in the sandy dirt and he lost control. The truck did a one-eighty all by itself. He hung on to the wheel anyway, stepped lightly on the brake and prayed for a clear path.

But tonight they were not going to be so lucky. Out of the darkness loomed a hefty-sized cactus. Dead ahead.

He slammed down on the brake, holding out his right arm in a vain attempt to keep Rosie backed into her seat. But it was too little, too late as the truck's momentum pushed them forward.

In the next instant, he heard his front bumper crunching against the cactus, and the truck came to an abrupt halt, though his body was still violently jolting in the seat. He vaguely heard the air bags deploy—immediately after his head smacked hard against the driver's-side window.

Then it was suddenly all over. Pain shot through his temple and everything faded to black.

Chapter 12

Rosie fought her way around the deflating passenger air bag, coughing at the dust in the air and battling with her seat belt. She scrambled over the center console to reach Jericho's side. His moans, coming from behind the driver's wheel, meant he must be alive. She was okay, so he should be all right. He just had to be.

Everything had gone so quiet. The truck's engine was still running, but it had stopped whining. When she reached Jericho, his inert body took the breath from her lungs with fear. She quickly checked him over and placed her ear to his chest. He wasn't conscious, but he also wasn't bleeding. His breathing seemed heavy but nevertheless steady. Thank heaven.

Just then she heard another noise that sent chills

running down her spine. Leaning over, she turned off the engine, listening intently. Yes, it was the other truck, and it was getting closer.

She tried to keep her head. What should she do? Run into the night and hide? But what about Jericho? She would never, ever leave him here, and there was no way she could carry or drag him away in time.

Without really thinking it all the way through, but minus a moment to consider, Rosie unbuckled Jericho's seat belt. That left her room to undo the safety cover on his holster. She carefully lifted his service weapon from its place, and tried to remember everything she'd learned from him about guns.

Stepping out of the pickup, she faced the road the same way they'd come and listened as the other truck's engine noise got louder and louder.

"Jericho?" she whispered, turning her face to him and silently begging him to wake up and take over for her.

But his soft moan told her that wasn't to be.

Standing in what she hoped was relative safety behind the pickup's open door, and holding Jericho's gun with both hands, Rosie pointed it in the direction of the oncoming engine noise. In the next instant, head-lights caught her in their glare as the huge truck navi-gated the first curve. Petrified, but determined to save both Jericho and herself, she aimed right above the headlights and held her breath.

Hold off, she cautioned herself. Let them get a little closer. That's what Jericho would do.

But Rosie could see that the truck was already slowing and turning more directly toward her as they no doubt had seen Jericho's headlights off the road. There wasn't going to be enough time for perfect shots.

She fired. But must've missed them. They were still coming. Firing once again, she heard a ping and knew that this time she'd at least hit the body of the truck.

That ended up being her last shot because right then the driver apparently caught sight of the cattle in the road. To avoid Rosie's bullets coming from his right and to miss colliding with ten tons of cow dead ahead, the driver dragged his wheel hard to his left.

For a moment or two more, Rosie could see headlights bumping off the road away from her. And then all of a sudden they disappeared. Disappeared!

After a crashing noise that sounded truly terrible to her ears, another unholy silence filled the air. Then, at last, Jericho called her name. She turned and scrambled back to his side.

"Who was doing the shooting?" he asked weakly as he shook his head and fought to untangle his own deflated air bag.

She heaved a deep sigh, so glad he was conscious and seemingly okay that she almost wept. "Me." Holding out his gun to show him, she began to shake. "Are you injured badly? What hurts?"

He gave her a curious look, took the gun and then turned to stare out the window past the cactus. "I'm okay. Where's the other truck?"

"I don't know. After they spotted the cows, the driver went off on the other side of the road. Then I heard a crash."

"The arroyo is over that way," Jericho said darkly. "It

was pretty damned steep and rough down in that spot the last time I saw it."

"Do you think they're still alive?"

Once again, Jericho's answer scared her. "It doesn't matter right now. We have to get out of here. This is still San Javier County. We're in danger every moment we stay here.

"I wonder if my pickup will still run," he added as he put his gun back in the holster, buckled his seat belt and straightened up in his seat.

"I turned it off," she told him. "And the motor was still going then."

He cranked the ignition and it roared to life. "Buckle up again, sweetheart. We're getting out of here. Only this time at a slightly safer speed."

"But shouldn't we check on…whoever that was? Maybe they need help."

"I'm real proud of the way you stood up to those bozos," Jericho said as he put the truck into Reverse and eased backward. "But you don't go sticking your hand in the hole, wondering if the rattlesnakes are doing okay. If they're still alive, that's the last place you should go. If they're not… Well, we'll call the sheriff in the next county and let him find out. Just as soon as we make it there safely ourselves."

Jericho listened from the bedroom of their suite at the bed-and-breakfast as water began running behind the closed bathroom door. Rosie was preparing to take her shower while he tried to sort through his emotions. It had been a very long night so far.

Thankfully, the sheriff in this county was an old friend and had been ready and willing to help. A crew of deputies was dispatched to Gage's Arroyo in the middle of the night to search for survivors. But when they'd found the smashed monster truck at the bottom of the dry arroyo bed, the driver and any passengers had been missing. The questions now seemed centered on whether any survivors had left the scene under their own power or had been thrown clear in the crash. A better search of the area would have to wait until daylight.

Meanwhile, Jericho could hardly arouse any real interest in those bastards. It was Rosie and his feelings toward her that had been hogging all his thoughts.

His old friend Sam Trenton, the sheriff of this county, had seen how beat up and tired he and Rosie had looked after all the questions were answered to the best of their abilities. Sam had called around and found them this one lone vacant suite in an entire county full of summer tourists who'd come for an arts-and-crafts festival.

Driving for a few hours to Esperanza had been out of the question. The pickup would run, but the tires were completely shot, the air bags needed to be replaced, the right front fender was crumpled and the headlight broken.

And the two of them needed rest.

From behind the bathroom door, the sound of running water changed over to the stronger noise of shower spray. Jericho sat down on the edge of the bed to consider what was going to happen when Rosie came out of the bathroom and they found themselves exhausted and alone together in a room with only a king-size bed and a sitting room with one tiny sofa.

His life had changed forever in one intense moment back there on that dark road. Gone was the guy he had once been, the one who'd wanted nothing more out of his life than a bachelor's existence. In his place was a man who would give anything to trade in his old ways for a chance at one red-hot lady who couldn't remember her baby's father. A lady who also easily remembered her weapons' training and thought nothing of wielding a weapon when backed into a corner.

For the last couple of hours, while he'd been checked over in a local clinic and had taken his own shower, he'd found himself thinking not about bad guys but about how best to remodel his cabin. How to change the house he'd built into a real home.

He looked over to the bathroom door. She was there— just on the other side. The only woman he'd ever met for whom he would gladly give up the rest of his life.

For her and for her child. He'd been thinking of her little one, too. More than anything, he wanted to be that child's father. He would make a great dad. He'd had the best example in the world.

For some reason, Jericho discovered he wasn't afraid of Rosie leaving him. Always before, when he'd come close to a serious relationship with a woman, he would call a halt to things sooner rather than later. Mostly due to his worrying about how long it would last before the woman up and left. Maybe that kind of thing was a legacy from his damned mother.

But not this time. If Rosie hadn't left him unconscious in the truck to save herself, and she certainly had not, he was positive she would never leave him at all. Not once she fully committed.

So that was what he was sitting here thinking about. How to go about making her *want* to stay as much as he wanted to keep her. But as usual, whenever he thought of her, the testosterone took over and he quit using his brain altogether.

In fact, right this minute his pulse pounded with need and his senses were on overdrive just knowing she was naked on the other side of that door.

Then with no warning, the door opened and Rosie stood on the threshold to the bedroom wearing nothing but a towel. Like a zombie he stumbled toward her with his arms outstretched.

Those brilliant sapphire eyes of hers swam with need, but she held out one arm to fend off his advance. "Jericho, wait. We have to think this through. I may be a terrible person. At the very least, I'm probably a thief. And obviously I slept with someone who didn't care enough about me to look when I went missing."

"You are my fantasy." It was all he could think to say. "The one I've waited for all my life." He took another step closer.

She backed into the bathroom. "But getting involved with me might bring you lots more trouble. Someone is still after me."

"Too late," he murmured. "I'm already involved. You stayed. You stayed and I don't care who or what you were before. I'll find a way to protect you from anything.

"And what's more," he added with a deep breath. "I hope we never find out who you were."

Her eyes went wide and she dropped the towel, holding out her arms to beckon him closer. It was all the invitation he would ever want.

She was stunning and he was breathless as he dragged her into his arms and pushed them both up against the bathroom counter. He slanted his mouth over hers and stroked her waiting tongue with his own.

Kissing like this, with him half dressed and her totally naked was pure torture. But also pure pleasure. His senses soared as he touched her everywhere. He craved her like a thirsty man craved drink.

Bringing a hand up to caress her breast, he reveled in the soft, weighty feel of it in his palm. She had such fabulous breasts. The joy of touching them intensified. His blood fired as he bent his head and took one rosy tip into his mouth.

She moaned and bucked against his hips. It was such a luxurious gift to hear her moaning under his touches and kisses. He spent another indulgent moment in licking and sucking her deep into his mouth, while at the same time letting his other hand slip easily between her legs to cup her.

Another moan came from her parted lips, and he lifted his head to kiss her again. To swallow her little sounds of pleasure and to push his tongue deep inside her, mimicking what he wanted them to be doing in other ways. He held her tight and felt himself growing harder.

Jericho wanted this to happen, more than he'd ever thought possible. But he also wanted to go slow. To draw out every precious moment—for both of them.

Nibbling his way down the satiny column of her

neck, he found her so sweet-smelling and fresh after her shower, and so compelling with her moist skin and soft moans that it nearly threw him off. He steeled himself against a too-soon ending to all this intimacy.

Rosie felt damned good under his hands, and he wanted her to experience something so special with him that she would never forget it. He needed to become familiar with every inch of her body. It seemed imperative to learn everything that she liked. What turned her on. What brought out those tiny mewling sounds of pleasure. What caused her to jump and shove her hips hard up against him, begging for more.

His fingers sought the nub to her core and rubbed there gently. Testing, exploring. Finally, teasing and tormenting.

"Jericho." His name came out like a whispered prayer. He was so turned on he almost missed that she was starting to come.

Crying out, she buried her hands in his hair and hung on. Her breathing came in short pants. He pulsed with anticipation next to her and gave an instant's thought to slowing her down just to bring her up again.

But in the next moment, when her body went taut and she jerked against him with a whimper, he knew this was so much better. To be able to watch her come apart in his arms was the ultimate pleasure. He'd done it once before but this time was even sweeter. This time there would be another and, he hoped, even another chance to make this happen. They had the time and he definitely had the desire.

Rosie trembled, clutching at him as he lifted her chin and kissed her. Kept on kissing her and touching her and rubbing up against her until she groaned again and reached down for his zipper.

"Please, don't leave me again," she whispered hoarsely as she fumbled with the button on his jeans. *"Please."*

He heard all the words she didn't say. *Come inside me. Become one with me. This is meant to be. I will never leave you.*

Helping her out, he slid out of his boots and shed his jeans while she leaned her bottom against the bathroom counter and watched him from under heavy lids. Then he was there. All for her.

Lifting her hips, he filled her. Pushing deep. Her head leaned back on a moan and her hips jerked forward, shoving him ever deeper.

She gripped his shoulders as he thrust once… twice…until his head was literally spinning. Her internal muscles tightened around him, clenching and stroking. Her body pulled at him, drawing him, locking them together in a primitive way and making sure he stayed with her.

Oh, he would stay with her, all right. Stilling, he looked down at her beautiful face, with her eyelids half-closed and with an expression that said she was lost in sensation. Her lips were parted and her breathing shallow.

Breathing deeply himself, he smelled sex, exotic and compelling. Both masculine and feminine shades of lust combined within the scent and drove him mad.

There was no time left. As much as he would've liked to go on forever, when she rubbed her hips to his again, he was undone.

He belted his arm around her waist and pulled her hard against him, thrusting again. The next few moments whizzed by in a blur of thrusts—deeper, deeper, again and again.

Higher and higher, lost and crazed, his muscles tensed and strained as he fought to hold on. He heard her scream, then curse something unintelligible as she twisted and lurched. She plastered herself to him, seeming to want the melding of the two of them into one entity.

That was all he needed. His climax surged through him like an earthquake. His whole body shook with the force. He braced his trembling legs and went along for the ride.

Bending nearly in two, he brought his mouth down on her neck, nipping and grazing and loving the sweetness and softness of her. One last thrust and his head came up as he gasped for breath.

Talk about your life-changing experiences.

He picked her up in his arms and headed for the bed. All he wanted now was another few hours. *Or* maybe, a whole lifetime of feeling this damned good.

Chapter 13

Rosie stretched out beside Jericho's sleeping body. Only moments before he'd laid her down on the bed and crawled in after her. Feeling limp and sated, she was amazed that her body still pulsed with pleasure. Surely there had never been anything in her previous life to compare to him and the things they'd done.

From that very first moment when he'd echoed her thoughts and said he hoped they never uncovered her past, she'd been all his. Forever. Whatever he wanted. For however long he wanted.

Still, at the beginning she'd felt compelled to tell him she loved him. That he was the only one there would ever be from this moment on. It had seemed so important to say the actual words. But quickly she'd come to the conclusion that words didn't matter.

He'd been such a master at telling her everything he was feeling without words. She'd felt his need throbbing inside her. She'd known his thoughts, begging her to never leave him as he'd worked hard to make sure she was fulfilled before taking his own pleasure.

For this short time with him, she'd forgotten all about her fears and the tension of having people after her. And now she wanted to find a way of forgetting them for good. To let Jericho become her permanent protector, so that together they could conquer all the bad things in the world.

He wanted that, too. She was positive. But just now she lay quietly racking her brain for the best way of communicating their mutual needs.

When he softly snored, she found the sounds of him beside her, seemingly so comfortable and sated himself, terribly endearing. He'd been through so much for her. He needed a little sleep.

Easing out from under his arm, she inched away and stood, turning back to look at him on the bed. So beautiful. She vaguely knew that wasn't how you were supposed to describe a man, especially a tough guy like this one. But she thought Jericho was simply gorgeous.

The strong chin. The hint of stubble. Those long lashes lying against the high curve of his cheek.

Whew. Despite the cool air-conditioning in the room, a trickle of sweat beaded at her temple and slithered down her neck. Rosie walked to the bathroom, found a glass and drank water, trying to cool off.

But knowing he was there on the bed, naked, brought her back to the doorway so she could stare at him some more. Just to look at those broad shoulders that had been absolutely perfect to hold on to during the throes of passion. They narrowed down to lean hips. And it was all sleek, flat muscle in between.

Half the time she thought he was some kind of throwback to the old West. The strong, silent type. But when they were alone together, his eyes told her something entirely different as they changed colors with his moods.

Granite when he was mad or taking his job seriously. Amber when he was being sincere or teaching her how to shoot. And almost jade-green when he was in the midst of giving her passion. That last image, the one of him gazing intently into her eyes with those fantastic green eyes, made her actually shiver as the heated desire skittered down her spine.

How could she explain that she wanted forever from him without scaring him or turning him off?

He stirred, rolling onto his back. The sight of all that manhood moved her to action. Thinking simply stopped.

She slid into the bed beside him, tempted beyond restraint. Taking him into her hands, she stroked and played and massaged. First she ran a forefinger down one long, smooth side. Next a tender touch to the rounded, slick tip.

When his body began to respond to her ministrations, she leaned in and took him into her mouth. A soft groan came from above her but what she was doing felt so indulgent, so right, that she refused to give it up.

Jericho came awake with a jolt of erotic sensation. When he looked down at the top of Rosie's head and realized what she was doing to him, he reached out for her. But she shied away from his hands.

Sweet mercy. The vibrations alone nearly caused him to come three feet off the bed.

Very much more of that and it would be all over. And though one day that might be a good plan to follow, it wasn't what he had in mind for tonight.

He wanted tonight to be all about her pleasure. Needing to make her see how much she meant to him. Desperate to make her understand that he did want her to stay with him forever. Tonight was supposed to be hers.

Tunneling his hands through her hair, he firmly eased her back. She lifted her head and looked at him and the sight of her glazed eyes and satisfied expression was a bigger turn-on than what she'd been doing.

Rock hard, he moved fast. Twisting their bodies with a roll and a plunge, he found himself inside her again. Right where he wanted to be.

Her body was slick with sweat but so was his. A momentary thought of moving this show into the shower came and went. Later. The next time. And there would be more. Lots more. Until both of them were weak and weeping and had no more questions about a future.

He eased out of her and then back inside again with a slow draw, setting up a rhythm he hoped to continue for a good long while. Hot damn but this was heaven.

She rocked hard against his hips, sending another blast of pure pleasure spinning through his veins. He reached down and cupped her bottom, holding her tightly to him.

Their bodies were on fire everywhere they touched. So damned hot he figured they might combust.

"Jericho, you feel so good."

"Back attcha, darlin'." *Good* didn't seem adequate. But so help him, his brain must be melting. Words were impossible.

He leaned down and kissed her, moving in and out and loving the feel of silky wet heat. Hoping somehow to make her see.

But he wasn't exactly positive about everything he wanted her to know. Except that he needed her to stay. Was that enough?

"I love you," she said on a moan as her body began tightening around him.

He thrust again on a long slow glide. Was this really what love felt like? Was that what he needed to say?

But before his mouth could catch up, she arched her back and her whole body went rigid. "Jericho!"

Nature took over then, freeing him from thinking, as his own movements came faster and faster. Pounding hard into her, too soon the orgasm broke through him on a flood of flashing sensation. He barked out a unintelligible curse and went with the flow.

Collapsing beside her afterward, he rolled them until he had her captured in his embrace and spooned against his chest. He lay there for a few seconds, smiling into the back of her head.

He breathed in the smell of her shampoo, and thought it might be the nicest scent ever invented. Not sure if it was some kind of flower or just the smell of clean, he figured he could certainly get used to it.

Running a hand along the smooth skin of her arm and amazing himself by becoming hard again so soon, Jericho figured he could certainly get used to this part, too. They were sure good together. Idly he wondered if they had the stamina to keep it up all night.

Then Rosie moaned, turning in his arms and moving in close. He felt her breath, hot along his neck. Her breasts pressed tight and hard against his chest. And without question he knew there was one thing for certain.

He had all the strength he needed for this night.

Rosie leaned back against the bed's headboard, a silly grin plastered across her face, and listened as Jericho shaved and finished getting dressed in the bathroom. What a wonderful night it had been. She didn't know if she'd ever had one quite like it before, but it didn't matter. Not now that she was sure she would be spending many more nights in the same way.

Well, that is if she could hold up. She probably hadn't gotten more than an hour's worth of sleep during the whole night. But at the moment she couldn't possibly feel any better even if she'd slept for days. She wasn't sick to her stomach and it was midmorning already. Maybe sex was good for that too.

She was in love. And though Jericho hadn't said it in so many words—that he loved her and wanted her to spend the rest of her life with him—he'd made his feelings perfectly clear in all the things he'd done and the ways he had treated her.

Hmm. *Mrs. Jericho Yates.* That seemed as good a name as any for her to take. In fact, a lot better than most.

Thinking about her missing name brought up a subject she would rather not consider. Her past. But more than her past, who was chasing her and why. Had she stolen something? If only she could remember.

She thought back to the one and only breakthrough to her past that her mind had yielded—the dream of a prince turning into a monster. The prince from her nightmare had looked a little like Sheriff Montalvo, only taller and much more sophisticated and suave.

Sheriff Montalvo. Her skin crawled just at the thought of him. Now *there* was someone to worry about. Rosie wondered what he was doing this morning. Had Jericho's friend, the sheriff from this county, contacted Montalvo about the attack and crash already?

Curious, she picked up a remote from the bedside table and turned on the television that was housed in a beautiful antique armoire across the room. Maybe there would be some news about the missing men. Flipping through the channels, trying to find a local station, Rosie caught the tail end of an image that stopped her cold.

Her mouth sagged open as she backed up the channels until the picture came onto the screen once again. Then all of a sudden, there he was. Her nightmare prince.

No mistaking him. The tall regal bearing. The dark brown hair combed in an impeccable style. Conveniently, the fellow was even wearing a tux. Whoever the man on the TV screen was turned then and gave the camera a generous smile. A deep dimple on his left cheek was all it took to make some things click into place for Rosie.

The man she was staring at, her nightmare prince, was also most definitely her baby's father. And there he was, live and in color, right on the television. Oh. My. God.

* * *

Jericho turned off the water and folded his towel. From behind his back he heard the TV running. Rosie must've turned it on while she was waiting for him to finish getting dressed.

The fleeting thought of her caused his lips to spread into another of the big, stupid grins that he'd been plagued with all morning. She was perfect. He could barely wait to begin their lives together. He wanted lots more nights. Lots more time to find ways of telling her how much he cared.

But not until after they got a few other things taken care of today. He needed to borrow a truck to get them back to Esperanza, and he wanted to go long before dark. His friend Sam had called a while ago to say Sheriff Montalvo had taken over the crews searching for crash victims in the arroyo. After all, the scene was located in his county.

But that knowledge did nothing to calm Jericho's nerves. He was positive Montalvo had had something to do with those men in the first place. And he didn't like knowing a man as powerful as a sheriff might be after Rosie.

Rosie. Another smile crossed his lips. One thing he needed to do today was tell her how much he wanted her in his life for good. Maybe while they were driving back to Esperanza would be as good a time as any.

He picked up his clean shirt, freshly laundered courtesy of the staff of the bed-and-breakfast, and shoved his arms into the sleeves. As he buttoned down, he tuned into what was happening on the television behind his back. It sounded like a news story. Had Rosie found a story about the attack and crash?

Turning and taking the few steps out into the bedroom, Jericho was shocked with what he saw. Rosie sat hypnotized by something she was watching on the screen. He glanced at it but didn't see anything exciting. It was nothing but a national news story about the presidential candidates. Still, Rosie's face had gone pale. Her eyes were glazed and her mouth hung open. She seemed paralyzed. Completely lost in something on the screen.

"What's the matter?" he asked as he moved to her side. "Is everything okay?"

No reply.

"Are you okay, darlin'?" He took her by the shoulders and gently forced her to face him.

He could see her fighting to bring his features into focus. Her features were contorted with fear. What on earth could be the matter?

"Rosie. Honey. Talk to me."

"It's him. I…I mean… It's starting to come back." She grabbed for his hand and he captured both of hers. They were ice-cold.

"What's coming back?"

"Jericho, look." She pointed at the television screen but all he saw there was the Texas governor, giving what seemed to be an ordinary political campaign speech for his run for the presidency of the United States.

"Governor Daniels?"

"Allan Daniels. Yes. That's him. That's my baby's father. I'm positive."

Worried about her growing hysterical state, Jericho

sat at the edge of the bed and gathered her close. "Calm down, sweetheart. I know you may think this is real, but it doesn't seem possible. Allan Daniels? How? Why?"

"I don't know." She frowned and knitted her eyebrows. "I can't remember any of that. My own name isn't even coming back. But I know this for sure. Allan Daniels is the man I was with. The only man. I know it."

Standing in tall grass at an isolated bend in the Rio Grande River, Arnie watched in the distance as a marked sheriff's SUV drove down the dusty side road, heading for the clearing. Montalvo. It was about time.

Glad his bleeding had stopped some time ago, Arnie fingered the cut across his cheek. Damn it. The thing would probably leave a deep scar.

Arnie needed help to cross the border so he could find medical assistance, and Montalvo was going to provide that help. The *boss* had said the sheriff would do what he could. And what the boss said, happened.

After all, it was Montalvo's brilliant idea that had gotten him into the big mess last night. What the hell had Arnie, a big-city guy, known about the range land after dark? Or of that arroyo area. Or of stupid dumb-ass cows for that matter.

Nothing. Zip. But he did know how to climb out of a busted SUV and scramble up the side of a brush-strewn arroyo to save his butt. And he also knew enough to drag the driver's dead body free and hide it good.

Most of all, Arnie had known to call the boss and beg for forgiveness and help. After all, there was no one else on earth who could help him if the boss refused.

The sheriff's SUV pulled into the clearing and stopped, the engine still running. A blacked-out side window rolled down and Montalvo stared at him from behind huge aviator sunglasses.

"It's about time," Arnie said. "I've been waiting."

"Shut up."

A chill rode up Arnie's spine and he secretly fingered the .45 hidden under his shirt. This was not going down well. Montalvo was always a snake anyway.

"Did the boss tell you what I need?" Arnie tried once more to be heard. "I just want an easy way across the river without the U.S. Border Patrol shooting me on sight. Nothing else. I swear."

"I know what your boss wants," Montalvo said menacingly and reached down as if for a weapon.

Uh-oh.

To hell with it. Arnie palmed his gun and fired point-blank exactly at the moment he twisted and headed for the river, going at a dead run.

Only thirty or forty feet from the steep riverbank to start, he knew he could make it in a few seconds if he wasn't shot dead before getting there.

For those few seconds nothing happened behind him. No sounds or shouting. No lights from Border Patrol units. Maybe he was home free. Maybe he'd plugged Montalvo. And maybe Montalvo had agreed to meet here because he knew this place had a gap in the Border Patrol area. Maybe.

That son of a bitch Montalvo. He'd meant to kill him.

If Arnie hadn't actually finished Montalvo with his lucky shot, he vowed to come back and do the job right. After he found safety in Mexico, of course.

Arnie hit the river running and never stopped. Splashing across the two-foot-deep water, it occurred to him belatedly that Montalvo would never have had the nerve to ambush him if the boss hadn't agreed. Hell. If the boss wanted him dead, he might as well stop breathing.

At the Mexican side of the river, Arnie took a huge breath and figured he had a few more hours to live. He would try to figure out something.

But then he looked up the bank and spotted a whole squad of Mexican *federales* staring down at him. Or at least they looked like they were part of the Mexican army.

Until…they pointed their AK-47s in his direction and began firing.

Chapter 14

"So what'd you do to her, man?" Clay Colton stood on his own front step with his hands on his hips, scowling down at Jericho.

Clay might be his best bud, and he'd been nice enough to let Rosie stay here at his ranch again last night. But Jericho would be damned if he would let Clay interrogate him. He stuck his hands in his pockets and looked away.

"It's none of your business," Jericho said through gritted teeth. "Is she ready to go?"

"Tamara is with her. Apparently she cried all night and has been sick to her stomach all morning. So what happened? Where are you two going today? 'Cause I heard her tell Tamara that she didn't want to go."

Yesterday Jericho had heard all Rosie's reasons for not wanting to go to Austin and confront the governor. But he was just as determined to show up for their appointment with Allan Daniels as ever. She was the one who'd insisted Daniels was her lover, after all.

Jericho would never forget it. Not if he lived to be a hundred. After their fantastic night, and just as he was trying to find a way to tell her he wanted her to be his forever. That's when she'd burst out with the news.

In so many words, she'd said, "Oh, by the way, thanks for saving my life and for one really great night. But I see my old life on the TV. And there's no way for you to live up to its sophistication and power."

Hell.

From that moment on they'd disagreed about calling the governor and arranging a meeting. But though it had taken him all afternoon and most of the night, Jericho had been determined that Rosie needed to confront her past—if Daniels really was that past.

He'd finally done it, too. Found an assistant to an assistant who agreed to get Rosie a moment with the governor. Between Daniels's regular duties and his busy campaign schedule, it had not been easy. And for the whole time, Rosie had begged him not to make her go.

Jericho didn't understand her. If she really was happy here with him, as she said, why bring up her past at all? He'd come to the conclusion that she wasn't happy and contented here. Either Daniels was her child's father and deserved to know about it. Or he wasn't and Rosie had invented the whole Daniels thing to ease out of a relationship with Jericho that had grown pretty intense.

Eventually, early last evening, he'd brought her out here to stay with Clay and Tamara for the night and then spent his own night brooding at home.

"Well?" Clay was waiting for some kind of answer.

"We're driving to Austin to check on a lead to her past. I don't know why she's saying she doesn't want to go."

"Maybe she's scared," Clay offered. "She's been kidnapped and shot at a couple of times. I know that would give me more than a moment's pause about driving around the countryside with you."

Jericho frowned again. "Thanks for the vote of confidence. But I think she might be okay from now on.

"Last night Sheriff Montalvo in San Javier County was found shot to death in his official sheriff's unit, parked down by the Rio Grande. They also found the body of a known hitman nearby in the river. The theory is that it was some kind of Mexican drug deal gone sour."

"Montalvo? Rosie said something about how creepy he seemed and that maybe he was behind the attack against you down by Gage's Arroyo the night before last."

Jericho nodded and heaved a sigh. "Yeah. I've come to the conclusion Rosie must've been somehow involved with Montalvo in her past. And that he was the one who hired those goons to come after her.

"I intend to keep investigating what his motives might've been and what precipitated the kidnapping. But with Montalvo dead, I think she should be okay."

He figured maybe she would be *more* okay with her old life rather than with him in a new one. At least she wouldn't have to keep looking over her shoulder. She could relax and heal. And while he worked to get over her and figure it all out, he wouldn't have to keep worrying about saving her life.

Twisting her hands together nervously, Rosie peered down the hall as they stepped out of the elevator. They were on the sixth floor of the Austin office building that supposedly housed the governor's campaign head-quarters. She really didn't want to be here. But Jericho had insisted.

She still couldn't figure out what had gone so suddenly wrong with him. All during their fabulous and intimate night, Jericho had given her everything. He'd made her every wish come true. She'd been so positive the rest of their lives would stay that way.

But right after she'd had the vision of her and Daniels, um, making a baby, Jericho had changed into someone else entirely. Someone angry and withdrawn.

He'd barely said a word to her since then. His attitude had surprised the devil out of her. After all, he had to have known *someone* else was the baby's father. But he'd suddenly started insisting they go to Austin and confront the governor rather than talk it over, figure out the truth and learn why no one had reported her missing.

Rosie wasn't too sure why she didn't want to see Daniels. But maybe it was for just that very reason. Why hadn't he cared enough to report her absence? Why weren't the Texas Rangers and all the county sheriffs out looking for her? He was the governor. He had the power to find her anywhere, if he wanted to.

She took a couple of steps along the rather ordinary-looking hallway behind Jericho and hesitated. Yes, this place did seem vaguely familiar. But it also seemed scary. She didn't like it.

"What's the matter? Come on." Jericho turned, and she wished she could see his eyes better but they were hidden under his broad-brimmed sheriff's Stetson. He took her by the elbow and gently tugged her forward. "We just barely managed to get this appointment. We can't be late for it."

"I don't…" She was shaking so badly that she couldn't speak. What if she'd been wrong and Daniels didn't even recognize her? They shouldn't be here. Everything just felt bad.

But right then Jericho stopped in front of the door marked as the Daniels's campaign headquarters. He opened it and drew her inside with him.

A couple of women stood at a reception desk. Both of them were engrossed in something on the desktop and didn't glance up. Directly behind them was a big open room with rows of long tables, all empty at the moment. Off to each side were a couple of office spaces with closed doors. Everything had a temporary and bare feeling.

Both of the women were dressed in pantsuits, very businesslike. One was in her twenties, blond and pretty. The other must've been in her fifties. She had salt-and-pepper gray hair, but it was cut with sophistication and made her face look fragile. Jericho cleared his throat to get the women's attention.

The older one looked up first. "Olivia! You're back. It seems like you've been out forever. How're you feeling? Are you finally completely well?"

Olivia? Rosie took a step backward, but Jericho held tight to her arm and kept her beside him.

The second woman had lifted her head by then. "What on earth did you do to your hair?" She tilted her chin to study Rosie. "I simply loved all your long blond hair, Olivia. It always made me so jealous. This style isn't too terrible, though…I guess. It frames your face. But the color. Why in heaven's name did you darken it? That shade doesn't do a thing for you."

Jericho moved forward a few feet, dragging her along. Rosie's feet didn't move willingly. In fact, her whole body was going numb. These women weren't the least bit familiar to her, even though they seemed to know her well.

"You know this woman?" Jericho asked them.

They both looked at him as though he had materialized out of the woodwork.

The older one recovered first. "Of course we do, Sheriff…uh…Sheriff…"

"Yates. Sheriff Jericho Yates from Campo County. I called about an appointment with Governor Daniels for our amnesia victim."

"Amnesia? Our Olivia? Really?" The older woman stared into Rosie's eyes.

"Then you do know her," he interjected, taking charge of the situation, as he usually did. "How? What's her full name?"

"Olivia Halprin," the younger of the two blurted out and then also came closer to study Rosie. "And we work with her. She's Governor Daniels's campaign treasurer. She's been out sick with the flu for the last ten days.

"Or at least that's what we all thought," she amended.

Rosie's knees were trembling and she was afraid she

might be sick again. Clinging to Jericho's arm, she fought to bring images to her mind. Any images.

The name *Olivia* did sort of ring a bell. Maybe Olivia was her real name. At least it could be. But that was all there was. Nothing else was making any sense.

One of the two side doors opened and Allan Daniels stuck his head out. "What's going on out here?" He turned to her and his eyes widened. "Olivia. Sweetheart. There you are. How are you feeling? Better, I hope."

A picture formed in Rosie's head of kissing those smiling lips. Of kissing the nightmare prince.

With legs collapsing under her, she started down a long dark tunnel. Where things began growing smaller and smaller, like *Alice in Wonderland,* until her whole world simply disappeared.

Sometime later Rosie lay back on the leather couch in Allan's office with her eyes closed and listening to Jericho finish explaining to Allan how he'd found her and about everything they'd been through for the last few days.

It all sounded fantastic. But to her it was the only reality. She still couldn't come to grips with an old life. A few shadows, like old black-and-white movies moved across her consciousness. But most of it didn't stick around long enough for her to bring it into focus.

Shifting a plastic baggie full of ice that one of the women had plopped on her forehead after she'd been carried to this couch, she remained quiet with her eyes closed. But she still paid attention as the two men talked about her as if she were someone else.

"I can't believe she's been through all that just in the

time she's been gone," Allan said. "We were lucky you were the one who found her, Jericho. You don't mind me calling you that, do you? I owe you a big debt of gratitude and I hope to find a way to pay you back."

Allan hesitated and Rosie could just picture him taking off his jacket and loosening his tie, the big phony. "So you believe this Sheriff Montalvo from San Javier County was somehow responsible for the things that happened to Olivia?" The image of Allan Daniels was now firmly formed in her mind. From her past. And from her present.

Jericho must've nodded his head because she didn't hear him agree. She might not be able to see him, but she was tuned into his responses. Feeling him growing colder, more distant, with every passing moment, she wished they could leave. She couldn't really blame Jericho. With every word and movement Allan seemed more snakelike and slimy. How could she have ever let herself be conned by the man?

"Well, then," Allan said to Jericho. "I would take it as a personal favor if you'd follow up on that. I'll put you in touch with Chief Aldeen of the Rangers. He'll see you get all the help you need for your investigation."

"Thank you, sir."

"You're…"

"Allan." Rosie decided it was time to come back into this life, though truthfully she was as hesitant as Jericho. Most of the things that belonged in her previous world were still only vague images. And not all of them would apparently be full of sunshine and light. There continued to be lots of dark, black holes that she couldn't—or wouldn't—fill in.

And all of it seemed to circle around the governor of Texas, for crying out loud.

"Olivia, you're up," Allan said as he came close and helped her to stand. "Are you sure you don't need to be checked out at a hospital?"

"No," she heard herself say. "A doctor looked me over in Esperanza. I'm going to be fine."

He gave her an odd look, and Rosie wondered if he had any idea she was pregnant. She would bet not. Well, it remained to be seen whether she ever told him the truth. At the moment, chances were slim.

Like a silent beacon of hope, Rosie felt drawn instead toward Jericho, who stood behind the desk. He was her savior. Her protector. Her love.

Shooting her a rather creepy and lecherous look, Allan let his gaze linger on her breasts. Her growing unease around him became an urgent sense that she needed to get out of here. Away from this man.

Allan put his arm around her shoulders, and a disgusted shudder skittered clear down her spine. Why was she so sure this guy was not who he seemed? She inched away without making a big deal.

"I just want to go home." Amazingly, she did remember where her old condo was all of a sudden. However, she found herself dearly wishing to go to the *home* a hundred miles southwest in a blip on the map called Esperanza.

Allan's pleasant expression turned frustrated. "I can't take you home right now. I have that $10,000-a-plate fund-raiser coming up in a couple of hours. You remember—you set it up."

She did not remember. Nor did she want to. It was all wrong. Wrong. Wrong.

Afraid Allan might insist she go with him, she began, "I can get there by…"

"I'll see her safely home, sir." Jericho had moved to stand at attention by the door, but he interrupted her firmly and came closer. "If you'll give me her address, I'd be happy to take care of it."

Jericho sounded like a damned bodyguard. Was that all their time together meant to him? Just because she was on the governor's campaign staff and probably had sex with the man—

"That would be terrific, Jericho, if you wouldn't mind," Allan said in what she vaguely remembered were his normal, charming tones. Then he turned to her. "There's always been a spare set of keys to both your condo and your car stashed in your office. Just in case of emergencies. Let's go see if they're still there. Then all of us can be on our way. And I'll contact you later at home."

"I wonder what happened to my car?" Rosie said absently as Jericho unlocked her condo and ushered the two of them inside.

She lived on the twelfth floor of a downtown building with parking below and a doorman in residence. Jericho wasn't surprised at the condo's sweeping views of Austin and the Hill Country from the floor-to-ceiling windows.

"You don't remember?" he asked as he hesitated just inside the threshold. "What kind of car do you own?"

"A Mercedes S550." After a silent instant, she continued with a grin. "Wow. A few minutes ago I couldn't have come up with that answer. Things are just flashing into my brain at lightning speed."

She strolled wide-eyed through the large foyer and stepped into the sunken living room. Gracefully, she walked around the room, touching white leather couches, staring at expensive artwork on the walls, marveling at marble sculptures. The furnishings seemed to bring memories back into her mind.

Jericho wasn't too pleased to see this much opulence. No expert, he still would bet there was several hundred thousand dollars' worth of art and sculptures skillfully placed around the room. And her car was a Mercedes. Of course it was. Daniels no doubt kept his girlfriend in diamonds, too.

How could his handmade cabin and seven-year-old truck ever compete with all this? How could he ever hope to compete with the *governor of Texas?*

The answer was simple, he couldn't.

But he could do his job and also do the governor his favor at the same time. "If you'll give me your license number and a description, I'll report your car as missing. We'll find it."

She nodded idly. "Thanks."

"Are more things coming back?" he asked, hoping against hope that they weren't. That she would only ever remember him and their time together. He had to guess it was already too late for that.

"A few," she told him. "Like the fact that my birth name is Olivia DeVille Halprin. The only child of Chester Halprin and Suzanne DeVille. And before he passed away, my father built an Internet empire that's been valued in the billions."

Oh? Maybe it wasn't Daniels's money that had provided all the opulence then. But that didn't give Jericho much comfort. He still couldn't live up to any of this. Never would.

"So your father is no longer alive. How about your mother? I'm wondering why she didn't report you missing?"

Rosie turned and graced him with a wry smile. "As cold and ruthless as my father was, Suzanne is just the opposite. Beautiful and outgoing and a pillar in hundreds of Texas charitable foundations. She has just never had much time for a daughter. She's much too busy devoting her life to really good causes.

"I haven't talked to my mother in months." Rosie continued a little too quietly. "In almost a year now, I think. But I'm sure she would've missed me eventually."

Jericho couldn't imagine such a family. Okay, so his mother had disappeared and never come back. But both his father and his brother had always been the rocks in his life. What would he have become without his family?

He took a step in Rosie's…no Olivia's…direction before coming up short. He didn't know Olivia Halprin, and he had absolutely nothing in common with her. She wouldn't want sympathy from him, and he couldn't stand to have her back out of his arms when she realized the same thing.

Olivia blinked a couple of times then said, "A *bath?*"

"Excuse me?" He hadn't said anything about a bath. She shook her head as though to clear it. "What? Oh, sorry. I don't know why I said that. I never take baths. But it just popped into my head while I was thinking that things seem a little off."

"A little off? How do you mean?"

Shrugging, she turned and walked over to open one of the many doors that led off the main room. "My office is in here. Let me see if it feels funny, too."

Jericho shoved his hands in his pockets and followed. Funny feelings were not in his jurisdiction.

Olivia's office was crammed with computer equipment. It made him wonder if she'd inherited her father's genius.

"Before I became the Daniels campaign treasurer," she began as she studied the machines up close, "I was a CPA. A Certified Public Accountant. That's just what I love to do. I know it doesn't sound interesting, but I specialized in forensic accounting. Chasing bad guys around inside their bank accounts."

She turned and smiled at him. A real smile. "Maybe that's why I fell under the spell of a lawman. You think?"

He couldn't talk to her about that right now, so he shrugged one shoulder and stayed quiet.

Her smile faded slowly, then she turned and moved one of the keyboards a few inches to the left. "I swear it feels like someone has been in here since I was last in this room. I'm sort of fussy—okay *anal* would be a better word—about my workspace. Everything has to be just so. Must be the accountant in me.

"And my things have been moved. I could swear to it."

"You sure it isn't just that it's been a while?" he asked soothingly. "Your security alarm was still armed when we came in. We had to disarm it. Besides, you've been through a lot over the last few days. Especially with your memory. Maybe things are still hazy in your mind."

She looked around. "Lots of things are still a little hazy. But not this room." Sighing, she turned back to him. "I guess I need more time. How long are we going to stay here? Do I have time for a bath?"

Those seemed like odd questions, but he decided it was past time for him to get out of town. Let her have her bath and anything else she needed. The lady was home. She hardly needed him to stick around anymore, despite the fact that leaving was bound to kill him.

"You go on and take your bath. I've got to be heading back to Esperanza. Just come see me to the door. Make sure your doors are locked and the security alarm is set behind me."

"You're leaving without me? But…"

"Look, *Olivia*. You're where you belong. You have a job and people who care about you. But I sure don't belong here. Let's just cut our losses while we still can."

Her face crumbled and big tears welled in her eyes.

"I'll stay in touch," he offered. "Let you know how the investigation is coming along. And I'll be sure to work on finding your car."

She sniffed and reached out a hand to him. "But can't you see that I don't belong here anymore, either? No one in my old life even bothered to check up on me. That would never happen in Esperanza. I need…"

Jericho needed to get out of there—fast. "You'll change your mind when more things start coming back. I mean, for one, yours would be the only Mercedes in all of Esperanza, Texas. And that's just for starters. There's no place to shop. We don't have any art museums. I can't think of anybody who would need the services of a CPA."

He waved his hand as if that explained everything. And to him, it did. He could never stand to work at making a life with her only to lose her back to the big city.

The worst had happened. She was regaining her memory and that meant he wouldn't stand a chance in the long run. Just like his mother, only for different reasons, she'd be off and running before he could turn around.

"Lock up behind me," he said as he turned tail and made a dash for the door. "I'll contact you."

Maybe. *If* his heart could stand the pain of hearing her voice and knowing his house would forever stand barren and lonely without her there.

Damn her all to hell for making him believe it could happen. Believe he could get what he wanted for once.

Well, Sheriff Jericho Yates would be just fine alone.

Chapter 15

Furious at herself for being such a hormone-raging wimp, Rosie slashed at the tears streaming down her cheeks. She'd finished locking up behind the retreating Jericho, and then had come to the conclusion that she might as well have that bath, so that's where she was headed.

How could he have left her here in Austin all alone?

She *should've* said he had to take her with him. That his job wasn't done and they hadn't even had a chance to talk. She *should've* said something about her things being still in his closet and that at the least she needed to say goodbye to the dogs. She *should've* grabbed him and kissed him senseless, just to remind him of everything they'd done together.

But she'd been so surprised, so thrown by the idea

of how shallow her old life had been, that she hadn't thought fast enough to get out a word. All the should'ves in the world didn't matter when the person you counted on turned his back on you and walked away.

In her old life it had been easy to blame her distant, cold father for all her unhappiness. But in truth, she remembered now how it really was. She'd tried desperately hard to become the most beautiful and successful daughter a father could ever want. No matter what she did, though, he'd never seen her efforts—not really. So to emulate her father, make him see her, she'd learned to appreciate art, as he had, and forced herself to like the other superficial things in life that meant a lot to him. But of course, *her* list of superficial things also ended up including dating gorgeous, powerful and successful men with no scruples.

That was how she'd been drawn to Allan Daniels in the first place. But giving up her old job to please him had been the craziest part. The only thing in her life that she'd ever done that made any real sense was to work at the forensic accounting consulting firm. She'd tossed it all the minute Allan crooked his little finger at her.

Rosie turned on the bath water and thought of Jericho— not Allan. Thought of how much better her life had been with the Campo County sheriff. In just a few short days, she'd turned herself into someone who could be appreciated and respected. Because of him. He had really taken time to see her for herself. Not for only the outside.

But stupid her, she'd just let him walk away.

Sitting on the edge of the filling tub, Rosie hung her head and wept for all the things she had not done or said that might've made a difference. Might've made Jericho wait for her. Want her.

This place—this life—weren't hers anymore. So she would refuse to stay here, by heaven. After she took this bath and rested a little, she would rent a car and drive right back to Esperanza, Texas. Back where she belonged.

An odd, instant and intense urge to put bath salts into the water had her reaching for the fancy jar she'd never opened but only used for decoration. Though once she had the clear bottle in hand, she *knew*. In her mind she could actually see herself hiding something deep inside the fuchsia crystals.

Standing up beside the vanity, Rosie dumped the contents of the salt jar out on the counter. The clunk of something hard and metallic captured her attention. What had she hidden? And why?

In another moment, at least the *what* was clear. Out of the baths crystals rolled a tiny flash drive. Hmm.

Fighting to remember more, she turned off the bath water and headed to her office. It should be easy enough to find out the *why* by plugging the drive into one of her computers.

The curiosity was killing her.

Cut and run! He'd done it again.

Jericho eased on the brakes of his borrowed SUV and pulled into a roadside park off the 290 that was not quite in Johnson City. A half hour out of Austin and he was finally getting his head on straight. About damned time.

With the engine idling, he beat his fists against the steering wheel and wondered what the hell was the matter with him. In his whole life, every time a woman got too close, he would shut down and split. That was just who he was. Call it pride. Call it not wanting to take a chance on being hurt. Whatever. But never before had it seemed this important, or this wrong to run.

All those other times the women were perfectly fine, and maybe he could've made a life with them. But this time. This time it was Rosie and she was…she was…
Everything.

Jericho drew a deep breath and tried to think instead of letting his emotions tie him up in knots. Why was he always like this, shutting down without a fight? Could he change this time? After all, he never backed down from other challenges in his life.

But with that thought in his mind, a picture of Allan Daniels leering at Rosie with a malevolent gleam in his eye and yet another picture of Rosie begging him not to take her there, made him rethink all that had taken place.

There were several missing pieces to the puzzle of Rosie. Big missing pieces. Like, what had those goons wanted from her? *It.* They'd kept mentioning an *it.* Was Rosie going to suddenly remember what that was and then be in terrible danger again?

Jericho had walked off the job before it was done. He had never done that in his life.

Putting the SUV in gear, he prepared to turn around. Had he been so intimidated by Daniels's position as governor that he'd lost his mind? There was nothing right about the whole scenario. If Rosie and Daniels had been such great lovers, then why hadn't Daniels gone to her condo to check on her when he'd thought she was sick? He knew if she'd been *his* girlfriend and had really been sick with the flu, Jericho would've stuck to her bedside like glue.

Who the heck had reported that she had the flu in the first place?

Lots of problems. Lots of big red flags that should've caught his attention.

But the worst of it was that he hadn't listened to Rosie. He hadn't given her a chance to talk. She had become his whole world and he'd turned his back? Stupid. Stupid.

Pulling out onto 290, he stepped on the gas and retraced his route back to Austin. Back to Rosie. Maybe she would give him a second chance. Maybe he could make her see that he was willing to fight to save her—fight to love her.

He just hoped to hell it wasn't too late.

Rosie sat staring at the monitor, too stunned to move. Everything—all the secrets and terrible truths—came back in a rush of clarity.

Allan Daniels was dirty. More, Allan was an embezzler who consorted with Mexican druglords—and he was running for president of the United States. Holy moly.

She remembered well her first instance of finding these horrible facts on an innocuous-looking flash drive in Allan's office. Almost ten days ago now. After convincing herself of the reality of what she was seeing, she'd been nearly hysterical wondering what she should do next. Who to go to who would not only believe her but who could do something to stop him.

The governor of Texas was the head of the Texas Rangers. So that was out. The police? The FBI? She remembered thinking they might laugh at her—or worse—ignore her. He was, after all, a candidate for the presidency, and everyone figured all his secrets were already out.

Not by half.

After taking the precautionary step of hiding the flash drive in her bath salts and making a copy to hide in her car, she'd done the only other thing that made sense. She'd contacted an old friend, a reporter for the *Dallas Morning News,* who was honest and who could start a secret investigation that could eventually bring Allan down.

Mary Beth Caldwell. My God. What had happened to her?

Rosie remembered their secret meeting at Stubbins Barbeque. Remembered distinctly sitting across from Mary Beth, who looked a lot like Becky French, in her early sixties, short and plump. But Mary Beth was a shark. Smart and well-connected, as an investigative reporter she could not be beat.

Mary Beth had not only believed her about Allan, but had agreed to hide Rosie until the authorities could be convinced. Rosie had already realized she was in dire trouble because Allan had called her cell while she was with Mary Beth. He'd wanted to know if she'd seen anyone strange near his office. Obviously, he'd already missed his flash drive and knew she was the only one who could've taken it.

She and Mary Beth had immediately left the barbeque joint and headed for Rosie's car. But before they got there, a couple of dangerous-looking men came up behind them. Rosie remembered running, then a thud coming from behind her. Mary Beth must've been hit, but she'd been too afraid to turn back to help. Oh, God. Rosie's stomach clinched.

She remembered dropping her car keys and running. Running for her life and not looking back. A trucker had picked her up down the highway, and she'd thought she might be okay if she got far enough away. When that good-guy driver dropped her off in Rio View, Rosie had done the smart thing and headed straight to the sheriff for help. Sheriff Montalvo.

Yeah, Montalvo had helped all right. He'd helped her find a motel to hide in. And then he'd apparently called the governor to help himself to whatever clandestine reward Allan must've been offering for her.

Now Montalvo was dead. Mary Beth was probably dead. With sudden clear panic, she knew she was as good as dead, too.

Oh, Jericho, where are you? She reached for the phone to call him at the exact moment when she heard a slight noise in another part of the condo. Not much of a noise. But enough to keep her from being surprised as the voice she'd dreaded to hear came from directly behind her back.

"Put the phone down, Olivia."

She did as he demanded and slowly turned to face what looked like a silencer attached to a huge gun. "Hello, Allan," she managed without looking at his face. "I thought you were at that fund-raiser. Where's your secret-service security detail?"

Oh, hell, she was done. She hadn't remembered enough of her past in time. With just a few more minutes, she could've been out the door and gone. Of course now that it didn't help her, she remembered that Allan had access to a duplicate key and knew her security codes. That was the very last thing she'd remembered and probably the last thought she would ever have.

He chuckled. "Yeah, I gave them all the slip. The secret service thinks I'm having a quickie fling in a hotel room not far from here. Smart and sly. That's me. It'll be a great alibi in case I ever need one."

Did "ever need one" mean that he wasn't planning on killing her? Or did it mean he imagined no one would ever question the governor?

"Look, Allan, there's something important you should know." Her mind raced to find some excuse to stay alive. Give her the break she needed to get away.

He waved the gun at her, and perversely she noted he was wearing a tux. "Shut up. Now that I've found my flash drive—" He pointed the barrel at the monitor as if that said it all. "I don't need to hear anything from you. I've already got a plan. You're going to be killed by whoever's been chasing you. They broke into your condo because you forgot to lock the door and set the alarm.

"*Tsk, tsk,* sweetheart. What a shame." He leveled the gun at her and took aim.

"Wait a second," she begged. "I made a copy of the drive. Kill me and you'll never find it."

Jericho heard the voices coming from Rosie's office and crept closer. He'd been alarmed when he'd arrived back here only to find her front door unlocked and ajar. He definitely remembered Rosie locking it behind him when he'd left.

That's when, on instinct, he'd drawn his service weapon and edged inside the door instead of knocking. Was that Daniels's voice? Absolutely. And Rosie's, too, sounding scared and on the verge of panic.

She'd been right about not coming here. Why hadn't he listened? The only thing he had in his favor now was surprise. That would have to do.

Sneaking up to the office door, Jericho eased it open and peeked inside. Daniels was standing with his back to him, but he was holding a weapon to Rosie's head.

"I said, shut up, bitch." Daniels screamed, clearly out of control. "Lies won't save your traitorous ass. You stole my property. You were going to use it to ruin me.

"If you made a copy and hid it, then where is it? I've had this place searched top to bottom." Daniels rammed the barrel of the gun against Rosie's cheek. "Better make me believe you by telling the truth."

Jericho's anger came up fast and hard. He wanted to shout at Daniels to take his hands off her. It was all he could do to tamp it down and think like the lawman he needed to be.

"Hold it, Daniels," he yelled, jamming the barrel of his 9mm into the man's back. "Drop your weapon. Now!"

Daniels stilled for the moment, but said, "You won't shoot. If you do, your girlfriend here is dead. You'd better drop your gun, sheriff, and we'll have a little conversation."

Nearly blinded by his furor at the man, Jericho fought

his emotions long enough to make the right move. Daniels would have to kill both of them now. It was his only out. But there would be two of them to his one. Jericho figured those odds were in their favor.

At least, he had to give surprise a try. Otherwise, Rosie was dead.

"Okay, Mr. Governor, you've got the upper hand," he said with as casual tone as he could manage. Under his shirt, his muscles bunched and tensed. "I'm going to put my weapon on the floor. Don't be surprised." He kicked the 9mm clear across the room and under a daybed. "See there. Now we can talk."

"Not until you come over here where I can see you," the governor snapped at him. "Carefully. Move to your right. Go stand beside your girlfriend's chair directly in front of me."

Daniels still had his weapon poking into Rosie's temple. Jericho raised his arms slightly, almost offhandedly, and took a docile step to the right.

"Easy there," he told the other man. "I'm moving."

But with his second step, Jericho deliberately stumbled a half a foot closer to Daniels. Surprised and panicked by the sudden move, the governor spun and pulled the trigger without aiming. The shot went wild, off into the ceiling.

Everything happened at once then. Rosie screamed and kicked out at Daniels's gun hand. The weapon flew out of his grip. And in that instant, Jericho was on him.

The two of them were on the floor, grappling and throwing punches. Daniels didn't stand a chance. Not with the superhuman power Jericho's furor provided him.

The son of a bitch had hurt Rosie. He'd planned to kill her! Jericho landed a right and heard Daniels's nose break. Well, let's just see how he likes being hurt.

Battering Daniels's head against the ground, Jericho didn't feel any of the other man's blows and could only think about Rosie. This bastard had been planning on taking away the one woman he loved. Never!

Daniels fought with incredible strength. Still, Jericho remained on top and was numb to any pain. Finally, Jericho edged free enough to ram his knee into the other man's groin. He felt gristle crunching underneath the slacks even as the other man shrieked in pain.

"Hope it hurts like hell, you bastard." A scarlet haze of pure hatred and anger developed in front of Jericho's eyes, as he just kept yelling and punching. Never noticing the other man go limp.

Hitting. Smashing. Landing blow after blow.

Rosie came to her senses and scrambled across the room to get a hold of Allan's gun. She pointed it at the two men on the floor. That was when she saw that Allan wasn't fighting back anymore.

"Jericho, stop." She put the gun down and moved closer when he didn't seem to hear. "Jericho!" she screamed.

Inching closer, she yelled again and got the nerve to shove at his arm. "Please, honey. Don't do this. Stop."

Tears sprang from her eyes and threatened to swamp her, but she kept yelling his name and shoving at his arms and back, desperate to make him understand. *Please, my love. Don't ruin your life—my life—over this piece of garbage.*

At last, Jericho quit swinging and turned to her. Shocked at what she saw, she reached out for him.

Tears rolled down his face, his fury clear but almost spent. Reaching for her, too, he stood and pulled her into his arms.

"Are you okay?" He swiped his face across his shirt-sleeve and choked back an obvious sigh.

His father had been right. There must've been a lot of anger buried in him for all these years.

She looked up into his beloved hazel eyes, now dark green with feeling. "You came back," she managed through her tears. "You came back for me."

"I shouldn't have left. If I'd been a few seconds later…" His words trailed off as she saw the deep emotions swirl across his face.

It thrilled her. Scared her. He seemed so intense. So full of concern for her.

To shake off the strong feelings she didn't know what to do about, she turned back to look at the limp body on the floor. "I hope you didn't kill him. He isn't dead, is he?"

Jericho seemed reluctant to let her go, but in a second she saw the sheriff return to his eyes. He stepped closer to Allan and checked his pulse.

"He's alive," Jericho said with authority. "He's going to live to spend a long time in prison. I can't believe how I missed seeing what a phony he was."

"Everyone missed it. The whole world missed it." She shook her head, heading toward her desk. "I'll call 911 and get an ambulance. Do you think we need to tie him up?"

Jericho reached out and pulled her to a stop. "I'll tie his hands and you can call in a second," he said gently.

"First, I have to apologize to you. I almost lost you. I should've listened when you didn't want to come here. I should've listened when you wanted to leave with me. I…" Again he seemed to choke on his words.

"You didn't know," she said, rubbing uselessly at his sleeve.

He drew in a deep breath. "No. I did know something, if only I'd just paid attention. I knew you loved me and I knew I loved you. That should've been enough."

"You love me?" The adrenaline must be spiking inside her again, because she thought she was hearing things and her whole body began to shake.

"More than anything. It would've killed me to lose you. Literally. I can't…I can't live without you.

"Whatever your name is now, Rosie-Olivia, marry me and change it. In fact, marry me as soon as we clean up here. Today. Tomorrow at the latest. I'm never leaving you again."

The tears started up again and Rosie damned her hormones. But laughing through the rolling rivers of salt on her cheeks, she managed to nod her head.

At last she would know for sure who she was. A woman worthy of respect and love. A woman so full of love for the man who provided it that she thought she might burst.

Epilogue

Pleased with himself for getting the seventy-two-hour waiting period waived and arranging for the justice of the peace on short notice, Jericho stood with his best friend and watched as his new bride talked to his father and brother on the other side of the yard.

"Are we supposed to call her Olivia now that her amnesia is gone?" Clay asked as he poured himself a drink from the temporary refreshment table set up in Jericho's backyard.

Rosie's backyard now, too, Jericho thought with a secret smile. He was simply amazed at how peaceful, how settled he felt since she'd said yes. What a lucky bastard he was.

The governor was recovering from his injuries in the

hospital jail, and many of the questions had already been asked and answered. The worst answer concerned finding the body of the reporter, Mary Beth Caldwell, in the trunk of Rosie's car at the bottom of a ravine. Rosie's testimony, the flash drive and the rest of the pending investigation would put Daniels away for good.

Tilting his head to Clay, Jericho answered, "Mrs. Yates will do for you." A little sarcastic maybe, but then he allowed the smile to show. "Really, she says she prefers Rosie. But she's willing to answer to either one."

Clay nodded as he too looked across the lawn to where Rosie stood. "It's nice your brother's leave isn't over yet so he could be here for your actual wedding. Family is so important at times like this."

Clay sounded so down all of a sudden, not like himself at all.

"You okay?" Jericho asked.

"Yeah. It's just...well, you know I've been writing to my brother, Ryder, in prison. My most recent letters came back as undeliverable."

"What does that mean?" Jericho could see that the news had upset his friend. Maybe a lot more than he was letting on.

"Not sure." Clay looked off at the sunset. "I'm planning on calling the warden to find out. But I've been a little hesitant, knowing it might be something I don't want to hear."

Jericho could understand that. Running instead of standing and listening was something he was real familiar with.

He put his hand on his friend's shoulder. "No matter

what it is, it's better to know the truth. Let me know if you need my help."

Rosie turned to him and their gazes met across the lawn. The thrill ran down his spine, landing squarely in his gut. Would it always be this way? The desperate hunger. The pulse-pounding wave of recognition when he looked her way.

As he walked toward her, he imagined it would probably last a lifetime. When he got close enough to put his arm around her waist, he was positive. This. This exhilaration and breathlessness would never go away.

"So, bro," Fisher began. "You two planning on a hunting trip as a honeymoon?"

Jericho kept his gaze locked with his bride's. "None of your business. Just let us handle the honeymoon."

Moving closer to him, Rosie felt the warmth of her new husband's love clear down to her toes. She stood, basking in both the sun and in the friendship and love she'd found with all these wonderful people.

What an amazing thing it was. Not more than two weeks ago she was a lonely, superficial woman with no family to speak of and no friends. Amazingly, if she'd given it any thought back then, she would've said she was happy. She'd had things, a prominent job and a part-time lover who had power and influence.

But deep down something big had been missing. She hadn't been able to put her finger on it then, just as she hadn't been able to come up with her past over the last days. But she'd kept on reaching—reaching for *love* as she now knew. And for family.

Family. She gazed at her handsome new husband

and then at his loving and gentle father and brother who were chuckling at Jericho's teasing. Well, she had a family now. A better one she never would've found.

Easing her hand over her belly in a protective motion, she reminded herself that there would be one more family member soon. A baby to love and cherish. How lucky could she be?

Smiling at her love, a secret smile that told him all that was in her heart, Rosie Yates decided all was right with the world at last. The sheriff's amnesiac bride had found her mind…her place…her love.

And she meant to hang on to them forever.

* * * * *

SOLDIER'S SECRET CHILD

BY
CARIDAD PIÑEIRO

Caridad Piñeiro is a *USA TODAY* and *New York Times* bestselling author of twenty novels. In 2007, a year marked by six releases, Caridad was selected as the 2007 Golden Apple Author of the Year by the New York City Romance Writers. Caridad's novels have been lauded as the Best Short Contemporary Romance of 2001 in the NJ Romance Writers Golden Leaf Contest, Top Fantasy Books of 2005 and 2006 by *CATALINA* magazine and Top Nocturne of 2006 by *Cataromance*. Caridad has appeared on various television shows, such as the FOX News Early Edition in New York, and articles featuring her novels have been published in several leading newspapers and magazines, such as the *New York Daily News*, *Latina* and the *Star Ledger*. For more information on Caridad, please visit www.caridad.com or www.thecallingvampirenovels.com.

This book is dedicated to the men and women
of the military and their families, without whom we
could not have the liberties that make our
daily lives possible.

Chapter 1

Macy Ward had never imagined that on her wedding day she would be running out of the church instead of walking down the aisle.

But just over a week earlier, she had been drawn out of the church by the sharp crack of gunshots and the harsh squeal of tires followed by the familiar sound of her fiancé's voice shouting for someone to get his police cruiser.

Her fiancé, Jericho Yates, the town sheriff and her lifelong friend. Her best friend in all the world and the totally wrong man to marry, she thought again, her hands tightening on the steering wheel. She shot a glance at her teenage son who sat beside her in the passenger seat.

"You ready for this, T.J.?"

He pulled out one earbud of his iPod. Tinny, too loud music blared from it. "Did you want something?" T.J. asked.

It was impossible to miss the sullen tones of his voice or the angry set of his jaw.

She had seen a similar irritated expression on the face of T.J.'s biological father, Fisher Yates, as he stood in his Army dress uniform outside the church with his brother—her fiancé. Fisher had looked far more attractive than he should have. As she had raced out into the midst of the bedlam occurring on the steps of the chapel, her gaze had connected with Fisher's stony glare for just a few seconds.

A few seconds too long.

When she had urged Jericho to go handle the incident and that they could postpone the wedding, she had seen the change in Fisher's gaze.

She wasn't sure if it had been relief at first. But the emotion that followed and lingered far longer had been more dangerous.

Now, there was no relief in T.J.'s hard glare. Just anger.

"Are you ready for this?" she repeated calmly, shooting him a glance from the corner of her eye as she drove to the center of town.

The loose black T-shirt T.J. wore barely shifted with his indifferent shrug. "Do I have any choice?"

Choice? Did anyone really have many choices in life? she thought, recalling how she would have chosen not to get pregnant by Fisher. Or lose her husband, Tim, to cancer. Or have a loving and respectful son turn into a troublesome seventeen-year-old hellion.

"You most certainly have choices, T.J. You could have failed your math class or gone to those tutoring sessions. You could have done time in juvie instead of community service. And now—"

"I'll have to stay out of trouble by working at the ranch since you decided not to marry Jericho."

It had been Jericho who had persuaded a judge to spare T.J. a juvenile record. The incident in question had resulted in rolls and rolls of toilet paper all over an old teacher's prized landscaped lawn and a mangled mailbox that had needed to be replaced.

"After postponing the wedding, I realized that I was getting married for all the wrong reasons. So, I chose not to go ahead with the wedding and I'm glad that I did. It gave Jericho the chance to find someone he truly loves," she said, clasping and unclasping her hands on the wheel as she pulled into a spot in front of the post office.

"I told you before that I don't need another dad," he said, but his words were followed by another shrug as T.J.'s head dropped down. "Not that Jericho isn't a nice guy. He's just not my dad."

Macy killed the engine, cradled her son's chin and applied gentle pressure to urge his head upward. "I know you miss him. I do, too. It's been six long years without him, but he wouldn't want you to still be unhappy."

"And you think working at the ranch with some gnarly surfer dude from California will make me happy?" He jerked away from her touch and wagged one hand in the familiar hang loose surfer sign.

She dropped her hands into her lap and shook her head, biting back tears and her own anger. As a recreational therapist, she understood the kinds of emotions T.J. was venting with his aggressive behavior. Knew how to try to get him to open up about his feelings.

But as a mother, the attitude was frustrating.

"Jewel tells me Joe is a great kid and he's your age. Maybe you'll find that you have something in common."

Without waiting for his reply, she grabbed her purse and rushed out of the car, crossed the street and made a beeline for the door to Miss Sue's. She had promised her boss, Jewel Mayfair, that she would stop by the restaurant to pick up some of its famous sticky buns for the kids currently residing at the Hopechest Ranch.

When she reached the door, however, she realized *he* was there.

Fisher Yates.

Decorated soldier, Jericho's older brother and unknown to him or anyone else in town, T.J.'s biological father. Only her husband, Tim, had known, and he had kept the secret to his grave.

The morning that had started out so-so due to T.J.'s moodiness just went to bad. She would have no choice but to acknowledge Fisher on her way to the take-out counter in the back of the restaurant. Especially since he looked up and noticed her standing there. His green-eyed gaze narrowed as he did so and his full lips tightened into a grim line.

He really should loosen up and smile some more, she thought, recalling the Fisher of her youth who had always had a grin ready for her, Tim and Jericho.

Although she couldn't blame him for his seeming reticence around her. She had done her best to avoid him during the entire time leading up to the wedding. Had somehow handled being around him during all the last-minute preparations, being polite but indifferent whenever he was around. It was the only way to protect herself against the emotions which lingered about Fisher.

In the week or so since she and Jericho had parted ways, it had been easier since she hadn't seen Fisher around town and knew it was just a matter of time before he was back on duty and her secret would be safe again.

She ignored the niggle of guilt that Fisher didn't know about T.J. Or that as a soldier, he risked his life with each mission and might not ever know that he had a son. Over the years she had told herself it had been the right decision to make not just for herself, but for Fisher as well. Jericho had told her more than once over the years how happy his older brother was in the Army. How it had been the perfect choice for him.

As much as the guilt weighed heavily on her at times, she could not risk any more problems with her son by revealing such a truth now. T.J. had experienced enough upset lately and he was the single most important thing in her life. She would do anything to protect him. To see him smile once again.

Which included staying away from Fisher Yates no matter how much she wanted to make things right between them.

Fisher was just finishing up a plate of Miss Sue's famous buckwheat pancakes when he looked up and glimpsed Macy Ward at the door to the café.

She seemed to hesitate for a moment when she spied him and he wondered why.

Did she feel guilty about avoiding him the whole time he'd been home or was her contriteness all about her change of mind at the altar where she had left his brother? Not that it had been the wrong thing to do. From the moment his kid brother Jericho had told him about his decision to marry Macy, Fisher had believed it was a mistake.

Not that he was any kind of expert on marriage, having avoided it throughout his thirty-seven years of life, but it struck him as wrong to be in a loveless marriage. Jericho should have known that given the experience of his own parents.

Their alcoholic mother had walked out on the Yates men when he was nine and old enough to realize that if there had been any love between his mother and father, drink had driven it away a long time before.

Macy finally pushed through the door and as she passed him, she dipped her head in greeting and said, "Mornin'."

"Mornin'," he replied, and glanced surreptitiously at her as she passed.

At thirty-five years of age, Macy Ward was a fine-looking woman. Trim but with curves in all the right places.

Fisher remembered those curves well. Remembered the strength and tenderness in her toned arms and legs as she had held him. Remembered the passion of their one night which was just another reason why he had known it was wrong for his brother and Macy to marry.

He couldn't imagine being married to a woman like Macy and having the relationship be platonic. Hell, if it were him, he'd have her in bed at every conceivable moment.

Well, at every moment that he could given the presence of her seventeen-year-old son T.J.

Which made him wonder where the boy was until he peered through the windows of Miss Sue's and spotted him sitting in Macy's car. His mop of nearly-black hair, much darker than Macy's light brown, hung down in front of his face, obscuring anything above his tight-lipped mouth.

Fisher wondered if T.J. was angry about the aborted wedding. To hear Jericho talk, the teenager had been none too happy with the announcement, but to hear his father talk, there wasn't much that T.J. had been happy with since T.J.'s father's death from cancer six years earlier.

Not that he blamed the boy. It had taken him a long time to get over his own mother's abandonment. Some might say he never had given his wandering life as a soldier and his inability to commit to any woman.

From behind him he heard the soft scuff of boots across the gleaming tile floor and almost instinctively knew it was Macy on her way back. Funny in how only just a couple of weeks he could identify her step and the smell of her.

She always smelled like roses.

But then again, observing such things was a necessary part of his military training. An essential skill for keeping his men alive.

His men, he thought and picked up the mug of steaming coffee, sweet with fresh cream from one of the small local ranches. In a couple of weeks, he would either be heading back for another tour of duty in the Middle East or accepting an assignment back in the States as an instructor at West Point.

Although he understood the prestige of being assigned to the military academy, he wasn't sure he was up for settling down in one place.

Since the day eighteen years ago when Macy had walked down the aisle with Tim, he had become a traveling man and he liked it that way. No ties or connections other than to his dad, younger brother and his men. People he could count on, he thought as the door closed on Macy's firm butt encased in soft faded denim.

A butt his hands itched to touch along with assorted other parts of her.

With a mumbled curse, he took a sip of the coffee, wincing at its heat. Reminded himself that he was only in town for a short period of time.

Too little time to waste wondering over someone who probably hadn't given him a second thought in nearly twenty years.

Chapter 2

What made the drive to the Hopechest Ranch better wasn't just that it was shorter, Macy thought.

She loved the look of the open countryside and how it grew even more empty the farther they got away from Esperanza. The exact opposite of how it had been in the many years that she had made the drive to the San Antonio hospital where she had once worked.

Out here in the rugged Texas countryside, she experienced a sense of balance and homecoming. When Jewel Mayfair and the California side of the Colton family had bought the acres adjacent to the Bar None in order to open the Hopechest Ranch, Macy had decided she had wanted to work there. Luckily, she and Jewel had hit it off during her interview.

It wasn't just that they had similar ideas about dealing with the children at the ranch or that tragedy had touched both their lives. They were both no-nonsense rational women with a strong sense of family, honor and responsibility.

They had bonded immediately and their friendship had grown over the months of working together, so much so that she had asked Jewel to be her maid of honor.

Because she was a friend and understood her all too well, Jewel hadn't pressed her since the day she had canceled the wedding, aware of Macy's concerns about marrying Jericho and her turmoil over the actions of her son.

Macy was grateful for that as well as Jewel's offer to hire T.J. to work during the summer months at the ranch.

At seventeen, he was too old for after school programs, not to mention that for the many years she had worked in San Antonio, she had felt guilty about having him in such programs. Before Tim's death, T.J. used to go home and spend time with his father, who had been a teacher at one of the local schools.

She pulled up in front of the Spanish-style ranch house, which was the main building at the Hopechest Ranch. The Coltons had spared no expense in building the sprawling ranch house that rose up out of the flat Texas plains. Attention to detail was evident in every element of the house from the carefully maintained landscaping to the ornate hand-carved wooden double doors at the entrance.

Macy was well aware, however, that the Hopechest Ranch wasn't special because of the money the Coltons lavished on the house and grounds. It was the love the Coltons put into what they did with the kids within. She mumbled a small prayer that the summer spent here might help her work a change in T.J.'s attitude.

She parked off to one side of the driveway, shut off the engine and they both stepped out of the car.

One of the dark wooden doors opened immediately.

Ana Morales stepped outside beneath the covered portico by the doors, her rounded belly seeming even larger today than it had the day before. The beautiful young Mexican woman laid a hand on one of the columns of the portico as she waited for them.

Ana had taken refuge at the Hopechest Ranch like many of the others within, although the main thrust of the program at the ranch involved working with troubled children. Despite that, the young woman had been a welcome addition, possessing infinite patience with the younger children.

Sticky bun box in hand, Macy smiled and embraced Ana when she reached the door. "How are you today, *amiga?*"

"Just fine, Macy," Ana said, her expressive brown eyes welcoming. She shot a look over Macy's shoulder at T.J. "This is your son, no?"

She gestured to him. "T.J., meet Ms. Morales."

"Ana, *por favor*," she quickly corrected. "He's very handsome and strong."

"Miss Ana," T.J. said, removing his hat and ducking his head down in embarrassment.

As they stepped within the foyer of the ranch, the noises of activity filtered in from the great rooms near the back of the ranch house and drew them to the large family room/-kitchen area. In the bright open space, half a dozen children of various ages and ethnicities moved back and forth between the kitchen, where Jewel and one of the Hopechest Ranch's housekeepers were busy serving up family-style platters of breakfast offerings.

Ana immediately went to their assistance as did Macy, walking to the counter and grabbing a large plate for the sticky buns. Motioning with her head, she said, "Go grab yourself a spot at the table, T.J."

As the children noted that the food was being put out, they shifted to the large table between the family room and kitchen and soon only a few spots were free at the table.

T.J. hovered nervously beyond, uncertain.

Macy was about to urge her son to sit again when a handsome young man entered the room—Joe, she assumed. He had just arrived at the ranch and she hadn't had a chance to meet him yet.

Almost as tall as T.J., he had the same lanky build, but his hair was a shade darker. His hair was stylishly cut short around his ears, but longer up top framing bright blue eyes that inquisitively shifted over the many occupants of the room.

He walked over to stand beside T.J. and nodded his head, earning a return bop of his head from T.J.

"I'm Joe," he said and held out his hand.

"Just call me T.J.," her son answered and shook the other teen's hand.

"Looks good," Joe said and gestured to the food on the table. "Dude, I'm hungry. How about you?"

The loud growl from T.J.'s stomach was all the answer needed and Joe nudged him with his shoulder. "Come on, T.J. If you wait too long, the rugrats will get all the good stuff."

A small smile actually cracked T.J.'s lips before he followed Joe to the table. He hesitated again for a moment as Joe sat, leaving just one empty chair beside a dark-haired teen girl.

The teen, Sara Engelheit, a pretty sixteen-year-old who had come to the ranch recently, looked up shyly at T.J., who mumbled something beneath his breath, but then took the seat.

Macy released the breath she had been holding all that

time and as her gaze connected with Jewel's she noted the calm look on her boss's face. With a quick incline of her head, it was as if Jewel was saying, "I told you not to worry."

Jewel walked to the kids' table, excused herself and snagged one of the sticky buns, earning a raucous round of warnings from the children about eating something healthy.

Grinning, Jewel said, "I promise I'll go get some fresh juice and fruit."

Heeding the admonishments of the children, she, Ana and the housekeeper helped themselves to the eggs, oatmeal and other more nutritious offerings and then joined Jewel at a small café bar at one side of the great space, a routine they did every day.

Some of the children had rebelled at the routine at first, but they soon fell into the security of the routine. Happiness filled her as she noticed the easy camaraderie of the children around the table.

While they ate, the women discussed the day's schedule, reviewing what each of them would do as they split the children into age- and need-defined groups before reuniting them all during the day for meals.

When they were done, they turned their attention to their charges. Ana took the younger children to play at the swing set beyond the pool so they could avoid the later heat of the Texas summer day. Macy took the tweens and teens out to the corrals that housed an assortment of small livestock and some chickens. They loved the animals and learning to care for them helped her reinforce patterns of responsibility and teamwork.

As the groups were established, Jewel faced T.J. and Joe who were the eldest of the children present. "I'm going to ask the two of you to go with me today. You're both new to the

ranch and I'd like to show you around. Give you an idea of
the chores I expect you to do."

The boys stood side by side, nodded almost in unison, but
as Jewel turned away for a moment, Macy noted the look that
passed between them as if to say, "What have we gotten ourselves into?"

In that moment, she knew a bond had been established and
only hoped that it would be one for the better given Jewel's
accolades about Joe.

"Hurry up, Mom. I promised Joe I'd get there early so I
can show him those XBOX cheat codes before breakfast," T.J.
said and raced out of their house. The door slammed noisily
behind him and normally she would have cautioned him about
being more careful, but she didn't have the heart to do it. He
seemed so eager to get to the ranch.

Rushing, she hopped on one booted foot, trying to step into
the other boot while slipping on her jacket at the same time.
Nearly pitching backward onto her ass, she grappled for the
deacon's bench by the front door and chuckled at her own
foolishness.

She was just so excited to finally see her son starting to lose
some of his surliness. He actually looked forward to something.

She finished dressing with less haste and minutes later, they
were on their way to the ranch, T.J. sitting beside her with his
iPod running. Unlike his slouched stance of a week ago, he
almost leaned forward, as if to urge them to move more
quickly toward the ranch.

The countryside flashed beside them as they left the edge
of town, the wide open meadows filled with the whites of wild
plums, the maroon and yellow of Mexican hat and mountain

pink wildflowers. Ahead of them a cloudless sky the color of Texas bluebonnets seemed to go on forever.

In less than ten minutes they were at Hopechest and she had barely stopped the car when T.J. went flying up the driveway and into the house. She proceeded more slowly, stopping to inhale the fresh scent of fresh cut summer grass and the flowers from a nearby meadow.

It was going to be a good day, she thought.

Inside the house, T.J., Joe and Sara were gathered around the XBOX in the family room, where as promised, T.J. was teaching them the cheat codes.

As the women did every day, they set up breakfast, ate and after they finished, Jewel announced to the kids that they had a special treat for them that day—Clay Colton was bringing over a mare to keep at the ranch for them to ride and care for.

T.J. and Joe had been at work all week in anticipation of the mare's arrival. They had cleaned up some of the stalls in one of the smaller barns on the property, placing fresh-smelling hay in one stall and setting up the other one to hold tack, feed and other necessities.

As the ragtag group walked to a corral on the property, the younger children were in front of the pack, followed by T.J., Joe and Sara.

Macy, Jewel and Ana took up spots at the side of the group, keeping an eye on the youngest as they approached the corral. Clay Colton waited astride his large roan stallion Crockett. A smaller palomino mare stood beside him and his horse.

Clay was all cowboy, she thought, admiring his easy seat on the saddle and the facility with which he swung off the immense mount. He ground tethered Crockett and then walked the mare over toward them.

"Mornin'," he said and tipped his white Stetson. Longish black hair peeked from beneath the hat and his eyes were a vivid blue against the deep tan of his skin.

"Mornin', Clay. We can't thank you enough for bringing the mare for the children," Jewel said.

"My pleasure. How about I show Joe and T.J. how to handle her for the younger kids?"

"That would be great, Clay. It'll be a big relief for both Jewel and me if the boys can control her. What's her name?" Macy asked.

Clay pushed his hat back a bit, exposing more of his face as he waved the two boys over. "Gentlemen, come on over and meet Papa's Poppy."

T.J. and Joe scrambled up and over the split rail corral fence, stood by Clay as he took the saddle, blanket, bit and reins off the mare. The horse stood by calmly as he did so and then later as Clay showed the boys how to place all the equipment back on.

T.J. already had a fairly good knowledge of what to do since he and his dad used to ride together. He seemed hesitant at first, but then Clay said, "That's the way, T.J. Good job."

His uncertainty seemed to fade then and before long, he and Joe had ridden the mare around the corral a time or two. The younger children were calling out eagerly to have a turn as well.

Joe slipped off the horse and handed the reins to T.J.

"Me? What am I supposed to do now?"

Clay clapped him on the back. "Keep her under control while Joe gets one of your friends up on her. She's gentle. You can handle it."

T.J. took a big gulp, but did as Clay asked and before long, the two boys were giving the remaining children their turns on the mare, Clay hovering nearby protectively until it was clear that T.J. and Joe were in charge of the situation.

He stepped over to where she stood with Jewel and Ana and said, "This will work out well for you, I think. Papa's Poppy is the gentlest mare I have."

"I insist on paying for her, Clay," Jewel said, facing him.

Clay shrugged and the fabric of his western shirt stretched tight against shoulders made broad by years of ranch work. "She was an injured stray I found a year or so ago. All scratched up from a fight with some prickly poppy she got tangled up in."

"Hence the name," she said.

"Yep and to be honest, you'd be helping me out by taking her. I need room for a new stud I want to buy for the Bar None."

"Are there many strays in the area, Clay?" Jewel asked as she leaned on the top rail of the fence, vigilantly keeping an eye on the children.

"Occasionally. Why do you ask?" he said and pulled off his hat, wiped at a line of sweat with a bandanna.

Jewel dragged a hand through the short strands of her light brown hair, suddenly uneasy. "I've heard noises in the night."

"Me, too," Ana chimed in. "It sounds like a baby crying or maybe a small animal in pain."

"Yes, exactly," Jewel confirmed. "Not all the time, just every now and then."

Clay jammed his white Stetson back on his head and glanced in the direction of the two boys, squinting against the sun as he did so. "I haven't heard anything up my way, but I can swing by one night and check it out for you."

He motioned with a work-roughened hand to the two boys. "They'll make fine ranch hands. Remind me of Ryder and myself when we were kids. We loved being around the horses more than anything."

Macy couldn't miss the wistfulness in his voice as Clay spoke of his younger brother. Much like T.J., Ryder had begun getting into trouble as a teen, but then it had gotten progressively worse until Ryder had ended up in jail for smuggling aliens across the border.

"Have you heard from your brother lately?" she asked, wondering if Clay had relented from his stance to disavow his troubled brother.

"I wrote to him, but the mail came back as undeliverable." A hard set entered his jaw and his bright blue eyes lost the happy gleam from watching the children.

"Maybe your brother was moved?" Ana offered, laying a gentle hand on Clay's arm.

He nodded and smiled stiffly. "Maybe, Miss Ana. I just hope it's not too late to make amends with my little brother. I'm going to try to call someone at the prison to see what's happening with him."

"I think you're right to put the past behind you and try to make things right with Ryder," Jewel added, but then stepped away to help the boys with one of the younger children who seemed to be afraid of the mare.

Ana went over as well to help since the child was Mexican and still learning English, leaving Macy alone with Clay.

"You'll work things out with your brother," she said, trying to offer comfort. Clay was a good man and she hated to see him upset.

"I hope so. It's never too late to make amends with the people from our past, Macy. You should understand that more than some," he said, surprising her.

She examined his face, searching for the meaning behind his words. Wondering if he somehow knew about her and Fisher. About T.J.

"I do understand," she said, waiting for him to say more so that she could confirm the worst of her fears, but he didn't. Instead, he shouted out his farewell to everyone, walked over to his stallion and climbed up into his saddle.

"Take good care of her, men. I'll be back later to show you how to groom her, handle the feeding and keep the stall clean," he added with a wave to the boys before leaving.

Both T.J. and Joe straightened higher at his comment. She hadn't been wrong in wanting to marry Jericho to give her son a man's presence in his life. It was obvious from just this slight interaction that both boys had responded positively to the added responsibility and to being treated as adults.

Small steps. Positive ones.

She should be grateful for that, but Clay's words rang in her head as she stepped over to help Jewel and Ana with the rest of the children.

It's never too late to make amends with the people from our past.

As much as she hoped that he was right, she also prayed that she would not have to make amends before T.J. was ready to handle it.

Chapter 3

The mare had been a wonderful addition to their program at the ranch, Macy thought as she watched the teens working together in the stalls and adjacent corral.

She and Jewel had discussed how to incorporate the responsibilities for the mare into a program for the children. They had broken them up into rotating teams that took turns with the mare's care and feeding. In addition, she worked with the tweens and teens, including T.J. and Joe, to improve how they handled the mare. Setting up a series of small tests, she encouraged each of the teens until they were all able to take turns not only outfitting and riding the mare, but watching and helping the younger children with the horse.

When T.J. and Joe weren't with the groups, they were off finishing up some of the other chores around the ranch, including a ride with Clay Colton to attempt to track down the elusive sounds that Jewel was still hearing at night. But they returned from that expedition with little to show for it.

She was grateful that T.J. and Joe seemed to have bonded so quickly and so well. As the eldest amongst the children at the ranch, the others seemed to look up to them, in particular the tweens and Sara, the petite young teen who had recently joined them.

It wasn't unusual to see the three of them together at meals and as they took an afternoon break at the pool during the heat of the day, much as they were doing today.

As she watched them frolicking in the cool waters, Jewel stepped up beside her.

"Things seem to be better," her friend said.

"I had hopes for it, but this is more than I expected so quickly."

"Let's take a break." Jewel gestured to a small table located on the covered courtyard where someone had placed a pitcher with iced tea and glasses. A few feet away from the table in the middle of the courtyard was a fountain. The sounds of the running water combined with the scents from the riot of flowers surrounding the courtyard were always calming.

With a quick nod, she sat at the table and poured tea into the two glasses, all the time keeping an eye on what was going on in the pool.

T.J. and Joe led the younger children in a game of Marco Polo, while Sara sat by the side, arms wrapped around herself in a slightly defensive stance.

"We've still got to get Sara to open up a bit," she said.

Jewel picked up her glass and took a sip. "She's been better since the boys got here, but she hasn't been willing to say much during our one-on-one sessions."

"Nothing about the bruises or why she ran away?" she asked, thinking of the purpling marks and fingerprints that had been on the girl's arms on the day she had arrived at the ranch a few weeks ago.

"Nothing and you know our rule."

"We wait until our charge is ready to talk. Do you have another session scheduled with her anytime soon?" She sipped her tea, sighed as the cool liquid slid down her heat parched throat. She hadn't realized just how hot and dry it had been as she and the teens had worked with the mare all morning.

"I have a group session with the older children this afternoon. I was thinking to ask T.J. and Joe to join us."

She thought of T.J.'s anger at his dad's passing and of Joe's adoption by the Coltons. Certainly both of the boys had things to unload and considering how well the group had been getting along, it seemed like a good idea.

"Both T.J. and Joe might have things they want to talk about. I'd ask to sit in, but I know T.J. might be more willing to open up if I'm not around."

Jewel laid a hand on hers as it rested on the table, shifting her iced tea back and forth in the condensation from the glass. "I know that hurts, but you're right. T.J. will likely be more open if you're not around. But I'll keep you posted about what happens. This way you'll know how to deal with it."

Macy took hold of Jewel's hand and gave it a reassuring squeeze. "Thanks. I'd appreciate anything you can say without violating doctor/patient confidentiality."

"Deal," she confirmed and then they sat back and took a moment just to enjoy the peacefulness of the midday break.

* * *

Macy was working with two of the younger children when she noticed the teens walking out of the living room where Jewel often held the group therapy sessions.

The two tween boys had their arms around each other's shoulders and their heads together, talking.

T.J., Joe and Sara followed behind closely, but then split away, walking through the great space and then out to the pool area. They kept on walking beyond the tract of grass with the swing set and Macy assumed T.J. and Joe were off to do the last of their afternoon chores.

Once in the great room, the tween boys headed immediately to the XBOX and she could hear them carrying on about the tricks Joe and T.J. had taught them.

She smiled at the worship of the older boys, but her smile faded as she noted Jewel's face. Excusing herself from the memory game, but urging the children to continue on their own, she approached her boss.

"You look wiped."

"Mark finally opened up today. Told the other kids about how his dad used to beat him."

Both of them suspected that Mark had been physically abused from his manner when he had first come to the ranch, but having him admit it was a good step to helping him deal with the trauma.

"How about Sara?" she wondered, thinking that maybe Mark's revelation would have encouraged the young girl to tell her own story.

Jewel shook her head. "Nothing. She just sat there, arms wrapped around herself. Silent."

"Sorry to hear that, but she is coming out of her shell. She seems to talk to T.J. and Joe a lot."

"That's a good start. Where are they?" Jewel asked as she scanned the great room and saw no sign of them.

"I saw them heading out back, probably to finish up their chores before the weekend. I'll go see what they're up to," she said and at her boss's cue of approval, she went in search of them.

As she suspected, they were at the corral, but not working. The two boys sat on the top rail of the fence, Sara between them, head bowed down.

She was about to approach to make sure everything was okay, but then T.J. brought his hand up and patted Sara's back in a familiar gesture. She had seen Tim do it more than once when comforting his young son and it twisted her heartstrings that Tim would not see the man T.J. would become.

Which was followed by a wave of guilt as she realized that maybe Fisher never would either if she didn't tell him about his son. If she didn't make amends for what had happened in the past between them.

Certain that the teens were better off without her presence at that moment, she returned to the ranch house and the game of memory she had left earlier.

But even then she experienced no relief as the children matched up the first few letters.

F.

S.

I.

Certainly someone somewhere was telling her it was time to consider what she would do about Fisher.

Fisher sat across from his dad in Miss Sue's, enjoying the last of his ribs and delicious fries.

It wasn't as if he and his dad couldn't have made themselves dinner. Since their mom had left, the three men had learned how to provide for themselves, but with it being Friday night and all, they needed a treat.

Plus, he hadn't wanted to waste time cooking when he could be spending it talking to his dad, especially since his time in Esperanza was ticking away quickly. Just a few more weeks and he would head back to the military.

As he ran a fry through the ketchup and ate the last piece of tender meat on the rib, the cowbell clanged over the door. A trio walked in—Macy's son with another boy and a teen girl.

They stopped at the door to wait to be seated. As the hostess showed them to a booth, they passed by.

"Evening, Mr. Yates," T.J. said to his dad and nodded at Fisher in greeting as well.

"Evening, T.J. Are these friends of yours?" Buck Yates asked, flicking his large hand in the direction of the other teens with T.J.

"Yes, sir, they are. Joe and Sara, meet Mr. Yates. He's the sheriff's dad and this is the sheriff's brother—Captain Yates."

Joe and Sara shook hands with the men and then the trio excused themselves.

"Polite young man," Fisher said, slightly surprised given the accounts provided by his brother about T.J.'s antics.

"He's a good kid, just a little angry ever since his pa died," Buck said and pushed away his empty plate.

"It must have been rough," he said, imagining how difficult it would have been on both Macy and T.J. His own brother had suffered greatly as well since Tim had been his lifelong best friend.

Luckily, Jericho had been Macy's best friend also and had

been by her side during the long months that Tim had battled cancer. At least Macy hadn't been alone, but it didn't stop the sudden clenching of his gut that maybe he could have been there for her, as well.

He drove that thought away quickly. Being away from Macy was up there on the list of reasons he had joined the military.

Maybe the top reason, he mused, thinking back to the night that had forever sealed the course of his life.

Chapter 4

Esperanza, Texas
Eighteen years earlier

Jericho stood at the plate, bat held high. His hips shifting back and forth, his body relaxed. He waited for the pitch.

Jericho's team was down by one. Tim Ward was on third base and another player on second with two men out. It would be the last inning unless they were able to get some runs on the board.

Fisher sat beside his dad on the bleacher and called out encouragement. "You can do it, Jericho."

His yell was followed by Macy's from where she sat a few feet away and a row down from them. "Go-o-o, Jericho-o. One little hit."

She sat beside Jericho's latest girlfriend. He couldn't remember her name because Jericho never kept a girl for too long, much like him. The Yates boys were love 'em and leave 'em kinds of guys, he thought.

Macy, on the other hand, wasn't a love 'em and leave 'em type of girl. Until recently, everyone thought she and Tim were a forever kind of thing what with them going off to college together. Except that in the past few weeks, Macy and Tim didn't seem to be a thing anymore, which meant that Tim had loved her and left her. That struck him as downright stupid.

The crack of the bat pulled his attention away from thoughts of Macy.

Jericho had lined a rocket of a hit up the first baseline and deep into the corner of the stadium. Tim would score easily to tie the game, but as people got up on the bleachers and started cheering, it was clear the ball was deep enough to maybe score the man from second.

The outfielder picked up the ball and with all his might sent it flying home, but the man from second was already well on his way to the plate. The ball sailed past the catcher as the man slid into home to win the game.

The wild cheering and revelry of the hometown crowd spurred on the players who ran out onto the field to celebrate the victory. After a few moments of exuberant celebration, both the players and the crowd finally quieted down and the players formed a line to shake hands with the other team.

As they did so, the crowd began to disperse from the stands.

"I'll see you at home, son," his dad said, clapped him on the back and waved at Jericho on the field.

He jumped down from the bleachers and weaved through the crowd of well-wishers until he reached Jericho, whose new girlfriend was already plastered to his hip.

Tim and Macy stood across from one another awkwardly, clearly no longer a forever kind of thing and surprisingly, he was kind of glad about that.

"Hey, big bro," Jericho said as he joined them. "Tim, Cindy and I are heading to Bill's for a post-baseball bash. Want to come hang with us?"

All three of them, but not Macy? he wondered and shot a glance at her as she stood there, hands laced primly together in front of her.

"No thanks, lil' bro. Just came down to say congrats on winning the game."

"We've gotta run. What about you, Mace?" Jericho said, either clearly oblivious to the tension between his two friends or choosing to ignore it.

"I've got…things to do," she replied, peeking up at him from the corner of her eye.

"We're history, then," Jericho said and left with Cindy bumping hips with him on one side and Tim on the other.

He jammed the tips of his fingers into the pockets of his jeans and rocked back on the heels of his boots, hesitant now that he and Macy were alone. "So what's so important for you to have to do on a Friday night?"

A blast of pink brightened her cheeks before she straightened her shoulders and faced him head on, determination in her brown-eyed gaze. "Well, since it's early, I was thinking of maybe grabbing a bite at Miss Sue's. Are you hungry?" After she asked, she worried her bottom lip with her teeth, belying her nervousness around him.

He was hungry, but not necessarily for anything other than a taste of that luscious bottom lip. Years earlier he'd had a taste during what was supposed to be a chaste holiday kiss, but he had underestimated the potency of her kiss. That encounter had made him realize that like Tim, he had been smitten by tomboy Macy Ward.

"I'm hungry, but won't Tim mind, you know...you and me. Friday night. Dinner."

She cocked her head at him defiantly. "What I do is no longer any of Tim's concern. So, dinner?"

Interesting, he thought, but quickly offered her his arm. "Dinner it is. My treat."

He wanted to lick the plate of the last remnants of Miss Sue's famous apple cobbler, but his dad had raised him to be a gentleman so he held back.

Macy must have seen the hunger that remained in his gaze since she offered up the last few bites of the pie on her plate. "You can finish mine."

His mouth watered at the site of those extra pieces, but he shook his head. "I couldn't take the last of your dessert."

"Go ahead. I need to watch my figure anyway," she said, moving aside his plate and pushing hers before him.

Fisher dug into the cobbler, but after he swallowed a bite, he said, "Seems to me you're worrying for nothing, Mace."

Truth be told, she had a wonderful figure. Trim and strong, but with womanly curves in all the right places. As he thought about that, he shifted in his seat as his jeans tightened painfully. He had imagined those curves next to him once too often since that fateful kiss.

"Something wrong, Fisher?" she asked, innocently unaware of the effect she had on him.

"Not at all," he lied, quickly finished the cobbler and paid the tab.

With his hand on the small of her back, he walked her out to the sidewalk where they stood there for a moment, enjoying the early summer night. Dusk was just settling in, bringing with it the cooler night air and the soft intimate glow of the streetlights along Main Street.

"Thank you for dinner," Macy said, glad for not only the fine food, but his company. He had always been a distant fourth musketeer to their little group and tonight she had been able to enjoy his presence without interference.

As he turned to look at her, she noticed the gleam in his green eyes. The kind of gleam that kicked her heart up into a hurried little beat. She might have been going out with Tim for as long as she could remember, but she could still recognize when a man found her attractive. And considering her breakup with Tim, it was a welcome balm that someone as attractive as Fisher appeared to be interested.

He smiled, his teeth white against his tanned skin and his dark five o'clock shadow. He was the kind of man who needed to shave more than twice a day. He was a man, she reminded herself, trying to ignore the pull of her attraction to him. Nothing like Jericho and Tim, even though Fisher was only two years older. There had always been a maturity and intensity about him that had set him apart from the others.

"It's early still," he said, the tones of his voice a soft murmur in the coming quiet of the night.

"It is," she said.

He leaned toward her and a lock of nearly jet-black hair fell forward onto his forehead as he said, "Too early to call it a night, don't you think?"

She met his gaze, glittering brightly with interest, the color like new spring grass. Kicking up that erratic beat of her heart and making her want to reach up and brush away that wild errant lock of hair.

"Did you have something in mind?" she asked in a breathless voice she didn't recognize.

"How about a drive? I'll even put the top down on the CJ."

She imagined driving through the night, Fisher beside her. The scents of the early summer wildflowers whipping around them as they sped along in the open Jeep through the Texas countryside.

"I think that sounds really nice."

They drove through the open meadows and fields surrounding Esperanza, the scented wind wrapping them in its embrace while bright moonlight lit the road before them until Fisher took a dirt road to one of the few nearby hills. He parked the CJ so it faced the lights of town and the wide starlit Texas sky.

She imagined she could see the lights of San Antonio, well to the south of their hometown. She and Tim had planned on going to college together there until Tim had said he was reconsidering that decision. She gazed at the lights of Esperanza and noticed the cars parked around Bill's house where Jericho and Tim would be with the rest of the baseball team. Where she might have been a few weeks earlier if things hadn't changed recently.

"Penny for your thoughts," he said and pushed back some strands of wind-blown hair from her face. The pads of his fingers brushed the sensitive skin of her cheek, sending a shiver rocketing through her body.

"Do you ever wonder if some things happen for a reason?" she asked.

"Meaning?" He arched one dark brow in question.

"Tim and me. His breaking it off." She shrugged and turned in her seat to face him. "If it hadn't been for that—"

"Being the nice girl that you are, you wouldn't be here tonight." He once again brushed the tips of his fingers across her cheek, then trailed them down to cup her jaw.

"Is that what you think I am? A nice girl?" she shot back, slightly perturbed, which was ridiculous. She was a nice gir,l unlike many of the women with whom Fisher had been seen around town.

"Don't get so riled, Mace. There's nothing wrong with being a nice girl."

The words shot out of her mouth before she could censor them. "And boys like you don't think about doing things with nice girls."

"Boys like me?" he asked with another pointed arch of his brow and a wry smile on his lips.

Macy fidgeted with her hands, plucking at the seat belt she still wore. "You know, love 'em and leave 'em types like you."

He chuckled and shook his head, but he never broke the contact of his hand against her chin. Instead, he inched his thumb up to brush softly across her lips.

"Let's get something straight, Mace. First of all, I'm not a boy, I'm a man. A man whose daddy would tan his hide for the thoughts he's having right now about the nice girl who happens to be sitting next to him."

The warmth on the pad of his thumb spread itself across her lips and with his words, shot through the rest of her body. "Thoughts? What kinds of thoughts?"

He chuckled again, only with something darker and dangerously sexy this time. "You always were the daring type."

"He who dares, wins," she reminded him.

The smile on his face broadened and he leaned toward her until the warmth of his breath replaced that of his thumb against her lips. "Then I guess I should dare," he said and brought his lips to hers.

The shock of his hard mouth against hers was quickly replaced by a sense of…rightness which surprised her considering that this was Jericho's brother. That up until a few weeks ago, she had thought she was about to embark on a life with another man.

Another man who had rejected her. Who had never made her feel the way Fisher now made her feel.

The tip of his tongue tasted her lips, gently asked for entrance at the seam of her mouth. She opened her lips and accepted the thrust of his tongue. Joined it with hers until they were both breathing heavily and had to break apart for air.

Fisher turned away from her and clenched his hands on his thighs, struggling for control. This was Macy, he reminded himself, rubbing his hands across the soft denim of his jeans. Jericho's best friend and Tim's intended, he recalled as he held back from reaching for her again.

Only she wasn't Tim's anymore, the voice inside his head challenged and then urged, *And now she can be yours.*

He faced her and seeing the desire in her eyes, he asked, "Are you sure about this?"

She nodded quickly and he didn't second guess her decision. Reaching into the backseat of the CJ, he grabbed a blanket he kept there and stepped out of the car. Swinging around the front, he met her by the passenger side door and slipped his hand into hers. Twined his fingers with hers as he led her a few feet away from the Jeep to a soft spot of grass on the overlook.

He released her only long enough to spread out the blanket and then he urged her down.

For long moments they lay side by side on their backs, staring up at the late May moon. Listening to the rustle of the light breeze along the taller grass and the profusion of wild-flowers that perfumed the air.

Fisher rolled onto his side and ran the back of his index finger along the high straight ridge of her cheek. He had known her all his life and had thought she was the prettiest woman he had ever seen.

"You're beautiful."

Much like before, an embarrassed flush worked across her cheeks as she avoided his gaze. "I bet you say that to all the girls."

He laughed and shook his head. "Now why do you think I'm such a hound dog?"

"Because I've seen you around town with all those dangerous women," she answered and the blush along her cheeks deepened.

"Jealous?" he asked, but then immediately confessed, "Because every time I saw you with Tim, I was jealous."

A little jolt of excitement rattled her body before Macy turned onto her side and cradled his cheek. His five o'clock shadow tickled the palm of her hand. As she met his gaze, made a silvery green by the light of the moon, she detected no deception there, just honesty.

"Why didn't you—"

"You were Tim's girl and Jericho's best friend. I wasn't going to be responsible for breaking up the Three Muske-teers," he said and shrugged.

"And now?" she asked, mimicking his earlier move by

bringing her thumb to trace the warm fullness of his lips which broadened into a sexy dimpled smile with her caress.

"He who dares, wins," he said and brought his lips to hers.

Chapter 5

"I've never seen a smile like that one before," Buck Yates said as he signaled for the waitress, who immediately came over.

"I bet I know what you'd like, Buck," she said as she picked up the empty plates from the table. "A slice of Miss Sue's famous cherry pie and some coffee."

"You know me too well, Lizzy. How about you, Fisher? Was it something sweet that put that smile on your face?" Buck teased.

Something sweet and hot, Fisher thought, recalling the taste of Macy's lips and the warmth of her body pressed to his as they had made love that long ago night.

Shifting in his seat to readjust his increasingly tight jeans, he looked up at the perky young waitress. "I'll take a slice of that pie with some vanilla ice cream, please."

He needed the chill to cool down his thoughts.

As Lizzy walked away with their empty plates and orders, Buck once again resumed the earlier conversation. "So what had you smiling like the cat that ate the cream? A woman, and I hope a decent one at that."

With some force, Fisher shook his head. "Come on, Pa. You know I can't offer a decent woman the kind of life she'd want."

"Nonsense," Buck began and for emphasis, jabbed a gnarly index finger in his direction. "Plenty of military men have wives and families."

He couldn't argue with his dad, although he understood how difficult it was for such men. Being away from their families for months on end. The fears and dangers that each new mission brought for those left behind.

"I don't think I could share my kind of life with a woman."

His father was about to speak when Lizzy returned with the pies and coffee, but as soon as she left them, his dad continued his plea. "You could if you took that teaching assignment at West Point."

For weeks since the offer had come, he had been debating between that and returning for another tour of duty in the Middle East. As captain of his squad, he had recently led his men safely through three tours. He couldn't imagine leaving them.

"I don't want to abandon my men. Besides, I like the military life. It's orderly. Disciplined."

"Lonely," Buck jumped in. "At the end of the day when you hang up that uniform with all those medals—"

"I'll know that I helped bring home alive as many men as I could. Their families will thank me for that," he replied and forked up a bit of the pie and ice cream. The taste was wooden in his mouth because a part of him recognized that on some level his father was right.

At the end of his career, no matter how successful he had been, his uniform would hang in a closet empty of any traces of a woman or family. Despite that, he couldn't picture himself as a father or husband. Solving a family's problems instead of those of his men. He wasn't sure how to handle such things.

While glancing down at his pie, he said, "I know you'd like grandkids to carry on the Yates name, Pa. Seems to me Jericho's the one you should look to for that."

"Hard to believe it's only been a couple of weeks since he met Olivia and married her," his father said.

"I admire that Jericho's willing to claim Olivia's baby as his own and if I know my brother—"

"He'll be wanting more with her. I can see how much he cares for Olivia and it really makes me happy. I always worried after what happened with your ma—"

"Don't blame yourself. You did what you could and we all know we were better off without her," he said and yet a part of him acknowledged that her leaving had ripped away a piece of each of them. That for him and Jericho, it had made them leery of loving a woman for fear of being abandoned again.

Like Macy had abandoned him, he thought, recalling how despite their one night of incredible passion she had walked down the aisle with Tim Ward just over a month later.

His dad must have picked up on his upset. "You shouldn't let your ma leaving eat away at your gut like that. Neither you or Jericho had anything to do with that."

"You're right, Pa," he said, wanting to foreclose any further discussion. Wanting to forget anything and everything relating to Macy Ward.

He wasn't meant for women like her or for a family kind

of life. The military was what had brought order and happiness to his life eighteen years earlier.

It was what would bring order and happiness to his life for the future.

For the first Friday night in too many months, Macy felt like she could actually just kick back and relax.

The change in T.J. in a little over a week was a welcome surprise. He had clearly bonded not only with Joe, but with Sara. She hoped that friendship would help the young girl come out of her shell and talk about her problems. The Hopechest Ranch policy was not to press for details, but offer refuge. She knew, however, that she did the most good when the children were finally able to talk about their traumas.

Maybe Sara's friendship with T.J. and Joe would help her trust them enough to share and begin the road to healing.

Much as T.J. seemed to be healing.

In addition to the bonding, T.J. and Joe had completed each and every task that had been asked of them at the ranch and eagerly helped out with the other kids during their free time. Because of his exemplary behavior, when T.J. had asked if he could go to town with Joe and Sara, she had unequivocally said "Yes."

Which meant she had time to just unwind. Rare time in her normally hectic life.

She had filled her big claw-footed tub with steaming hot water and added some fragrant rose oils that Jewel had given her as an engagement gift. She had attempted to return them after she cancelled the wedding, but Jewel had insisted she keep them so she could treat herself.

Treat herself she would, she thought, tying the lush terry

cloth robe around herself and pouring a glass of wine to take with her to the bath. On the way, she snagged her brand-new romance novel from the nightstand in her bedroom.

Tim had always teased her about her romances until she had insisted he read them to her at night before bed.

He had never complained again after that, she thought with a smile as she set the book and wine on the painted wrought iron caddy. It perfectly matched the Victorian look of her bathroom, her one touch of fanciful in her otherwise modest and plain home.

She might have taken the Victorian theme further in the house, but realized it might have made it a little too girly for T.J. and had refrained from doing so. But in here and her bedroom—her private domain—she let herself give into her fantasies.

She slipped into the tub and the heat of the water immediately began to soak away some of the aches and tiredness. She loved working at the ranch, but with half a dozen children and the two teen boys, it was always a whirlwind of activities and quite physical.

The activities, however, were clearly making progress with some of the children. In the months she had been at the ranch, she had seen noticeable improvements not only in their academic skills, but their social ones. Kids who had once been loners were finally coming out of their shells.

It was what made her career so rewarding.

Grabbing the book off the caddy, she cracked it open and began to read, only she hadn't realized it was a book with a hero in the military. It normally didn't bother her, but her emotions were too unsettled with Fisher in town and so she set the book aside and picked up her wineglass.

As she took a sip, she recalled the sight of him and Jericho standing outside the church. Jericho had been so handsome in his tuxedo, but it had been Fisher standing there in his Army uniform, medals gleaming in the sun, that had caused her heart to skip a beat.

Even if she hadn't had any doubts about her marriage to Jericho before then, that reaction alone would have made her realize she was making a big mistake.

No matter how much she tried to forget it, her one and only night with Fisher had left an indelible memory. One she had driven deep inside her heart when she had made the decision to marry Tim Ward.

The right decision, she reminded herself as she took a small sip of the wine.

She and Tim had been destined to be together, their short breakup in high school notwithstanding. Tim was kind and patient and honorable. When she had told him she was pregnant just a short time before their wedding, he had been understanding and had even talked to her about telling Fisher.

She had considered it back then and in the many years since. But Jericho had been going on and on about how happy Fisher was in the Army and since their night together, Fisher never approached her again.

Talk had been that Fisher was the kind of man who couldn't commit and back then she felt he had loved and left her. When she had heard about his enlistment in the Army, it had made no sense to ruin his life by telling him about a child he probably wouldn't want.

But then she recalled the way he had looked at her on the steps of the church. Imagined she had seen desire in his gaze along with hurt. Not that she could hurt him unless he actually had feelings for her. Something which she didn't want to consider because it would complicate things.

Forcing her mind from such troubling thoughts, she placed her nearly untouched glass of wine on the caddy and sank farther into the bone-melting heat of the water. The fragrance of roses wafted around her, reminding her of the profusion of wild rose bushes tangled amongst the small stands of trees just outside the Esperanza town limits.

Reminding her of how the night had smelled while she made love with Fisher.

She shot upright in the bath, mumbling a curse, but then the phone rang and she mumbled yet another curse.

She had left the portable phone in her room.

As it continued to ring, demanding her attention, she climbed out of the bath, grabbed a towel and wrapped it around her. She raced to her bedroom to pick up before the answering machine kicked in.

Unfortunately, the answering machine engaged just as she reached it and heard across the speaker, "Mrs. Ward. This is Deputy Rawlings."

Her stomach dropped at the identity of the caller. At his next words, sadness and disappointment filled her soul. "I've got your son down at the station."

Chapter 6

T.J. walked out of the sheriff's office beside her, his body ramrod straight and stiff with tension. He hadn't offered up much of an explanation for the speeding which had led to his running into another car just on the outskirts of town.

Luckily the damage to both cars had been minor and no one had been injured. But because of their age and the speeding, the Deputy had decided to take the boys in and call her and Jewel.

She looked over her shoulder at her boss who walked beside Joe. The teen had a hangdog look on his face and clearly seemed to be sorry for what had happened.

Unlike T.J.

As they exited the police station, she spotted Fisher strolling out of Lone Star Square. Judging from the activity in the square, the movie had apparently just let out in the theater on the other side of the plaza. Some of the people headed to the cars parked all along the edges of the central space while Fisher and another couple waited to cross the street. He noticed them leaving the police station and condemnation flashed across his features.

It made her want to go over and wipe that critical look from his face, but she plowed forward. Speaking with T.J. about what had happened tonight needed to be her number one priority right now.

As they approached the parking lot, she inspected yet again the damage to T.J.'s car—a big ugly dent along the front bumper and part of the passenger side panel of the 1974 Pontiac GTO.

The GTO that his dad had bought as a rusty heap and had been restoring for years before his death. The GTO that T.J. had also been, as he called it, "pimping."

She paused before the car and stared at the damage before she looked up and met Jewel's concerned gaze, Joe's sheepish one and T.J.'s stony countenance.

"Luckily no one was hurt and the damage to both cars can be repaired. When we get home, we'll discuss how you're going to pay for those repairs and the speeding ticket," she said. Handing T.J. the keys to the GTO, she finished, "I'll follow you home."

Turning to Jewel, she noticed her friend's concern, but also Jewel's interest in Fisher as she glanced back across Main Street toward where he still stood on the edge of Lone Star Square, watching them.

She laid a hand on her friend's arm. "Can we talk about it in the morning? It's late and we should all be heading home."

Jewel nodded, faced Joe and said, "Let's go. You and I have a lot to discuss, as well."

As the two walked away, Macy waited for T.J. to get in his car and then she went to her own late model Cherokee, starting it up and then idling it until T.J. pulled out of the parking lot.

T.J.'s pace as he exited was slow.

Slow enough that it gave her yet another chance to see Fisher, the disapproval still stamped on his face as he observed them.

"Tell me again what happened?" she pressed, sensing there was something off about T.J.'s version of the speeding and accident.

"It was just an accident, Ma," he said, slouching negligently in his chair in the kitchen.

"Tell me again why you were speeding?"

His big hands, like those of Fisher, man's hands on a boy's body, flopped up and down before settling on the surface of the table. "I didn't mean to only… There was another car. It was fast. It kept getting in our face—"

"In your face? As in threatening you? Why didn't you pull over? Use your cell phone to call the police?" Macy asked as she rested her hands on the table where T.J. sat, leaning closer.

A glimmer of fear flickered across his features, impossible to miss. "No, not like that. You know like…challenging us. Trying to prove their car was better."

She understood about men and cars. Entire industries had been built about proving who was faster, better, fancier. She also understood about men and cars and girls.

"Sara was with you?"

Another small flinch rippled across his body and T.J. couldn't meet her gaze as he answered, "We had already dropped Sara off at the ranch."

She hadn't had time at the police station to ask Jewel

whether Sara had been home at the ranch when the call had come from Deputy Rawlings. She certainly would ask tomorrow because she was sure T.J. wasn't telling the truth.

"So you were drag racing? And because you were speeding, you couldn't stop when that car pulled out?"

An indifferent shrug greeted her queries, infuriating her, but she knew she had to keep her cool. Nothing would be gained by anger.

"You've already earned enough at the ranch to pay me back for the coach's mailbox. What you earn from now on will pay for the repairs to both cars and the speeding ticket. Do you understand?"

He nodded without hesitation, but never raised his gaze to meet hers.

"You're also grounded for a month. You come home after your work at the ranch. On the weekends, I'll have chores for you to do around the house. Understood?"

A shrug greeted her punishment.

"I'm going to bed. It's late and we both need to go to work tomorrow," she said, but she didn't want the night to end angrily.

She kneeled before her son, cradled his jaw with her hand and gently urged his face upward. Reluctantly, he met her gaze. "*You* are the most important thing in the world to me, T.J. You can trust me with anything. Anything," she said in the hopes of having him tell her the truth about what had really happened that night.

A sheen of tears glimmered in her son's eyes. He gulped, holding back emotion before he said, "I know, Mom. I love you."

"I love you," she said, sat up and hugged him, believing that all would be right with him as long as they still had love to bind them together.

* * *

She was a coward, she thought, not looking forward to speaking with Jewel about what had happened the night before. Because of that, and knowing Jewel's sweet tooth, she was on her way to Miss Sue's again for yet more sticky buns.

Luck was on her side as there was an empty parking space directly in front of Miss Sue's. But then she noticed that Fisher was once again sitting at a booth in the restaurant.

Didn't he ever eat at home? she wondered with irritation as she took a deep breath to fortify herself, exited the car and entered the cafe.

As she passed by the booth where he sat finishing up a mound of Miss Sue's scrambled eggs with bacon, cheese and hash browns, he met her gaze. Rebuke filled his green eyes and within her, annoyance built. At the counter, she forced a smile to her face as she ordered the sticky buns.

The waitress smiled warmly and offered her sympathies. "Boys will be boys, Macy. Don't let it get to you."

She nodded, but said nothing else. She also didn't turn to brave the rest of the people in the restaurant, although she sensed their stares as she waited. In a town the size of Esperanza, Miss Sue's was Information Central and everyone already knew about what had happened the night before.

Her sticky bun order came up to the counter. She paid quickly, eager to make her exit, but as she headed out, she noticed Fisher's attention was on her once again and something inside of her snapped.

In one smooth move, she slipped into the booth across from him, surprising him with her action. Calmly she said, "You don't know me or my son, so don't presume to judge us so quickly."

Fisher slowly put down his mug of coffee. Lacing his fingers together, he leaned forward and in soft tones said, "And I don't intend to get to know you…again. Once Jericho returns and I'm sure all is right with him, I'll be off and out of your way."

Out of her way, but also in harm's way, it occurred to her guiltily. "There's no need to rush back to the Army on my account."

He tossed up his hands in emphasis. "The Army is all I know and need. Discipline. Order. Respect."

The condemnation lashed at her once again. Discipline, order and respect clearly being things that he seemed to find lacking with her and her son. Sadly, she acknowledged that she, too, wished she had more of those traits in her life. Because of that, she tempered her response.

"I'm glad the military makes you happy. I hope you stay safe when you go back."

She didn't wait for a reply. She swept her box of sticky buns from the booth's table and hurried out the door.

In her Cherokee, she handed the box to T.J., who placed it in his lap and said, "What was that?"

"Excuse me?" she said as she pulled away from the curb.

"You and Captain Yates. It looked…intense," her son said and she realized that T.J. had seen everything through the plate glass window of Miss Sue's.

Striving for a neutral tone, she said, "Nothing important. I just asked him if he'd heard from Jericho. I expect he and Olivia will be back soon from their honeymoon."

T.J. snorted loudly and shook his head. "You're not a very good liar, Mom."

Her hands tightened on the wheel, but she said nothing else

which prompted T.J. to add, "Maybe you should practice what you preach. Maybe you should talk about what's up with you and Captain Yates."

What was up with her and Fisher was more than she suspected T.J. could handle at the moment. He'd been walking a very fine line lately and she was concerned that telling him the truth about Fisher would push him over the edge. If he crossed that line, she worried that the next trip to the sheriff's station would result in more than community service or a speeding ticket.

Because of that, she kept her silence as they drove toward the ranch.

T.J. also kept silent, guarding his own secrets she suspected since she still believed he was not telling her the whole truth about what had happened the night before.

At the ranch, it was Jewel who opened the door when they pulled up in the driveway. There was no mistaking the look on her boss's face that said she intended to get to the bottom of things.

Taking a deep breath, Macy braced herself as she approached the door to the ranch.

Chapter 7

The sticky buns became an after lunch treat as she joined Jewel and Ana in the shade at a patio table near the pool.

Jewel had opted to say little to the boys other than to assign them a mess of chores that would keep them busy until she intended to speak to them. That kept Sara with the other children rather than with her two new best friends. During their absence, the young girl retreated more deeply into her shell.

Ana's face was flushed by the midday heat as she slowly lowered herself into a chair at the table.

Macy placed a tall glass of milk before her, but two iced coffees before her spot and Jewel's. Then she set a sticky bun at each place before sitting beside Ana. Jewel came by a few minutes later after reminding the children in the pool about the rules.

Jewel's face was also flushed from the heat and wisps of

her short wavy brown hair curled around her face. Dark circles marred the fragile skin beneath her cocoa brown eyes.

"I'm sorry about last night. I know you couldn't have slept well afterward," she said.

Jewel nodded, her lips in a grim smile. "I didn't. The call about the accident brought back painful memories."

"You were in an accident?" Ana asked, leaning forward and examining Jewel's features.

Jewel looked away and gripped the glass of iced coffee. With her thumb, she wiped away the condensation on its surface and said, "My fiancé and I were in an accident on the night he proposed to me. He was killed. Although I survived, I lost the baby I was carrying."

"*Perdoname.* I didn't mean to pry," Ana replied and dipped her gaze downward to her own pregnant belly. Almost protectively, she ran her hand across the rounded mound.

"It's all right, Ana. You couldn't have known," Jewel reassured her. "I was lucky to have Joe and Meredith Colton by my side, otherwise I think I might have lost my mind."

"The Coltons seem like wonderful people," Macy chimed in.

Jewel nodded emphatically. "They are which is why I'm so happy that with Daniels being exposed and jailed, Joe's presidential campaign has taken off. His nomination seems like a sure thing now."

"Definitely. I can't imagine how Olivia must have felt when she regained her memory and realized it was Daniels who was trying to kill her," she said and a sudden screech from the pool snagged her attention, but it was only two of the kids engaged in a splashing match.

Jewel had also whipped around at the noise, obviously on the edge. But when she realized it was nothing serious, she returned her attention to her friends. "Olivia's lucky to have found Jericho only... How are you dealing with canceling the wedding? Are you—"

"Convinced it was the right thing to do. It wouldn't have been right for me and Jericho to be together. Even though we love each other as friends, he deserves more from a marriage and Olivia will give him that," she admitted. She grabbed her glass of iced coffee, light with milk and sweet with sugar and took a big gulp. The cool helped chase away some of the heat of midday.

"Do you think what happened with T.J. has to do with you and Jericho? That he's angry about it?" Jewel pressed and then quickly tacked on, "Or is it about Fisher Yates?"

The heat that pressed down on her now came from Jewel's inquiry and her own guilt about both the Yates men. "T.J. was upset with my decision to marry Jericho. He said he already had a dad."

"And Fisher?" her friend repeated.

She recalled T.J.'s words about how maybe she should talk about it, but she still wasn't ready to reveal the secret she had kept for so long. "That's a complicated story. Plus, I don't think that it has anything to do with the boys and last night."

Taking another bracing sip of her drink, she met Jewel's too perceptive gaze and realized her friend knew it was time to back off about Fisher. That she would talk only when she was good and ready. "I'm sorry about last night, Jewel. I've talked to T.J., but I feel as if he's only telling me part of what really happened."

"I've spoken with Joe as well, only..." Jewel hesitated and then picked up the sticky bun, tore off a piece. "There's something not right about their story," she finally said.

She nodded. "I agree, although I can't put my finger on what's wrong."

"They say they dropped Sara off, but I don't remember if she was home when I got the call. Do you, Ana?" Jewel asked.

Ana rolled her eyes upward as she tried to remember, but then shook her head. "I do not know. She was home later. When you and Joe came home."

"So maybe Sara was with them when the accident happened?" Macy said and glanced over at the young teen, who deprived of her two friends thanks to their chores, was sitting alone on the edge of the pool.

"If she was with the boys, why didn't the police see her?"

"And if she was with them, why would they lie about that?" Jewel wondered aloud.

"She has many secrets, I think," Ana added and absent-mindedly rubbed her hand over her belly once again.

"If she doesn't want to be found, she wouldn't want to be involved with the police," she said, considering the police were bound to discover who she was.

Jewel took another piece of sticky bun and motioned with it as she said, "But that doesn't explain why they were speeding, does it?"

"T.J. said there was another car out on the road. One that was challenging them to prove their car was better."

"A drag race? Joe says they didn't realize they were speeding. That they didn't see the other car until it was too late to stop," Jewel said, but then she turned in her seat to glance at the pool and Sara in particular. "I don't know what to believe, but my gut says it involves Sara."

"Boys, cars and girls. A familiar mix, don't you think?" she suggested, remembering her own teen years and the many times that mix had caused problems in town.

"I hope that's all it is," Jewel said, finishing off the last of her sticky bun and pointing at Macy's, which remained untouched before her. "If you're a true friend, you'll eat that," she said.

"Why is that?" she asked.

"Because otherwise I'm going to devour it and you don't want me to get fat." A hesitant smile spread across Jewel's face and Macy realized she was trying to lighten the moment.

As another playful shout came from the pool, Macy grabbed her sticky bun and with a playful snort said, "Fat. Right. That's why Deputy Rawlings is always making goo goo eyes at you."

· "Goo goo eyes?" Ana asked, slightly confused by the expression.

"That means he's interested in Jewel," she explained and Ana smiled broadly, nodded with some spirit. "Definitely. I've seen how he looks at you whenever he visits."

The blush that now blossomed across Jewel's face wasn't from the warmth of the day. "I've tried my best to discourage him. I'm just not ready for another relationship."

Neither was she, although she had been hard-pressed to forget about Fisher during the day thanks to their encounter that morning. "Me, either," she chimed in and finished off the last of her sticky bun.

Ana was done as well with her treat and as Macy glanced at her watch, she realized their lunch hour was almost over.

"Do you want me to work with the older children on their study skills while Ana and the younger kids do some craft work?"

Jewel nodded. "I know school is still some time away, but it would be good for them to be ready. It'll also give me some time to talk to the boys."

The three women split up to finish their work for the day.

As she aided Sara and the two other older children with their study exercises, her mind was half on what was happening with Jewel, T.J. and Joe in the library where Jewel often met with the children privately.

It came as no surprise to her later that Jewel had not been able to get any other information from them.

It also didn't surprise her to see T.J., Joe and Sara huddled together by the corral later that afternoon, clearly engaged in some kind of animated conversation. As soon as the rest of the group neared in order to take some rides on Papa's Poppy, the conversation stopped.

Their actions worried her, but with T.J. grounded for a month due to the speeding and accident, the trio was unlikely to get into trouble anytime soon.

Anytime soon hopefully being long after Jericho had returned from his honeymoon and Fisher had left town.

She knew which Yates brother she could count on to help her and it sure wasn't Fisher, she thought.

Relative quiet ruled over dinner that night.

T.J. didn't have much to say about either his discussion with Jewel or what he, Joe and Sara were talking about at the corral.

In truth, she didn't push too hard for the information. If she did, T.J. would become even more tight-lipped and remind her that she had something she needed to get off her chest as well.

Namely Fisher.

She hadn't been able to get him out of her mind all day and as she slipped into bed that night, he once again invaded her dreams as if to remind her that she had been about to marry the wrong Yates brother.

* * *

A small crowd gathered around the steps of the church. Jewel and Ana. An assortment of Coltons. Jericho and a pregnant Olivia, her rounded belly larger than it had been just a few weeks before. Buck Yates stood beside them, a broad smile on his face.

As she neared the group, she stumbled on something and looked down.

She had stepped on the hem of her dress—her wedding dress.

Confused, she paused and stared back up at the gathering of friends and family, only everyone had disappeared, leaving only two people on the steps—Fisher and T.J.

T.J. looked solemn and too grown-up in his dark blue suit—the suit she had bought for him to wear for her wedding to Fisher.

No, not Fisher.

Jericho, she reminded herself, but as she stared at her son and the man standing next to him, she realized just how much T.J. looked like Fisher, his father.

It was there in the squareness of their jaws and the lean build of their bodies. T.J.'s hair was darker than hers, closer to Fisher's nearly black hair much like T.J.'s eyes were a mix of Fisher's green and her brown.

The physical similarities between the two men was undeniable.

She wondered why she hadn't seen it before. Why others hadn't seen it over the years. Suddenly, she realized everyone had gone.

Everyone except Fisher who stood there, lethally handsome in his Army uniform. The dark blue of the fabric intensified the green of his eyes while the fit of the jacket lovingly caressed the broad width of his shoulders and leanness of his waist.

She remembered those shoulders, she thought as she took a step toward him and the distance between them vanished.

Suddenly in his arms, she braced her hands against those strong shoulders only they were bare now beneath the palms of her hands much as she was now bare, the wedding dress having evaporated into the ether of her dreams.

His skin was warm against hers as he pressed her to his lean muscled body. A man's hard body, she thought, recalling the strength of him on the one night they had shared so long ago. Remembering the emotions he had roused that had shaken her to the core of her being.

She met his gaze, her own likely confused as she said, "I've never forgotten our one night."

"Neither have I," he said and lowered his forehead to rest against hers. His tones soft, he said, "Why did you marry Tim?"

She had loved Tim with all her heart. Loved him in a way that was different from how she felt for Fisher and yet…

She had loved Fisher as well after that night. And because of that emotion, she hadn't been able to ruin his life when she had heard of his enlistment and excitement to be leaving Esperanza.

At her hesitation, he smiled sadly and said, "Still not talking? You didn't want to talk after that night either."

No, she hadn't wanted to talk. She had wanted to show him how she cared in other ways and so she did that now, rising up the inch or so to press her lips to his.

Fisher groaned like a man in pain at that first touch, but then he answered her kiss, meeting her lips again and again. Tenderly breaching the seam of her mouth with his tongue to taste her. To unite them until every move and breath became as one between them and just kissing wasn't enough.

He gently lowered her to the ground and the softness of well-worn fabric, smelling like her mama's detergent, dragged her eyes open.

It was night out and they were lying on a blanket on the overlook, much as they had done eighteen years before.

The sky above them was a deep endless black dotted with hundreds of stars and a bright summer moon that silvered all below as it had so many years earlier.

As she met his gaze, he cupped her cheek and ran his thumb across the moistness his kisses had left behind on her lips.

"I never forgot that night," he said once again.

"Neither did I," she admitted and gave herself over to his loving.

Chapter 8

Macy bolted upright in bed, breathing heavily. Her body thrummed with unfulfilled desire.

She yanked a shaky hand through her hair, troubled about the dream. Troubled because it had hit too close to home regarding her feelings for Fisher.

No matter how hard she had tried to forget him during the last eighteen years, he had always been with her. In her brain and in her heart.

Tim had known and understood. Had realized that her love for him was strong and true, but that Fisher had touched a part of her that could not be his.

She had admired Tim for that and for claiming T.J. as his. It had allowed both her and Fisher to get on with their lives in the ways that both of them had wanted.

And what about T.J.? the niggling voice of guilt

reminded. What about Fisher not knowing he has a child? it lashed out.

Shaking her head as if to clear out that nagging voice, she slipped from bed and walked down the hall to T.J.'s room.

The door was open and as she peered at her sleeping son, the guilt flailed at her repeatedly. T.J.'s features were stamped with Fisher's, she thought again. If Fisher had stayed in town, or visited more often than during his occasional breaks between tours of duty, she would not have been able to keep her secret for so long.

It made her wonder why the other Yates men hadn't seen the resemblance, or if they had, why they hadn't said anything?

With such thoughts dragging at her, she returned to bed only to find sleep was impossible.

Grabbing her romance novel from her nightstand, she read, knowing it would give her the happily-ever-after that she seemed unable to find in her own life.

Fisher sat before the fireplace in his father's home, staring at the pile of logs ready to be lit when fall came and brought with it the cooler weather.

He had been tempted to light the fire tonight to chase away the chill from the jog he had decided to take earlier that evening. That chill had registered in his thirty-seven-year-old bones, he told himself, but the annoying voice in his head chastised him. Warned him that what he was feeling was something else.

Guilt, maybe?

The hurt look on Macy's face that morning had chased him throughout the day, especially when despite that hurt, she had wished him to stay safe.

Safe. A funny word.

For the eighteen years he had been in the military, he had regularly kept himself and his men safe. Not that there hadn't been injuries or times when he had thought he'd never see home again. But through it all he'd kept his head and made sure each and every man had come home alive.

Coming home being so important except…

He didn't feel safe here.

Being near Macy reminded him of all that his home lacked. Hell, it wasn't even his home, but his dad's, he thought, glancing around at the place where he had grown up and to where he returned after each tour of duty was over.

He rose from the couch and to the breakfast bar that separated the living room from the kitchen. A single bottle of bourbon sat on the bar and he poured himself a finger's worth of the alcohol and returned to sit before the fireplace.

After a bracing sip of the bourbon, he winced and considered what it would be like to have his own home. Wondered what it would be like to have someone like Macy to come home to. Not that Macy would be interested because she hadn't been interested eighteen years earlier.

Not to mention there was T.J. to consider.

As he had seen Macy and her son leave the police station the night before, he had thought, much as his brother and father had said, that what the boy needed was a strong man in his life to help set things straight.

He chuckled as amusement set in because he had no doubt that the headstrong and independent Macy would tan his hide for such a chauvinistic thought. Not to mention that it was ridiculous to consider that he might be that man. He wasn't the kind to settle down into the whole home and hearth thing.

Of course, his brother Jericho hadn't seemed like that kind of man either. He took another sip of the liquor, leaned his head back onto the couch cushions and considered his surprise at how happy his brother had looked marrying Olivia.

That look had confirmed to him that maybe his brother was the marrying type, but also that his brother's plan to wed Macy had been totally wrong from the outset. For starters, you didn't marry out of obligation and you sure shouldn't plan on having a platonic relationship with your wife.

A bit of anger built inside of him at both his brother and Macy at that thought. Macy for relying on her friendship to even consider the marriage and at his brother for agreeing to it, especially since he couldn't imagine lying next to Macy in bed and having it stay platonic.

His gut tightened at the thought of his kid brother making love to the only woman who had ever managed to break her way into his heart.

Since his mom had left, he hadn't had much faith in women and had sealed shut his heart…until Macy had somehow slipped through a crack.

Of course, after her abandonment, he had walled off his heart from hurt once again, but the memory of her had stayed locked behind those barriers. And now with her involvement with Jericho, it had roused all those old memories.

Slugging back the last dregs of the bourbon, he rose from the sofa, went to the kitchen and washed the glass. Slipped it into the dish drain sitting there holding an odd assortment of china and cutlery.

A single man's mix of mismatched items, he thought.

A woman would have made sure all the cutlery and plates were the same and that something wouldn't be sitting in the dish drain for days. It would be washed, dried and put away in anticipation of the next family meal.

Like when Macy and T.J. sat down to their next meal, he thought, but couldn't picture himself there beside them. She and T.J. had too many issues and it would be best for him to lay low until Jericho came home.

Once his brother returned, he would be back on his way to the Army, although he hadn't decided whether it would be to another tour of duty in the Middle East or the instructor's position at West Point.

The former was familiar, but he understood the importance of the latter. Even acknowledged how it could be a new adventure for him. A different mission.

Teaching up and coming officers was as significant as being out in the field with his men. After all, the nation needed excellent military men to lead and his many years of experience could help those cadets become better officers and save lives.

But as Fisher walked to his bedroom—the same one in which he'd slept as a child—he wondered if he would grow bored with living in one place and having the same basic daily routine. For nearly eighteen years he'd avoided that and he couldn't imagine changing now unless…

It would take something really special for that kind of change, he realized as he stared at his cold and lonely single bed.

Fisher drove from his mind the picture of Macy waiting for him in that bed because he feared that maybe Macy could be that something really special to change his life.

As he undressed and slipped beneath the chilly sheets, he reminded himself that Macy needed more than a man in her life. Her son needed a father figure and once again it occurred to him that he wasn't the right man for that job.

But as he drifted off to sleep, visions of her seeped into his dreams, reminding him of just how much he was missing in life.

Chapter 9

Macy awoke tired and grumpy. Her night's sleep—or lack of—had been dominated by thoughts of both Fisher and T.J.

None of her deliberations had been good, she thought as she and T.J. drove to the ranch. But then blushed as she remembered her dreams of making love with Fisher.

Of course, any pleasure had been wiped out by her son's surly mood. That morning he had complained about how hard he and Joe had worked the day before until she had pointedly reminded him of how much it had cost for the speeding ticket and repairs.

His cold silence had replaced the complaints during the short ride to the ranch.

When they entered the house to share breakfast with the others, he became slightly more animated, taking a spot by Joe and Sara and striking up a conversation with them.

She watched their camaraderie and was more convinced than ever that Sara had something to do with the speeding and accident.

Her intuition was confirmed when she sat with Ana and Jewel and her boss leaned over and said, "Some of the kids mentioned that they thought Sara wasn't home when the Sheriff phoned about the accident."

"She was with the boys?" Ana asked softly, keeping her tone low so that the conversation would remain with them.

"I thought so. Boys, cars and girls just seem to create problems when you mix them together," Jewel replied and took a sip of her coffee.

Macy ran a finger along the rim of her cup as she considered Jewel's words, so similar to the thoughts she'd had herself. T.J. had been working hard on restoring the muscle car and quite proud of not only the vehicle's looks, but the power beneath the hood. And even though she had thought that, she also sensed there was more to it.

Meeting her boss's gaze, she said, "That may be true, but I would feel a lot more comfortable if we knew more about Sara. About why she's here and why all three of them would be lying about her being with them that night."

Jewel paused with her mug in midair, then slowly lowered it to the table. "You know the Hopechest policy. We offer refuge without qualification. Without making any demands that our residents reveal anything."

She was well aware of the Hopechest policy. They had taken in each of the children and even Ana without question.

She nodded and said nothing else of it as they finished breakfast, instead turning to a discussion of what Jewel wanted them to do that day with the children. As she had done the day before, her boss piled on a load of chores for the two boys and after breakfast, they all went their separate ways.

Despite the work assigned to them, she noticed that the two boys managed to spend their free time with Sara. At the midday lunch break and then again during the afternoon rides at the corral, T.J. and Joe were engaged with Sara, their heads bent together in discussion.

She had hoped to speak to T.J. about it on their way home, but he was exhausted and irritated once again, not to mention smelly from mucking out the mare's stall. Wrinkling her nose, she said, "Please shower while I make dinner."

He yanked one iPod earpiece out and angry music blared from it as he faced her. "What if I'm not hungry?"

Considering how hard he had been working, she couldn't imagine him not needing to refuel his growing body, but she wouldn't get into a war of words with him.

"Then I'll eat alone."

His mouth flopped up and down like that of one of the sunfish they used to pull out of the small pond behind the high school, but he said nothing else.

He did shower as she had asked and met her at the dinner table where he silently shoveled in the burger and fries she had made. He even deigned to sit with her for a slice of a home-baked apple pie, à la mode of course.

But after that, he excused himself, saying that he was tired and planned on going to bed early.

She didn't argue with him, recognizing that the space might help him get over his pique.

After he left the kitchen, she turned on the small television tucked into a corner cabinet and took her time cleaning up. Washing the pans and dishes by hand, slowly and methodically since she found the simple work relieved her mind of thinking of more complex things.

It was barely eight when she finished, went up the stairs and passed by the door of T.J.'s room. His door was ajar and she peered within. As her son had said, he was in bed and asleep.

Relieved at the momentary peace that his slumber brought, she retired to her room where she changed into her pajamas, slipped beneath the covers and grabbed her book, intending to finish it.

A few hours passed and she was near the end of the novel when she thought she heard a noise.

T.J.? she wondered and eased from her bed to check on him.

He was still tucked safely in bed and she returned to her own, finished off the last few pages, smiling at the ending.

It was with those happy thoughts that she turned off her light and lay down to sleep.

She drifted off in that blissful state, her mind turning to thoughts of happier times. With T.J. and her husband Tim before the cancer had robbed him of life. With Fisher on the one night that had forever changed her destiny.

Her memories muddled together in dreams, becoming ones of her, Fisher and T.J. together until the phone rang beside her, rudely pulling her from her dreams.

Barely awake, she grabbed the phone, raking her sleep-tousled hair away from her face as she realized that it was barely six in the morning.

No good news at such an hour.

"Macy?"

It was Jewel on the line and she came instantly awake.

"What's wrong, Jewel?"

"Sara's missing."

* * *

The police combed every inch of the ranch house looking for clues as to Sara's disappearance.

They questioned everyone on the ranch, including T.J. and Joe who unfortunately, had little to offer as to Sara's possible whereabouts or why she would run away from the ranch.

When the police had left, Jewel and she had questioned the two teens once again, but they had little information to offer. Sadly, she knew as did Jewel that the two boys were being evasive. Despite that, hope remained within her that T.J. was not involved. He had eaten dinner with her and gone to bed early. She had seen him in his bed last night not just once, but twice.

Twice because she had heard something, she thought.

As she watched T.J. and Joe during the afternoon break, she wondered what it was that she had heard. If there had been more to it that she hadn't realized.

Her worst fears were confirmed when Deputy Rawlings returned to the ranch shortly after four.

As he walked toward the corral where they were offering the children rides on Papa's Poppy, she understood it was no social visit and so did the children. They stopped what they were doing and huddled together by the split rail fence. In the corral, T.J. and Joe helped the one child down from the horse and then also stood there, clearly anxious.

Deputy Rawlings dipped his head as she and Jewel approached him and removed his hat. "Miss Jewel. Miss Macy."

"Do you have news, Adam?" she asked, striving for a friendly tone.

He looked down for a moment, seemingly ashamed before he lifted his face and looked at her directly. "We started asking some of the Hopechest's neighbors if they had seen anything."

He continued with his report, his tone hesitant. "About a half mile up the road, one of the neighbors heard a car door slam. It was late so she looked out the window to see who it was."

A cold chill filled her as he motioned to T.J. and Joe with his hat. "She saw a young girl getting into a car with a dented front fender. From her description of the girl it seemed like it could be Sara. When we showed her pictures of the boys, she picked T.J."

Jewel laid a hand on her shoulder and stepped closer in a show of support. "You don't think T.J. had anything to do with—"

"I'm afraid I'll have to take him into custody. Ask him a few questions and find out why one of your neighbors thinks that she saw him last night with Sara."

"Can't you just question him here?" she said and he shook his head.

"There's procedures to follow and—"

"Jericho wouldn't do this," she insisted.

A strong flush of color filled his cheeks and a muscle ticked along his jaw. "Sheriff Yates isn't here and he left me in charge. There's procedures I have to follow, Mrs. Ward."

Without waiting for her, he once again motioned to the boys and called out, "T.J. I need you to come with me, son."

Her stomach clenched as she waited, hoping that he would be obedient. That he wouldn't give the deputy anything else to use as ammunition against him.

Blessedly, he did just what Deputy Rawlings asked.

With a worried look that he shot at Joe, who clapped him on the back, T.J. turned the reins of the horse over to his friend and walked to the edge of the corral. Easing beneath one of the rails of the fence, he approached the officer and said, "I haven't done anything wrong."

But she realized that with those words, he also wasn't denying any involvement with Sara's disappearance.

"Thank you for cooperating, son."

"I'm not your son," T.J. said with gritted teeth.

Deputy Rawlings nodded, laid a hand on T.J.'s shoulder and walked him around the side of the house toward the driveway.

Macy glanced at Jewel out of the corner of her eye and said, "I need to follow them into town. Find out what Adam plans to do."

Jewel squeezed her shoulder reassuringly. "I'll go with—"

"No, you stay here. The kids will need you to talk about this and so will Joe," she immediately said, appreciating Jewel's offer. The children were clearly upset by what was happening which was understandable. Some of them may have had run-ins with the law or been disappointed with the systems put in place to protect them. They would need Jewel's reassurance about what was happening.

"I'll call you as soon as I know anything more," she added and without waiting, rushed after T.J. and the police officer.

As she caught up to them, Deputy Rawlings eased T.J. into the backseat of the cruiser, then he took the wheel.

Macy quickly got settled in her own car and followed a safe distance behind the cruiser. She followed it into the parking lot for the police station and got out of her car, but as she headed toward the door, Deputy Rawlings stopped and faced her.

"It might be best for you to go get a coffee while T.J. and I talk."

She thought about her son being interrogated by the officer. She didn't like the thought of it, but she also didn't want to anger the deputy. Taking a deep breath, she looked away and realized Fisher and his dad were across the street in front of Miss Sue's.

They watched intently, clearly aware that something was up. A condemning look immediately came to Fisher's face, but Buck's features were more supportive. A second later, the older man took a step toward them and after some initial hesitation, Fisher followed his dad.

Shaking her head, she returned her attention to the police officer and decided to voice her concerns. "I'm not sure it's such a good idea that T.J. speak to you alone."

Chapter 10

Deputy Rawlings' lips tightened into an ascetic line as he ripped off his hat, frustration and anger evident in every brusque movement. "Why do you want to make this difficult? I'm not taking T.J. into custody. I just want to ask him a few simple questions."

"Is there a problem, Macy?" Buck Yates asked as he stood beside her.

She glanced up at Buck, avoiding Fisher when he took a spot just to the right of his dad. "One of the teens has gone missing from the ranch and Deputy Rawlings wants to speak to T.J. about it."

Buck nodded and pushed his hat back, adopting a stance that was more casual than that of the officer. "I'm sure the deputy understands how troubling this is for both you and T.J. That he needs to handle this carefully. Right, Deputy?"

A muscle clenched along the officer's jaw, but he nodded slowly. "Certainly, Buck. I know how to deal with this."

"Good. How about you join Fisher and me for dinner, Macy? Give the deputy and T.J. some time just to chat."

Protest gathered within her, ready to erupt, but Buck slipped his arm around her shoulders and hugged her so she kept her tongue. When the deputy took her son away, she forced a weak smile at the older man.

"Thank you for the invite, Buck, but I'm not sure I could eat a thing right now."

"I won't take no for an answer," he said and applied gentle pressure to turn her around. He guided her in the direction of Miss Sue's, Fisher quietly following behind them.

Inside the restaurant they were quickly seated at a booth. Buck took the one bench and sat in the middle, giving her no option but to slide along the vinyl of the other booth bench until Fisher could sit beside her.

The waitress came over and handed them menus.

She had intended not to take one, lacking any appetite, but Buck's half-lidded look brooked no disagreement.

After a short perusal of the menu, she ordered a soup and a half of a fresh roasted turkey sandwich, earning a satisfied nod from the older man.

Neither Fisher nor he seemed to have any problem with their appetites since they ordered the blue plate specials, which included not only the soup of the day, but chicken-fried steak with white gravy, squash and cheese casserole, green beans and a choice of dessert.

After taking their orders, the waitress brought over tall glasses of iced tea, a dish of summer slaw and a basket heaped with warm corn bread and sweet cream butter.

The enticing smell of the corn bread made her stomach growl. She placed a hand above her belly, but Fisher picked up the basket and offered it to her. "Would you like some?"

She smiled and thanked him. After buttering the corn bread, she took a bite and sighed as the dulcet flavors of the corn and butter filled her mouth.

"This is good," she said, but then quickly added, "but not as good as that jalapeño corn bread you used to make for us when we were kids, Buck."

"That was really tasty with your five alarm chili, Pa," Fisher said, but then stuffed a big piece of buttered corn bread in his mouth.

Buck laughed and forked some of the summer slaw onto his bread dish. "The four of you could sure eat," he said with a chuckle.

Fisher nodded, recalling the many nights that Macy and Tim had joined his family for a meal. "Those were good times."

"Yes, they were," Macy said. A sad sigh followed, however.

"It'll be okay, darlin'. Don't worry about T.J.," Buck offered, but Macy dipped her head down until her chin was nearly burrowing a hole in her chest.

Upset by her dismay, Fisher reached beneath the table and laid his hand over hers. "It will be okay," he also reassured.

With a long inhale and a sniffle, Macy nodded. "Yes, it will be okay. I'll make it okay."

He had no doubt of her sincerity, but worried about whether she could make good on it. T.J. seemed to be bringing her nothing but trouble and possibly the boy needed a man's influence in his life. A man who would be there for him.

When the waitress brought their meals, he withdrew his

hand from hers and they all dug into their dinners, hunger bringing a long stretch of quiet to the table.

Macy finished her meal quickly, but he and his dad had quite a lot to eat. While he ate, he offered Macy a small piece of his steak and she tried it, murmured her approval. Slowly he and his father finished their meals and by the time dessert came, they convinced Macy to get some peach cobbler.

When they were finally finished, Macy offered to pay to thank them for their company, but his father insisted it was their treat and that they should do it more often.

"I'd like that, Buck," she said.

Then something inside of him—something Fisher didn't understand and didn't want to acknowledge—had him saying, "I'll go with you to the sheriff's office."

Her mouth opened as she prepared to refuse him, but then she abruptly snapped it shut. "I'd appreciate that," she said instead.

In front of the restaurant she hugged Buck and thanked him again before the two of them silently walked side by side to the sheriff's office.

Inside the police station, one of the other deputies manned the front desk. As he realized who had entered, he sheepishly glanced down at the papers on his desk, but Fisher wasn't about to be dissuaded.

"You know me better than that, Bill. Where's Deputy Rawlings?"

Bill shuffled the papers into order before addressing them. "Deputy Rawlings is still with the suspect."

"The suspect?" Macy nearly croaked. "When did he become a suspect?"

Before the other man could answer, Deputy Rawlings stepped from one of the back rooms. He grimaced when he noticed them standing by the front desk, but swaggered over, his shoulders thrown back. Hands cocked on his hips.

"Macy. Fisher," he said with a curt nod.

"Evening, Adam. I came to see when I could take T.J. home," she said, bracing her hands along the edge of the front desk.

Adam looped his thumbs through his belt loops and swayed side to side on his feet for a moment. "I'm sorry, but I've decided to keep T.J. overnight while we continue our investigations."

The other deputy rose from the desk, wisely making himself absent for the discussion that would follow.

"Excuse me," Macy said, her voice rising with each syllable, prompting Fisher to reach over and place his hand on her shoulder to try to calm her.

"We need to be sure there's no foul play," the deputy said and beneath his hand, the tension escalated in Macy's body.

"Come on now, Adam. There's no reason—"

"A young girl is missing. We have a witness who claims to have seen your son with her on the night she disappeared."

Macy inched up on her toes, ready to erupt, but he applied gentle pressure to keep her in control. Macy didn't normally have a temper, but when it involved her family, he didn't doubt that she would tenaciously defend her son.

"You know Jericho wouldn't do this," she urged and he had no doubt about that. Jericho would not be handling this situation as badly as Deputy Rawlings, but he could see that the man was not responding well to being challenged.

He opted for a different approach, hoping that he could calm the deputy until his brother returned in a day or two. "No one doubts your concerns, Deputy, but wouldn't it be possible to release T.J. into his mother's custody? I'm sure she can—"

"Handle him?" The deputy chuckled harshly and shook his

head. "Mrs. Ward hasn't done a very good job of controlling T.J. so far. Until we know that there's been no foul play, I'm going to hold him overnight. Maybe even longer."

Macy's body trembled beneath his hand, but she somehow kept her cool. "Please don't do this, Adam. I promise to bring T.J. back in the morning—"

"I don't think so," the deputy said and Fisher was about to jump in and offer his assurances, but bit the words back. He knew little about T.J. other than that both his brother and dad believed he was good, but confused. Worse yet, he knew nothing about how to deal with the boy and even if he did…

He would be gone in another couple of weeks.

Becoming involved in their lives not only made little sense, it would be cruel since he could promise nothing of permanence. But he needed to help Macy now.

"Let's go, Macy. We'll come back in the morning."

Macy shot a worried look at him and while glancing her way, he said, "The deputy knows what he needs to do. He'll take good care of T.J."

He faced the other man and left no doubt about his words. "You will take good care, right?"

Adam stalked the remaining distance to the front desk and leaned over the barrier toward him. "That's not a threat, is it?"

"Just a reminder," he said, dipped his head and smiled, making sure that the other man understood it was a promise of what might happen if T.J. wasn't cared for. Then he urged Macy back from the desk. "We'll see you bright and early, Adam. Have a nice night."

Slipping his arm completely around Macy's shoulders, he steered her out the door of the station and onto the steps, where she shrugged off his touch and wrapped her arms around herself.

"Jericho wouldn't do this. He would know that T.J. could never hurt that girl," she said.

"But is T.J. involved in her disappearance?" Fisher asked, but as Macy's face paled at his words, he cursed beneath his breath.

"I'm sorry," he said and took her into his arms.

She was tense at first, but then she slowly relaxed and embraced him. Laying the side of her face on his chest, she said, "Thank you. I was a little tired of going it alone."

He suspected that up until her cockamamie idea to marry Jericho, she had been going it alone ever since Tim's death nearly six years earlier.

As she raised her face and her brown eyes, shimmering with unshed tears met his, he wanted to tell her that she didn't need to go it alone anymore. That he would be there for her, but he couldn't. But he also couldn't resist the pull of that emotional gaze or the desire to soothe the spot on her lower lip that she was worrying with her teeth.

He bent his head as she rose up on tiptoe. Licked the abused spot on her lower lip before covering her mouth with his.

She pressed into him, cupping the back of his head with her hand and he dug his fingers into the silky lushness of her shoulder-length brown hair.

When she opened her mouth to his, he pressed on, sliding his tongue along the perfect edge of her teeth before dancing it against her tongue. He wrapped his one arm beneath her buttocks and brought her full against him and with that dangerous full body contact, sanity returned.

They pulled apart abruptly, both of them breathing hard and obviously shocked by the intensity of the emotion they had unleashed with one simple embrace.

"Macy, I'm—"

She raised her hands to stop him. "Please don't say you're sorry because I'm not. There's no need for apologies or regrets. All I want to say is thank you for being here for me."

He dragged a hand through the short-cropped strands of his hair and held back on telling her what he wanted—that he wanted her again. Wanted her next to him. Wanted her lips beneath his, opening to his invasion. Inviting him to take it further.

Instead, he took a deep breath and stuffed the tips of his fingers into the pockets of his snug jeans to keep from reaching for her again.

"You're welcome. I'll see you home."

She wrapped her arms around herself once more and shook her head roughly, sending her hair into movement with the action. "You don't need to do that—"

"I do. Until Jericho is home, I want to make sure you're okay."

She looked away then, but he couldn't fail to see the tear as it slipped down her face and she said, "I understand, Fisher. I won't mistake what just happened for anything else."

He longed to take her into his arms and shake her until she did understand, only he wasn't sure he knew why they were both standing there, trembling with desire. Hungry for another taste, but fighting it.

Because of that confusion, he said, "How about I just watch you walk to your car. If you need me in the morning—"

"I'll call," she said, but as she walked away, he understood that she wouldn't.

Chapter 11

Macy spent the night tossing and turning, worried not only about T.J., but about the kiss that shouldn't have happened. The kiss that had rocked her world, reminding her how Fisher continued to move her. That she was still immensely attracted to him.

But she wouldn't call him.

Her life was complicated enough without adding Fisher to the mix. But the little voice in her head kept buzzing in warning. Guilting her that Fisher should know T.J. was his son. Urging her to explore the emotions he roused.

She ignored that stubborn buzz and focused on what she had to do that morning.

Rising early, she made herself some coffee, but was too nervous to eat. After showering, she phoned Jewel and asked for the day off so she could head to the sheriff's office to deal with Deputy Rawlings and T.J.

Sympathetic and supportive, her boss offered to meet her there to help in whatever way she could, but Macy couldn't accept it. She needed to deal with her problems on her own, much as she had since Tim's death.

With that focus, she rushed to the sheriff's office in the hopes of securing T.J.'s release.

Bill was at the front desk again, looking as uncomfortable as he had the night before.

"Good morning, Macy," he said, rose and held up his coffee mug. "Can I get you a cup?"

"Will I be here long enough to need one?" she said with a forced smile.

"I hope not. Let me go get Deputy Rawlings." He walked away, cup in hand, and to one of the offices, where he knocked.

Someone ripped the door open and Bill jumped back.

Deputy Rawlings stepped out from the office. As he realized she was there, he tempered his attitude. He walked to the front desk and swung open the waist-high door in invitation.

"Why don't you join me in my office?" he said and held his hand out.

"Can I take T.J. home now?" she asked as she passed by him and walked toward his office.

"Let's discuss this in private," the deputy replied, his tone obviously annoyed.

She wondered why they needed privacy much like she was still questioning why it had been necessary to keep T.J. overnight. She guarded her tongue since it would not accomplish anything if she lost her cool.

In his office, she sat before his desk and kept quiet, waiting for him to set the tone of the discussion.

He leaned back in his chair and laced his fingers together

on his flat stomach. "I spoke to T.J. at length yesterday. He clearly knows more about Sara's disappearance than he's saying, Macy."

"Sara and he are friends, Adam. He wouldn't do anything to hurt her. If anything, he's probably trying to protect her."

"I don't doubt that. In fact, our investigations so far seem to indicate that there isn't any foul play." He shot forward in the chair, opened a file on his desk and quickly moved some papers around.

"At least a week ago, Sara may have been at a local honky tonk about ten miles from here—the Amarillo Rose. One of the bartenders remembers a young girl being there and getting into a truck with someone."

She shifted to the edge of her seat and said, "So it's possible she's gone off with the same person again?"

The deputy shook his head and chuckled harshly. "Could be, although I'd put my money on T.J. But there's nothing so far that says she didn't go willingly or that any harm has come to her. Because of that, I'm going to let T.J. go—"

"Thank you," she said and popped up out of her chair, eager to go get her son.

Deputy Rawlings picked up his hands and waved for her to sit back down. "Easy now, Macy. Don't be in a rush because even though I'm letting T.J. go now, you need to keep an eye on him. Make sure that if he knows anything about Sara, he lets us know before something bad does happen."

As angry as she was at the deputy's heavy-handed tactics, she couldn't argue with what he was asking. "If I find out anything, you'll be the first to know."

"Good to hear. I'll go get T.J. Why don't you meet us out front?"

Dismissed, she rose and headed to where Bill sat at the desk, sipping his coffee. As she approached, he said, "So you're taking T.J.?"

"I am," she answered, grasping the handles of her purse before her.

The sound of metal grating against metal snagged her attention—the jail cell opening. A second later, her son popped out, looking tired and haggard. As he saw her waiting for him, however, a smile quickly flashed across his face before he controlled it. He walked toward her slowly, hesitant, but when he stood before her, she reached out and hugged him hard. His body relaxed and he returned the embrace.

"We're going home, T.J."

She stepped away, but kept one arm around his shoulders, reluctant to lose contact with her son.

He didn't battle her but kept close to her side as they walked out the door of the sheriff's station.

She shot her son a sidelong glance. Relief washed over her as he met her gaze and another timid smile blossomed on his face. Everything would be okay, she thought until she nearly walked into the man standing before them on the steps of the sheriff's station.

Fisher.

In wickedly tight blue jeans, a chambray shirt that hugged his lean chest and abs, and a black Stetson that made his green eyes pop brightly in the morning sun.

"Fisher," she said out loud, a little more breathlessly than she liked.

"What are you doing here?" T.J. said and came to stand before her, placing himself between her and Fisher in an obviously protective gesture.

She placed her hand on T.J.'s shoulder and urged him back to her side. "Fisher and his dad were nice enough to keep me company last night. We had dinner together at Miss Sue's while I waited to see if Deputy Rawlings would let you go home."

T.J.'s mouth quirked with displeasure before he mustered some politeness. "Thank you for taking care of my mom."

Fisher seemed taken aback by the unexpected gratitude, but quickly recovered. "My pleasure. I'm sure Jericho would have done the same if he were here."

Disappointment stung her ego followed by confusion at the disappointment. Snagging her keys from her purse, she handed them to T.J. and pointed to where her car was parked across the street.

"Fisher and I need a moment alone. Why don't you go wait by the car for me?"

T.J. nodded, but before he left, he chanced an assessing look at Fisher. Then he did as she had asked, walking down the steps of the sheriff's office and to the corner, where he waited for the light to change so he could cross.

Macy shifted her attention to Fisher. "What are you doing here?"

He shrugged, looked away and dragged off his hat, bouncing it back and forth in his hands. With his head hanging down, he said, "I wish I knew."

She wished she knew as well and was about to press him for another answer when the squeal of tires rent the air. Loud, harsh and angry.

Both she and Fisher whirled toward the sound in time to see a large black sedan lurch wildly toward T.J. as he was crossing the street. Smoke came off one of the tires as the car burned rubber with the driver's haste to pick up speed.

"T.J.," they both shouted in unison and sprinted toward him, intent on getting him out of the path of the oncoming car.

He had noticed the car as well, but for a moment he stood there, stunned as the vehicle accelerated toward him. Then in a blur, he raced for the side of the street, trying to avoid the sedan which made no attempt to avert hitting him. If anything, it picked up speed, veering toward where T.J. had run to escape.

At the last minute, her son sidestepped the car like a matador might a bull as the vehicle traveled past him, but it still struck him a glancing blow. He flew into the air and against one of the parked cars as the sedan hurtled down the road, its engine racing as it continued to pick up speed.

She and Fisher rushed to where T.J. lay sprawled in the street as did a number of other pedestrians who had witnessed the accident.

When they reached his side, T.J. was attempting to rise, but Fisher laid a gentle hand on his shoulder. "Stay down, son. You could have some broken bones."

T.J. didn't argue, clearly dazed. A large gash on his temple bled profusely and he had a number of other cuts and scrapes along his face and arms.

Her hands shook as she passed a hand along T.J.'s forehead. As she glanced up the block, she noticed the flashing lights of an approaching ambulance and it filled her with relief. "Take it easy. Help will be here soon."

T.J. nodded, but even that small action seemed to hurt. He closed his eyes and lay there quietly, his face pale, frightening her.

Fisher sensed her fear. He placed his hand at the nape of her neck to steady her and said, "Don't worry. He'll be fine."

She sucked in a shaky scared breath and it rocked him all

the way to his gut. He wanted to make her feel better, but he was failing miserably.

Luckily, the EMTs arrived a second later and urged them both to move away.

He kept his contact with her as she stood there, arms wrapped around her waist. Her body tight with anxiety as they waited for some kind of word from the paramedics.

The young man finally looked up at them over his shoulder. "Nothing serious from what I can see, but we'll take him to the hospital just to confirm that."

The EMT quickly had the rest of his crew getting T.J. ready for transport. At the periphery of his vision, he noticed that Deputy Rawlings and one other officer were talking to the crowd, getting witness statements, he assumed. He wondered if anyone had gotten the license plate number. He had been too rattled to think about it, which shocked him. He was a man of action and trained to stay in control in stressful situations.

That he had lost that control scared him more than he wanted to admit.

But despite that, he knew he had to be in charge now for Macy and her son.

As the paramedics finished getting T.J. on a gurney, he took command. "Can his mother go with him in the ambulance?"

The EMT nodded. "Yes, but there's only room for your wife, sir."

"I'll follow in the car, Macy," he said and she nodded, murmured a strained, "Thanks."

He stood by her until T.J. was loaded into the ambulance and then he helped her climb up into the back. One of the paramedics came by and closed the door of the ambulance, leaving him standing there awkwardly until the sirens kicked in, reminding him he had something to do.

He had to follow them to the hospital and be there for them.

He had to do that, but not because it was what Jericho would have done.

He had to do it because his heart told him it was the right thing to do.

Chapter 12

Macy held T.J.'s hand as the paramedic placed a temporary bandage on the cut along his temple. When he was done, he strapped T.J.'s head in place to keep it from moving during the drive.

Apparently comfortable that T.J. didn't have any major injuries, the paramedic slipped into the seat beside the driver and left them alone in the back of the ambulance.

"How are you feeling?" she asked.

"A little sore, but I'll be okay," he said and squeezed her hand.

Macy thought back to the moment when she had heard the squeal of the tires and the car hurtled forward toward T.J. The fear of that moment fled, replaced by questions.

"I didn't recognize the car, did you?" Esperanza was a small town and almost everyone knew what kind of car everyone else drove.

"I didn't," her son replied, but something in his voice didn't ring true.

"Do you recollect anything about the car? The make or model? Did you see the face of the driver?"

"No, Ma. I was too busy trying not to get run over," he answered, the tone of his voice part annoyed but a greater part evasive.

"Are you sure—"

"I'm sure I was trying to get out of the way," he shot back and withdrew his hand from hers, bringing it to rest on his flat belly.

She focused on that hand, skinned along the knuckles. Drops of blood had congealed at various spots and there were more abrasions on his other hand. As she swept her gaze up and down his body, she noticed the angry road rash along one arm, from his elbow down to mid-forearm.

In her brain came the recollection of the low thud as the car caught him along one hip and he went flying, smacking into another car before falling to roll along the ground from the impact of the blow. A chill took hold in her center and she tried picturing the sedan again. Closed her eyes and attempted to remember what she could about the car, but it had all happened too fast.

The image of the vehicle was just a black blur as it sped toward T.J.

She was sure of that. The car had intended to hit her son. She had no uncertainty about that which made her wonder why T.J. might be lying to protect someone who had tried to hurt him.

The ride to the nearby hospital was blessedly short and the emergency room relatively empty. It didn't take long for them to examine T.J. and determine that there were no broken bones or a concussion. Although he would be bruised in a number of spots, especially along the one leg where the car had clipped him, there was no reason for the doctors to admit him.

Macy sighed with relief as the doctor made that pronouncement and finished sealing the cut on T.J.'s head with some butterfly bandages before taping a gauze pad over the wound. Another large bandage covered the road rash that they had cleaned while yet more gauze was wrapped around the knuckles on both hands.

As T.J. noticed her examining his various injuries, he barked out a short laugh and said, "You should see the other guy."

She chuckled and embraced him as he sat on the edge of the bed. "I was so scared."

"I'm okay, Mom. Really."

When she stepped away, he eased from the bed to stand upright, wincing as he put pressure on the leg which had taken the brunt of the hit from the car. It took him a moment to fully straighten and his first step was a little gimpy until he seemed to stretch out a kink.

With her arm around his shoulders, they walked out into the emergency room waiting area.

Fisher sat there, bouncing his black hat in his hand. He shot up out of the chair when he saw them and approached. Grimacing as he noted the bandages on T.J., he forced a smile and said, "I hope the other guy looks worse."

To her surprise, T.J. grinned and nodded. "He does."

Fisher motioned to the exit. "I brought your car from town. I'll go get it and drive you home."

The accident had rattled her nerves and having Fisher drive them would be a welcome respite. Concern remained about why someone would try to hurt T.J. and why he would cover up the fact that he might know who was responsible. As she and T.J. followed Fisher out of the hospital, she realized that she needed to tell someone about what was up with T.J. Needed to confide in someone who could help her deal with the problem.

As she watched Fisher pull up to the curb and saw how carefully he handled getting a sore T.J. into the car, she realized that Fisher might just be the someone she needed.

At seventeen, T.J. wouldn't have normally needed her to get him settled in bed, but he was aching enough now to require her assistance. She helped him take off his jeans. Managed to control her reaction at the sight of the large bruise which had already formed along his hip and thigh in addition to the smaller purpling marks along his other leg and ribs.

"Get some rest," she urged as she tucked him beneath the covers.

He nodded and closed his eyes, obviously drained by the events of the day.

She walked into the hall and left his door open, wanting to be able to hear him if he needed anything. She began to walk down the stairs, but paused a few steps down, peering through the open doorway of his room just to check on him again.

He seemed to be asleep already.

She breathed a sigh of relief that his injuries had been so minimal and finished her walk down the stairs. At the landing, she proceeded a few more steps and then turned into the kitchen.

Fisher stood at the counter by the coffee machine, pouring water into it. He slipped in a filter and then the coffee. Hit the button to get it going.

His actions were so domestic that it seemed incongruous

until she remembered how often she had seen Jericho do the same thing both in her home and his. They had grown up in a household full of men and such routine activities would likely be almost second nature to them.

She allowed herself the pleasure of watching him finish up the task, his movements sure and totally comfortable. Totally masculine. When he finished, he turned and realized she was standing there.

Fisher leaned back against the counter while he examined Macy. She appeared in control and he admired her strength in the midst of yet another crisis. Her strength being one of the things that had always attracted him.

"How's he doing?"

"Tired and sore. He's already fast asleep," she said and went to the small island in the middle of the kitchen, bent and retrieved two mugs and a sugar bowl which she placed on top of the island counter.

"And you?" he asked, raising one brow to emphasize the question.

She braced her hands on the edge of the counter, suddenly uneasy it seemed to him. She took a deep breath, held it before releasing it in a rush. Then she met his gaze directly and said, "I need your help."

"Just what kind of help?" he asked and from the corner of his eye he noticed that the pot of coffee was almost done. He took it from the machine, walked over and poured them both a cup of coffee.

She picked up the mug, her hands slightly shaky. She blew on the coffee and took a sip before placing the mug down. Bracing her hands on the counter once again, she looked away and said, "I think T.J. knows who was driving the car that hit him, but he's not admitting it. Normally I would have asked Jericho—"

"I'm not standing in for my brother, Macy. I'm not Jericho."

Her head whipped up and she nailed him with her gaze. "You're right that you're nothing like your brother. But you can't refuse to help."

He snorted and shifted his brow ever higher. "Really? Please tell me why I can't refuse."

No sign of emotion or distress marked her face as she said, "Because T.J. is your son."

Chapter 13

Sucker-punched.

That was the only way to describe how he was feeling.

She had sucker-punched him years ago with her first kiss and then again the night they'd made love.

Now she had done it again.

"Excuse me?" He came round the corner of the island until he stood directly beside her. She had looked away immediately after her pronouncement. Now he grasped her arms and applied gentle pressure to turn her in his direction. Placing his thumb and forefinger beneath her chin, he angled her face upward so that she couldn't continue to avoid him.

"T.J. is my son? My flesh and blood?" His tone was deliberately calm, displaying nothing of the maelstrom of emotions churning through his gut.

"The one night that you and I—"

"We used protection," he reminded her and she nodded, bit her lower lip as he had seen her do so often when she was upset.

"We did, but it must not have worked. I found out I was pregnant right before I was supposed to marry Tim—"

"And you didn't tell him?" he said and ripped away from her, pacing across the room with a ground-eating stride or two before facing her once again.

Her brown eyes sparkled with indignation at his attack. "I could never mislead someone like that," she said, but then pulled back, obviously acknowledging that she had misled him. That he had a right to be angry and he definitely was angry. Probably more furious than he'd ever been before—except possibly on the day that he had learned Macy had decided to marry Tim.

Sucking in a rough breath, he walked back toward her, but stopped when he was about a step away. He didn't trust himself to get any closer at that moment. Fisting his hands tightly, he kept them at his sides, struggling for control.

"Why didn't you tell me?"

She shrugged and looked down once again before lifting her face. Her eyes glimmered with tears as she said, "Jericho was going on and on about how happy you were to join the Army. How you were looking forward to seeing the world and leaving Esperanza behind."

"And you assumed—"

"I didn't want to stop you and…you never called me again and Tim… He was a good man. I knew he would be a good father." A tear finally leaked out and trailed down her face, but she did nothing to swipe it away.

Nor did he. Instead, he took the final step to bring him close and leaned down until they were nearly nose-to-nose. "*I'm* a good man—"

"I know you are. You're a real hero. One who's made a difference to so many other people. Saved lives. That wouldn't have happened if you had stayed here…with me," she said and reached up, cradled the side of his face.

Her tender touch nearly undid him, but he couldn't leave it at that. "Did you love me? When you walked down the aisle—"

"I loved Tim with all my heart."

He had thought he was over the pain of losing her to another man, but the ache deep in the center of him told him otherwise. Her words were creating as much hurt now as her actions had eighteen years earlier.

But he couldn't retaliate and wound her, even if he was in agony with her admission.

He also couldn't let her continue to hide behind her love for Saint Tim.

Cradling her cheeks with both hands, he finally wiped away the trail of tears on her face with his thumb. Stroked the soft skin of her cheek and bent that final inch so that his lips were close to hers. He whispered, "You wanted me then and you want me now."

Then he kissed her like there was no tomorrow because he knew there might not be. As honor-bound as he felt to help Macy now that he knew T.J. was his son, he was also sure that he was not cut out for family or civilian life.

There was just too much uncertainty unlike the orderly military life that had worked so well for him, he told himself even as he kept on kissing Macy. Opening his mouth against hers over and over until it wasn't enough and he finally slipped his tongue within to taste the sweetness of her breath.

She responded to him willingly, going up on tiptoe to

continue the kiss. Pressing against him until he needed more. He slipped his hands beneath her buttocks and lifted her until her backside was on the edge of the counter and her legs were straddling him.

Macy shivered as the hard jut of his erection brushed the center of her, awakening a rush of desire that dragged a moan from her.

The sound penetrated the fog of want that had wrapped itself around them, tempering their kisses. Creating a short lull during which she managed to murmur a soft, "I'm sorry. I should have told you about T.J."

The reminder of her deception stilled his actions and he lifted his lips from hers, but remained close, his hands tangled in her hair. His body intimately pressed against her.

"Macy, I wish that things could be different, only—"

"Ma, I'm hungry," they heard loud and clear from T.J.'s bedroom upstairs.

The typical teen moment shattered the emotional angst and lust that had overtaken them.

Fisher released a rough sigh and stepped away while she called up to her son, "I'll be up with something in a minute."

She slipped off the counter and gestured to the oak kitchen table. "Will you stay for lunch?"

He nodded, but quickly added, "Let me help you with it."

She sensed that the hero in him intended to help her with more than lunch, much like she had asked. As much as she appreciated that he would do so, she also hoped that she wasn't making a mistake that would not only break her heart, but hurt her son.

When she acquiesced to his request, she quickly pulled out a can of condensed tomato soup from one cabinet and handed it to him. "Can you make this while I put together some sandwiches?"

"Can do," he said and she headed to the fridge for the fixings for lunch. She had some leftover roast beef that she could slice up for sandwiches and as she prepared them, she kept half an eye on Fisher as he made the soup.

He went into the fridge and removed a bottle of salsa and some shredded cheddar cheese. After opening the can and adding the water, he proceeded to put in a few heaping spoonfuls of the salsa to the soup. As she plated the sandwiches, he poured the steaming hot soup into bowls and topped them off with some of the shredded cheese.

Grabbing a tray from beneath the island counter, she prepped T.J.'s lunch, added a glass of milk to the tray and took it up to him.

The short nap he had taken seemed to have made a difference. He appeared more alert and not as pale as before and so it was with a lighter heart that she went back to the kitchen.

Fisher had set the table, laid out the soup and sandwiches for each of them along with fresh mugs of coffee.

"Thank you," she said and offered him a tired smile as she sat down beside him.

"You may not be thanking me when this is all over," he said and picked up half of his roast beef sandwich.

"Why's that?"

Fisher thoughtfully chewed the bite of sandwich before responding with, "Because if I'm going to help you, I intend to make sure that T.J. is being totally upfront with you, me and the sheriff."

She paused to consider him as he resumed eating and realized that he was in his military mode, where there were rules that needed to be followed and the failure to do so had consequences. She had tried to follow the same basic principles in raising her son, but too often since Tim's death, she had cut T.J. slack about the consequences part. In retrospect, she had done so to try and soften his father's loss, but had Tim been alive, he wouldn't have put up with T.J.'s behavior.

Fisher wouldn't either and that might be a good thing. "I agree that we need to get to the bottom of why T.J. isn't telling us what he saw today."

Fisher paused with his soup-filled spoon in mid-air, clearly surprised by her agreement. When he realized she was on board with him, he said, "And what's actually up with the missing girl. Sara, right?"

"Sara Engeleit," she confirmed and finally took a spoonful of the soup. The salsa and cheese had transformed the simple soup and her stomach growled noisily in appreciation.

"It's delicious," she said and quickly ate another spoonful.

"A bachelor's got to know how to take care of himself," Fisher said, but knew he had made a mistake when Macy's eyes darkened with sadness. Despite that, he had no doubt that it made sense to remind her of what he was and what he would continue to be once he was done helping her.

"Tell me about Sara," he said in an attempt to draw her attention to something besides their confusing and basically non-existent relationship.

With a shrug, she said, "Not much to tell. She came to the ranch about a week and a half ago. Right before T.J. and Joe started working at the Hopechest."

"Do you know where she's from?" After he asked the question, he took a bite of his sandwich.

Macy likewise took a bite, rolled her eyes upward as if

trying to gather all that she knew about the girl before responding. "She's sixteen and from Dallas, we believe. When she arrived at the ranch, she had some bruises on her arms and hands, but she seems to be from a family that's fairly well-off judging from her clothes and behavior."

"What about your boss? Does she know anything more?"

"Yesterday morning Jewel mentioned hiring a private investigator since Sara was missing. She was supposed to get a name from Joe Colton, but I haven't talked to her since then."

"Maybe after lunch—"

"I'll call her," she said and after that, the two of them quickly finished up the last of their soup and sandwiches.

While Fisher cleared off the table and tackled the dishes, she phoned Jewel to fill her in on all that had happened, beginning with the hit-and-run incident with T.J.

"Is he okay?" her friend asked, her concern evident in the tones of her voice.

"Bruised and banged up a little, but nothing serious luckily."

A heavy sigh filled the line. "I'm not liking this, Macy. There's just too much going on for it all not to be related."

"I agree, but without any more info—"

"Actually, Joe Colton was able to provide me some information about the man he believes to be Sara's dad—Howard Engeleit," Jewel said and relief flooded through Macy that they might finally have something to go on.

"Mr. Colton knows him?"

"When I mentioned Sara's last name, it rang a bell with Joe. Apparently Howard Engeleit had once worked with him. He says he didn't care for the man and that they'd had a falling out. He left Joe's company some time ago," Jewel recounted.

"Does he know where Howard is now?" she asked as

Fisher finished washing the dishes and stood there, drying his hands on a towel as he listened.

"Howard started his own company and made a good chunk of money. He and Joe see each other occasionally. The last that he had heard, Howard was in the middle of a nasty divorce battle, but Joe couldn't recall whether or not Howard had any children."

Although the information wasn't yet complete, she was relieved that at least now they might have something more to go on in their search to discover what was going on with her son and Sara. "Thanks for all the info. Fisher and I—"

"Fisher and you? Are you a team now?" Jewel said teasingly, unaware of just how problematic being together with Fisher was for her.

"We're going to check into some things and keep you posted. If you find out anything else, could you call me?" she responded, steering clear of any further discussion of her and Fisher.

"I understand, Macy. When you're ready to discuss it…"

"I'll let you know. Talk to you later," she said and hung up.

Fisher had walked back to the table and now he stood there, hands braced along the top rung of one of the kitchen chairs.

"You've got something to go on," he said.

"Something, but we need a little more. Seems like there's one sure way of finding out more about Howard Engeleit," she said, picked up her hands and mimicked that she was typing.

"The Net is bound to turn up something. Where's your computer?"

Chapter 14

Their Internet search on Howard Engeleit immediately revealed hundreds of hits on the man.

As Macy skimmed through the various Web search results, it became apparent that Joe Colton wasn't kidding about Howard making himself money as a mover and shaker. There was account after account of Howard's business dealings, including some questionable ones. Much as Joe had said, Howard was in the midst of a difficult divorce but as luck would have it, the news articles mentioned a young daughter. Sara.

On one Dallas gossip page, there was even a picture of Howard, his wife Amanda and their daughter Sara. Howard's presence dominated the photo and Macy immediately got vibes from the submissive body posture of both his wife and daughter.

With Fisher sitting beside her and reading along, she gestured to the two women in the photo and pointed out how they seemed to be uneasy. "See their body posture and their eyes are downcast. Howard's clearly the one in control here."

Fisher nodded and agreed. "I've seen the same kind of body language on fresh recruits. He's definitely the one calling the shots."

"It may be more than that. Sara had bruises on her arms and hands when she first got to the ranch. If Howard was responsible, Sara might feel powerless to say anything about the abuse."

Fisher leaned back in his chair and rubbed his hand across his lips, thoughtful for a moment. "He's wealthy and connected, so who would believe her?"

She nodded emphatically. "Exactly. And if he's suing for custody of her—"

"He would have free rein to keep on abusing her." Fisher shook his head, sat up in the chair and clasped his hands together tightly. "It's sad that a father would do that to his child. That she feels there's no one there she can turn to."

"It's probably why she came to the ranch."

Fisher glanced up the stairs toward T.J.'s room. "Do you think he knows about the abuse? Is that why he's protecting her?"

She thought of T.J. and how much he was like the man who had raised him. Tim had been good-hearted and prone to helping others. But also, deep within her son were the genes from the man sitting beside her. A man of action. A hero. Combine the two and it was starting to make sense that T.J. was somehow involved with helping the young woman.

"I think that T.J. believes he's doing what's right for Sara, but the best thing would be to tell us what's happening so the authorities can handle this," she admitted.

He nodded, but then his gaze dropped down at his hands for a moment before he faced her. "There are times when a man has to make his own stand no matter what the rules say about what's right."

She heard him, but couldn't agree. Laying her hand on his tightly clasped ones, she said, "But he's not a man, Fisher. He's a boy. A scared and confused young boy."

Fisher eased his hands away from hers and pointed to the monitor. "You said that the deputy mentioned that Sara had been at a place up on the highway before she came to the ranch. We should print out that picture of her and check out that honky tonk. She might have run back there again."

She felt dismissed much as she suspected his men might feel when he gave them an order. She tried not to take it personally, telling herself that he was a man used to being in charge and making decisions.

But she was also used to being in control of her own life. Some might say she hadn't done a good job of it—heck, she even felt that way at times—but she had tried her best.

Her silence must have registered with him since he shifted his attention from the monitor and the prints he was making and back to her.

The strain on Macy's face was evident and Fisher struggled for a moment with a reason for it until it finally came. "Do you want to go that place on the highway or is there something else you think we should do?"

"I know you're used to taking control—"

"It's a hard habit to break," he freely admitted. In his life a delay in decision-making could cost someone their life, but he understood this wasn't the military.

"I didn't mean to order you around only...I feel like you and T.J. are my responsibility now." He paused as the strain on her face increased and sadness crept into her eyes. He wondered at it once again, although she was quick to make the reasons clear.

"Is that all we are? A responsibility?"

He mumbled a curse beneath his breath, regretting that his time alone and in the Army had seemingly cost him so many of his skills with women. Needing to reach her, both physically and emotionally, he cupped her cheek and tenderly ran his finger along the ridge of her cheekbone.

"I'm so not good at this, Macy," he confessed.

"This? As in—"

"Family life. Personal relationships. I don't know how to deal with the kinds of things you've had to handle. Difficult things like Tim's death and T.J.'s problems."

"I've done the best I could," she replied, defensiveness in every line of her body and the tight tone in her voice.

"You have and asking for my help isn't a bad thing…I don't think. But there's a lot I have to deal with also and I'm trying to do it the best that I can as well." He couldn't say it, but his reawakened feelings for Macy and the surprise announcement that he had a son were creating doubt within him. Doubt about the decisions he had made in his life. Doubt about the future he had thought to be fairly certain.

Now nothing seemed sure anymore except for the fact that he had to help Macy and T.J. His honor demanded it. He just hoped his heart would be intact when it was all over.

Macy nodded and after a shaky inhalation, her words came out on a rushed breath. "We'll do the best we can together for now."

Together for now. It seemed like the best thing they could hope for at that moment.

"Do you want to go to this honky tonk?" he asked again, trying for that togetherness.

The tension ebbed slowly from her body. "I think that's a good idea. I just want to check on T.J. first. Is that okay?"

"That sounds fine."

She laid her hand over his as it rested on her cheek, the action achingly tender and causing a funky tightening in his heart.

"Thank you for trying."

He bit back the words he had been about to say—that it was the least he could do. He had never believed in doing the least of anything in his whole life and Macy and T.J. certainly deserved more from him. Instead he said, "I will give it my all to make sure this comes out right."

A glimmer of a smile came to her face. "I'm certain you will."

Her trust in him moved him once again, choking his throat tight. Unable to say more for fear of what he might say, he nodded.

"I'm going to go check on T.J. and then we'll go, okay?"

"Okay," he managed to eke out and returned his attention to printing out larger pictures of Sara, both alone and with her parents.

He heard the tread of her steps going up the stairs and past the whir of the ink-jet printer, the soft and loving way she called T.J.'s name. A moment later, she descended the steps again and reentered the kitchen carrying the tray with the empty plates and glasses with T.J.'s lunch.

"He's sound asleep again. I left him a note that we were stepping out for a little while," she advised and went to the sink to clean the plates.

"That's good. It'll give us some time to visit this place and try to figure out where Sara may have gone." With a final *thunk-thunk,* the printer spit out the last sheet of paper with the photo of Sara.

He stood, picked up the papers, folded them neatly and tucked them into the pocket of his chambray shirt. Macy joined him just a second later.

"Are you ready to go?"

She nodded. "As ready as I'll ever be."

The Amarillo Rose sat on one of the smaller county roads, but one well-traveled by truckers avoiding the some-times more crowded state highways. Sitting smack dab in between Esperanza and another rural town, the location made it a great watering hole for the truckers who were headed from the Corpus Christi area to Lubbock or other northern cities.

The paint on the sprawling one story structure was a faded color which had probably once been yellow based on the name of the place and the slightly more colorful neon sign of a yellow rose close to the roadway. A couple of tractor trailers were parked off to the side of the building and a Chevy Silverado that was at least a decade old sat near the door.

As they walked by the truck, they noticed the name of a fish company painted on the door along with a Dallas address.

Macy took it to be a good sign.

She entered first, her eyes adjusting to the dimmer light. A small podium stood by the door and beyond that, a long bar to the left. In the center of the space were dozens of tables and chairs and to the far right, a small dance floor and bandstand.

Plastic bunting in red, white and blue emblazoned with

the name of a local beer hung from the ceilings. The walls were adorned with yet more ads and neon signs for an assortment of beers.

At the bar, a bartender was filling a glass with beer while a waitress laid out a plate for one of the three customers seated at the counter.

Fisher placed a hand at the small of her back and after a quick exchange of gazes, urged her toward the bar. She took a seat as did he and the bartender approached after setting the beer in front of one of the patrons. He slapped down paper coasters on the relatively clean surface of the bar.

"What can I get you folks?" He inclined his head in Macy's direction.

"An iced tea for me," she answered and Fisher immediately added, "And another for me."

The bartender quickly shifted away to get their orders and the waitress came to their side, held the menus before her as she said, "Can I get you folks some food? We've got a mean five alarm chili today as well as a to die for peach cobbler."

Fisher met her glance for only a second. "Peach cobbler for me. With vanilla ice cream if you've got it."

"We sure do, honey. What about you, ma'am. Same thing as your husband?" the waitress asked.

Macy was about to protest her mistake, but then thought better of it. If the waitress thought they were concerned parents searching for their daughter, she might be more inclined to help them. "I'll just have the cobbler, thanks."

The waitress walked away to fill their orders while the bartender came by with their drinks. "Here you go, folks. Is there anything else I can get you?"

Fisher pulled the photo of Sara from his pocket and as he

did so, she quickly spoke up. "My husband and I are looking for our daughter, Sara."

Fisher masked his surprise well, she thought, as he pushed forward the picture they had taken off the Internet.

"We think she might have come through here. Maybe a couple of weeks ago," Fisher said.

The bartender peered at the photo and then called out to one of the men sitting farther down the bar, "Maybe only… Hey, Billy Joe. Didn't you say that you gave a young girl a ride a few days ago?"

Billy Joe, a grizzled older man sporting a trucker's hat, slid off his stool and approached them. Leaning toward the picture on the bar, he placed his hands on his lips and tipped the hat back, exposing his Marine-buzzed salt and pepper hair.

"Yep. Picked her up just outside of Esperanza on…" The man rubbed the thick graying stubble on his cheeks as he tried to recollect. Finally, he said, "I think about two nights ago. She was on the road all by herself trying to get back to some ranch just outside of town."

"The Hopechest Ranch?" she asked and the old man nodded.

"I think that was the place. Dropped her off at the end of the driveway and she hightailed it up to the front door and went in."

"Your company's from Dallas, though, right. Do you do the drive from there regularly?" Fisher asked.

"I do. Funny you should mention that," the old man said, still rubbing at his cheeks. "When the young lady saw the name on the truck, she asked me if I was headed to Dallas. Seemed to me she didn't want to go back there if she could avoid it."

"Have any other strangers passed through here recently?" she asked, glancing back and forth between the bartender and truck driver. The waitress came over at that moment with their cobblers as the bartender said, "Have you seen any new faces around, Alice?"

A frown created a ridge above the older woman's eyebrows as she considered the question. "Just that salesman who said he was on his way to San Antonio. Didn't seem like much of a salesman to me."

"Why's that?" Fisher questioned.

"Got the most expensive thing on the menu. Didn't ask for a receipt and left a lousy tip," she said and wiggled her fingers to indicate that she wanted to see the photo.

After Fisher handed it over and she examined it, she said, "Don't remember the girl."

He pulled the other photo from his pocket and passed it to the waitress. "Was this the salesman?"

She glanced at it, but shook her head and placed the photo on the counter of the bar. "Don't recognize him."

"Me, neither," said the truck driver as did the bartender.

She exchanged a glance with Fisher, who handed the bartender the photo of Sara. "Do you think you could keep this just in case Sara comes by again? We can give you a phone number where you can call us."

"Sure." The bartender plucked a pen from inside his apron and jotted down the cell phone number that Macy provided.

Although they had ordered the desserts, she had no appetite thanks to the disappointment of discovering virtually nothing about Sara. The only worthwhile information they could pass to Jericho when he returned in a day or two would be the name of the company that the truck driver worked for and the license plate number. It wouldn't be all that much harder for Jericho to get the man's name based on that and their description of the truck driver. She didn't believe the older man had done anything, but Jericho could hopefully confirm that the man had no prior record.

Fisher bent close to her and whispered in her ear. "Do you want to go?"

"I'm not really very hungry," she admitted.

He brushed a kiss along her brow and laid his arm around her shoulders. "Let's go home then. Maybe T.J. will be able to tell us more once we tell him what we know about Sara's dad."

The tenderness of that caress chased away some of the disappointment. "Let's go home," she confirmed.

Chapter 15

They were on their way to Macy's, but it must have occurred to her that they would have to go past the Hopechest Ranch to reach her house.

She laid a hand on his arm as he drove the Jeep along the country road. "Do you mind if we drop by the ranch and speak to Jewel? I'd like to share what little we have and see if she maybe has some information for us."

"Not a problem." He slowed the Jeep as they neared the driveway for the ranch, then turned onto it and drove up to the front of the house.

After he had parked, he said, "Do you want me to go with you?"

"Of course. Together, right?"

Together for now, he thought, but couldn't disappoint. She had been too discouraged after their visit to the roadside canteen. Because of that, he nodded and followed her as she walked to the front door and entered, calling out Jewel's name as she did so.

A very pregnant woman—Mexican, young and pretty— was the first one to respond.

"Macy. Miss Jewel is in the library with Joe," the woman said. "Is something wrong, Ana?"

Ana wrung her hands together and glanced toward the back of the house. "Joe said he had to talk to Miss Jewel. That he had something to tell her about Sara."

Macy placed her hand over her stomach and wavered on her feet. Fisher was immediately there, his hand at her shoulder to offer support and comfort.

"Let's go see if Jewel can talk to us," he said and squeezed her shoulder.

She reached up and placed her hand on his, seeking his solace and he offered it, easing his hand down so that she could grab hold of it.

Together they walked the few steps back to the library, a moderately sized room filled with books, a leather sofa and chairs as well as a small table where the children could read or study with some measure of quiet.

The door was ajar as they approached and Macy could hear the gentle tones of Jewel's voice as she spoke to Joe.

She knocked on the door, but no one responded. She was about to knock again when Jewel came to the entrance to the library.

"Macy. I'm so glad you're here." Her sharp-eyed gaze immediately went to Fisher behind her, down to where their hands were joined and then back up to her face.

"You have news?" Jewel asked.

"Not all that much unfortunately. And you?"

Jewel opened the door wide and held out her arm. "Why don't you come in. You need to hear what Joe just told me."

Her stomach did a little flip-flop, sensing the news would not be good. She tightened her hand on Fisher's.

They entered the room. Joe was seated on the maroon leather coach, but stood as he saw them. He nodded his head in greeting and said, "Mrs. Ward. Mr. Yates."

As anxious as she was, she couldn't muster the energy for niceties. "Your aunt tells us that you've got something we should hear."

The boy shifted from foot to foot and stuffed his hands in his pockets. He inhaled deeply and held it before finally speaking. "I saw Sara and T.J. together the afternoon before she disappeared. They were by themselves at the corral and Sara seemed upset."

"Upset with T.J.?" Fisher asked, but the boy quickly shook his head.

"I don't think so. It seemed like T.J. was trying to make her feel better. I think he has a crush on her," Joe said.

Jewel came up to stand by Joe and placed her arm around his shoulders. "Tell them what else you heard."

Joe fidgeted once again, clearly uneasy about what he would say and possibly, about betraying a friend's confidence. Macy understood that and so she tried to relieve that concern.

"I know you want to protect your friends, but if it's something that could get them hurt—"

"T.J. was telling Sara not to worry. That he would take her to a place where no one could find her."

"Was there someone Sara was afraid of? Someone who had found her here at the Hopechest?" Fisher asked.

"Maybe," he began and shrugged. "The other night—the night of the accident—another car started following us. Sara got worried and that's why T.J. was speeding, to get away from that car."

She recalled T.J.'s explanation that the other car had been challenging them, but this made a great deal more sense. If Sara's father had sent someone to try and find her, they might have spotted her in the car with the boys and decided to follow them to see where she might be.

"She was with you the night of the accident," Macy said, wanting to confirm her suspicions.

Joe exchanged a pained look with Jewel and nodded. "She was with us, but after we got into the accident, that car that had weirded us out was driving by. Before T.J. and I realized it, she had slipped out of T.J.'s car and somehow got back to the ranch without us."

Macy sensed something even more troublesome approached and at the thought of it, her knees began to shake. If Fisher hadn't already been gently guiding her toward one of the wing chairs, she would have sagged into one ignominiously.

"There's more, isn't there?"

Joe dropped his head until the only thing she could see was the tousled mass of his dark brown hair. He mumbled something, almost beneath his breath, but at Jewel's prodding, finally spoke up.

"I saw Sara getting into T.J.'s car the night before she disappeared. I'd heard some noises out by the one barn and went out to check. There wasn't anything by the barn, but on the way back, I saw a car in the distance and someone running to it."

"Are you sure, son? It was nighttime and you were quite a distance away," Fisher said.

Joe nodded and as he raised his blue-eyed gaze to them, it was filled with guilt. "I'm sorry, but it was T.J. and Sara. I saw their faces when T.J. opened the door and the lights came on."

She sighed and buried her head in her hands. If what Joe said was true—and she had no reason to doubt him—T.J. was headed for major trouble once the deputy found out. Before he did, she had to get to the bottom of what was really going on with her son.

Rising, she stepped up to Joe and her boss, her hands clasped tightly before her. "I know this is a lot to ask—"

"We're not supposed to speak to Deputy Rawlings until tomorrow and actually, I was hoping to wait until Jericho came back. He's due any day now, isn't he?" Jewel asked, her head cocked in Fisher's direction.

"Dad says he'll be back either tomorrow or the next day, although the next is more likely," Fisher replied. He laid his hand on her shoulder once again and said, "That gives us time to talk to T.J. and find out what's going on."

She nodded and embraced Jewel. "Thank you for understanding."

Jewel hugged her hard and brushed a lock of stray hair away from her face. "Call us as soon as you know anything. In the meantime, I'm going to speak to Clay Colton about those noises again. Find out if he can go out on the range to see if it's an injured animal."

"I'll call as soon as we have something." Turning, she took hold of Fisher's hand and they left the ranch house, jumped in the Jeep and raced home.

She knew something was wrong from the moment they pulled up into her driveway. There was something just too… quiet about the house. After she exited the Jeep, she immediately walked to the garage doors, stood on tiptoe and peered in through the glass windows.

T.J.'s GTO was gone.

Running to the front door, she threw it open and shouted his name.

When silence answered, she tore up the stairs, the house's old bones creaking from the force of her strides.

At T.J.'s door, she stared at his empty unmade bed.

He wasn't anywhere in the room.

Things had just gone from bad to worse.

He was getting slow in his old age, Fisher thought as he bounded up the stairs, chasing Macy after her mad dash from the garage and into the house.

He nearly barreled her over as she stood silently at T.J.'s door, her shoulders nearly heaving as she apparently struggled for control. He realized why as he stood behind her and peered over her shoulder into the room.

Her son...*their* son was gone.

Disappointment slammed into him as he thought of how T.J. had broken the rules of his punishment. He couldn't imagine how Macy felt, but he could see it in the lines of her body.

He stepped close and embraced her from behind, wrapping one arm across her waist while stroking her hair with his hand. "It'll be okay, Mace. We'll find him."

She sucked in a ragged breath while her body vibrated with tension. "Why would he do this? Why couldn't he talk to me?"

He remembered himself at T.J.'s age, all full of perceived male empowerment, but struggling with the confusing emotions about Macy, his mom and his life in Esperanza. Although he had been close to his father and brother, he hadn't been able to talk to them about all that he was feeling. He'd been too prideful, too perplexed and most of all, too angry.

"This isn't about anything you've done wrong, Mace. He's young and probably unsure of the situation he's gotten himself into with Sara. Women can do that to a man."

Another shuddering breath ripped through her body and transferred her pain to him and because he wanted to ease her anguish, he said, "I promise that this will work out. That we'll make this okay."

A big promise.

As she turned in his arms and wrapped hers around him, holding on to him as if for dear life, regret slammed into him that the promise he had just made might be one he would break because he didn't know how to make it okay. Had it been a mission with his men, he'd know the plan and what to do. Even if the plan got all messed up out in the field, he could find a way to make the mission work.

But this wasn't a mission and family things… They were far more complicated at times than a military mission and he feared he lacked the skills to be able to keep his promise.

Awkwardly he patted her on the back, held her as she cried out her frustration. He wasn't used to dealing with a woman's tears. Or a son's disobedience.

He couldn't tell her there was no crying in the military. Well, he could but it would be a lie because he had shed more than one tear over his men and their injuries. He also couldn't punish T.J. with a week in the brig for disobeying his mother.

In reality, he couldn't bring the kind of order he had in the Army to this family, but as Macy's tears finally subsided with a tiny hiccough that wrung his heart, he realized what he could do. He could bring her peace for a moment. Soothe her hurt and maybe make her smile.

As for T.J....

He needed a man's guidance to get him in line and he would try his best to help T.J. put his life in order. To fulfill his promise to make it okay before duty called for him to return to the Army.

Bending slightly, he cradled her face in his hands. Her cheeks were wet with her tears and slightly flushed. He wiped away the tears with his thumbs, brought his forehead to rest against hers once again and repeated his promise.

"It will be okay. *We* will make sure that everything is put to right."

As she nodded and gazed up at him, her brown eyes shimmering from her spent tears, he realized she believed in that promise. Believed in him.

His heart constricted again at the trust she had in him and he vowed to do his best not to disappoint her which meant that as difficult as it might be, they had to decide what to do about T.J.

Chapter 16

An open bottle of wine sat on the kitchen counter and he poured them each a small glass before making them a quick dinner.

Macy had protested, saying she wasn't hungry, but he had insisted. She needed to keep her strength up so that they would be ready to figure out what T.J. was doing and where he might have taken Sara, since both of them now had no doubt that he knew where the girl was.

Between the trip to the Amarillo Rose and the stop at the ranch, it was already dusk. T.J. had likely been gone for hours and what made the most sense was for them to refuel, get some rest and prepare to find T.J. the next day.

He also insisted on Macy helping him, hoping that the simple chores would help take her mind off things. As they worked together in the kitchen, he intentionally kept the talk away from T.J., wanting Macy to relax. If she felt more at ease, it might prompt some idea of where T.J. might have hidden Sara.

While Macy chopped onions and red peppers for the omelets, Fisher took out the eggs and found some bread to toast.

"There's only six eggs," he said, glancing down at the plastic egg tray from the refrigerator.

"There's only two of us," Macy replied with surprise.

"A man's got to get his protein," he said with a smile and rummaged through her fridge until he found a ham steak. Taking it out, he walked with it to the island counter where she was working and laid it before her.

"If the veggies are ready—"

"They are," she said and handed him the cutting board with the chopped peppers and onions. She grabbed another so she could cut up the ham.

"I'll get them cooking up," he said and little by little, with the two of them working side by side, the omelet and toast took shape.

Within less than half an hour, they were seated at the table, eating a delicious omelet. Silent as they finished the simple meal and sipped the last of the wine in the bottle. After, they cleared the table and cleaned the dishes together at the sink.

By the time they had finished, Macy was obviously more in control. More relaxed and truthfully, so was he. Being beside her…

It made him imagine what it would be like to have a family of his own. To do everyday things together like they had tonight. Simple things which somehow brought a peace to his heart that he hadn't experienced in some time.

She walked him to the door, but then they both stood there,

awkward. Uncertain. Lingering at the door, heads hanging downward. He wondered if she was as reluctant as he about all that had happened that day. About leaving her, although he was hesitant to admit that.

"Fisher," she said, her voice rising in question although she didn't pick up her head.

He bent a little, trying to see her face, but couldn't in the dim light of the bulb at the front door. He placed his thumb and forefinger beneath her chin and gently tipped it upward so that he could see her face.

"Macy?"

She kept her eyes downcast as she said, "I don't want to be alone tonight. Would you stay?"

Stay. With her?

It tightened his gut to imagine being with her. Lying beside her and yet…

She was vulnerable and he was…decidedly too puzzled about what she made him feel. Regardless of all that, as she finally tipped her eyes up shyly and the need there slammed into him, he realized he couldn't deny her request.

"I'll stay."

As they walked back into her home, he finally took the time to appreciate her house's simplicity. No fripperies or excessive feminine touches. He wondered if she had kept this home simple and feminine-free for Tim and T.J. If it was the kind of house she wanted or one she had settled for because of the men in her life.

Was this the kind of house they would have shared if things had been different or if she would have taken the time to stamp their home with her unique personality.

As she opened the door to her bedroom, he finally saw traces of her.

He knew little about design, so the best he could do was call it feminine. Lacey things adorned the rich mahogany furniture in the room. Floral curtains were at the two windows and a bedspread with a similar pattern of roses covered a queen-sized bed. To the far right of the bed sat a big soft chair and ottoman in a floral chintz pattern. A romance novel sat on the ottoman. The cover was up with the open pages facing the ottoman, marking the spot where she had stopped reading.

Macy paused in the middle of the room and gestured to a door at the other end. "The bathroom's in there in case you need to…you know."

He didn't need to do anything, but decided to give her a moment to collect herself. With a courteous nod, he went to the bathroom and shut the door behind him.

The decor of the bathroom was even more feminine. Lace decorated the one window and the light rose-colored towels were adorned with beige lace. A painted wrought-iron stand by the bathtub was fanciful as was another by the window which held an assortment of African violets blooming in shades of purple and pink.

He smiled at the flowers, which added so much life to the space, and walked over to touch the velvety surface of one bloom. Soft and lush. Like Macy's skin.

Wrong, wrong, wrong, he reminded himself. He needed to be in control if he was going to survive the night.

He walked to the pedestal sink, turned on the cold water and splashed his face with it over and over again until he had restored control.

Drying his face and hands with one of the very feminine towels, he then folded it neatly and laid it on the rack to dry.

When he walked back into her bedroom, her door was closed and the room was dimly lit by one small lamp on a nightstand by the bed. Macy was on top of the covers, fully clothed, her back turned toward the bathroom.

He wrung his hands nervously, then wiped them up and down on his jeans before taking a stutter step toward the bed.

She turned at the sound he made, leaned back on one hand as he approached. Her brown-eyed gaze looked him up and down, hesitant but hungry as he stopped at the edge of the bed.

"Are you sure?" he asked.

"I don't want to be alone tonight. I haven't been alone in this house since…"

"Tim died?"

Shaking her head vehemently, she said, "I bought this house and everything in it a couple of years after Tim died. T.J. and I…we needed a change. There were just too many sad memories at the old place."

Relief washed over him then. Relief that he wouldn't be lying in another man's bed. Beside another man's memories.

He sat on the edge of the bed and pulled off his boots. Tossed them aside and they landed with a thud on the polished hard wood floor.

Facing her, he copied her pose, leaning back on one hand as he considered her. "It must have been hard for you."

She lay down on her back and nodded. "I didn't want to believe it at first—that Tim was really going to die. Since we found out that he…"

She shuddered and closed her eyes before shifting to grab

the crocheted throw at the foot of the bed. She pulled it up around her, as if she was cold.

It tugged at him with the vulnerability it exposed and he shifted quickly, moving to her side and embracing her. Bringing her to rest beside him as he stroked his hand up and down her side, trying to soothe her.

"I know I said I was sorry at his funeral, but—"

She slipped her hand over his mouth. "Can we talk about something else?"

He frowned, confused until she said, "Could we talk about you? Why you chose the Army?"

He wanted to say "Because of you" but bit the words back. He had already been considering the Army before what had happened with her. What had happened with her had only cemented the decision he had already been about to make.

"My dad did a great job of giving Jericho and me stability after Mom left and I needed that after high school. Community college just wasn't doing it for me. I needed more."

"And the Army gave you that?" She cradled his cheek and stroked her thumb across the roughness of his afternoon beard.

He nodded, but it seemed to not be enough for her.

"Did you ever miss Esperanza while you were gone?"

He should have lied. It would have made things that much easier, but he was a man of honor and couldn't lie to her.

"I missed home more than I thought I would."

Macy told herself not to read anything into his words. "Jericho and your dad miss you a lot. They worry about you. So do a lot of people in town—you're our hero."

He smiled tightly, clearly uncomfortable with the praise. "I'm just doing my job."

"A job that could get you killed." She shifted her hand

down to rest on the hard muscles of his chest. Beneath her palm his heart beat strongly. Steadily, much like the man beside her.

He covered her hand with his, his palm rough on the back of hers. The thin white line of a scar marred one knuckle and another larger one was close to his wrist. The hand of a warrior.

"Almost more than anything, I want you to be safe and to be happy," she said, finally admitting to what had been in her heart for far too long.

"Almost more? Can I guess that what you want even more is to see T.J. safe and happy," he questioned, tenderly rubbing his hand back and forth against hers.

"Definitely."

He slipped his hand from hers and slid it into the short waves of her hair, softly cupping her head. "And what about you?"

"Me?" she asked, slightly befuddled until she met his brilliant green-eyed gaze and his meaning was clear. "What do I want?" she asked, just to be sure.

"Yes, what do you want for yourself?" he said, leaving no room for doubt about the answer he expected from her.

What did she want that was only for herself? she wondered, but then the answer came too swiftly to be denied any longer.

"I want you."

Chapter 17

A tremor rocked through the hand in her hair and beside her his body tensed.

"Macy," he said, his tone low and tinged with an odd combination of exasperation and need. He rolled onto his back, breaking contact with her.

She raised herself up on one elbow. "You were right when you said that I wanted you back in high school and that I want you now, but you know what else?"

He looked away, unable to meet her probing gaze as he asked, "What?"

"Want without love is empty. That's what I realized back in high school. That's why I married Tim," she finally confessed, thinking that he deserved a complete explanation after so many years.

The pain in his heart was almost more than he could bear

and so strong that he wanted to lash out at her. Before he could control himself, he had flipped and pinned her to the mattress, his body holding her down while he held her hands above her head.

"You never even gave me a chance to prove to you it was more," he said, his breath ragged in his chest from his distress.

"No, I didn't and that was wrong. I should have given you a chance, especially when I found out I was pregnant with T.J., only…"

"Only what, damn it! I deserve an answer as to why you kept my son from me for his entire life," he barked out.

"I was afraid of what I felt for you. I was afraid that if I gave you my heart, you'd break it when you left." Tears shimmered in her eyes, but she battled them back, biting her lower lip in a gesture that was all too telling and all too tempting.

He slowly loosened his grip on her hands and bent his head, bringing his lips to a hair's breadth from hers. "Maybe if you had asked, I wouldn't have left," he said and then closed the distance between them and kissed her. Put all of his heart and soul and eighteen years of frustration into showing her just what might have been between them.

The shock of his kiss, filled with such need and yearning, overcame any doubts Macy might have had about whether it was right to explore this. She opened her mouth to his and pressed her body upward, meeting the hardness of his muscled physique. The short strands of his dark hair were soft against her hands as she held his head to her, urging him on.

Over and over they kissed until they were both trembling. Until it wasn't enough and she lifted her hips against the press of his erection, so full and hard against her belly.

She shuddered and between her legs, her muscles clenched

on the emptiness there, but she reminded herself of her earlier words to him. About how empty want was without love.

She had no doubt she cared for him. About him. She had no doubt she could be falling in love with him. With his strength and goodness.

But she also knew that if that love was to grow true and strong, taking this any further tonight would be wrong. Fisher must have sensed it as well since he gave her one last kiss before slowly pulling away.

"I'm willing to wait until you're ready, Macy," he said, brushing away a tousled lock of her hair.

She nodded, but had to ask him. "What happens then, Fisher?"

Fisher wished he knew what to tell her. He wished he knew whether she ever would be ready for a relationship with him or whether he could commit to her if she was. Commit to having a wife and family after so many years in the military.

"I'm not sure," he confessed.

She faced away from him as she said, "Jericho said you might not sign up for another tour of duty. That you might teach instead."

Damn his brother for being such a busybody, he thought. Hadn't Jericho ever heard the old saying that loose lips sink ships?

"I've been offered a teaching post at West Point."

"And had you given any thought to it?" she asked, turning toward him once again, the resoluteness in her brown-eyed gaze drilling into him, daring him to lie to her, but he couldn't.

"I had given it some thought," he admitted and that seemed to be enough for her for the moment.

"I think it's time we got some rest," she said and flipped onto her side.

He nestled against her, his front to her back, spooned as close as he could be, and dropped his arm to rest across her waist while pillowing his head on his other arm.

"Good night, Mace."

"Good night, Fisher," she said and laid her arm over his.

For long moments he lay there, listening to her breathe until the rhythm of it deepened and lengthened, confirming to him that she slept. Even then he clung onto wakefulness, trying to experience this peaceful interlude. Wondering how it might be if she lay beside him every night. What it would be like to sample the passion he had experienced but for a brief moment earlier that night.

As he drifted off, the taste of her on his lips and the memory of her pressed close, it occurred to him that maybe family life might not be such a bad thing.

That maybe it was worth giving that teaching position more than just a thought.

He awoke to the smell of fresh coffee and Macy. Her scent lingered on the sheets long after she had left the bed.

He took his time to snuggle her pillow close and savor that rose-filled scent. Maybe even memorize for the future if it turned out to be that his nights were meant to be without her.

Realizing he couldn't dawdle for long, however, he rose and went to the bathroom where he relieved himself and after, washed his face and hands. Put a little of her toothpaste on his finger and scrubbed his mouth out the best he could.

Thankfully, it took just his fingers to rake smooth the short strands of his hair and then he was on his way downstairs and to the kitchen, where Macy was standing at the counter, fork-splitting some English muffins.

"Good morning," he said and came up behind her, dropped a quick kiss on the side of her face.

"Mornin', Fisher. I walked over to the corner store and got some more eggs. Figured I'd make us a bite to eat while we decided what to do today."

"Let me help," he said, grabbed the muffins and brought them to the toaster while Macy cracked the eggs.

After he popped the muffins into the toaster oven and got it cranking, he leaned back against the counter and asked, "Have you given any thought to where T.J. might have taken Sara?"

She shook her head as she scrambled the eggs and said, "I've been thinking about that ever since yesterday. Joe said T.J. thought no one would find her there…"

Her voice trailed off and she stopped whipping. She put down the fork and bowl and said, "We used to go hiking and camping about thirty miles from here in the Texas hill country."

Wiping her hands on her apron, she headed toward a side door in the kitchen and he followed.

The door opened into the two-car garage which had a recessed area on one side. Shelves and a large plastic storage bin were tucked into the recess and Macy immediately went to the storage bin and pulled up the top.

"The camping equipment and knapsacks are gone. T.J. must have taken them and if he did that…I bet that's where he took her. We used to go up in the hills and camp. We even found a cave one time."

"Was the cave big enough for someone to hide in or stay for any length of time?" he asked.

"Definitely. We slept there one night when it was raining,"

she said with a quick bob of her head. "T.J. and his dad used
to go there often until... I only went a few times, though.
Hiking and camping were not my thing."

"Do you think you could take us there? Find the trail that
T.J. would be most likely to use to get to the cave?"

"I think so. It's been a while, but I'm good at remembering places. We'll need some supplies—"

"I've got camping gear back at Dad's house and we can
stop by the feed and supply to pick up some MREs."

"MREs?" she questioned, clearly unfamiliar with the term.

"Ready to eat meals. Dad has everything we need in his
camping section," he explained.

"I'll get changed and pack some warmer clothes. It can get
cold in the hills."

"And they're predicting heavy rains. I hope T.J. knows
enough to stay to the high ground and away from those
arroyos. They can be dangerous if there's a flash flood."

Macy paled a little, but kept her cool. "I hope he knows
that as well. I'll be down in a few minutes."

"I'll finish cooking breakfast. The food will help us to be
prepared for a long day."

As Macy walked back into the kitchen and he went about
finishing the meal, he only hoped that by the end of the day,
they would have a better idea of where T.J. and Sara might be.

Fisher had called Buck Yates ahead of time and his dad had
a few days worth of rations as well as some maps of the area
ready for them when they arrived at his feed and supply store
on the outskirts of town. Combined with the camping equipment that Fisher had picked up at his dad's house, they would
be well-prepared for a trip into the hill country.

As Buck helped them stow supplies in their knapsacks, Fisher asked, "Is Jericho still due home tomorrow?"

Buck nodded. "As far as I know he is."

Fisher shot a look at her and said, "Tell him that we think T.J.'s helping Sara and that they're hiding up in the state park. We'll check in with the park ranger when we get there, but Jericho should try and reach me on the cell phone as soon as he can."

When their bags were packed, they tossed them into the back of Fisher's Jeep, climbed in and started the ride to the state park. It was about thirty miles away in the hill country and easily reached along a small interstate.

The weather station had predicted torrential rains for that afternoon. Macy hoped that they could reach the park and pick up T.J.'s trail before the rains came and obliterated any sign of him and Sara.

The weather forecast was on her mind during the entire ride along with concerns about what would happen if Deputy Rawlings decided to come by the house to question T.J. Would he assume the worst if he found them all gone? If he did, would he issue an all points bulletin for T.J. as if he were a fugitive?

At her prolonged silence during the ride, Fisher glanced at her out of the corner of his eye. "Don't worry. We'll find them before there's any more problems," he reassured her.

"If Deputy Rawlings—"

"Jericho will be home soon enough and I think Rawlings is smart enough to know that Jericho would be less than pleased with the kind of grief he's already given you. He's not going to escalate this."

She shook her head, recalling the dour look on the deputy's handsome face when she had gone to pick up T.J. "He seemed pretty determined to me."

"Focus on what we'll do once we get to the park. Which trail we'll take and where T.J. might have hidden Sara," he urged and she did, forcing herself to remember the two or three trips she had taken with Tim and T.J. up into the hills. Trusting that between that and Fisher's military expertise in tracking, they could find where T.J. and Sara might have gone.

Hoping that whoever it was that had tried to run down T.J. or had been asking questions back at the honky tonk would not already be on the teen's trail.

Chapter 18

When Fisher pulled into the main lot of the state park, her heart skipped a beat.

Stationed at the farthest corner, beneath some thick oaks, was T.J.'s GTO. She pointed at it and Fisher drove to the car and parked beside it. As she stood beneath the canopy of the oaks, she realized why he had chosen the spot. It would be difficult for anyone searching from above to spot the car.

Fisher kneeled by the driver's side door, observing some impressions in the gravel by the car. He tracked the impressions to a dirt path besides the gnarly pines surrounding the parking lot. "The footprints lead from the car to here, but there's only one set that I can see."

"From last night when he came back to where he'd hidden Sara," she said.

He nodded, lifted his hand and pointed to the small ranger

station about thirty feet away on the opposite side of the lot. "Why don't you stay here while I talk to the ranger?"

If someone was chasing the teens, they might also have a picture of her and be showing it around. Better she lay low as well, she thought and eased back into the Jeep to wait for Fisher's return.

Nearly half an hour went by as she sat there, tapping her foot and fidgeting with her cell phone. She was on the verge of calling Fisher when she saw him via the rearview mirror, exiting the ranger station. He had a piece of paper in his hand which he glanced at once or twice as he came closer.

When he reached the car, he eased back in and laid out the paper—a map of the park areas—in the space between the two seats. "The ranger says there's at least three trails into the hills. One of them starts right here where T.J. parked."

He pointed to a spot on the map and she leaned over, followed the meandering uphill path of the trail on the paper until it arrived at an overlook.

She remembered such a spot at which she, Tim and T.J. had stopped on at least two of their hikes. Thinking back on it, the scenic hillside site had taken them nearly three hours to reach and she mentioned that to Fisher.

He examined the map and said, "Assuming you were only walking about two miles an hour, this overlook would be about six miles away so it seems as if this might be the trail T.J. would take since he was familiar with it."

Trailing her finger along the path, she stopped and circled one area on the map. "The rock face around here had a lot of openings. That's where we found a cave that one time and stayed inside overnight."

"Could be where T.J. stashed Sara," he said and then his

mouth tightened to a grim line as he jabbed at another spot on the map. "This is a bridge over an arroyo. Let's hope that it's more than a foot bridge and that they have the sense to stay away from it if the rains are as bad as they say they'll be."

Her stomach turned at the thought of how bad a flash flood could be high up in the hills. The water would come churning down the arroyos, sometimes ripping up small bushes and trees. Cascading with powerful roughness against anything in their path. Anyone caught up in the way of the raging waters faced serious injury or death.

"He'll know better," she said, but it was almost as if she was trying to convince herself.

"Are you ready to go? If we're lucky the rains will hold out until we've got a solid grasp on where T.J. was headed."

"I'm ready," she said. As she eased on the knapsack and adjusted its weight on her shoulders, she worried about why Sara had run away and why T.J. would have found it necessary to hide the young girl.

But then she remembered the bruises on Sara's arms when she had arrived at the ranch and T.J.'s comments about the driver who had challenged him a few nights ago. The teens had clearly been afraid of whoever was responsible for both.

Because of that, she hoped she and Fisher would find the teens before anyone else did.

Although heavy rains were expected later that day, it had been at least a week since it had rained and the ground was hard and dusty. Despite that, Fisher was able to track the impressions in the gravel by T.J.'s car to a distinctive set of sneaker treads on the dirt path leading to the trail.

"What size shoe does T.J. wear?" he asked.

"A thirteen," she responded and stood by him as he kneeled to examine the footprints.

"That's about the size of this shoe which confirms that T.J. probably went up this trail."

He rose and adjusted the straps on the knapsack, making sure they were tight so that the pack would not shift as they headed up the trail. From the trunk, he removed a rifle, eased the strap over his head and settled the weapon securely beside the pack on his back. Then he faced Macy, reached for her straps, but paused by the bindings on her knapsack.

"May I?" he asked.

She nodded and he quickly adjusted her pack to keep it from shifting and then gestured to the trail. "I'll lead the way. If I'm going too fast—"

"Believe me I'll let you know."

He smiled, ripped out a baseball cap from his back pocket and plopped it on her head. "Put this on. There'll be glare on the footpath and once it starts raining, it'll keep you dry."

"Thanks."

He grabbed his cowboy hat from the backseat of the Jeep and also put on a pair of polarized sunglasses which would help cut down on the glare. Taking the point, he focused on the sneaker tread pattern and followed it up the trail.

T.J. had not tried to hide his tracks. The footprints were clearly visible along the path. He had been in a hurry, however, judging from the wide distance between his steps. If he recalled T.J.'s height correctly, the space between the footprints indicated that he had been almost jogging up the trail.

If Macy hadn't been with him, he would have done the same, eager as he was to find the teens and put to right what was happening so Macy could have some peace of mind. But she was with him and so he kept his pace reasonable, his mind focused on tracking T.J., but also aware of how she was doing as she followed behind him.

About a mile up the path, T.J.'s stride began to shorten and about a quarter of a mile after that, they became the length of a normal walking step. He paused then and perused the path ahead of them as well as the open country all around.

Pines and oaks dotted the rolling hillsides. In between the stands of the trees were patches of grass and larger meadows which in the springtime would be awash with the colors of Texas wildflowers. Even now there were spots of bright color from some of the later blooming plants and stretches of prickly pear cactus. Up ahead of them, the trail wound through stands of trees before a limestone rock face rose up to the left, leading to the overlook Macy had identified on the map.

"It's beautiful, isn't it?" she asked as she stood beside him.

"It is," he said and pointed to a herd of fallow deer feeding on grass in one distant meadow, their almost white coats bright against the dull brown of the parched grasses.

Macy leaned against him and took hold of his hand as she witnessed the sight. "I wish that one day…"

He didn't need her to finish. He knew what she wished and inside of him, something had been slowly taking root since last night. Something that said maybe what they both wished wasn't so far apart.

Looking up the trail, he said, "You mentioned a cave?"

She nodded. "There's quite a few of them up ahead, but I think the biggest one is quite a ways up. Probably past the overlook and closer to the bridge."

Once again concern rose in him as he cast his gaze upward at the thickening clouds above. Inhaling deeply, he could smell the coming rain and hoped the forecasters were wrong about the force of the storm.

"Let's get going. The rain will be here soon," he said and they once again set off, following T.J.'s sneaker prints in the dust of the trail.

They had been on the winding path for another half an hour when the first fat raindrop plopped on the brim of his cowboy hat. He quickly removed two large rain ponchos from one of the pouches on his pack and helped Macy ease hers on over the backpack. Then he slipped on his own as the drops grew more frequent and quite heavy in a matter of seconds.

There was little shelter on the trail as they continued upward, just an occasional stand of oaks here and there, but they couldn't pause for any delayed shelter under the trees. The impressions of T.J.'s sneakers vanished quickly beneath the onslaught of the rain. The trail in front of them became a difficult morass of mud.

As they struggled ever onward, he kept his eyes trained on the areas around the trail to make sure T.J. had not detoured off the path. There wasn't any sign that he had deviated from continuing up the trail. If anything, up ahead he found an impression protected by a thick oak beside the trail. Bending down, he examined the footprint more closely just to make sure. It was T.J.'s.

Beneath the canopy of the oak, he offered Macy a drink and short respite from the mud and pounding rains they had been battling for nearly an hour.

She took a deep draw from the canteen and pulled off her baseball cap to wipe away a line of sweat from her forehead. "We're not even halfway to the overlook."

No, they weren't, he thought. He cradled her cheek and

said, "Don't worry. If we're moving this slowly, so is T.J. He won't get that much farther ahead. For all we know, he's taken refuge in one of the caves to wait out the storm."

Macy considered his words and prayed they were true. That would give them a chance to catch up to her son and Sara.

She dragged her hand across the back of her neck. She had tucked her hair up into a ponytail to try and stay cool, but with the rain the ponytail was dripping wet. Beneath the plastic of the rain poncho and heavy backpack it was hot, although once the sun went down, the temperature would cool quickly.

She glanced at Fisher who seemed as fresh as he had when they had first started the trek. Of course he would. As a soldier he was used to exercises like this. It was why he had taken the bulk of the supplies in his pack. She appreciated it since even the lighter weight in hers began to feel like a ton of rocks.

"How much farther will we go today?" she asked although she was determined to follow Fisher even if she had to crawl up the trail.

"Depends on how bad the footing becomes and how quickly it gets dark. We can't risk losing our balance once we're higher up on the trail."

She eased the baseball cap back on, pulling her dripping wet ponytail through the hole in the back. "I'm ready to go."

He smiled and tenderly passed his fingers down the side of her face. "I know you are."

Turning, Fisher once again set off up the trail, but as they cleared the protection of the oak, the rain pounded them once again. Beneath their feet, the ground was even more unsteady and their boots sank into the mud, making each step that much harder. At one point she slipped and fell to one knee. The cold of the rainwater soaked through the fabric of her jeans and she prayed T.J. had been sensible enough to take shelter from the storm.

As she struggled to rise in the muck, Fisher was there to help her up.

She took hold of his hand, but he didn't release it as they continued onward, slipping and sliding. Pressing ever onward until dusk came and darkness threatened. By that point, they were beside the limestone rock formations that held an assortment of crevices and breaks.

Fisher stopped at one, examining the size of the opening which was big enough for someone to slip through.

He turned to her and as he removed his pack, he said, "I'm going to check inside."

Leaving his pack propped up against the face of the limestone hillside, he easily sidestepped into the opening and exited quickly into a small cave. Clearly, someone had stayed inside. The cold remains of a firepit were in the center of the area and a small pile of tinder and wood sat along the wall.

He could barely stand upright, but there was enough space for a few people to comfortably sit or sleep. He snared a small penlight from his belt loop and flashed it along the edges of the cave. The exterior wall was fairly straight and toward the back of the cave another opening led deeper into the rock hillside. Stalactites had formed near that opening from beyond the sounds of dripping water echoed from deep within the cave.

Although the cave smelled damp, there appeared to be fresh air flowing through it, which would explain how they could build the fire within the small space. As he turned his penlight on the dirt floor of the cave, T.J.'s easily identifiable sneaker tread was visible in several spots along with a much smaller footprint.

T.J. and Sara had been there recently. Maybe last night, he hoped, thinking that if the two teens were up ahead they were also finding a dry place to spend the night. If he and Macy got an early start in the morning, they might be able to make up some ground on the teens.

He eased back out through the opening to where Macy stood huddled against the rock face, the rain pounding against her.

"T.J. and Sara were here recently. We can stay in the cave tonight."

Stepping beside her, he helped her slip off her pack and then led her through the opening before heading back out to bring in his own supplies.

Inside the cave, he gestured to the firepit. "Think that you can get a fire going?"

She pulled off her baseball cap and then her poncho, setting them by the entrance to the cave opening to dry. "My Girl Scout skills are a little rusty, but I think I can manage," she said, reached into her pocket and pulled out a small package which she wiggled in the air. "Your dad handed me some waterproof matches on the way out of his store."

He grinned and nodded. "There may be some deadfall just off the trail. It'll be wet, but should still get dry if we get a good fire going. There's some tinder and a small supply of wood just over there," he said and motioned to the far side of the cave wall.

He had left his pack and the rifle by the entrance of the cave as well and stopped to remove a small hatchet from the main storage area on the pack. Exiting the cave, he carefully eased down a side of the trail that had some small brush, saplings and luckily, the deadfall from an oak tree. With a few sharp strokes, he chopped away some larger branches which he carried back up to the cave before returning once again to gather some more wood.

When he had a good enough pile, he returned to the cave, set the hatchet by his pack and slipped off his dripping poncho and cowboy hat. His boots were soaked as well and so he took them off and placed them besides Macy's.

Turning, he realized she had a nice fire going. The smoke from the fire was being drawn back toward the interior of the cave. He suspected there was a break somewhere allowing the air to vent. Macy had also laid out a tarp on the cave floor and had their sleeping bags ready for later use. A cooking frame was set over the fire and she heated water in a small kettle beside another pot where something was steaming flavorfully.

"Smells great," he said as he placed the damp wood close to the fire to dry.

"Thank your dad for the prepackaged stew." She stirred the mixture in the pot before reaching beside her and grabbing a plastic bag. "We've got some biscuits I'll heat up as well."

"Do you mind?" he said and motioned to his wet jeans.

Macy gulped as she imagined what lay beneath the faded denim, but it made sense. She had planned to remove her own wet jeans as well once the meal was closer to done.

"Go ahead." She kept her eyes trained on the stew and once it bubbled, she tore open the package with the biscuits and laid them on the grate of the cooking frame to heat.

Before she knew it, Fisher was kneeling beside her, his sleeping bag wrapped around his hips.

"Why don't you get out of your wet things while I finish this up?"

She handed him the spoon for the stew and stepped away only long enough to peel off her damp pants and set them on top of her pack to dry. As he had done, she wrapped her sleeping bag around her waist and returned to sit by the fire.

Fisher gingerly flipped over the four biscuits with his fingers and he shot a quick glance at her. "Would you rather have tea or coffee?"

"Coffee would be great." After he had sprinkled grounds in the pot with the boiling water, she picked up the two divided plates she had removed from his backpack, held them out to him.

He snared the biscuits from the grate and placed them on the plates, then quickly spooned up the stew into one of the sections of the dish. As one they shifted away from the fire and sat, using the cutlery that came with the mess kits to eat.

Hunger took control and it was quiet as they both savored the meal. The heat of the fire helped chase away the damp and chill of the rain.

Macy watched as Fisher sopped up the stew sauce with the last of his biscuit and took pity on him, handing him her second biscuit.

"Are you sure?" he asked even as he was reaching for it.

"I'm full," she said and she was. The stew and first biscuit had been surprisingly filling. She grabbed a pot holder and picked up the coffeepot, swirled the liquid and grounds around before setting it back down on the grate to continue brewing.

While she did that, Fisher rose and removed a large thick plastic bag from his pack and placed the dirty dishes inside. "We'll wash them up later."

She nodded, grabbed the two mugs she had put by the fire earlier and poured them both steaming cups of coffee. She opened a plastic bag which contained dry creamers and sweeteners. After they had fixed their coffees, they sat and quietly sipped them.

The sound of the rain coming down continued outside and Macy grimaced. "Do you think it will let up soon?"

He blew on his cup of coffee and took a sip before answering. Shaking his head, he said, "Weatherman said the storm front would be with us until tomorrow night, but it shouldn't be as heavy during the day tomorrow."

Macy cradled the hot tin mug in her hands, enjoying the warmth of it more than the coffee within. When she finally took a sip, the coffee was strong and sweet. She peered over the edge of the mug to where Fisher sat, drinking his coffee and adding some wood to the fire.

The wood was still damp and as it heated; it began to snap and pop. Hissed as steam escaped from the log.

The heat grew pleasantly in the intimate space of the cave and she unzipped the sweatshirt she had put on, allowed the heat of the fire to soak in. But her growing comfort made her guiltily think about the kids and how they might not be as restful.

"Do you think T.J. and Sara—"

"They were in this cave. Probably last night. I'm sure they took shelter again today."

His words reassured her, until it occurred to her that she would once again be sleeping beside him. Sharing intimate space and given last night's talk, trusted feelings.

A scary and exhilarating realization.

Chapter 19

As he looked up from where he had been poking at the fire, trying to get it banked for the night, he didn't fail to notice the battling emotions on her face. He could even understand.

He would be sleeping beside her tonight. Again.

It scared him. Each time that he was beside her made it harder to think about leaving. And it terrified him to think about what would happen if he released the control he had exerted last night and finally explored his feelings for her.

Which brought an unwelcome tightening to his gut which he had to tamp down like the fire he was so diligently managing.

Yanking his attention back to the flames, he said, "Do you want any more coffee? I'm going to go clean the mess kits."

"I'll help—"

"No," he said more forcefully than he had intended. Repeating it softly, he said, "No, just stay warm and get comfortable. I think Dad packed some inflatable pillows in your bag."

She handed him her mug and he piled up everything from the mess kits. Balancing it all, he went to the opening of the cave and the flow of air through that gap chilled the bare skin of his legs. Lucky for them, however, since that ventilation kept the cave free of the smoke and other toxins from their fire.

Easing through the gap, he used the rainwater to rinse off their plates and after, to clean the coffee pot and refill it for the morning.

His shirt was damp by the time he was done and he shivered. At his pack, he pulled off his shirt and grabbed a dry sweatshirt, slipping it on.

Macy had also changed into a different sweatshirt and lay by the fire, watching him. Her gaze was wickedly tempting as he imagined lying beside her and shedding the clothes they were both using as defenses against their emotions.

He padded back to the fire and gave it one last poke. He would have to keep an eye on it during the night to make sure it was under control. Then he slipped into the sleeping bag beside her and lay his head on one of the pillows she had inflated.

A nice comfort considering the hard ground beneath them and the tarp which crinkled noisily as they moved about. Of course, he'd slept in worse conditions.

"It's not so bad. We're warm and dry," he said, striving for neutral.

"I'm still a little chilled," she admitted.

"We could zip the bags together and share our body heat," he said before his brain had a second to think about the consequences of those actions.

Her eyebrows shot up in surprise at the suggestion and

worry settled onto her face. She bit at her bottom lip and mulled over the suggestion before finally saying, "Do you think that's a good idea?"

He thought about lying beside her. Remembered the press of her body against his last night and the softness of her cheek beneath his hand. He imagined the softness of her in other spots and immediately answered.

"It's probably the worst idea I've ever had."

She chuckled, shook her head and toyed with one of the ties on the sleeping bag. "I always knew you were an honest man."

Honest? An honest man might confess to what he was feeling and the conflicting emotions she roused in him. But then again, he was an honorable man and surprisingly, honor sometimes meant being less than honest.

"I guess I should be glad you feel that way about me."

Macy sensed hurt in his words and hadn't meant to cause it. Cupping his cheek, the rough beard on his face rasped the palm of her hand. "I didn't mean anything bad by it. I always admired you."

"Did you? Lots of women thought I wasn't a happily-ever-after kind of guy," he said.

She thought back to those days and the women he had dated—none of them had been the kind to have lasting relationships with. Except her. Which made her wonder aloud, "Why me?"

A flush stained his face and he looked away at her perusal. "Why you? That night, you mean? Why you and not someone else?"

The words escaped her on a tortured breath. "Yes, why me?"

He met her gaze then, his resolute and hard. "I dated the kind of girls who didn't want commitment, but I knew you were different. I knew you and Tim… I had wondered for a while what it would be like if it was you and me."

Much as she had questioned afterward what being with Fisher would have been like.

"Do you ever think about it now? I mean, with the teaching offer and all?"

She couldn't bear to look at him as she finished and concentrated on the ties of the sleeping bag, twirling them around and around her finger as she waited for his answer.

And then waited some more.

Finally, she had no choice but to meet his gaze.

"What do you think?" he asked.

"I'd like to think that maybe you had thought about it. About us," she finally admitted, deciding that after eighteen years of doubt, it was time to put an end to it.

"I have, only now there's T.J. to consider as well. A son that I didn't know I had."

"I'm sorry that I didn't tell you before. With Tim's death and all that started happening afterward, I wasn't sure T.J. could handle that kind of revelation," she admitted.

"And now?" Fisher asked and tipped her face up so he could search her features. "What makes now any different?"

Tears filled her eyes. "I always worried whenever you went on a mission. I prayed for you to be safe so that maybe one day you and T.J. could get to know one another."

"Did you maybe pray a little for yourself? That maybe one day you and I—"

"Yes, I did," she blurted out and shifted closer to him. Cupped his cheek and brought her lips close. "I prayed that one day you and I could finish what we started."

"Then let's finish it," he replied and kissed her, taking

her lips over and over again until she was clinging to his shoulders. Pressing her body tight to his except the thickness and tangle of the sleeping bags kept them from really being close.

Without breaking the kiss, he unzipped both bags and dragged her body to his, his hands splayed against her back. The bare skin of their legs warm as they twined their legs together.

He needed to feel more of her skin and inched his hands beneath her sweatshirt. The flesh at the small of her back was damp. Slick as he moved his hands upward.

She copied his actions, shifting her hands beneath his shirt to grasp his back. Moaning impatiently before reaching back down for the hem of his shirt, in one swift move she had pulled it over his head, baring him to her gaze.

She stilled then as she laid her hands on his chest. They trembled for a moment before she eased her one hand down to the scar along his ribs—a stray piece of shrapnel and a minor injury. She ran her finger along that scar before shifting to another on his arm.

"Don't think about them. I'm here and I'm alive. I want to explore the feelings between us," he urged, knowing that if she focused on those old wounds for too long, her fear would overwhelm everything else.

"How about I think about the way your heart skips when I do this," Macy said and moved her hand to cup his pectoral muscle. Beneath her palm, his nipple hardened into a tight nub. She shifted her hand so she could strum her thumb across the hard peak.

He sucked in a breath and at her back, his hands clenched against her skin.

"Not fair, Mace."

"All's fair in love and war, Fisher. You should know that," she teased, bent her head and took his nipple into her mouth.

He cupped the back of her head to him and murmured his approval, but even as he did so, he slipped his hand between their bodies and cupped her naked breast. Rotated her nipple between his thumb and forefinger and she gasped against his chest.

"That feels good," she said.

"Then this will feel even better," he said and pulled her shirt up and over her head, encircled her waist and brought her breasts to his mouth, where he greedily suckled, shifting his lips from one breast to the other as he pleasured her.

She held his head to her, kissing his forehead and encouraging him with her soft sighs and the press of her hips against his hard body.

"Touch me, Mace," he pleaded.

She reached down between their bodies with her one hand and covered his erection. The cotton of his briefs was smooth over the long hard length of him. She ran her hand over him, but when he bumped his hips forward, she answered his silent plea.

She slipped her hand beneath the cotton and surrounded him with her hand. Stroked the smooth soft skin of his erection as he teethed the tip of her breast, yanking a harsh moan from her.

The sound of her passion and the gentle caress of her hand nearly undid him.

Fisher eased her onto her back and while he continued suckling her breasts, he moved his hand downward until he encountered the edge of her low-rise panties. She sucked in a breath and held it, creating a gap between her skin and the panties and he pressed forward, delving beneath the fabric. Moving beyond the soft curls between her legs to the center of her, where he stroked her with his fingers. Felt her swell and grow damp beneath his fingers until he shifted his hand downward and eased his finger within.

She arched her back and called out his name in a satisfied surprise. "Fisher. Please tell me this is about more than want."

"It's about more," he said.

Smiling, she brought her lips to his and said, "Then make love to me."

Chapter 20

He groaned, so loudly that it made his body rumble against hers. He jerked beneath her hand, clearly at the edge and threw his head back with a shuddering breath.

"Damn, Mace. I don't have any protection."

Tenderly she stroked him while with her other hand she cradled his jaw and urged him to face her once again. "I've been on the Pill since Tim got sick and just never stopped taking it, hopeful I would find love again. I'm safe."

"I'm safe also," he confirmed and there came a flurry of movement as they dragged off their underwear.

Spreading her legs, she guided him to her center where he poised for a moment, the tip of him brushing her nether parts. Her muscles clenched in anticipation of welcoming him. Accepting him into her warm depths.

He looked down to where they were about to join, leaving

her staring at the short dark strands of his hair. She needed more. She needed to see the look in his eyes as they took that step. As they started to finish what had begun eighteen years earlier.

Asserting gentle pressure on his jaw, she urged him to meet her emotionally the way he would soon join her physically.

His green eyes glittered brightly and a slight flush worked across his cheeks as he breached her center with just the tip of him, holding himself away from her with shaky arms.

"Are you sure?" he asked, almost as if he needed to convince himself as well.

"I've never been more sure of anything in my life," she said and flexed her hips downward, surrounding him as she did so.

They both held their breath at that union. Held steady as their bodies reunited and their minds processed the fact of that joining.

He was thick within her and hard. All of him was hard against her, she thought as she laid her hands on his shoulders. Stroked the broad width of them, broader even than he had been at twenty. Stronger.

"You feel…" She stopped, unable to find the words. How familiar and yet different in a way that was exciting, she thought as she ran her hands all across his well-defined arms and shoulders. Across the deep muscle in his chest and down the six-pack abs that came from real honest work and not a gym.

He held himself steady, allowing her that exploration before he braced his weight on one hand and picked up the other to caress her breast. He ran his thumb across the tip of her and then took her nipple between her thumb and forefinger, tenderly tweaked it, creating a pull deep within her legs that caressed him. Urged him to move.

Slowly he did, easing out with almost agonizing tardiness

before he stroked deep within again, pleasing her with the fullness of him and the friction of his movement.

Fisher gritted his teeth and held on for control. Nothing had prepared him for how good it would feel to be inside her. To have the warm wet depths of her hold him as he moved in and out of her body. As he stroked her breast and knew that just touching wasn't enough. He had to taste…all of her.

He bent his head and sucked her nipple into his mouth as he continued his tarried penetrations, drawing her ever closer to a release. She clutched his head to her, shifted her other hand down to his buttocks to urge him on, but he withdrew from her, wanting that taste.

At her protest, he trailed his mouth down the center of her. Over the softness of her flat midsection and the sweet indentation of her navel. He paused there to tongue that valley before quickly moving past the nest of darker brown curls between her legs and to the center of her.

She yanked in a ragged breath as he tongued the nub between her legs and eased his fingers into her. Stroking her as he then kissed her there and sucked, building her desire with his hands and mouth. Feeling the pulse of her passion intensify beneath his mouth and fingers until her back arched up off the ground and she came, calling his name and holding tight to his shoulders.

He feasted on that release with his mouth, but before it had ebbed, he quickly shifted upward and joined with her again.

"Fisher," Macy cried out, holding onto him as his penetration brought her to the edge again and she shuddered.

He smiled, bent his head and kissed her. She could taste herself on him and realized that now she wanted a taste as well.

Pushing on his shoulders, she urged him onto his back and

straddled him, increasing his penetration and her pleasure. It was all she could do not to come again, but then he cupped her breasts. Tweaked her taut nipples and urged her on.

"Come for me, Mace. Tell me how much you like this."

She shuddered and climaxed, the explosion of damp and sensation ripping deep between her legs.

"That's it, Mace," he said, but then groaned as she rocked her hips up and down on him, dragging all that moist pulsing heat along the hardness of his erection.

He brought his hands to her hips to guide her, helping her set a rhythm. Picking up his head to lick at her breasts as she rode him and built toward another climax, but she still wanted that taste before it happened.

She eased off him, earning a strangled protest until he realized her intent and then he lay back, offered himself up, laying his hands to his sides. Exposing every bit of him to her.

She started at his chest, licking and biting his deliciously brown male nipples while she encircled him and stroked him, the wet of her from her possession of him slick beneath her hand. As the trembling in his body increased with her caresses, she trailed her mouth down the center of him, but she paused to kiss the scar along his ribs and murmured.

"I never want you to be hurt again," she said, but even as she did so, she worried that she might be the one to cause that hurt if things didn't work out with them again.

Shifting downward, she traced the edges of his defined abdomen with her tongue before playfully biting the skin over his nearly flat navel. He chuckled and cupped the back of her head, urged her downward until her mouth brushed the tip of him.

His big body jumped beneath her and she slowed the stroke

of her hand, tightened her grasp as she finally took the head of him into her mouth.

He groaned then and closed his eyes, arched his back to ask for more and she gave it to him, sucking him deep into her mouth while continuing to fondle him with her hand until he inhaled roughly and held his breath. She tasted the first hint of his release, but knew she wanted him deep within her when he came. Wanted to come with him and share in their passion for one another.

She held him tight and straddled him again. Guided him to the center of her and then sank down on him.

Their gazes locked at that union and she leaned forward, grasped his hands where they rested at his sides and brought them up and over his head. Twining her fingers with his, she watched his face as she began to move. Welcomed the surprise and acceptance in his gaze as their bodies strove toward the same goal. As the rush of pleasure and satisfaction drew them closer and closer to release.

Her body was shaking as was his when she finally bent her head and brought her lips close to his. With her eyes locked on his intense gaze, she whispered, "Love me, Fisher."

"God help me, but I do, Mace. I love you," he said and released the explosion of passion between them.

The muted call of an early morning bird filtered into her brain followed by the hard warmth of him spooned against her. The cadence of his breath changed, confirming that he, too, was awakening. His body definitely was, she thought as his erection stirred against her buttocks, arousing fresh desire within her.

She hadn't thought it possible given how often they had made love throughout the night, but she couldn't deny it now.

Pressing herself against him, she waited expectantly.

"Are you sure?" he asked as he splayed his hand against her belly.

When she nodded and urged his hand downward, he eased his thigh between hers and then pressed his erection into her.

She was slightly dry and the friction of him was rough at first, but he stilled to allow her time to adjust. Found the center of her with his fingers, caressing her. Bringing his other hand around to tease her nipples until she was wet and throbbing around him.

He let her set the pace, murmuring encouragement as she rocked her hips back and forth, her movements slow at first, but growing more determined as he brought her to the edge with his hands.

As her strength flagged, he somehow rolled and brought them to their knees. She braced her arms on the ground and accepted the strong thrusts of his body which pushed her ever closer to her release.

When he leaned over her and cupped her breasts from behind, rotating her tight nipples with his fingers, she came roughly as did he. But he was still there to hold her. Support her as her body shook with the force of her climax until they both dropped to the ground, bodies still joined.

The passion ebbed from their bodies, but the comfort of being beside him remained. Bittersweet because she knew there were still many tests their reborn love would have to survive.

From outside came more morning sounds as the hill country awakened, but mixed in with those sounds was the distinctive patter of rain against the ground and rock face. Inhaling, she smelled the rain in the air and hoped that T.J.'d had the sense to remain in whatever shelter he had found.

She and Fisher would not have the same luxury.

They had to find T.J. and Sara and return to Esperanza in order to set things right. She hoped that by now Jericho had returned from his honeymoon. Before she could say anything, Fisher said, "I can feel you drifting away."

Almost prophetically, his body slipped from hers, breaking the physical connection of their bodies. Trying to deflect his concern, she said, "Only until we have time alone again."

"Will we have that kind of time again?" he pressed, not falling for her attempt to avoid any serious discussion.

She flipped onto her back and he pillowed his head on one hand, braced his elbow on the floor so he could face her. "I want to. Once we find the kids and deal with whatever is going on with them—"

"We'll deal with us? With telling T.J. the truth?"

She thought about how difficult that might be, but recognized it was well beyond time to confront that past history and heal those old wounds so they might build a future. If he wanted to build a future, that was.

"Will you think about the teaching position?"

He nodded. "I already had, but now it seems as if I have even more reason to consider it."

She wanted to press for more, but decided she already had received more of a promise than she had ever expected. Rising up, she dropped a kiss on his lips and afterward said, "We should get going."

As she went to move away, he eased his hand around the nape of her neck and dragged her close for a deeper kiss. She clung to him for a second before he finally broke away.

"Just to make sure you know" was all he said as he rose

and went to the fire, tossing on some kindling and firewood to ignite it once more.

Once a small flame sprung up, he kindled it while she dressed and stowed away their sleeping bags and pillows. By the time she turned back to him, he had also dressed, gotten the pot of coffee going and had some oatmeal with fruit cooking on the campfire grate.

"Smells good," she said and sat down on the tarp beside the mess kits he had cleaned the night before.

"It'll provide solid energy and chase away the chill from the rain."

It wasn't much longer before they were eating the delicious warm oatmeal and drinking the coffee. He had made enough in the pot to fill up a small thermos he had in his pack. With the ever present rain, it would feel nice to have something warm to drink once they were back on the trail.

She helped him clean up and finish putting away their supplies. Once again they slipped on the ponchos, careful that the plastic covered their packs. Using the hoods and their hats to shield their heads from the worst of the rain.

Outside the downpours from the night before had abated somewhat, but the ground beneath their feet was sloppy. It was immediately clear their climb today would be arduous.

Despite that, they pressed on, Fisher in the lead, constantly alert to the ground and area around them in the hopes of finding any sign of the teens. About two-thirds of the way up, almost within sight of the overlook, Fisher held up his hand and motioned for her to stop.

A few feet ahead of him was another gap in the rock face along the left of the trail. A big enough gap that he was able to enter with his pack on his back. She followed.

As in the earlier cave, a firepit rested in the middle of the space and beside the firepit, something heartbreakingly familiar.

She rushed to the stones near the pit and picked up the piece of bright silver foil. "It's T.J.'s favorite granola bar," she said.

Fisher knelt and motioned to the footprints all around the foot of the cave. "T.J.'s tread and Sara's smaller shoes from the looks of it."

He held his hand over the ashes and remnants of burnt wood surrounded by the stones of the makeshift firepit. "Still warm. They can't have left all that long ago. Maybe they were waiting during the morning for the rain to let up—"

"And when it didn't, they left. So maybe they're not so far ahead."

"Maybe," he said and jerked his head in the direction of the gap in the rock face. "Do you think you can pick up the pace?"

Her legs ached from the constant sucking and pulling of the mud as they hiked, but if it meant finding T.J. faster…

"I'll go whatever speed you want."

With a nod, he rose and walked toward the break, but he stopped before her, cradled her cheek and said, "I always said you were a hell of a woman."

She smiled at the compliment, gratified by his praise. Back out on the trail, however, she was sorely tempted to curse him as he took her up on her word and pushed her at a grueling pace. Finally the trail leveled off a bit. Luckily, the sun was trying to poke through the clouds. While it would bring heat and humidity, it would hopefully dry up the ground for an easier hike.

They were near a bend that would put them on the final part of the trail to the overlook when she heard what sounded like a shout and the sudden intense roar of rushing water. Fisher must have heard it as well since he hurried around the bend.

She followed and smacked into him since he had stopped dead on the trail. As she glanced ahead, she realized the reason why.

Barely twenty feet before them was a wide arroyo spanned by a rickety wooden footbridge.

On the footbridge were two people—T.J. and Sara—hanging onto the flimsy wood and rope balusters of the bridge as it swayed and bucked from the force of the water cascading across it and down the arroyo.

"T.J.!" she shouted and rushed toward the bridge.

Chapter 21

Fisher took off after Macy, fearful that she would attempt to cross the bridge to reach the teens.

He had barely gone a few feet when a sickening crack and groan filled the air as the moorings for the footbridge closest to them gave way.

The end of the bridge rushed downward, propelled by the flood waters while T.J. and Sara bravely clung to the ropes and what remained of the bridge. The remnants of the bridge, with them hanging onto it, slammed into the far side of the arroyo, nearly unsettling the teens. The rush of the water covered them and the bridge pieces and then with another loud snap, the other end of the bridge likewise collapsed, plunging the teens into the flood waters.

Since the water sluicing down the arroyo actually brought them closer to where he stood, he jumped off the trail and careened almost wildly down the slope toward the edges of the arroyo. Seconds later, as he reached the bank and searched for T.J. and Sara, he heard Macy pound down the slope behind him.

"Do you see them?" she shouted over the loud noise of the raging flash flood that continued to surge down the arroyo.

On the opposite bank was a tangle of wood and rope from the footbridge, caught up in some tree roots and rocks. He thought he saw a glimmer of a red jacket amongst the debris, but couldn't be sure.

Tossing off his poncho and pack in the event he would have to go in after the teens, he waded into the edge of the waters. The immense force of the current pulled at him. Cursing under his breath because he doubted he could make it across the flood waters to the remnants of the footbridge, he withdrew back to drier land.

As he did so, some of the remaining bits of bridge gave way and were swept down the arroyo, but luckily, it revealed that T.J. and Sara were directly opposite them, clinging to each other.

When he looked at them more closely, he realized that T.J. had managed to grab hold of a sapling that had been along the edge of the arroyo. T.J. had one arm around the sapling and another beneath Sara's arms. The young girl was clutching him frantically, holding on to his arm and the fabric of T.J.'s red windbreaker.

He had to act and quickly. Sara looked like she couldn't hold on for much longer and the torrent of the waters was quickly eroding the ground securing the sapling.

He untied his rope from his pack and formed a lasso. He was a bit rusty, he thought, as he twirled the rope round and round, building up enough force to then toss it out across the twenty or so feet separating them from the teens.

It fell short of the mark but was in the right general vicinity.

He quickly reeled the rope back in, once again twirled the lasso over and over until he let it sail and it landed smack between the teens.

T.J. shouted at Sara to grab the rope and she did, but Fisher had other ideas.

"Tie it around the two of you—"

"The water's too strong and we'll be too heavy," T.J. shouted back. "Take Sara across first."

"T.J., please," Macy shouted from beside him, but he glanced at her and said, "T.J.'s right. It'll be too hard and we'll lose them both."

Macy hated that the two men were right. She also hated that by pulling Sara across first, they might risk T.J.'s life if he lost his shaky grasp on the small tree. But continuing to argue only increased the risk of that happening.

"Hold on tight, Sara," she shouted out and watched as one-handedly, her son somehow managed to get the rope up and around Sara's arms, securing her to the lasso.

Fisher had tied the other end of the rope around a tree on the bank and as T.J. released Sara, the waters carried her downward. Fisher began to pull her in, the muscles in his arms straining as he battled the force of the waters.

He had her halfway across the arroyo when a shot rang out.

By his head, a bit of bark flew off the tree beside him.

Someone was shooting at them, she realized, but she hadn't even finished the thought when Fisher blocked her body with his and continued reeling in Sara.

Another shot rang out, close to his head once again. He mumbled a curse, pushed her back behind the protection of

he tree trunk while he held on to the rope, fighting to not lose
his grip on it.

"Can you handle the rope?" he said and she immediately
grabbed it, sensed the pull of the water and Sara's weight
threatening to drag it from her hands.

She dug in forcefully, firmly planting her feet in the wet soil
and leaning back to get the leverage she needed while Fisher
grabbed his rifle. As she pulled in the rope, dragging it in hand
over hand, Fisher used the scope to search for the shooter.

Another shot rang out, dangerously close to Fisher, but he
grunted with apparent satisfaction.

"Now, I've got the bastard," he said and opened fire.

Her arms trembled from the force she was exerting, but she
kept at it, protected by Fisher's body and shooting.

As Sara neared the bank of the arroyo, the muddy dirt by
her feet flew up.

The shooter had turned his attention to her.

Fisher reacted immediately, rushing to block Sara's body
with his and urge her in the direction of the tree.

Sara plopped down behind the trunk, shivering from the
cold of the water. Her hands shook as she slipped the rope
from around her body and handed it to Macy.

Wet hair covered most of her face, but her fear was evident.
Her teeth chattered from the cold as she said, "Y-y-ou n-n-eed
t-t-o get T-t-J."

She peered across the surging waters cascading down the
arroyo. T.J. was still holding onto the sapling, but he was
deeper in the water as the roots of the tree began to give way.

She didn't have much time to save her son.

To save their son.

While Fisher continued to pin down the shooter by returning fire, she undid the rope from around the tree and stepped toward the bank of the arroyo. Fisher shifted his body to keep her covered. She swung the rope as hard as she could and when she thought she had enough momentum, released it.

It flew across the waters but landed below T.J.'s position.

Mumbling a curse, she quickly pulled the rope back in and gave it another try, aiming for a spot well above him.

As the rope flew across the waters this time, it landed a half a dozen or so feet above and was quickly carried downward by the waters.

With a sickening knot in her stomach, she watched T.J. lunge outward with one hand for the rope. As he did so, the sapling in his other hand gave way and he surged down the arroyo. She feared she had lost him, but suddenly there came the rough pull of the rope in her hands. Strong enough to almost upend her, but she braced herself and wrapped the rope around her arm.

T.J. had managed to grab the rope.

Using all her might, she made her way back to the tree and braced herself against the tree. She used the trunk to help her inching around the tree with the rope. Suddenly Sara was beside her, helping her to tie the rope to the tree.

Then another shot hit the trunk beside them, gouging a deep wound in the wood, but Fisher was immediately shooting at their assailant, trying to protect them.

As Fisher returned fired, she and the young teen began to reel in T.J. Together they managed to bring him onto the bank and once he was there, he slogged out of the water and mud and rushed to their side.

The happy reunion was short-lived, however, as the shooter opened fire on them again.

The three of them ducked down behind the meager protection of the tree and Fisher.

Fisher kept firing on the location of the shooter. It was only a matter of time before someone got hurt since they were too exposed on the banks of the arroyo. If he could backtrack on the trail and get behind the shooter, he could disarm them.

Glancing back at Macy where she huddled with the two kids, he said, "Can you grab the rifle and cover me? I need to take out that shooter."

Macy vehemently shook her head. "I'm a suck shot."

"I'll do it. My dad taught me how to shoot," T.J. said, standing up and holding out his hand for the rifle.

He ignored the ache in his gut at T.J.'s mention of his dad. Of Tim. Of how it could have been him who had taught T.J. to shoot the same way his dad had taught him and Jericho.

Driving away the pain, he handed T.J. the rifle and then stood beside him to point out the location of the shooter. Luckily, their attacker decided to fire, providing a needed view of his muzzle fire to confirm his position. T.J. immediately returned fire, his shot striking on the rock right by where he had seen the muzzle fire.

"Great shot. Keep that up, son," he said and patted the teen on the back. "I'm going to double-back along the trail and then come up behind the shooter."

"I'll cover you."

He nodded. "As soon as I've got a hold of him, I'll signal you so you can come down."

T.J. confirmed that he understood and then Fisher shot a look at Macy as she huddled next to Sara behind the tree trunk, trying to comfort the young girl. As their gazes met, he gave her a look that hopefully communicated his intent to stay safe.

At her nod, he rushed back up the slope and to the trail. While he did so, he whipped his cell phone out and called down to the ranger station, advising them of what was happening. Although the ranger immediately answered, he gave Fisher the answer he suspected.

"The sheriff and I won't be able to reach you any time soon," the ranger advised.

"I understand. He's got three of us pinned down and I need to get this shooter under control."

"Understood. The sheriff and I will be on our way shortly."

"I'll keep you posted," Fisher said and tucked the phone back into his pocket.

During the conversation, he had managed to make it halfway down to where the shooter was located. Moving as quickly as he could along the sloppy trail, he kept his eyes focused on the shooter. Listened as the ping and ricochet of gunfire echoed through the hills and arroyo.

Well aware of the shooter's position, he slipped from the trail, careful to stay out of view of their attacker, but unfortunately, he knew he might be out of view of T.J. and Macy. It meant he would likely need to deal with the shooter on his own, but he was well-prepared to do that.

In retrospect, it was the only way to keep them safe which was all important to him.

Important enough to risk his life.

With that awareness, he forged ahead.

Chapter 22

T.J. had his one arm propped against the trunk of the tree which shielded the bulk of his body from the shooter. The rifle was up against his other arm and he kept up a steady, but careful return of fire. Macy nestled with Sara behind the tree.

The girl was shivering in her arms and softly whispering, "It's all my fault."

Macy did what she could to comfort and reassure her. "It's no one's fault, Sara. Don't worry. We'll be fine."

She suddenly heard the hollow click as T.J. fired. The rifle was empty. Ducking down next to them in the meager protection provided by the tree trunk, he quickly reloaded the weapon with the ammo she had removed from Fisher's pack. Then he rapidly reassumed his position and began a brisk return of fire.

When he paused for a moment, she glanced up at him and asked, "Is something wrong?"

"I'm not sure. I think I saw Mr. Yates for a moment." He kept his weapon trained on the attacker, but held his fire.

She only hoped the shooter had not seen Fisher as well. When there was a continued lull in the shots from down below, T.J. dropped back down next to her and said, "We should head down. See if Mr. Yates needs our help."

"I'll go for the trail first. If it's clear, then you and Sara can follow," she instructed.

As she was about to move back up to the footpath, T.J. resumed his position at the tree, ready to fire, but no one shot at her as she headed up the embankment and back to the trail.

The ground was slippery and the weight of her pack made speed of any kind laborious, but she couldn't delay.

Fisher might need help.

Ironic how in all the years that she had worried about him being killed while on a tour of duty, he was probably in greater danger right here at home because of her and T.J.

She forced such negative thoughts from her mind and focused on the trail, remembering where she had last seen Fisher before he left the footpath to double back on the shooter. From behind her came the sounds of T.J. and Sara plodding along, gaining ground on her.

The lack of shooting was almost as scary as being fired upon. *Had Fisher subdued their assailant?* she wondered, refusing to consider the other possibility as she paused at the edge of the trail. She peered back up at where they had been pinned down by the shooter. It seemed far enough down and as she took the first step off the trail, she noticed that a few feet away, the brush and soil was torn up, as if someone had recently come that way.

Fisher, she thought, and rushed downward, at one point

losing her footing and ending up on her backside, sliding down the muddy bank of the trail. The weight of the pack dragged at her as she struggled to rise and she opted to release the bindings keeping it on.

She could move more quickly without it and if Fisher needed her help …

Free of the encumbering weight, she charged forward and came upon a small clearing where Fisher was fighting with a bigger, but slightly older man. A man who still held a rifle and was trying to bring it around to shoot.

"Fisher!" she called out and raced ahead.

Macy shouted his name and from the corner of his eye, he saw her plowing toward them, heedless of the fact that their attacker still had his weapon. Putting herself in danger.

The larger man took advantage of that millisecond of distraction and sharply hammered the butt of the rifle into his ribs. The blow drove the air from him, but he couldn't let the pain or lack of breath hold him back.

He had been tempering his actions up until now, keeping from using deadly force in the hopes of subduing the man, but Macy's presence had changed all that.

His years of military training took over.

When the man swung around to try and raise the rifle to fire, he unleashed a roundhouse kick to the man's head which dazed him for a moment. He followed up with a penetrating jab to the man's solar plexus, but the man somehow kept his hold on the rifle.

Charging him head on, he tackled their assailant to the ground and the impact of the landing finally loosened the man's hold on the weapon which went sailing a few feet away.

"Mom," he heard as he wrestled the man to his stomach and got him in a choke hold. Applying pressure, the cartilage in the man's neck crunched beneath his arm. With just a little more pressure it would give and end the battle. But as he shot a look out of the corner of his eye, he realized that T.J. and Sara had arrived. T.J. had shouldered the rifle again and now had it trained on them, ready to fire.

"It's okay, son. I've got him under control," he said and loosened his grip on the man's throat while grabbing hold of the arm he had twisted behind the man's back.

"Get his rifle, Mace," he instructed and she did so, picking up the discarded weapon before resuming a spot a few feet away beside the teens.

"Get up," he commanded the man, although he dragged him upward as well and maintaining his grip, made him face Macy and the teens.

"Dad!" Sara exclaimed, stepping from behind T.J. to stare at the man he had subdued.

He finally allowed himself the luxury of examining the man and realized he was one and the same as the picture that he and Macy had found online of Howard Engeleit.

Macy realized it as well. She stepped forward and looked up at him. Shook her head and said, "You're Sara's dad. You were shooting at your own daughter? Why?"

Engeleit sneered at Sara and said, "Because that little bitch is just like her mother. She was going to ruin my life."

Fisher increased his pressure on the man's arm, forcing him up onto his tiptoes to avoid the pain. As he did so, he asked, "Care to explain in a little more detail?"

"Sara saw my wife and I arguing—"

"You were always screaming at us and then you hit her. I

had to do something and realized I had my cell phone camera. I recorded him yelling and hurting my mom."

Howard sagged in his arms and his tone was pleading as he said, "You didn't understand what was going on, Sara. It was all a misunderstanding."

"I know what I saw," she shot back. "You were abusing mom and you were lying to the judge about her being unfit," she immediately continued and advanced on him until she stood right before him. She was petite and Howard's big bulk nearly dwarfed her, but she got up on her tiptoes until she was right in his face and said, "You only wanted custody of me so you could keep her quiet about how you mistreated us. But now I have proof of what you are."

Even though Fisher had a firm hold on him, the man lunged at his daughter. He yanked him back and T.J. took a protective step forward, the rifle pointed right at the man's head.

Howard stepped away and as if finally realizing that he was defeated, drooped in Fisher's arms until he was on his knees, his head downcast as he bemoaned his likely fate. "You're going to spoil everything, Sara. Once people see that video, I'll be ruined."

It was T.J. who spoke up next. "The night of the accident, someone chased us. Sara thought it was you."

Howard shook his head. "It was one of my investigators. I had him trying to find Sara. I just wanted you home safe and sound, honey," he cried, his tone cajoling, but Sara remained unconvinced.

"What you wanted was my cell phone with the video, that's why you tried to take it from me. You said you'd kill me if I didn't give it to you."

She faced Macy. "That's why I ran away and why I had those bruises on my arms—from fighting him off." She reached into her pocket and pulled out the cell phone. She had put it into a plastic bag and despite her soaking from the rain and flood waters, the cell phone appeared undamaged.

She dangled the bag with the phone in front of her dad. "Even if you take it now, it won't do you any good. T.J. and Joe helped me upload a copy of the video. It's safe now and I'm going to give it to Mom. I hope the judge gives her everything she's asking for in the divorce."

"And we're going to show it to the police," Macy said, coming to stand beside the young girl. She placed her arm around Sara's shoulders and said, "It's going to be all right now."

The young teen nodded. "It is. Thanks to T.J. and all of you, I finally feel safe."

From across the distance separating them, Macy met Fisher's gaze and the pride on it was evident. Their son had only been trying to keep Sara protected all that time. She only wished he had trusted them so they could have avoided a lot of misunderstandings and the risk to their lives.

"We should get down to the ranger station," she said and Fisher inclined his head in T.J.'s direction. T.J. had shouldered his pack for the trip down the trail.

"There's cable ties in the top pouch to the left, Macy. If you can get some, I'll get ol' Howard here trussed up for the trip down the hillside."

While T.J. continued to keep his rifle trained on Howard, she quickly removed the cable ties and handed them to Fisher who expertly secured Howard's hands behind his back.

After he was done, he said, "I'll take the pack now, T.J."

"I can handle it. Why not take Mom's?" he said and with a nod, Fisher shouldered the smaller pack as well as Engeleit's rifle which he used to prod the man and get him moving down the trail. As he walked, he called ahead to the ranger station to apprise the ranger of what had happened. When he hung up, he said to them, "The sheriff will be waiting for us down at the bottom of the trail."

She nodded and took up a spot just behind him while T.J. brought up the rear, Fisher's rifle cradled in his arms.

The downhill journey took a few hours, but it was much shorter and easier than the uphill climb. The sun had finally emerged, bringing with it the heat and humidity which she had expected, but also drying the ground somewhat, making their footing and journey less severe.

At the end of the trail, the local sheriff and park ranger were waiting for them. The sheriff took Howard Engeleit into custody, promising them that he would make sure Engeleit was held without bail in light of the threat he posed to Sara and his attempt to murder them along the trail.

With the sheriff gone, the ranger offered them the use of the ranger station to rest a spell before they went home.

Macy wanted nothing more than to head to Esperanza and clear up things about T.J., hopefully with Jericho and not Deputy Rawlings. But before she did that, she realized something else needed to be done.

She faced Fisher and held out her hand. He took it with his and smiled gently, although a hint of confusion colored his features. "I want to thank you for everything you've done for us."

T.J. stepped up to his mother's side, placed his arm around her shoulders and said, "Yes, thank you for taking care of my mom and me, Mr. Yates. I know my dad would have appreciated all you did also."

A pained look crossed Fisher's features and Macy knew it was the right time to act. Turning to her side, she took hold of her son's hand and said, "There's something you need to know, T.J."

Before either she or Fisher could say anything else, T.J. surprised them by saying, "Mr. Yates is my biological father, isn't he?"

Once again pain flashed across Fisher's features, but he schooled his emotions quickly. With a nod, he said, "Yes, I am. How did you know?"

Sara jumped in at the moment to say, "I think you all need some time alone. I'll be waiting in the ranger station."

After she walked away, T.J. said, "While we were on the steps of the church, I overheard someone say how handsome father and son looked. They were talking about you and me. Then I realized how much we looked alike. How we were standing alike."

And as they stood there facing one another, Macy once again noted the physical similarities between the two that marked them as father and son. Guilt swamped her, creating a knot in her stomach. She took a deep breath and slowly released it before she said, "I'm sorry you learned the truth that way. Your dad… Tim and I should have told you."

"Tim Ward was my father," T.J. began, his voice shaking with emotion.

Fisher laid a hand on T.J.'s shoulder and the young man didn't pull away. A good sign, he thought.

"Tim Ward was a good man. I never want to replace him in your heart, T.J. But I would like to get to know you."

Beneath his hand, tension radiated in T.J.'s body, but then the teen relaxed a bit. After a moment's delay, T.J. nodded and said, "I'd like that."

He didn't know how it happened, but a second later, they

were embracing and his heart swelled with love and pride at the fact that this young man was his son. "I'm proud of how you protected Sara and helped me up on the trail."

"Thank you for all that you did for us. For helping Mom, Sara and me," T.J. replied again before easing away to stand before Macy.

She slipped her arm around his shoulders and gave him a hug. "You're welcome to visit any time you'd like, Fisher. I know that with your military life that may not—"

"Actually, I may be seriously considering that job up at West Point," he said, wanting her to know that things had changed between them. Aware that in time, he might be asking her and T.J. to go with him, although he kept that to himself for the moment. Too much was happening right now to add that to the mix.

"I'm glad, Fisher. I always worried about you when you went on tour," she said and added, "It's time we all headed home."

"Let's go get Sara and maybe get the two of you into some dry clothes," Fisher suggested.

"I lost my pack with all our stuff when the bridge gave out," T.J. said.

Fisher motioned to his bag and Macy's which were on the ground by T.J.'s feet. "The clothes may be big, but you and Sara can take stuff from our packs."

T.J. immediately grabbed one pack and went off in the direction of the ranger station, his long strides quickly putting some distance between them. Fisher picked up the other pack and together, and much more slowly, he and Macy strolled to the station.

As they walked, she glanced up at him, almost shyly. "You were serious about considering that teaching position?"

He thought about leaving the life he had known for so long. A life that had brought him order, discipline and stability. But as he met Macy's gaze, he thought about all that he had missed with her and all that they could still have. With a smile and a nod, he said, "I've never been more serious about anything in my life."

Her smile was the only answer he needed.

Chapter 23

"I don't know what's going to happen with my mom and dad, so I'd like to stay on the ranch for now," Sara said, her brown-eyed gaze skittering over each of them before finally settling on T.J. as he sat beside Joe on the couch.

Jewel Mayfair contemplated Sara's request a moment before responding. "I hope the three of you realize how much danger you put yourselves in by not trusting us with the information about what was happening."

Macy watched as if almost orchestrated, the heads of all three teens bobbed up and down in unison. Bodies slouched, they were clearly aware of how their behavior had jeopardized not only their lives, but hers and Fisher's.

Jewel continued. "I have no problem with you staying as long as you'd like, Sara, but we need to let your mom know what's happened, and also Sheriff Yates."

"I've already talked to Jericho," Fisher offered from his spot beside her. "I phoned him from the ranger station, plus the local sheriff faxed him a copy of his report a short while ago. He'd like to interview all of you tomorrow so that he can complete his part of the report on Howard Engeleit's activities."

T.J. perked up and said, "Does that mean I'm no longer in trouble with the law?"

"You're out of trouble with them, but not with me," Jewel advised. Facing the two boys, she said, "Starting tomorrow, I expect both of you to get back to work bright and early. Even though you did what you did for a good reason, T.J. still needs to pay off his mom for the damage to the two cars and the speeding ticket."

Jewel then faced Macy, "Don't you agree?"

"Wholeheartedly," she said with a nod.

"I'm glad that's settled. I'd like to talk to Macy and Fisher alone for a moment, but afterward we're going to call your mom, Sara."

The young girl nodded and the three teens rose and went off to the family room to join the other kids, while Fisher and she remained behind in the library.

Jewel rose and closed the door, let out a tired sigh. "Am I glad that's all over."

"So am I. I'm sorry about how T.J. acted," she began, but Jewel waved her off and sat back down in her chair.

"He was confused and trying to help. Luckily it worked out well, only...I had actually thought we'd find him and Sara somewhere on the ranch property."

Fisher shifted to the edge of the couch and leaned his elbows on his thighs. His large hands were clasped before him as he said, "Why do you say that?"

"For several nights I've been restless with worry about T.J. and Sara and have been going for walks outside. For the past few nights I've heard noises while I walked. What sounded like crying—"

"Like what you heard before that you mentioned to Clay Colton?" she asked.

Jewel confirmed it with a shake of her head. "Similar, only this time I thought I heard hushed voices as well which is why I thought it might be the teens."

"Did you call Jericho and tell him?" Fisher asked.

Jewel shrugged and said, "I figured he had enough on his plate what with his just getting back from his honeymoon and all that was happening with the kids. Besides, when I mentioned it to Clay again, he said he would check around once more."

Fisher shifted back onto the sofa beside her. "If it continues, you should mention it to Jericho. It could be nothing or it could be—"

"Serious. I know. I should listen to the advice I gave the kids and talk to the sheriff about it."

Macy considered what her friend and boss had said and grew concerned that the noises might truly be something to worry about. "Do you want Fisher and me to stay here tonight? Help you keep an eye on things?"

Jewel shook her head. "No need right now. Clay is going to look around, but if it keeps up, I'll call Jericho. Besides, I figure the two of you need some time together. Or am I wrong about that?"

Hesitant, she risked a glance in Fisher's direction, but there was no uncertainty there. He quickly answered, "You wouldn't be wrong about that, Jewel. There's a lot for me and Macy to work on."

A broad smile came to Jewel's face. "Well, I'm glad to hear that. If you need to, take another day or so, Macy. Ana and I can handle the kids."

She appreciated her boss's offer and thanked her as she rose from the sofa. Turning to Fisher, she said, "I think it's time we took T.J. home and let Jewel get some rest."

Fisher stood up and eased his hand into hers. "I'd like to go home with you, if that's okay."

Macy grinned. "It's better than okay. It's what's right."

Fisher was used to sitting down to dinner with his men or his father and brother. Maybe it was because they were generally taciturn men that he found the back and forth between Macy and her son—no, their son—to be so lively.

T.J. was busy filling her in on what Joe had to report about the goings on during his absence.

"He says Deputy Rawlings was totally pissed off when Sheriff Yates told him that he was assuming control over Sara's case."

Macy carefully and methodically cut into the steak on her plate, clearly thoughtful about T.J.'s comments. "I think the Deputy is interested in Jewel, so maybe he had hoped to spend some more time around her thanks to the case."

"I don't like him," T.J. said without hesitation and then stuffed a chunk of sirloin in his mouth.

"That's understandable," he offered. "He was kind of rough on you."

"Damn straight," T.J. replied with a determined nod while he chewed the steak.

"T.J.," Macy warned, but the teen quickly swallowed and renewed his protest.

"He wouldn't cut me any slack, even when I told him the accident wasn't my fault."

"Let's just say he had past history to consider. Sometimes it's tough to overcome that kind of past although what you did for Sara will count for a lot," she said.

T.J. glanced over in his direction as if waiting for his take on things and then Macy looked his way as well. Considering T.J.'s actions that day, there was only one thing he could say.

"You were a hero today. You helped keep us all safe, only… Next time you should trust your mom more. Tell her if you or a friend are in trouble."

"What about you? Can I tell you if I'm in trouble?" he challenged and at his words, Macy looked away, obviously uncomfortable and possibly nervous about the answer.

To quell her discomfort, he laid his hand over hers as it rested on the table and said, "You can count on me, T.J. I'll be there if you need me."

"Will you be here for my mom?" he pressed and Macy's hand tensed beneath his.

"Your mom and I…there's lots for us to discuss and whether I'm here, that's for your mom to decide."

T.J. shot a glance between the two of them, without a doubt wondering about them, but he kept silent and resumed eating.

He and Macy did the same, polishing off the rest of the quick and simple steak and potatoes meal they had prepared.

After dinner, T.J. helped clear off the table and then walked to the door of the kitchen. "I'm kind of tired, so I'm going to my room to turn in early."

Fisher thought about saying goodnight. Thought about leaving the two of them that evening and every evening thereafter. It was more difficult to imagine than he had expected.

Macy solved the problem for him, coming to stand by his side while addressing T.J. "Would you mind if Fisher stayed with us tonight?"

"With us?" T.J. echoed and then picked up a finger and pointed it between the two of them. "You mean, like with the two of you like a mom and dad kind of stay with us?"

Heat flared across his face and as he shot a glance out of the corner of his eye, he realized Macy was likewise blushing at T.J.'s directness. Despite that, she nodded and answered, "Yes. As in Fisher and me staying together tonight like a mom and dad."

T.J. thought about it for a moment before he said, "Could I speak to Mr. Yates for a second, man-to-man?"

With a nod, Fisher walked up to him and then the two of them stepped outside the kitchen and into the hall. T.J. stood face-to-face with him and he was struck once again by how much the boy looked like him and wondered why no one had ever noticed before or if they had, why they hadn't said anything.

"What can I do for you, T.J.?" he asked, his voice pitched low so that Macy would not hear.

"You do mean to do what's right for my mom, don't you?" the boy asked, his tones seriously adult.

"I do, but I also want to do what's right for you. I've been thinking about whether to accept a teaching position at West Point—"

"I think Mom would like that," T.J. said and then quickly added, "And so would I. It would let me get a fresh start somewhere and get ready for college. That is if I'm included in your plans."

He imagined what T.J. might feel like, being faced with so much change in so short a time. So much life altering change.

but then he realized he didn't have to imagine so hard. He had lived through such upheaval when his mom had abandoned them. He was living through the same abrupt change now with the discovery that he had a son and was still in love with Macy.

Even with his own confusion about the recent changes, he had no doubt about the answer to T.J.'s question.

"You're my son and I want what's best for you. If you and your mom wanted to stay here until you finished high school—"

"I'll do whatever will make Mom happy. I know I haven't made her life easy lately, only…I really missed Dad…Mr. Ward…"

"Your dad. Tim Ward was your dad, T.J., but I'd like for us to get to know one another. For your mom and I to possibly share our lives as well."

T.J. nodded and before Fisher could anticipate it, the teen hugged him hard, but then just as swiftly, turned and raced up the stairs.

Emotion swelled up in him, so strong it nearly choked him. Taking a few steadying breaths, he walked into the kitchen where Macy had just about finished cleaning up. As she dried her hands on a dish towel, she faced him. Worry clouded her features as she asked, "Is everything okay?"

He smiled and said, "Better than I could have expected."

"Really?" She walked toward him, stopped about a foot away and looked up at him. "T.J. is…okay with things?"

"As long as you're okay with things, only you and I really haven't decided what the future holds for us."

Macy was nearly strangling the dish towel in her hands and he stepped up and took it from her. "Why don't we go up to your room and talk."

She narrowed her eyes, as if taking his measure. "Is talk all you want to do?"

He grinned. "What do you think?"

Taking the final step to close the distance between them, she slipped her index finger beneath the waistband of his jeans and tugged him even closer. "I think that if you don't plan on kissing me soon, I may go crazy."

Clay Colton glanced out over the Hopechest Ranch from the small hill at the edge of the Bar None. All seemed quiet down below and he had yet to hear the strange noises in the night about which Jewel had complained.

Pressing forward, he headed down the incline to the metal fence which separated the two ranches and helped keep his livestock from wandering off. He followed the fence line, thinking that possibly one of his animals or even a wild animal had gotten caught up in the fencing. Or maybe they had been hurt by the barbed wire and lay injured nearby, accounting for the crying sounds that Jewel had heard.

Riding slowly along the fence, he kept his eyes trained for signs of any animals or possible problems and then something caught his eye in the bright moonlight.

He eased off Crockett and ground tethered the horse as he approached the fence. Squatting down, he realized there were boot prints near the fence and also, a few cigarette butts close by. He picked up one of the butts. There was something familiar about it, although he couldn't quite put a handle on what it was.

Taking a bandanna from his back pocket, he slipped that butt and two others into the bandanna, intending to show them to Jericho. As he stood and tucked the bandanna into his pocket, something glinted in the moonlight once more up ahead on the fence.

As he approached, he realized that the bottom line of barbed wire had been cut. Recently, since the ends were still silvery and unrusted like the rest of the wire. With the bottom wire cut, it would be easy for an animal or a person to slip through and as he looked around more carefully, he noticed more boot prints on the Hopechest side of the fence.

Strange, he thought and rose, searched out the countryside for signs of any strays or humans, but saw no one. He did notice, however, that he was near some caves where he and his kid brother Ryder had used to play as children. They would head down into the caves to avoid the heat of the summer day and had even camped out overnight in one of the larger ones a time or two.

He and Ryder had sure shared some fun times back then, before the problems.

His baby brother Ryder, he thought once again as he had often thought about him in the past few weeks. He'd had no luck reaching him in the prison where he was being kept. No luck finding out anything about how his brother was doing.

As he let out a low whistle for Crockett and the horse came over, he thought about writing to Ryder once more, but then decided that it would probably be another futile endeavor. Grabbing Crockett's reins and hoisting himself back up in the saddle, he decided he had to do something more if he was going to find out what was up with his little brother.

Tomorrow he would phone the prison and after, head into town to tell Jericho about his findings along the fence. He

hoped his friend would be able to help him figure out wha
was going on between the Bar None and the Hopechest an
possibly decide what to do about Ryder.

Chapter 24

Macy held Fisher close, arching her back as he slowly shifted in and out of her, slowly building her climax.

As she reached the edge and sucked in a rough breath, he stopped and arms braced on either side of her, looked down at her. "Are you okay?"

She was more than okay, but there was T.J. to consider just a few doors away. Reaching up, she cradled the back of his head and urged him down until she could murmur softly against his lips, "More than okay, love."

He kissed her then and whispered, "I understand, Mace."

He continued kissing her as he began to move within her again, dragging her to the edge time and time again, holding his own release back until his body was shaking above her. Raising her hips, she deepened his penetration and dragged a rough moan from him which she muffled with another kiss.

"Come with me," she urged against his mouth and with a few stronger strokes, he did, joining her as her release washed over her. Swallowing her small scream of satisfaction with another kiss before he lowered himself onto her, breathing heavily.

It took a minute or so before they could move, easing onto their sides so they were facing one another. It took less than that before they were touching each other again.

As Fisher cupped her breast and shifted his thumb back and forth across the tip of it, he said, "I can't get enough of you, Mace. I can't imagine how I survived all this time being without you."

"I'm here now, Fisher," she said and ran the back of her hand over the ridges of his abdomen before moving lower and encircling his softness which immediately began to harden beneath her hand.

He stilled his motions and as she glanced up at him, he asked, "I want more than now, Mace. Can you give that?"

"Whatever you decide, I'll be here for you, Fisher. I don't want to lose you again."

He groaned once more and his body shook against her from the force of his emotion.

"You won't lose me, Mace. I promise," he said and pressed her down into the mattress as he began loving her anew.

Macy held him tight, her hands clasped on his shoulders. Her body welcoming his as they tried to make up for all the time they had lost. As she tried to store up the memories to keep her in the event he decided to go back on another tour of duty.

He must have felt her stiffen in his arms since he bent his head and repeated his earlier promise. "You won't lose me."

As she released her heart and body to him, she prayed that was a promise he could keep.

Jericho flipped through the pile of envelopes that Clay had handed him. Each bore Ryder's name and cell number neatly printed in Clay's handwriting. He noticed that the postmarks on the envelopes went back for several months. Leaning back in his chair, he rubbed his finger across his lips and contemplated the man sitting before him.

Clay Colton sat tensely on the edge of the hard wooden chair, juggling his Stetson between his large work-worn hands.

"You say the warden had nothing to tell you."

Clay nodded and released a heavy sigh. "Warden said he wouldn't tell me anything about Ryder and couldn't give me a reason why the letters had been returned unopened."

Even though Ryder's actions years earlier had created a rift between the two brothers, Jericho had no doubt that Clay sincerely wanted to make amends and was concerned about his younger brother. Unfortunately, there wasn't much he could offer for the moment.

"I'd take a ride to the prison and demand to speak to the warden and Ryder. Hear what they've got to say to your face. In the meantime, I'll make some calls and see what I can find out."

A tight smile came to Clay's lips. "I'd appreciate that." He juggled the hat up and down once more, clearly uneasy.

"Something else you want to say?" Jericho asked.

"I hate doing this to you so soon after your return, but I'm a little worried about something I found up at the border between the Bar None and the Hopechest."

The other man explained about Jewel's concerns about the

crying noises in the night and how he had gone out and discov ered the boot prints, cigarette butts and the recently cut fence

"Rustlers, you think?" Jericho asked, but Clay emphati cally shook his head.

"All my horses are accounted for and I've asked around. N one's missing any livestock or seen anything out of the ordinary.

A relief, Jericho thought. With him and Olivia just bac from their honeymoon and still recovering from their run-i with Allan Daniels, he had been looking forward to a littl quiet at his return. Of course, given all that had been goin on with T.J., Macy and Fisher, quiet was the last thing that seemed he was going to get.

"I'll send the deputy to make some extra rounds at nigl and take a ride up myself to see what's happening. I'll let yo know what I make of things."

Clay rose from his chair and held out his hand. "I'd appre ciate whatever you could do on both counts."

He stood, shook Clay's hand and nodded. As Jericho wa sitting back down, he noticed Fisher coming through the fron door of the sheriff's office.

"Welcome, bro," he called out and waved his brother ove to his door.

Fisher seemed tired and considering what had happene during the last few days, it was understandable. But as Fishe approached the door, he noticed the happy gleam in hi brother's eyes. When they embraced, there was somethin more relaxed in his brother's normally militarily rigid postur

"It's good to have you home, Jericho," Fisher said an after, sat in the chair before his desk.

"You seem to be doing okay, all things considered."

Fisher leaned his elbows on the arms of the chair and lace

his fingers together before him. "All things considered, I'm doing better than okay although…"

His brother surged forward in the chair, his hazel eyes glittering brightly. "There's a lot I've got to say and I'm going to ask you to let me finish it all before you start asking any questions."

Jericho nodded and leaned back in his chair which squeaked from the weight of his body. As he grasped the arms of the well-worn leather chair, the bright gold of his new wedding band caught Fisher's eye.

Once again he thought about how his brother hadn't seemed like the home and hearth type, but then again, until lately, he hadn't thought of himself that way.

That was, until lately.

"I'm thinking of taking the teaching position at West Point instead of signing up for another tour of duty in the Middle East. I'll miss my men and worry about them, but I think I can do a lot more good teaching new officers."

He waited for Jericho to comment, but his brother just sat there, although a broad smile slowly leaked onto his face.

"Nothing to say?"

"You told me not to say anything until you were finished and I suspect that's just the start of your announcements."

He chuckled. His kid brother knew him all too well. Shaking his head with amusement, he met his brother's happy gaze and continued. "Do you know why I was angry about your planned marriage to Macy?"

"'Cause you wanted her for yourself?" his brother offered, surprising him.

"You knew that?"

"I suspected, but she needed my help—"

"And you were always one to help a friend. Much like Tim helped Macy when she told him she was pregnant," he said, but before he could continue, Jericho jumped in.

"I always thought she and Tim kind of rushed things. Her being pregnant out of wedlock explains—"

"No, it doesn't explain everything, bro. Macy was pregnant with *my* child."

Silence followed for long moments until Jericho plopped forward in his chair and splayed his hands on the top of his desk, his eyes wide and a look of shock on his face.

"T.J. is your son? And you never knew?"

"Never. I suppose you never suspected it," he said and examined his brother's features as the surprise slowly faded from Jericho's face.

"Never. I mean, T.J. didn't look that much like Tim, but I always thought he favored Macy." He paused and shook his head in disbelief.

"You have a son. I have a nephew," he said with a dazed tone in his voice.

"I have a son and yes, you have a nephew. Not to mention that Dad…well, Dad's a granddad."

"And he'll have another grandchild soon. I imagine the old man will be as pleased as a racehorse put out to stud. His family's growing by leaps and bounds," Jericho said and once again shook his head as he thought about everything.

"What do you and Macy plan to do? I mean, you've told T.J., I assume—"

"We have," he said and bounced his joined hands up and down nervously. "He seems to be handling it well. He says he'll do whatever will make his mom happy."

Jericho covered his mouth with one hand, his actions thoughtful as he rubbed his hand across his lips.

"What will make you happy, Fisher?"

"I can't imagine being without Macy again, Jericho. I think I'm going to ask her to marry me."

Jericho let out a small whoop, hurried around the desk and wrapped him up in a powerful bear hug. "I'm glad to hear that, Fisher."

He returned the embrace and when they parted, Jericho sat on the edge of his desk and picked up one of the envelopes there. Holding it up, he said, "Seems like we're not the only ones in a marrying kind of mood."

He held out the fancy off-white envelope and Fisher took it, removed the invite from within—one to Georgie Grady and Nick Sheffield's wedding. The event was barely a week away and he chuckled as he thought about good ol' Georgie Grady finally tying the knot after so many years.

"Seems like Cupid's been busy in Esperanza lately."

Jericho eyeballed him intently. "Are you complaining, big bro?"

He thought about going home to Macy later that day and warmth and happiness filled him.

"Not at all, lil' bro. Not at all," he confessed.

Chapter 25

A week later, they gathered for Georgie and Nick's reception at the local catering hall. The wedding had taken place earlier that day at the church where less than a month before she had planned on marrying Jericho. Where Jericho had married Olivia three weeks ago.

She held Fisher's hand beneath the table where they sat, listening as Clay relayed the information he had been able to obtain about Ryder after visiting the prison.

"The warden wouldn't see me at first, but I insisted. That's when he finally let me into his office and told me that Ryder had died a few months ago," he said and beside him, his wife Tamara covered his hand as it rested on the table and tenderly twined her fingers with his.

When Clay spoke once again, his voice was tight and slightly hoarse from holding back his emotions. "It's hard to elieve he's gone. I feel like he's still alive. I still feel as if ne day I'll be able to make amends for the distance between s over the last few years."

Jewel, who was sitting beside Jericho and Olivia at the able and her date, Deputy Adam Rawlings, leaned closer as he music from the band grew a little louder, making conversation slightly more difficult. "I know how you feel. When I ost my fiancé and baby…it took a long time for me to really ccept that they were gone."

She had experienced the same emotions after Tim's eath. For the longest time, she would roll over in bed, expecting him to be there. She would even smell him sometimes and recounted those sentiments in an effort to omfort Clay.

"Tim used to have this funky aftershave that T.J. had ought him for one Father's Day. For months after he was one I imagined that I could still smell it," she said and Fisher ightened his hold on her hand, offering her solace.

Clay's eyes narrowed at her comment. "I thought I smelled Ryder the other day. He used to smoke these fancy cigarettes hat had this weird odor…" His voice trailed off, but then he uickly added, "I think they were like the ones I found by the ence separating the Bar None and the Hopechest Ranch. You ave the butts, right, Jericho?"

"I do, Clay. I sent one of them on to the state police for nalysis."

"We appreciate you doing that. It'll be nice to know there's o worries to have about the kids," Jewel said and glanced in he direction of a large table at the other side of the room vhere T.J., Sara and Joe sat together with Georgie's little girl nd the other kids from the Hopechest.

"They're having a nice time," her boss said and suddenly the band launched into a Texas two-step.

Jericho stood and pulled his newlywed wife Olivia to her feet. "Come on, darlin'. I've got to teach this city girl how to dance before you get too big to move around."

Macy smiled as Olivia eased into Jericho's arms and the two of them hurried to the dance floor. It pleased her that Jericho seemed so happy and as she shot a glance at Fisher, there was no doubting the contentment on his face. Even Clay, with his sadness over his brother's loss, seemed to have an easier burden with Tamara beside him.

As her gaze skipped to Jewel, she wished her boss would find happiness and as if some fickle Cupid somewhere was listening, Adam leaned toward her and said, "Would you mind taking a spin with me, Miss Jewel?"

To her surprise, Jewel's lips tightened with displeasure. "Thanks, Adam, but I think I'll sit this one out."

The deputy's face went white with anger before flushing red from embarrassment. His jaw clenched tightly, he dipped his head, rose from beside her and walked away to the bar at the side of the room. He stood stiffly while waiting for a drink.

"You okay, Jewel?" she asked.

Her friend shrugged and looked away from the deputy. "There's just something about him lately… I guess I'm a little angry about how he handled everything with Sara and T.J."

She understood completely. She'd had her moments of hostility about the deputy's actions, but she didn't want that to create problems for her friend. "I understand, but don't be mad at him on my account. I kind of thought he had a crush on you."

"Which I guess explains why he asked me to be his date for the wedding, although I'm wondering why I agreed to come with him. I mean, he's nice and everything, but the more I think about it, the better it is to wait for the right person. I mean, just look at Graham Colton over there," she said and motioned to where the older man sat, watching all the goings on, but physically and emotionally alone.

"He never was one to join in, but I think he really did love my mom," Clay said, surprising everyone with his comment.

"Too bad he didn't know how to show it," Fisher said and glanced her way, his gaze hot and intense, leaving no doubt that he knew how to demonstrate his affections for her.

As heat pooled in her center at just how he would show her once they were home, she leaned close to him and whispered a warning. "Fisher, please. You'll have to wait until later."

Jericho and Olivia returned just then, slightly sweaty and winded from their two-step adventure. As Jericho glanced their way, he said, "You two have a secret?"

Fisher chuckled and wrapped an arm around her shoulders. "Actually, it seems as good a time as any to make this announcement—Macy and I are getting married. She and T.J. are going to join me at West Point where I've accepted a teaching position."

Congratulations and hugs erupted all around the table and she found herself going from one person to the other, accepting all their good wishes. She finished making her rounds by going to Jewel, who hugged her hard.

"I'm so happy for you, Macy. Fisher seems like a wonderful man."

"He is," she said and brushed back a lock of her friend's

short light brown hair. "I know that one day, you'll meet a wonderful man, as well."

Jewel grinned and playfully tugged on her hand. "I hope you'll let me be your bridesmaid again."

"Without a doubt. Fisher and I will be setting a date shortly and finalizing all the plans soon. I'll stay as long as you need me at the ranch."

"Don't worry about that. Ana and I can handle things for a little longer," her boss reassured her, but Macy didn't want to leave her in a lurch.

"With Fisher accepting the appointment, we'll have some more time in Esperanza and I'll help you find my replacement. Get things settled at the ranch before I go."

"I'd appreciate that," Jewel said and after, they all sat back down around the table to enjoy the rest of the wedding.

As Fisher took her hand in his again and they shared an intimate glance, she realized that soon they would be gathering to celebrate her wedding to Fisher. Her son...no, their son would be standing beside them, blessing their union. Making them a family finally.

Her secret was out in the open and as she faced Fisher and brought her lips to his, she whispered, "Are you sure?"

His grin erupted against her mouth, calming any of her fears. "I'm sure that our being together is about eighteen years overdue. And you?"

She chuckled against his lips and said, "I'm sure that if I do want I want to right now, Jericho will have to lock us up."

He joined in her laughter and closed the distance to her lips, kissing her deeply until an amused cough drove them apart.

"Bro, I think it's time you and Macy went home," Jericho said, his eyebrow arched in amusement.

Fisher jumped to his feet, her hand in his. "For once, I'm not going to argue with you."

The deputy's patrol car had passed him along the edge of the road, but he had flattened himself to the ground in a small ditch and gone unseen. When the car returned on its rounds and skipped by him on its way back to town, he waited for a few more minutes before rising from the ditch and making the nearly mile long trek to the cut in the fence.

He moved swiftly and quietly, slipped through the cut barbed wire on his way to the small stand of trees and the caves where he and Clay had played as kids.

Clay, he thought, thinking about his older brother and how he had looked the other day when he had come out to inspect the area and noticed the cut in the fence.

Ryder had been hiding by the trees, watching him. Wanting to reach out and let Clay know he was there, but he couldn't do it just yet.

He paused by the fence along the edge of the Bar None and Hopechest, glanced down toward Esperanza. He had noticed the traffic around the church earlier in the day and later, the gathering of cars and people at the one big hall in town.

Another wedding in Esperanza.

There seemed to be a lot of them lately and he wondered who was getting married today. Wondered whether any of the people at the wedding were aware of what was happening right beneath their noses.

Of course not, he told himself, pushing away from the fence and heading toward the caves. Not even the sheriff had a clue about what was going on or that the big bad little brother was back to get to the bottom of it. To redeem himself for all the wrong that he had done as a young man. The wrong that had driven a wedge between himself and his older brother Clay.

As he paused at the edge of the trees, he looked back toward town again and smiled at the thought of returning home.

"Soon," Ryder told himself and slipped into one of the caves, intent on completing his redemption.

Jericho and Fisher waited on the steps of the church, T.J. beside them much as they had stood there nearly a month earlier. Only there was no doubt now about who Macy was wedding and that this would be a real marriage.

Clasping his hands before him tightly, he rocked back and forth on his heels, prompting T.J. to ask, "Are you nervous?"

Nervous. Excited. Happy.

"I am," he confessed and examined his son. "Are you?"

T.J. shrugged, but the fabric of his dress blue suit barely moved since the jacket was slightly big on him. Not for long, he knew, thinking back on how both he and Jericho had filled out in their senior year.

Clapping a hand on T.J.'s shoulder, he said, "I'm glad we'll have the time to get to know each other."

"I'm glad, too," T.J. responded.

A second later, a limo pulled up in front of the church. Jewel stepped out first, looking beautiful in a pale pink bridesmaid's dress that hugged her slender figure. As she noticed them waiting on the steps of the church, she waved at them.

"Time for you to head inside. It's bad luck to see the bride before the wedding," she called out in warning, but before they could take a step, Macy slipped from the limo.

The dress she wore this time was nothing like the one she had purchased for her wedding to Jericho. This one was …

Amazing, he thought, taking note of the intricate skirt of the pale ice blue dress with its yards and yards of palest white lace. The bodice hugged her curves, accentuating her tempting shape and her shoulders were bare, making him want to touch her.

As his gaze skimmed up to her face and hair, he realized that she had gone all out. Makeup expertly done and her shoulder length brown hair stylishly cut and set in a tousled style that screamed sexy.

"Fisher?" his brother prompted.

He faced him and T.J., blushed as he saw the look on his brother's face and T.J.'s amused look as he said, "Aw, come on, Fisher. That's my mom."

"She's beautiful, isn't she?" he said and with a wink at Macy, he once again clapped T.J. on the back.

"Ready to become a family?"

T.J. shot a quick hesitant look back at his mom, but then a wide grin erupted on his face. "You love her, don't you?"

"I do. With all my heart."

"Then I guess it's okay," T.J. said. "I'll go get Mom."

Fisher watched as he walked away, went to Macy's side and slipped his arm through hers.

He was about to head into the church when T.J. shouted, "Wait up, Fisher."

To his surprise, T.J. hurried Macy over and then slipped his arm through Fisher's. "A family, right?" T.J. said as he stood between them.

He met Macy's gaze which was shimmering with tears of happiness. Grinning, he said, "A family, T.J."

Looking up at Jericho, who was waiting beside Jewel, he said, "Come on, bro. The three of us have places to go."

As they followed Jewel and Jericho down the aisle of the

church, he felt the secrets of the past slip away, replaced by the excitement of his new tour of duty—building a life with Macy and T.J.

It was a mission he knew would bring nothing but happiness for the three of them.

* * * * *

Don't miss the next book in this exciting series:
Baby's Watch *by Justine Davis and*
A Hero of Her Own *by Carla Cassidy,*
available October 2009 from
Mills & Boon® Intrigue.

Tall, Dark and Lethal
by
Dana Marton

He would kill a man before the day was out. And—God help him—Cade Palmer hoped this would be the last time.

He'd done the job before and didn't like the strange heaviness that settled on him. Not guilt or second thoughts—he'd been a soldier too long for that. But still, something grim and somber that made little sense, especially today. He'd been waiting for this moment for months. Today he would put an old nightmare to rest and fulfill a promise.

In an hour, Abhi would hand him information on David Smith's whereabouts, and there was no place on earth he couldn't reach by the end of the day. He'd hire a private jet if he had to. Whatever it took. *Before the sun comes up tomorrow, David Smith will be gone.*

He headed up the stairs to his cell phone as it rang on his nightstand. Wiping the last of the gun oil on his worn jeans, he crossed into his bedroom. He was about to reach for the phone when he caught sight of the unmarked van parked across the road from his house.

The van hadn't been there thirty minutes ago. Nor had he seen it before. He made it his business to pay attention to things like that. At six in the morning on Saturday, his new suburban Pennsylvania neighborhood was still asleep, the small, uniform yards deserted. Nothing was out of place—except the van, which made the hair on the back of his neck stand up.

The only handgun he kept inside the house—a SIG P228—was downstairs on the kitchen table in pieces, half-cleaned. He swore. Trouble had found him once again—par for the course in his line of work. Just because he was willing to let go of his old enemies—except David Smith—didn't mean they were willing to let go of him.

"Happy blasted retirement," he said under his breath as he turned to get the rifle he kept in the hallway closet. From the corner of his eye, he caught movement. The rear door of the van inched open, and with a sick sense of dread, he knew what he was going to see a split second before the man in the back was revealed, lifting a grenade launcher to his shoulder.

Instinct and experience. Cade had plenty of both and put them to good use, shoving the still-ringing phone into his back pocket as he lunged for the hallway.

Had he been alone in the house, his plan would have been simple: get out and make those bastards rue the day they were born. But he wasn't alone, which meant he had to alter his battle plan to include grabbing the most obnoxious woman in the universe—aka his neighbor, who lived in the other half of his duplex—and dragging her from the kill zone.

He darted through his bare guest bedroom and busted open the door that led to the small balcony in the back, crashing out into the muggy August morning. Heat, humidity and birdsong.

At least the birds in the jungle knew when danger was afoot. These twittered on, clueless. Proximity to civilization dulled their instincts. And his. He should have known that trouble was coming before it got here. Should have removed himself to some cabin in the woods, someplace with a warning system set up and an arsenal at his fingertips, a battleground where civilians wouldn't have been endangered. But he was where he was, so he turned his thoughts to escape and evasion as he moved forward.

Bailey Preston's half of the house was the mirror image of his, except that she used the back room for her bedroom. Cade vaulted over her balcony, kicked her new French door open and zeroed in on the tufts of cinnamon hair sticking out from under a pink, flowered sheet on a bed that took up most of her hot-pink bedroom. Beneath the mess of hair, a pair of blue-violet eyes were struggling to come into focus. She blinked at him like a hungover turtle. Her mouth fell open but no sound came out. Definitely a first.

He strode forward without pause.

"What are you doing here? Get away from me!" She'd woken up in that split second it took him to reach her bed and was fairly shrieking. She was good at that—she'd been a thorn in his side since he'd moved in. She was pulling the sheet to her chin, scampering away from him, flailing in the tangled covers. "Don't you touch me. You, you—"

He unwrapped her with one smooth move and picked her up, ignoring the pale-purple silk shorts and tank top. So Miss Clang-and-Bang had a soft side. Who knew?

"Don't get your hopes up. I'm just getting you out."

She weighed next to nothing but still managed to be an armful. Smelled like sleep and sawdust, with a faint hint of varnish thrown in. Her odd scent appealed to him more than any coy, flowery perfume could have. Not that he was in any position to enjoy it. He tried in vain to duck the small fists pounding his shoulders and head, and gave thanks to God that her nephew, who'd been vacationing with her for the first part of summer, had gone back to wherever he'd come from. Dealing with her was all he could handle.

"Are you completely crazy?" She was actually trying to poke his eyes out. "I'm calling the police. I'm calling the police right now!"

She was possibly more than he could handle, although that macho sense of vanity that lived deep down in every man made it hard for him to admit that, even as her fingers jabbed dangerously close to his irises in some freakish self-defense move she must have seen on TV.

"You might want to hang on." He was already out of the room. Less than ten seconds had passed since he'd seen the guy in the van. "And try to be quiet." He stepped up to the creaking balcony railing and jumped before it could give way under their combined weight.

She screamed all the way down and then some, giving no consideration to his eardrums whatsoever. Once upon a time, he'd worked with explosives on a regular basis. He knew loud. She was it.

He swore at the pain that shot up his legs as they crashed to the ground, but he was already pushing away with her over his shoulder and running for cover in the maze of Willow Glen duplexes in Chadds Ford, Pennsylvania.

Unarmed. In the middle of freaking combat.

He didn't feel fear—just unease. He was better than this. He'd always had a sixth sense that let him know when his enemies were closing in. It wasn't like him to get lulled into complacency.

"Are you trying to kill us? Are you on drugs? Listen. To. Me. Try to focus." She grabbed his chin and turned his face to hers. "I am your neighbor."

He kept the house between him and the tangos in the van, checking for any indication of danger waiting for them ahead. No movement on the rooftops. If there was a sniper, he was lying low. Cade scanned the grass for wire trips first, then for anything he could use as a makeshift weapon. He came up with nada.

"Put me down!" She fought him as best she could, a hundred and twenty pounds of wriggling fury. "Don't do this! Whatever you think you are doing, I know you are going to regret it."

He did already.

"Are you crazy?"

He could get there in a hurry. He put his free hand

on her shapely behind to hold her in place. Smooth skin, lean limbs, dangerous curves. He tried not to grope more than was absolutely necessary. Yeah, she could probably make him do a couple of crazy things without half trying. But they had to get out of the kill zone first.

"Let me go! Listen, let me—"

They were only a dozen or so feet from the nearest duplex when his home—and hers—finally blew.

That shut her up.

He dove forward, into the cover of the neighbor's garden shed. They went down hard, and he rolled on top of her, protecting her from the blast, careful to keep most of his weight off. The second explosion came right on the heels of the first. It shook the whole neighborhood.

That would be the C4 he kept in the safe in his garage.

Damn.

"What—was—that?" Her blue-violet eyes stared up at him, her voice trembling, her face the color of lemon sherbet.

There were days when she looked like a garden fairy in her flyaway, flower-patterned clothes with a mess of cinnamon hair, petite but well-rounded body, big violet eyes and the cutest pixie nose he'd ever seen on a woman. She had no business being wrapped in silk in his arms, looking like a frightened sex kitten as he lay on top of her.

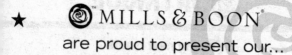

◎™ INTRIGUE

Coming next month

2-IN-1 ANTHOLOGY

BABY'S WATCH by Justine Davis

Bad boy Ryder is shocked by the connection he feels to the baby he helped deliver, as well as her mysterious mother Ana. But can he put his life on the line for them?

A HERO OF HER OWN by Carla Cassidy

From the moment she arrived in town, Jewel caught Quinn's attention. They're both overcoming tragic pasts, but does Jewel trust Quinn enough to let passion in?

2-IN-1 ANTHOLOGY

BENEATH THE BADGE by Rita Herron

Nothing matters more to Hayes than the police badge he wears. Protecting heiress Taylor is his sworn duty, but could she become the object of his desire too?

MATCH PLAY by Merline Lovelace

Special Agent Dayna jumped at an undercover assignment overseas. However she didn't expect to find former lover air force pilot Luke awaiting her arrival…

SINGLE TITLE

VEILED TRUTH by Vivi Anna
Nocturne

Lyra's skills as a witch can't help her solve a series of gruesome murders. She distrusts brooding Theron, but he could have the answers she seeks. And with the gateway to hell opening, it's imperative the two find common ground…

On sale 18th September 2009

 **INTRIGUE**

Coming next month

2-IN-1 ANTHOLOGY

CHRISTMAS SPIRIT by Rebecca York

Michael doesn't believe in the ghosts said to haunt
Jenkins Cove. Can Chelsea change his mind – or will
they be forced to confront the spirits of Christmas past?

BEAST OF DESIRE by Lisa Renee Jones

Only in the throes of lust and battle does Des embrace
his dark side. But in protecting Jessica from the
Darkland Beasts, it is the animal in him that must rule!

SINGLE TITLE

THE HEIRESS'S 2-WEEK AFFAIR by Marie Ferrarella

Detective Natalie never got over former love Matt, and now
he could be the key to helping her find her sister's killer.
But can she keep a professional distance?

SINGLE TITLE

TALL, DARK AND LETHAL by Dana Marton

With dangerous men hot on his trail, the last thing Cade
needs is Bailey seeking his help to escape her own
attackers. Now it's up to him to tame the feisty free spirit…

On sale 2nd October 2009

From No. 1 *New York Times* bestselling author Nora Roberts

Nightshade available 2nd January 2010

When a teenager gets caught up in making sadistic violent films, Colt Nightshade and Lieutenant Althea Grayson must find her before she winds up dead…

Night Smoke available 5th February 2010

When Natalie Fletcher's office is set ablaze, she must find out who wants her ruined – before someone is killed…

Night Shield available 5th March 2010

When a revengeful robber leaves blood-stained words on Detective Allison Fletcher's walls, she knows her cop's shield won't be enough to protect her…

Passion. Power. Suspense.
It's time to fall under the spell of Nora Roberts.

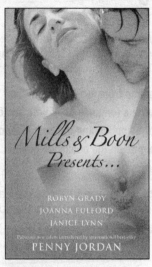

millsandboon.co.uk Community

Join Us!

The Community is the perfect place to meet and chat to kindred spirits who love books and reading as much as you do, but it's also the place to:

- **Get the inside scoop from authors about their latest books**
- **Learn how to write a romance book with advice from our editor**
- **Help us to continue publishing the best in women's fiction**
- **Share your thoughts on the books we publish**
- **Befriend other users**

Forums: Interact with each other as well as authors, editors and a whole host of other users worldwide.

Blogs: Every registered community member has their own blog to tell the world what they're up to and what's on their mind.

Book Challenge: We're aiming to read 5,000 books and have joined forces with The Reading Agency in our inaugural Book Challenge.

Profile Page: Showcase yourself and keep a record of your recent community activity.

Social Networking: We've added buttons at the end of every post to share via digg, Facebook, Google, Yahoo, technorati and de.licio.us.

www.millsandboon.co.uk

2 FREE BOOKS
AND A SURPRISE GIFT

We would like to take this opportunity to thank you for reading this Mills & Boon® book by offering you the chance to take TWO more specially selected books from the Intrigue series absolutely FREE! We're also making this offer to introduce you to the benefits of the Mills & Boon® Book Club™—

- **FREE home delivery**
- **FREE gifts and competitions**
- **FREE monthly Newsletter**
- **Exclusive Mills & Boon Book Club offers**
- **Books available before they're in the shops**

Accepting these FREE books and gift places you under no obligation to buy, you may cancel at any time, even after receiving your free books. Simply complete your details below and return the entire page to the address below. You don't even need a stamp!

YES Please send me 2 free Intrigue books and a surprise gift. I understand that unless you hear from me, I will receive 5 superb new stories every month, including two 2-in-1 books priced at £4.99 each and a single book priced at £3.19, postage and packing free. I am under no obligation to purchase any books and may cancel my subscription at any time. The free books and gift will be mine to keep in any case.

Ms/Mrs/Miss/Mr _____ Initials _____

_____

Surname _____

Address _____

_____

_____ Postcode _____

Send this whole page to: Mills & Boon Book Club, Free Book Offer, FREEPOST NAT 10298, Richmond, TW9 1BR